HELLO, DAHLI

S.J. CUNNINGHAM

Hello, Dahli
by S.J. Cunningham

© Copyright 2025 S.J. Cunningham

Paperback ISBN: 978-1-964369-09-9
Paperback Edition

This edition published by S.J. Cunningham: www.sjcunningham.net.

To Rachel:

My fiercely independent, successful, beautiful, life-changing daughter.

You are an inspiration.

Happy birthday!

PART 1

CHAPTER 1

—Hello, Dahli. Looking forward to this afternoon.

Dahli Reed's eyes skim over the words of the text on her watch. She smiles, but the smile wavers. This afternoon, her life may change. The knot of anxiety settles in her sternum.

She takes a deep breath, filling her water bottle under the stream of filtered water from the faucet of the kitchen sink.

She reaches for her phone, sliding it from the fitted pocket of her spandex running shorts.

Dahli is about to type out a reply when her husband's low voice rumbles in the darkened silence.

"Who the hell are you texting at five in the morning?"

Dahli startles, then recovers. Her face is neutral and impassive as she slides the phone back into place. Turning, she manages, if not a smile, what she hopes passes for an affable expression.

"You're up early," she remarks. "Did I wake you?"

"Couldn't sleep."

Her gaze skims over her husband illuminated in

the dim light above the stove.

Jeremy Reed is dressed in black shorts and a T-shirt with the name of a band from their college days. It features the image of a melting face and the word 'HUMAN' in large block letters printed across his chest. His thinning hair stands up in pillow-styled spikes, and he smells stale and sour. "Thought I'd go work out."

She doesn't respond, though the slow simmer of anger has started to bubble. She's training for a marathon in Virginia. Jeremy's told her it's both odd and silly to go north to run a marathon.

But she's been following a rigorous training plan; this morning's run is thirteen miles. If she can hold to ten-minute miles, she'll be back around six-thirty. The problem is, she won't hold ten-minute miles. Her calves have been tight, and she knows better than to push her aging body. At thirty-five, she feels the years in every muscle and joint. Her body isn't what it once was. For many reasons, Dahli isn't what *she* once was.

Before her mind goes down a familiar path of ruminating on the unknowable future and submerges her in panic, she stuffs the thought away.

She'd risen early to give herself time to return by seven. Plenty of time to get Luke and Maeve to school and herself to work.

If Jeremy is also leaving the house, she won't be able to go on her run. She won't be able to train.

She slams her bottle down on the counter.

Jeremy looks up from the protein bar he's just un-wrapped. "What's your problem?"

"Nothing," she says, though her voice belies her.

"You're going to wake the kids." The admonition is clipped and condescending. Smug. Her lip curls up as she bites back a retort.

He chews his protein bar and looks to the coffee machine. "No coffee?"

The implication is that she should have made some. For him.

She seethes as he moves to the refrigerator and pours a glass of orange juice instead.

She stares at him as he takes a long swallow of the liquid. He stares back.

Breathe, she demands of herself. She has no interest in engaging in a civil discussion with Jeremy, and maybe she has no right to a civil conversation either. Not after what she's done.

But she knows she needs to talk to her husband.

Just a little while longer until she knows which way her situation will head, she reminds herself. How the next part of her life may unfold.

She exhales, before speaking in a soft voice, the opposite of how she feels, "Jeremy, my problem is—"

"Oh, here we go…" he interrupts. He arranges his face into an exaggerated expression of anguish.

She opens her mouth. Shuts it. This time, she counts to five, then continues in that same soft voice.

"I'm training, Jeremy. You know this. We've *discussed* this. And now I can't train because you've decided you need to go to the gym. Even though we never discussed a change in the morning's routine."

He rolls his eyes. "Do you always have to be so damn dramatic? No one's stopping you from going on your run." He puts undue emphasis on the word 'run', as if the word is code for something else.

Dahli ignores his implication and steers the conversation back to its original intent. "*You're* stopping me, Jeremy. You don't care about me or what I want. You only think about yourself."

Her voice has become accusatory and whiny. She doesn't want to feel this way, but she can't help it. She may as well not even exist for all the attention her husband pays to her interests, her pursuits. Of course, there's more to it than that. There always is. But for the moment, she decides to focus on him rather than on *herself* and her own shortcomings.

He sneers. "Oh, so I'm supposed to, once again, acquiesce to your schedule because you're training for a marathon? You're just so fucking accomplished, aren't you?" he says sarcastically. "Fuck that."

"Fuck *you*."

Jeremy wheels around. He's not a large man, but he's taller than her. And when he suddenly approaches, his presence seems to expand, making him appear larger—menacing.

He was once handsome—is still handsome—but she's stopped seeing it. She takes a step back, taking in his flashing eyes, shaggy brown hair, unshaven face, and bared teeth.

Her movement of submission seems to calm him enough to cool his growing temper. Or maybe it's the thought of waking the kids. Whatever the cause, he stands down and turns back to his orange juice. "You can still go on your fucking run. Luke is twelve, Maeve is eight. At Luke's age, I was babysitting Sammy."

Jeremy had practically raised his younger brother, but times were different then. Where he'd grown up was different.

"Maeve sleeps like the dead," he continues in a more reasonable tone, as if he hadn't just physically threatened his wife. "And we'll lock the door behind us."

Dahli remains silent. She stands still, heart pounding as she leans against the porcelain slab countertop of their refinished kitchen.

After a moment, Jeremy comes close to her. She forces herself to stand her ground. But this time, he places his arms around her body from behind, pulling her against him. She remains rigid, but he doesn't let go. He smells of the fusty odor of sleep mixed with oranges and the peanut butter protein bar he has just eaten.

"They'll be fine," he says at her ear. His breath is

warm. Fetid.

She turns her head away.

Jeremy will never apologize with words; this is as close as he'll get. After thirteen years of marriage, she knows this about her husband.

He pushes his groin into her backside, and she can feel him harden. "Unless you'd like to just say 'fuck it' and go back to bed."

Dahli would rather do just about anything than that. Frankly, she's shocked by the suggestion. They haven't been intimate for ages. "I'll go for my run," she says quickly. She wriggles from his grasp. "I'll be back before seven," she mumbles as she laces her running shoes.

She doesn't wait for his response—doesn't even look behind her—as she pulls the door shut.

Outside, Dahli exhales. She can breathe. The October air is cool in their South Carolina suburb. They are not close to the ocean, but they're not far either. She detects a brininess to the air—faint, but there nonetheless—from the nearby lowland watershed.

She surveys the front lawn, its new landscaping half done. A fresh wave of frustration rises. She hadn't wanted to spend the money, but Jeremy had insisted on contracting a landscaping company to resod the entire lawn, bring in new rocks, plants, and trees. It will look nice, she knows. Already, it's starting to take shape. But in this neighborhood, they won't get the value back should they decide to sell the house. And that's been on Dahli's mind. Something is going to happen, and in no future scenario can she imagine herself staying in this house with Jeremy.

Dahli walks for a few minutes past the houses on Linden Lane, warming up her body. She stops at the end of the street to stretch, lunging and touching her toes. She feels the burn in her calves and hamstrings. Then she crouches low and butterflies her thighs, stretching her groin muscles.

She begins to jog—the same route she takes nearly every morning for the past few months.

She runs past the same houses, the same trees, the same buildings. She veers off to take the loop leading toward Goose Creek. The loop is about six and a half miles total, so she will run the route twice, down Pulaski Street and onto the trail that parallels Red Bank Road. Her pace and her heart rate increase as she times her breathing with her footfalls.

Despite the cool temperature, she begins to sweat, and the tension from the morning—the text message, the exchange with Jeremy—begins to ease from her mind and body as she relaxes into the run.

This will likely be the last marathon she participates in for a while, but she reminds herself of new beginnings.

And who knows—maybe in another few years she can start training all over again. The future is wide open.

It is exhilarating.

It is terrifying.

When she passes the Naval Nuclear Power Training Command Station, she picks up speed. The morning shift workers are reporting to the base but there's no one else around; no one else running this early in the morning. She feels as though she's being watched, and while she knows there are cameras in the area recording her every movement, she also feels like there are eyes on her.

This is silly. No one cares what Dahli Reed is doing. At least no one out on this lonely road.

Still, she breathes a sigh of relief when she finally turns off Red Bank Road onto Marrington Avenue. While this road is much more desolate, she feels safer here.

She moves swiftly past the marshy ponds, and in the rising sun, birds soar low and silent in the thick morning air. It smells of marsh and salt and sea.

A splash sounds at the edge of one of the nameless ponds to her right, and she watches an alligator's powerful tail disappear under the surface of the water.

Dahli will never tire of this part of the country. As someone who'd grown up in the middle of the flat and unremarkable cornfields of central Ohio, she decided a long time ago she'd never go back north.

She'd been class valedictorian at tiny Ellisville-Rose High School near Carbon Hill and earned a full ride to

Furman where she'd maintained a 4.0 grade point average. Her mistake, she knows now, had been to continue her long-distance relationship with Jeremy, who'd graduated from high school in the same year and opted to stay closer to home and attend Central State University.

The rearview mirror always gives a clearer perspective than the windshield.

She'd married Jeremy young, and after finding herself pregnant with Luke following her wedding, she'd struggled to find her footing. It wasn't supposed to have been that way.

But she'd been lucky. When Luke was a toddler, she'd taken a job as a marketing assistant at Mosswood Real Estate Developers in North Charleston.

By the time Luke turned five she'd worked her way up to manager, and her income combined with Jeremy's (as a project analyst at an electrical power management company) meant they'd been easily able to afford childcare. Jeremy had insisted she stay home, but thank goodness she hadn't listened—now she was Vice President of Public Relations and External Affairs for Mosswood, the company growing right along with her. She is more successful than she ever could've dreamed.

Jeremy, on the other hand, has found himself in a funk. He'd received a promotion the year before and was now leading a large digital transformation for the company. Both he and the project are struggling. Dahli knows this, and it is terrible, but she can't help feeling a little bit smug about it. It's not that she thinks she is better than him. It's that *he's* always felt he is better than *her*. Smarter. Superior. As it turns out, he is wrong.

As Dahli's run becomes more hypnotic, her mind regresses into the familiar complaints about her husband. When she tells him about her day, his meetings always have to be more impactful, his projects more stressful, the workplace politics more cutthroat, the drama more absurd. And so Dahli has stopped telling Jeremy about her day.

As she cuts through the deserted Menriv Park then bears left onto Vetr Road, she tries to focus on something else. She doesn't want to think about Jeremy. If she thinks about her husband, her thoughts will lead to the question of what to *do* about him. About their marriage. And she doesn't want to think about their marriage. Not this morning. Not this day. Not when she has so much on the line this afternoon.

She lets her thoughts wander again, but this time she finds herself savoring the anticipation. She should feel guilty, but she doesn't. Not even a little bit. Then she feels guilty about not feeling guilty.

Though the run feels good and her body is fluid, by the time Vetr Road turns back into Pulaski, Dahli has started to feel depleted. In her haste to escape the house—escape Jeremy—she'd abandoned her water bottle, and at mile six and a half, she feels the dehydration. She contemplates cutting the run short and veering south along North Rhett Avenue toward home.

But there's a cold-water fountain at the Marrington Plantation Trailhead. Only three more miles. She can do it.

The traffic is heavier now with people going to work along Red Bank Road, heading to the Naval Command Station and to the water treatment plant tucked within the swampy lowlands of the Cooper and Black Rivers.

Past the Cooper River is inhabited swampland: the small city of Wando, forests, dunes, and eventually Highway 17 which hugs the outside curve of the state along Bulls Bay which eventually opens into the Atlantic Ocean.

Dahli and Jeremy have taken drives out there. In happier times, they'd visited Sandy Point Beach and Cape Romain Lighthouse. They'd driven up to Santee and dined on fresh crab and barbeque. They'd taken the kids out that way, and they'd laughed and reveled in their young lives and bright future.

At one point, they'd even discussed buying a small cabin in the wilderness for solitude and weekend getaways. Jeremy had talked with a real estate agent and explored properties in person.

Like so many of their other dreams, nothing had

come of it.

Where had it all gone wrong? she wonders for the trillionth time.

Once again, Dahli turns onto Marrington Avenue. Her pace is slower now. She has no idea of the time, but if she hurries, she thinks she can still make it back by seven.

She has very little left in her tank.

She takes a sharp right into the Marrington Plantation Trailhead parking lot. There is one lone brown van pulled cattywampus into the furthest spot from the small latrine. Its windows are black.

Dahli surveils it; there could be a camper inside, asleep, or just someone out for an early morning run. Still, she eyes the vehicle from her periphery, wishing she'd brought her shrieking keychain whistle or pepper spray. In her haste, she'd thought of neither.

Still perspiring heavily, she approaches the water fountain next to the latrine. She bends to drink deeply; the water is cool running down her chin and throat. It wets her nylon shirt.

She cups a hand and splashes water on her face and neck. A rivulet runs inside the collar of her T-shirt and into her sports bra between her breasts.

A twig cracks behind her and Dahli whirls around, her heart pounding from more than just the run. She scans the trees but sees no movement. Multiple paths lead into the forest of cypress and pine and maple.

The van sits silently. Ominously.

Is someone watching her watch them?

The thought gives her chills, but she stands motionless.

She's not sure how long she remains in the same spot, watching and waiting. But it occurs to her she is not safe here alone. There's no one else around. The small black camera affixed to the top of the latrine building is old and its cord frayed. She doubts it's operational.

Her heart still hammering in her chest, she runs out of the trailhead parking lot fast, and turns right, back onto Marrington Avenue.

The sun is up now, and she relaxes as she passes an older couple—one with a pair of binoculars, the other with a camera fitted with a telescoping lens—likely birdwatching in Menriv Park. They nod a hello; Dahli wants to laugh with relief. She'd been silly to think there was danger. She's read too many fearmongering news reports. Seen too many true-crime documentaries.

She is safe.

She turns the corner where Marrington intersects with Vetr.

When she hears the sound of an engine approaching from behind, she moves to the very edge of the roadway. The vehicle slows, and all the relief she'd just felt vanishes. Somehow she knows it's the brown van.

She prepares to sprint fast, scanning her surroundings for any other people, any vehicles, any cameras. There is nothing and no one.

But when she looks in her periphery, it isn't the brown van. It's a black sport utility vehicle.

She knows the car.

The window powers down.

She startles. She knows this person.

"Hello, Dahli."

"Hi," she says, breathless from both fear and exertion. And also surprise. "What are you doing way out here?"

"Do you think we'd be able to talk?" The voice is low and conciliatory.

She hesitates. She doesn't want to talk. Not here. Not now. "I mean, I'm just…" She points behind her. "…I'm heading back now." Her words trail off. She isn't prepared for conversation, especially looking as she does. Sweating. Ugly. Weak.

"I know it's unexpected. I'm sorry…"

The voice is uncertain, and Dahli offers a smile. She can make this work, she thinks. Perhaps it's better this way.

"It's okay," she says. "You know, maybe I can cut it short." It's not a bad idea. She's tired, and she's late. "A ride might be good actually."

The driver looks relieved, and she hears the door latch disengage as the engine idles.

"Hop in."

She crosses in front of the car and opens the passenger door, sliding into the front seat.

The smiling face before her twists, and in a flash, the hand moves toward her. Dahli is so surprised, she doesn't have the sense or the time to react.

The last thing she remembers is a cruel laugh before her world goes dark.

CHAPTER 2

Jeremy Reed pulls his midsize SUV into the garage next to his wife's Lexus. He sits in the darkness for a minute, his mind racing. He can't seem to calm it.

He glances at the time. It's late, though he knew he'd be later than he wanted. It doesn't matter, he reminds himself. He'd accomplished *something*, at least.

This year has been shit. His job has been shit, his confidence has been shit, and he fears his marriage is circling the drain, too. He has always thought himself a man of action, but lately he's felt impotent, in more ways than one.

This morning, at least, he's taken steps forward. Steps toward the future. His heart is still galloping. He can't say he feels better, but he at least feels productive. It's something. He hopes this is the step he needs to take in order to get his life back on track.

He inhales, and his thoughts veer from the past to the future.

Jeremy is dreading the presentation scheduled for later this morning; the meeting where he'll explain to his boss and his boss's boss why the project is so far over budget and behind schedule. It's not Jeremy's fault. He knows it, and the company knows it. But the board of directors will want answers and consequences. A likely consequence is someone getting fired. And if they're looking for a scapegoat, Jeremy will be their guy. He's not convinced they didn't put him in the role for that specific purpose a year ago.

If he gets fired…

He runs his hand through his hair, which over the past year has begun rapidly disappearing.

If he gets fired…well. That will be that.

He blows out a breath and climbs from the car, pushing the button on the garage door. As the door cycles down its track, he glances outside. Even though it's well past seven, no one is around. The Timmons, who live in the house to the right, are retired. Jill and Bill, on the left, work from home, each holed up in separate offices on their second floor, facing the back yard.

They are all friendly, but they mostly keep to themselves. Jeremy likes it that way.

The lots across the street are wooded and empty, which is just fine with him. When they'd moved into the house nearly a decade ago, the community had plans to develop the neighborhood along with those wooded lots, but that hadn't happened.

Given the state of the economy and the housing

market, he doesn't know if those lots will ever be built out.

Of course, Dahli would have an opinion on the subject. *The brilliant, attractive, accomplished Dahlia Reed.*

Dahli, for short.

He sneers. Whatever her opinion, he can guarantee it's the exact opposite of his. She would never say as much aloud, but that morning, she'd look at him with that familiar twist of her mouth and superior expression that always overtakes her face when she thinks he's an idiot. Which is most of the time, if not *all* the time.

She tries to hide it, but he knows what she thinks of him.

With his hand on the doorknob leading into the kitchen, he takes another breath.

Then he enters.

The house is silent. He walks into the room, which is exactly as he'd left it. He listens for half a minute for movement.

"Dahli?" he finally calls.

He walks into their shared master bedroom. The salmon-colored sheets and matching quilted comforter are still heaped and tangled. He moves into the ensuite bathroom. The shower is dry, and Dahli's side of the sink is free of the usual hair and makeup products from her morning routine.

Jeremy hears a noise and walks out of the bedroom.

Luke has emerged from his room, bleary-eyed and wearing only a pair of boxer shorts on his thin pre-adolescent frame.

His father's heart lurches, and he has to clear the emotion from his throat before asking, "Where's your mom?"

Luke shrugs. "I just woke up."

Jeremy glances at the watch which has been paired to his phone. "She didn't say anything to you about a change in routine this morning?" His words are slow and enunciated.

Luke shakes his head, unconcerned, and heads into the second bathroom to shower.

"You're sure she didn't say anything?" Jeremy calls after his son, who looks back, an annoyed expression on his young face. "No, Dad. I just told you."

Luke turns around and shuts the door behind him.

Jeremy walks down the hall to Maeve's room. His daughter is still sleeping, one scrawny arm flung over the side of the bed, her hair a dark cloud of disarray against the pale pink pillowcase.

He must now rush to get Maeve to the sitter and drop Luke off at school, then hustle into the city in time to prepare the printouts for his meeting.

He grabs his phone and dials Dahli. It trills four times, then goes to voicemail.

Hi, you've reached Dahlia…or Dahli, if you'd prefer.

I can't take your call, though I'd love nothing more than to ring you back. Leave me a message, and we'll connect later.

His wife's voice is sprightly and confident. It's also cute—with a sensual raspiness to it. A bedroom voice, he'd once told her.

At one time, her voice had turned him on. Now, it makes him angry.

He debates leaving a message but decides against it. The missed call should do it.

"Maeve…" he says roughly, reaching down and shaking his daughter awake. The movement isn't gentle.

She blinks her brown doe eyes up at him and makes an incoherent sound as she rejoins the world of the living. She looks like a miniature version of his wife.

"Come on. Get up and get dressed."

He goes to her closet and takes a blue shirt from one of the hangers, throwing it behind him onto the bed.

"Daddy, no." Her voice is a whine.

He turns around.

She's now sitting up. Her face is a pout. "I don't want to wear that."

"Jesus," he says under his breath. "Then find something you *can* wear. And do it now. You need to get ready."

She makes a sound between a sigh and a cry.

"Don't even start. Not this morning."

"I have to pee." She draws out the 'ee' sound and adds an 'ah' at the end of the word.

"Then go."

She sticks out her lower lip, climbs from the bed, and slides past him into the hallway.

"Luke is in there," she whines again. "Luke!" she yells through the door and over the sound of the shower. She bangs the heel of her small hand against the wood.

"Use my bathroom," Jeremy orders and holds his phone back to his ear. This time when the call goes to voicemail, he does leave a message. "Dahli, where are you? You should be home by now. The kids are going to be late to school." He pauses, then adds, "Call me back."

He ends the call and stands alone in the hallways for a moment.

Luke and Maeve come out of separate bathrooms at the same time, and Jeremy thinks about the best way to do this. He tries to calm himself.

"Look, kiddos," he says, "your mom isn't home, so it's going to require some teamwork to get you where you need to be this morning. Can you help me out?"

Luke, who is mercifully responsible, nods solemnly, but Maeve says, "Where's Mommy?"

"I don't know where she is, which is why I need

you to get yourself dressed. Okay?"

"I want Mommy to help me."

"I do too. But she's not here, Maeve. We're going to have to do this without her this morning, okay?"

His daughter throws her shoulders back and makes that same pretend crying noise before stamping her foot against the vinyl flooring. "But she's going to braid my hair."

"I can do it," he says. He can do no such thing.

Maeve knows this and gives him a look. It's so close to the look he's become accustomed to from his wife, a wave of rage flows through him. It shouldn't be directed at his eight-year-old child, but he can't help it. Dahli has taught the girl condescension.

"Go get fucking dressed, for Christ's sake!" he explodes.

There is a moment of shocked silence by all three of them before Maeve bursts into tears. Real ones this time.

Luke doesn't look at Jeremy, but says, "Come on Maeve. I'll help you." He's still holding a towel around his slim waist. His children walk away from him as if he isn't standing there.

Jeremy manages to shower and dress with, by his estimation, just enough time to drop both kids off and get to the office. There is no breakfast that morning, and both Maeve and Luke will have to buy a school lunch, a prospect that doesn't make either of them happy. But both still spooked by his earlier outburst, they don't argue. There's that, at least.

He has not planned this well at all.

When Jeremy reaches the office, his young capable deputy, Kara Fletcher, is waiting for him. Her lips are pressed together in a thin line.

"The meeting's in ten minutes."

It doesn't need to be said, and neither does the censure he also knows sits unspoken on the tip of her tongue.

Kara has printed the slides, but Jeremy hasn't had time to go through his notes again. He is rushed and feels unprepared.

You know this information, he tells himself. *You've been living this job for the last year. You've got this.*

But when he and Kara enter the executive conference room, he feels a fresh rush of panic. Jeremy's boss, Carter Brooks, is already sitting at the long, polished table, frowning down at his phone in front of him.

Jeremy sets his phone and a copy of his notes on the conference room table.

Carter looks up, the frown transferring to Jeremy. "You just get in, Reed?" he asks, using Jeremy's last name.

"Dahlia didn't get back—" Jeremy starts to say

before Senior Vice President Alan Powell—Carter's boss—and his posse of useless management hacks enter behind him.

"What did you say about Dahli?" Carter asks, ignoring the others who have entered the room.

Jeremy doesn't bother to answer.

Alan has brought with him an air of impatience, and he takes a seat at the head of the table. He steeples his hands and stares at Jeremy. "I'm looking forward to hearing about how you're going to unfuck this situation." He glances at Kara. "Pardon my French."

Kara waves away the apology.

The man's head of white hair is brushed back, and his white buttoned collar is fastened tight just below the waddle of excess skin on his neck.

Jeremy swallows and takes a breath as Kara connects the laptop to the screen, which displays the meeting deck. He stands at the opposite end of the table, next to the screen displayed on the far wall of the room. Perspiration wets the fabric of the armpits of his shirt.

Then he begins to speak.

He recites the schedule, explains the resource constraints, the operational disruptions, and finally defends the financials. But when he glances at the faces around the table, he feels as though he's being met with blank stares and bored expressions.

Finally, Alan puts one hand up.

"Look, Mr. Reed, this is all well and good, and I appreciate the status update, but what I want to know is what you're going to *do* about it." Alan Powell's voice is deep and slow. It drips with southern charm over a spine of steel. He glances at Carter, not waiting for Jeremy to speak. "I thought I'd made that clear."

"You did, Alan. Of course you did."

Both Alan and Carter stare at Jeremy, waiting.

Jeremy presses his lips together.

So that's how this is going to go, he thinks. He has an answer to Mr. Powell's question—he has lots of answers, in fact. The problem is, he doesn't have the authority to execute any of those answers. Those solutions.

He pauses to think of an acceptable way to explain this conundrum to Mr. Powell.

The room is silent. Waiting. It has a pulse that thrums with expectation.

Kara leans forward, as if she's going to speak, but she doesn't. He realizes she's willing *him* to speak.

Carter rests his elbows on the conference table in front of him then folds his hands below his chin. He doesn't try to help Jeremy out. He puffs out his cheeks.

When Alan sits back, Jeremy finally finds his voice. "Well, sir, what I would do—"

"Don't tell me what you *would* do, boy!" Alan Powell explodes. He slaps a hand on the table. "I want to know what you *will* do."

The room has gone silent, all eyes either trained on Jeremy or lowered to the floor. They are watching his demise, but not everyone has the stomach for it.

"I…I…" He swallows. "If I could get approval for some extra resources—"

"You got a business case and a resource plan?"

"Well, no, sir. I thought that's what this meeting was for. I'd intended—"

"Let me tell you what *I'd* intended, Mr. Reed. I'd intended you to come in here with a plan to get us back on track. Not a status update with some whiny excuses for why you shit the bed and it's not your fault."

Jeremy isn't sure how to respond. And in the pause that follows, his phone vibrates loudly against the polished mahogany table where he'd set it down.

"Jesus," Alan Powell says and pushes his leather seat away from the table. He turns to Carter. "Deal with this, would you?"

The rest of the team at the table also push their chairs back with lowered eyes. No one speaks as they file out of the room. Only Kara remains seated.

Carter says, "Come see me in my office at noon, Jeremy." Then he strides out, too.

When Jeremy and Kara are alone in the room, Kara finally looks up at him. Jeremy has the humiliating urge to cry. He manages to breathe through the lump in his throat. "I didn't think it would be quite that bad," he said.

She nods almost imperceptibly. "It's not your fault."

Kara is in her late twenties. She's pretty in a girl-next-door kind of way. Fresh-faced, bubbly, and uncomplicated. She's engaged to be married in June. He and Dahli are invited to the wedding.

"You think I'll get fired?"

"They don't fire many people around here," she answers slowly, evasively.

"You want to get a drink after work?" The question is sudden, and Kara's eyebrows arch up.

He manages a smile and a helpless shrug. "I have a feeling I'm going to need one."

She hesitates then says, "Sure. Yeah."

She feels sorry for him, but right now, he'll take it.

Two hours later, Jeremy taps on the glass door to Carter's office. Carter looks up from his laptop and motions him in.

It's a good sign that no representative from Human Resources is in the office.

"I'm just finishing up this email," Carter says. "Have a seat."

Jeremy lowers himself into the padded chair on the other side of the desk. As Carter types, Jeremy studies a photo on his desk of his boss standing with a young man who looks remarkably like him. They are in a tropical setting, dressed in triathlon gear and holding up medals.

Jeremy doesn't want to think about how accomplished Carter is. Carter is maybe ten years Jeremy's senior, but the man has done so much more with his life. He is handsome, fit, athletic, successful.

Jeremy and Dahli had attended a Christmas party at Carter's home over the holidays. There had been no wife, and Jeremy couldn't help but notice the way Dahli had not only laughed at his boss's jokes, but had spoken seriously to him about Charleston's economic development and politics—the two of them huddled in the corner with their glasses of red wine and flushed cheeks.

Dahli saw Carter as her equal, and that infuriated Jeremy. He'd felt as if he'd been relegated to a second-tier character in the mind of his own wife.

He has a sudden, unexpected thought. The night before Carter's party had been the last time he and Dahli had made love.

Jeremy swallows and looks down at the folder in his lap, trying to force his thoughts to the present. After the disastrous morning meeting, he'd returned to his desk and created an updated resource plan for the project. It isn't quite finished yet, but if he can get Carter to listen to reason, maybe he'll be able to save himself. Save his career.

If he loses this job… The thought trails off. What *would* he do if he lost his job? Especially now?

He thinks about the purchase he's made recently: what had started off as a romantic surprise for his wife…before he'd suspected her of cheating on him. He'd never even told her about the cabin in the woods near the Francis Marion National Forest.

His heart starts to pound again, remembering.

Now he has another problem to consider.

He forces himself to remain calm and pulls out his phone to check his emails, but before he can open the application, Carter finally lifts his face to him.

Jeremy places his phone on the edge of Carter's desk.

Carter doesn't smile, but he doesn't seem angry either. "Want the good news or the bad news first?"

Jeremy opens his mouth and starts to hold up the resource plan, but before he can speak, Carter interjects. "Scratch that. The bad news won't make sense without the good, so I'll start there."

Jeremy's phone begins to buzz with an incoming call. Carter glances down at it, and Jeremy fumbles to silence the damn thing, dropping the folder. The pages skitter like leaves across the floor. He scrabbles to collect them, aware that they're now in the wrong order.

Carter blinks, annoyed with the interruption. And Jeremy's phone has begun to buzz again.

"Do you need to get that?" Carter asks.

"No." Jeremy shakes his head. "I'm sorry. Please continue."

"I'm serious. If you need to take it—"

"No," Jeremy says again, forcefully. He hasn't even looked at the caller. "It's not important."

Carter pauses for a second longer, then says, "The good news is you're not losing your job."

The air leaves Jeremy's lungs in a rush of relief. Thank God. He nods at Carter, the damn lump in his throat rising once again. "Thank you," he says quietly.

"Don't thank me. Mr. Powell is the one who agreed to keep you on."

Jeremy nods, but he's fairly certain Carter would have had to sell Jeremy's continued employment pretty hard after what had happened that morning.

"Now, the bad news."

Jeremy's phone buzzes once more, and again he fumbles to silence it. "Sorry."

"Seriously man. Just get it."

Jeremy glances at the display. It's a number he doesn't recognize, but his phone has given him a clue. 'Maybe Olivia Mitchell' is displayed at the top of the screen. Dahli's administrative assistant.

He frowns and silences the call again, but his heart thrums. He swallows. "It's fine." He places the phone in his back pocket, where it immediately starts to vibrate.

Carter gives a small shake of his head and takes a breath. "We are going to have to replace you in your position. You'll still have a place on the team, and we can talk about what responsibilities you might assume, but we're taking you out of the project manager slot."

Jeremy loses some of the feeling in his extremities. A demotion. While his wife is a vice president, he's relegated to individual contributor.

It's always been that way with him. Dahli leading the charge and Jeremy bringing up the rear. It shouldn't surprise him anymore.

Still…resentment toward his wife rests heavy in his chest.

"You'll now report to Kara Fletcher—"

"Kara!" Jeremy exclaims. "But she's not ready for that role. She's too new—too green." The phone buzzes again in his back pocket, and he shifts.

Carter spins around in his chair and picks up a manilla folder similar to the one that now rests in Jeremy's lap. When Carter turns back, he hands the paperwork to Jeremy who flips through it. It appears to be a resource plan—tabbed and itemized with job descriptions and responsibilities, suggested names, time allocation, backfill pitches, and rematriculation proposals. The document is a thousand times more comprehensive than the useless, misordered pages he'd been about to share.

"What is this?"

"This is what we'd wanted you to come to the meeting with."

"Okay…but where did you get this?" he asks, holding up the folder.

"Kara sent it to me."

Jeremy blinks, confused. "She didn't share it with me." He flips through the pages again.

Carter shrugs.

The phone buzzes.

"When did she send it to you?"

"Last week."

Jeremy continues to stare at the printout, but he's stopped looking at the words. "Did you know what was going to happen during the meeting?"

"No," Carter says, but there's a hesitation. "This role was yours to lose, Reed. Until the very end."

Jeremy is torn between a feeling of uselessness and a deep anger. Anger at himself for allowing it to get to this point. But much of his anger is directed at Kara, who has betrayed him. And, inexplicably, at Dahli. He can't help but think this is all her fault. That everything is her fault.

The phone buzzes again.

"Fuck," he swears. Carter's eyebrows raise.

Jeremy pulls the phone from his back pocket. "I gotta take this."

Carter puts his hand out, palms up. "You and Kara can work out your new assignment. Kara will report back to me once she agrees to a plan forward for you."

Jeremy doesn't bother to acknowledge Carter's comment. He leaves the office and accepts the call. "What is it?" he says forcefully. "I'm at work."

There's a moment's silence. "I'm sorry, Mr. Reed. This is Olivia Mitchell from Mosswood. I work with your wife, Dahlia."

"I know who you are," he snaps.

Another pause. "I'm calling because Dahlia didn't come into work today, and she's missed a number of important meetings. Her calls are going straight to voicemail, and it doesn't appear her texts are being delivered. Is she okay?"

Jeremy brushes a hand through his hair and walks toward his office. His eyes meet Kara's, and she has the grace to look embarrassed, but the nerve to hold up her hand as if she's summoning him. *Fat chance*, he thinks.

He ducks into an empty meeting room and shuts the door behind him.

"Mr. Reed?"

"Of course Dahli's okay."

"Did she say anything about missing work when you spoke with her? Was she ill?"

"No, she was fine. She was going for her morning run."

A silence stretches over the line.

Jeremy says, "Look, everything is fine."

"It's just…" The woman pauses. "It's not like Dahlia not to check in."

Jeremy wants to say, *How the fuck would you know what my wife is like?* But instead, he says, "Maybe you don't know her as well as you think you do."

The next pause is longer. Tense. Then Olivia says, "We're worried about her well-being, Mr. Reed. Please have her call us as soon as you hear from her, okay? We want to make sure she's safe."

"Of course she's safe, Ms. Mitchell. I'm her husband. I think I would know."

CHAPTER 3

Weston Moss the fourth runs the fingers of one hand over the sides of his mouth.

He'd arrived at the office later than normal, forced to deal with unexpected developments at home. Even now, the frenetic scene causes his vision to waver and his head to pulse behind his eyes.

He'd told his assistant, Kelly, that he was not, under any circumstances, to be disturbed.

His heart lurches at what he must do. How the hell has it come to this? He's usually so smart, so careful, so steady. He's not risk-averse, but the risks he takes are calculated, with careful consideration of drawbacks and mitigation plans. His recent actions have been careless and barely manageable.

He'd been tempted, and he'd given in to that temptation.

He'd been a damn fool.

And this next part has the potential to cause just as much, if not infinitely more, damage to his life. It depends how he handles things moving forward.

"Fuck," he swears out loud, louder than intended.

Through the open door, he sees Kelly look up sharply. She frowns and looks back down.

He needs to pull himself together, he thinks, pacing the length of floor and out of the view of the lobby. He glances at his phone. It's nearly eleven o'clock and he has a meeting with the operations team about an issue on the West Ashley property.

The issue has the potential to bring in some bad press, and he *should* bring Dahlia in, but he can't do that. Not today.

Weston forces himself to straighten when he exits his office and walks into the reception area.

Kelly says, "Mrs. Moss called." His assistant's voice is tentative. "She said it was urgent."

He just bets it is.

"Call her back and tell her I'm taking care of everything, and I'll be home for dinner, as planned."

"Yes, sir," Kelly responds.

He starts down the hallway, then turns back. "I have an unplanned meeting offsite this afternoon. Can you add it to my calendar?"

"Of course. Any details you'd like me to include?"

Mosswood has an open calendar policy, which means all employees can access the calendar details of everyone in the company, from the CEO to the interns. "No details," Weston responds. Kelly nods once in acknowledgment.

He pictures his wife's face. Josephine Vance Moss's

beautifully sculpted face had been distorted with rage as she'd spat at him the previous evening.

His wife—transformed by her long-ago marriage to Weston from low-country commoner to refined Southern lady—is no stranger to business herself.

Unsatisfied with the limited roles of mother and socialite early in their marriage, she'd opened a small clothing boutique along historic, charming, fashionable King Street. The boutique has been successful enough that she's since opened four more—in Savannah, Asheville, New Hope, and Provincetown. She's been grooming their daughter Adeline to take over management of the chain, Vamoose, a whimsical play on her two last names.

And Weston had already begun the process of grooming their son Aiden to take the reins at Mosswood once the boy had completed his degree at Clemson.

After a few years, Weston and Josephine would relax for once in their lives. Perhaps they'd travel. Perhaps they'd return to the couple they'd once been.

If only he could get his wife to release the stranglehold she had on Aiden. He'd rarely said anything, but Josephine's attention on their boy seems unnatural to him. Since Aiden has gone to college, the preoccupation seems to have eased, but he still sees echoes of it.

Some of it is his fault. He'd always been focused on Mosswood, and sometimes on…other diversions.

Like Dahli Reed...

He swears. His marriage may be irreparably frayed. All because of him and his damned ego. And that's something he can't afford.

He picks up his pace. There's no doubt he'll fix the situation. But the solution will require some very distasteful acts indeed.

He reaches the conference room where his chief operating officer has scheduled the meeting, draws himself up and walks in, hoping no one sees behind his veil of uneasiness or catches the twitch under his right eye which causes his flesh to quiver and jump.

When he exits the meeting nearly an hour and a half later, he has plenty of text messages from Josephine, demanding to know if he's done what he said he'd do. He doesn't respond. But heart thrumming, he heads to the other side of the building now.

He feels the change in the air when he walks down the inner hallway where his senior staff sit. Relaxed postures straighten, internet windows are minimized, hallway conversations abruptly stop. This effect is not normally something that bothers him, or even something he notices, but today he is hypersensitive to any unwanted attention.

He reaches his destination and is both alarmed and

relieved to find Dahlia Reed's office darkened.

His mouth pulls down at the corners and he catches the eye of the young woman sitting in the cubicle outside Dahli's office. The nameplate affixed to the cubicle wall outside her desk reads Olivia Mitchell.

When Weston's father had established Mosswood in 1960, he'd known the name of every employee until the day he'd retired. Given the company's growth since the time Weston had been installed at the helm, that type of recognition had become untenable. But there were times he regretted it. Like now.

"Ms. Mitchell." His powerful voice booms across the tops of the cubicles. Olivia jumps even though she's looking right at him.

"Yes, Mr. Moss…" Her voice is high and clipped.

"I was hoping to talk to Dahlia. Is she in?" He inadvertently glances at the phone in his hand.

"She isn't here, and I haven't heard from her. I thought maybe she'd told you her plans."

"What would make you think that?" He says this too quickly.

Olivia clears her throat. "You're her direct supervisor."

Weston blinks. "Have you called her cell phone?"

"Several times. It goes to voicemail." As if to prove her point, she presses a button on her desk phone, then shrugs and hangs up.

Weston holds his own phone up and does the same

as if he might get a different result. But Dahli's familiar sultry voice says from the speaker: *Hi, you've reached Dahlia…or Dahli, if you'd prefer. I can't take—*

Weston ends the call.

He considers what to say next. "Is there someone else we can contact?" He, of course, knows Dahli is married.

"Her husband?" Olivia asks.

"Okay, yes."

Olivia looks at him. "I've tried him already."

"Go ahead," he prompts.

Olivia appears as though she might argue, but then she frowns and presses a button.

As they wait, a man hurries in, flustered and out of breath. He rushes by Weston, bringing a cloud of foul-smelling air with him. Weston's nostrils twitch. The man reeks of mothballs and decay.

He may need to have Kelly send out a note about proper hygiene practice.

The man nearly trips over his own feet when he notices Weston. Then he settles into the cubicle over the wall from Olivia, mumbling something about an appointment.

"He didn't answer," Olivia says, ignoring the disturbance caused by her neighbor.

Weston feels queasy. "Did it go immediately to voicemail?"

She shakes her head. "It rang through."

"Call it again."

She does. Then again and again.

Finally, her expression shifts, and she says, "I'm sorry, Mr. Reed. This is Olivia Mitchell from Mosswood. I work with your wife, Dahlia."

Weston stares at Olivia, but he's aware they've attracted a crowd of interested bystanders.

"I'm calling because Dahlia didn't come into work today, and she's missed a number of important meetings. Her calls are going straight to voicemail, and it doesn't appear her texts are being delivered. Is she okay?"

A pause.

"Mr. Reed?"

Another pause.

"Did she say anything about missing work when you spoke with her? Was she ill?"

A frown creases Olivia's forehead. "It's just…" She hesitates, then says, "It's not like Dahlia not to check in."

Although Weston can't hear the other end of the conversation, from Olivia's deep frown and tense questions, he imagines the inquiry isn't welcome.

This, he thinks, is a comfort.

"We're worried about her well-being, Mr. Reed. Please have her call us as soon as you hear from her, okay? We want to make sure she's safe."

Olivia hangs up. "He says she's fine."

Weston glances toward Dahli's office. Then he looks at his phone.

"Should we call anyone else?"

Weston can tell she's wrestling with the amount of emotional capital to invest in the situation. He knows how she feels, but he's got a hell of a lot more invested than anyone else does.

He puffs out his cheeks while he considers the next step. Olivia was right about one thing—disappearing is not in Dahli's character. He's rarely met a more attentive, ambitious, responsible, or thoughtful person. In fact, he's never met anyone quite like Dahli Reed.

"Perhaps she's at home, in bed," says Weston, and the irony of uttering this statement aloud to his employees is far from lost on him. "Let's give it a few hours, and we'll talk again."

Olivia nods; the employees milling around look more concerned than they probably need to be. He stifles the urge to tell them to go back to work. That would make him appear insensitive.

He heads back to his office where Kelly is waiting. "Mrs. Moss has called several times," she says. Her color is high, and Weston imagines his assistant may have caught some of the fire intended for him.

"I'll take care of it." He hesitates, and Kelly looks at him expectantly. "Dahlia hasn't happened to call, has she?"

"Dahlia Reed?"

He doesn't bother responding. There is only one Dahli.

"No, she hasn't."

But Weston already knew that.

He nods and moves to the door, about to shut it behind him, when Kelly adds, "Have you checked with Candace?"

Candace Witten, Mosswood's consultant for regulatory and government relations, is in Washington DC this week. Candace Witten is also his wife's niece. It's a connection neither of them go out of their way to publicize.

Weston pauses with his hand on his door handle. "Why would I do that?" he asks slowly.

"She and Dahlia are good friends."

Weston swallows. He hadn't realized that. He knows Dahlia and Candace work together, of course, but Dahli's never mentioned a friendship. Nor has Candace.

The skin at the back of his neck prickles.

"I'll give her a call," he mumbles distractedly before he shuts the door.

He'll do no such thing.

CHAPTER 4

Eugene Ryan glances at Dahli's darkened office and listens to what's happening over the wall of his cubicle. He resists the urge to poke his head up, only listening, like the rest of the prairie dogs in the maze of cubicles encircling the outer perimeter of the office.

The executives at the company—led by useless CEO Weston Moss—act like the plebians were gifted from on-high their labyrinth of low-walled cubicles. They spout scripted talking points about natural light and a collaborative work environment. But all they've really done is install higher walls for the illusion of privacy, or at best save some money by not building more offices.

Eugene listens to Olivia's exchange with the person he assumes is Dahli Reed's husband.

Eugene has never met Dahli's husband, and he doesn't want to. Dahli is precious—an angel. No man is good enough for her. He thinks of her long brunette waves, those kind brown eyes. The way her pillowy lips curve into a smile when she sees him.

The daydream doesn't last long before the familiar

wave of anger rises up, washing away the serene image of Dahli from his thoughts. She can never be his. Not fully.

The anger gives way to anxiety, and he does his best to stay calm.

Weston Moss speaks from over the wall, a rare indecisiveness in the man's powerful voice.

Eugene mops his brow with his forearm, and despite everything else going on, he smiles. Weston's discomfort is a bright spot in his otherwise awful day.

From Olivia's responses he can tell Dahli's husband isn't as concerned as Olivia and Weston are about Dahli's absence.

Dahli's husband is an idiot, Eugene thinks. If he possessed someone like Dahli, he'd never let her out of his sight.

His smile fades.

If only he had Dahli all for himself…

He stares at his blank brown fabric wall; her face reappears. She smiles at him. He tangles his fingers into her thick hair while the fingertips of his other hand caress her lips, which are dry and matte against his skin. He cups her cheek with his palm while his other hand slides down the creamy, delicate skin of her throat. His finger travels lower to the collar of her shirt, dipping just below the hem—

"Eugene!"

Olivia's voice breaks Eugene's reverie. He looks up.

"Dahlia Reed didn't say anything to you about being out today, did she?"

He blinks. "Why would she?"

"She has an appointment on her calendar. It says, 'Check in with Eugene'."

Eugene's breath catches. He's only ever spoken with Dahli directly a few times, and he isn't sure if she's ever said his name. He imagines her forming the two syllables in her husky voice that spills from tender pink lips…

"Eugene…" Olivia's strident voice propels him back to reality.

He looks up.

The woman shoots him a disgusted look. "Why were you meeting with her?"

Eugene makes a show of looking at the calendar tab on his laptop, but he knows there's no meeting with Dahli scheduled. He has an idea why she may have wanted to talk with him, though…

Olivia clears her throat.

"No meeting." He holds his palms up in submission.

The woman gives him a hard look before she sits back down. She makes another phone call—he's not sure to whom—and asks about Dahli. She says something quietly that Eugene can't hear, then replaces the handset. It's quiet for a few minutes before Olivia stands and leaves her cubicle. The light goes on in

Dahli's office.

Eugene's palms are sweating. He wipes them on his cheap chinos. He takes a drink from the bottle of water on his desk and forces his breathing to a normal rhythm. He isn't sure there's anything to be worried about, but the air feels charged and the atmosphere quivers in anticipation. Semi-hidden within the walls of his cube, he rubs the back of his neck then leans toward his glowing laptop. He will attempt to concentrate on work.

The fat moon-face of his mother floats in front of his eyes, and he blinks, willing her away.

"Fuck you, Glenda," he says under his breath. It's bad enough he has to deal with the woman at home. He doesn't want to think about her at work, too.

She sneers at him.

Loser, she says, panting. Her lips are dry, like Dahli's. They are also pale and cracked. The skin of the face isn't soft and smooth, but red and broken and ugly.

He tries to conjure Dahli's gentle face. Her soft voice.

They're going to find out what you've done, his mother rasps. The loose skin of her neck wobbles. *They're going to know about you, Eugene.*

"Fuck you," he says, louder this time.

A few cubicles away, a man clears his throat, and Eugene slouches lower in his ergonomic chair. He opens Mosswood's property inspection software. The company employs a number of third-party inspectors who enter their data into the prescribed application. Eugene's job is to ensure the reports are complete and then track the status of the inspections in Mosswood's master schedule. It isn't taxing work, and it doesn't pay well, but Eugene makes enough money from the job to comfortably afford the extra necessities he and Glenda need. His disabled mother's meager monthly income is not enough to subsist even in their modest home in North Charleston. Not in this economy.

Once he's able to force his thoughts onto his work, he spends the next hour studying the submitted reports, searching for anomalies, and updating the master schedule with the status of the inspection reports.

When his tasks are complete, he checks the time, then stands to make his way to the conference room on the second floor for the scheduled status meeting on the Park Circle project. Normally, he'd call into the meeting from his desk, where he'd say nothing and give a four-word answer when his name was called. "No change in status." It's far too early in the project for any inspections. But today, he will attend in person.

Before he leaves the area, he glances over the wall of the cubicle divider; he notices the website for the Charleston Police Department open on Olivia's screen. Again, his breath hitches in his chest. He walks quickly away.

In the conference room, other than for a few curious glances, no one pays him much attention. He takes a seat in a chair at the far end of the room, away from the table, as conversations swirl around him. A man named Pete talks to a woman named Susan about the trouble they're having with the city in obtaining an environmental permit.

Another man whose name Eugene has forgotten is animated while he describes a round of golf—and a particularly good shot—to the project manager, Kent. Kent is only half listening as he connects his laptop to the video screen.

There are around ten participants in the conference room and a number of other employees dialed in through the video feed. A few of them are on camera but many have cameras turned off, the boxes along the side of the screen displaying only disembodied initials.

Eugene takes this all in anonymously.

Kent checks the time and says, "Let's go ahead and get started." He frowns as he surveys the employees. "Do we have Dahlia Reed or someone from her team here? There's an unflattering opinion piece that mentions the project in the *Post and Courier*. I want to make sure she's tracking."

No one in the room seems to have heard the rumor that Dahli hasn't shown up for work. There is nothing but blank looks and shrugs around the table. Eugene monitors these reactions, but the meeting participants don't seem suspicious or concerned.

Kent sighs. "I'll catch up with her offline." Then he starts the meeting.

Eugene tunes out until it's his turn to give an update. He utters the same four words. "No change in status." Likely because he's reciting those words in person, instead of as one of the disembodied boxes on the screen, Kent and everyone else in the room look at him curiously.

While Eugene hates the attention, he's accomplished what he's set out to do. He leans back and holds his breath before they all shift their attention and move on.

After the meeting ends, he foregoes the sidebar conversations and other pleasantries, and stops by the vending machines in the breakroom to purchase a bag of pretzels and a diet soda with his slightly damp and crumpled five-dollar bill. He hadn't had time to prepare his usual soggy peanut butter and jelly sandwich earlier. And after he'd prepared Glenda's large breakfast, he hadn't thought to eat his own.

When he gets back to his desk, he opens the pretzels and wakes his sleeping laptop.

Olivia moves around on the other side of the wall. Her desk phone trills just as Eugene is taking a drink of soda.

"Mr. Moss," she says. Her tone is tight and efficient. There's a pause. She lowers her voice when she says, "No, nothing yet."

Eugene moves closer to the thin wall separating him from Olivia.

"I didn't bother. It didn't seem like he wanted to talk to me the first time."

He carefully replaces the cap on his soda bottle. Two women who are laughing loudly walk around the corner and stop in the main hallway immediately in front of Eugene's desk. They prattle on about a child; Eugene shoots them a disgusted look. They don't notice.

He can't hear anything Olivia is saying.

He stands and says, "Excuse me. Some of us are trying to work."

Their heads swivel toward him. The woman on the left, with dirty-blonde hair and a tight plaid dress, looks as though she might laugh. The slimmer woman on the right, wearing a beige cardigan over an ugly green shirt and loose, unflattering khaki slacks, mumbles, "Sorry." But they move along, heads down, shoulders quaking. He doesn't care that they're laughing at him.

He sits back down and assumes his position close to Olivia. She is in the middle of a sentence.

"…not our place to call them."

The volume of Olivia's voice fluctuates and becomes louder. Eugene realizes she's swiveled her chair toward him in an effort to huddle away from her officemates.

"Candace Witten? She's in DC this week at a conference."

Eugene's pulse thrums. Dahli and Candace are friends, though he doesn't think many people at the office know about their friendship. He's seen them having lunch together, shopping on the weekends, and walking through the historic district with their heads bent close together.

"Yes, I can get ahold of her."

Olivia sighs after she disconnects from the call.

Eugene quietly places the pretzel bag in his trash bin and waits.

A moment later, Olivia, still apparently huddled in his direction, says, "Hi, Candace. This is Olivia Mitchell, Dahlia Reed's assistant. I'm glad I caught you. Have you, by chance, heard from Dahlia today?"

A pause.

"Well, she didn't call in and she didn't cancel any of her standing meetings. And she was scheduled to meet with Mr. Moss this afternoon."

Another pause.

"I spoke with her husband, and he seems to think everything is fine. Frankly, he sounded annoyed I'd called."

A man walks down the hallway and peers at Eugene hunched against the wall. Eugene makes, then breaks eye contact and pretends to retrieve something from the floor under the desk.

The man moves on.

"Don't you think that's a little invasive?" Olivia asks, then answers, "Of course not… Okay, I can go… Yes, I'll let you know." She mumbles a thanks and replaces the handset. Then she exhales loudly and clacks away at her keyboard before shuffling objects around her desk.

The unmistakable clinking of keys meets Eugene's ears before Olivia stands and steps outside her cubicle.

Eugene half-stands and watches Olivia's broad back as she slips on a light jacket and moves down the hallway.

Quickly, he locks his computer and hurries after the administrative assistant, meeting her at the elevator bank in the center of the building. She doesn't look at him, but shifts slightly away as he stands next to her.

"Are you going to check on Dahli? At her house?"

Olivia spares him the briefest of glances before looking away. "What makes you think that?" He can hear the alarm in her tone.

"I sit right next to you. Hard not to hear. Do you want some backup?"

"No." Olivia fixes her stare on the digital floor numbers above the elevator doors.

"It might be smart to have someone with you. In case you find something you hadn't expected."

Though she doesn't look at him, her expression

shifts. He can tell she's considering any number of possibilities that might meet her at Dahlia Reed's house.

Olivia is in her mid-thirties, unmarried, childless. She's at least fifteen pounds overweight, keeps her limp brown hair cut in a blunt, shapeless style, and dresses in bargain-store shirts and slacks. Eugene imagines she spends her evenings glued to true-crime documentaries on her television set. He imagines she's pictured herself in any number of those unfortunate scenarios that tend to befall single, lonely women.

The elevator doors slide open.

"Fine," she says tightly, and Eugene enters the car before the doors slide shut.

He bites the inside of his cheek to suppress his smile.

When they exit the building into the midday sunshine, Olivia hesitates. He can tell she doesn't want him to know what car she drives—a 2019 white Kia hatchback. It's parked in the second row.

But she seems to decide that inviting him into her car is preferable to getting into his, and after a brief pause, she walks resolutely toward the Kia, unlocking it with her fob as they approach.

After they're both settled, Olivia enters Dahli's address into an app on her cell phone, and a woman's voice announces the route.

Eugene could have navigated them to their destination without the help of technology, but he keeps his mouth shut.

They drive north toward the Hanahan suburbs in silence. With normal midday traffic, the route takes them approximately twenty minutes, during which zero words are exchanged between them.

This is fine with Eugene. He has nothing to say and is comfortable in silence. But it makes Olivia fidgety. The few times she seems on the verge of speaking, she immediately stops herself and swallows her words.

Eventually, they pull up to a blue one-story cement-sided home of modest size. The driveway is empty, and half of the front yard is torn up with a landscaping project. But the neighborhood is quiet. A delicate white butterfly flutters around a pile of sod.

Eugene sweeps his gaze around the lawn, then he and Olivia exit the vehicle. He follows her onto a covered porch ringed by a white railing. Two wooden rocking chairs shift ghost-like in the breeze.

Olivia presses the bell. When there is no immediate answer, she peers through the door's frosted decorative window.

Eugene hears the chime echoing inside the house and makes a show of listening for Dahli's voice to come through the bell's intercom.

Silence.

Olivia presses the button again, and Eugene moves to the center of the porch in front of the large bay window framed by two black shutters.

Through gauzy white curtains, he makes out a tastefully decorated room filled with an oversized sofa, loveseat, and chairs. There's a painting above the sofa, the subject of which he can't make out. An upright piano rests against the far wall, and a television set has been mounted on the wall opposite the sofa. There's no sign of disorder.

There's no sign of Dahli.

"I don't think she's here," Olivia says, her voice tentative, unsure.

Eugene walks off the porch toward the garage. Of average height, he must stand on his toes to survey the interior of the bay. He looks through the row of windows at the top of the retractable door.

He can make out one vehicle parked inside the dark space, but it's impossible to determine whether it's Dahli's dark blue Lexus.

Olivia has moved to Eugene's side. She also stands on her toes, but she's not tall enough to see into the windows. "What do you see?"

"A car. I can't tell what kind."

"Dahli drives a Lexus." Olivia has begun hopping, as if the movement might propel her upward. She glances at Eugene, and for a second he thinks she might ask him for a boost.

Then she deflates with a huff of breath and places her hands on her hips. "What now?"

Eugene has no idea. He marvels that he's standing in front of Dahli's home in full view of the entire neighborhood.

He moves from the garage and walks to the backyard, peering over the white fencing into a grassy enclosure shaded by the reddening leaves of the blackjack oak trees. More white butterflies flutter in the breeze. A children's playset—with swings, a sliding board, and a rope ladder—has been erected in the back corner of the carpetlike lawn. A covered back porch is decorated with white wicker furniture, lush green plants, and a stainless-steel grill.

It's all so idyllic; so perfect. He imagines himself standing in front of the grill while the children play. Dahli is lounging on the wicker loveseat, a glass of white wine between her elegant fingers. She's smiling up at him. The children laugh and chase a yellow lab that prances around the lawn.

"Do you see anything?"

Eugene startles. Olivia is at his elbow.

A scowl crosses his face, and he instantly dashes the expression away, replacing it with a blank look. He shakes his head and walks back to the front of the house where a man is standing at one side of the driveway.

At first, Eugene thinks this might be Jeremy, Dahli's husband. But upon closer inspection, he realizes the man is older.

"Can I help you?" the man asks. His voice is mildly curious and not unfriendly.

He's looking at Eugene, but it's Olivia who answers. "We're co-workers of Dahlia Reed. She didn't come into work today, and we came by to check on her."

He frowns. "I haven't seen her. I've been home all morning."

"Do you live around here?"

He points to a house next door with faded siding and a sparse lawn.

"Did you see Dahlia leave for work this morning?"

He shakes his head. "Not that I recall. I saw Jeremy leave with the kids, but I didn't notice Dahli."

Olivia frowns. "Dahlia is usually the one who drives the kids to school."

The neighbor shrugs, unconcerned. "Maybe she had another meeting somewhere. She's kind of a big deal, I hear." He chuckles, and his lips quirk.

Eugene isn't sure what the guy is implying, but he doesn't like it. He takes a step forward, but no one notices.

Olivia nods and says, "Maybe." The word is skeptical, but the man isn't paying attention.

He turns his attention back to Eugene and gives him a onceover. "Do I know you?"

"I don't think so."

"You look so familiar. I know I've seen you somewhere..."

Eugene resists the urge to turn around. He keeps his breathing regular and his expression passive. He doesn't respond.

The man examines him for a second longer before giving up the search of his mind. He aims his thumb over his shoulder and toward his house. "I've got to get back to it, but if I see anything, I'll be sure to let you know. Do you want me to tell Dahli you've been looking for her when I see her?"

"That would be great," says Olivia, and the man nods.

"The name's Bill, by the way. I should have asked…have you called Jeremy?"

Olivia shifts her weight from one foot to the other. "We spoke to him earlier. He said everything was fine."

"Well, there you go. Nothing to worry about."

The neighbor holds out his hands, smiles, then turns away and walks across his lawn toward his front door. Eugene notices there isn't a security camera installed on his home. Likewise, the residents on the other side of Dahli's home have not installed one either.

Just as Olivia and Eugene reach the car, the man turns back around and calls loudly, "Bingo."

They both glance up.

"I've seen you with your mother at the senior center in North Charleston."

Eugene exhales slowly. It's been months since he's

taken Glenda to the senior center. It's been months since she's been well enough to leave the house.

"How's she doing?" the man calls.

Eugene doesn't answer immediately. Even from this distance, he recognizes the mix of sympathy, curiosity, and amusement most people have when asking about Glenda. It never fails to provoke embarrassment, shame, and anger in him.

Bill waits a beat longer, but when it becomes clear Eugene isn't going to answer, he says, "Well. I'll be sure to tell Dahli you stopped by."

They climb in the car and Olivia starts the engine, but she doesn't move.

They both stare at the empty windows of Dahli's home.

Olivia makes a noise at the back of her throat, then says in a voice just above a whisper, "I'm not sure if Dahli's coming back."

Eugene doesn't answer.

But he thinks, *Neither am I.*

CHAPTER 5

Candace Witten glances down at the phone buzzing on the white tablecloth in front of her. She snatches it up along with her notepad and briefcase and wends her way briskly through the tables in the cavernous auditorium where the Deputy Secretary for the Department of Housing and Urban Development is giving her address.

By the time Candace reaches the double doors at the back, her phone is quiet.

The conference center is connected to her hotel, and she finds an empty chair in the lobby near the front windows. The mid-afternoon foot traffic is heavy in the metro center, and she observes the passersby while she redials Olivia Mitchell's number.

The call connects on the first ring, and before Olivia can utter a greeting, Candace says, "What have you found out?"

"Not much," says Olivia. "We went to Dahlia's house, but no one answered the door. Nothing seemed amiss. We spoke with a neighbor who seemed to think there was nothing to worry about."

"Who is 'we'?"

"Excuse me?" Olivia says, and Candace says impatiently, "You said 'we' went. Who did you go with?"

"Oh. Eugene went with me."

"Who the fuck is Eugene?"

Olivia's voice falters. "He's…he works here. He sits outside Dahli's office. We thought it would be safer. You know. In case…"

Candace rests her elbow on her bare knee and her forehead on her palm. "This Eugene guy knows she's missing?"

"He knows Dahlia didn't come to work today. A lot of people know that. I'm not sure any of us know she's *missing*." Olivia emphasizes the word, then says hopefully, "For all we know, she could have come down with a gastrointestinal issue and is too ill to answer her phone. Or the door," she adds.

No, thinks Candace. Not Dahli. Unless she was on her deathbed, Dahli would have dragged herself to work. This job means everything to her. And if she really were that sick, she'd have let someone know.

She would have let Candace know.

But Candace isn't sure that's necessarily true. Not after the last lunch they'd had together a week earlier.

"Have you tried her husband again?" Candace asks in a clipped voice.

"Yes." Olivia's voice tightens. "He didn't answer."

Candace watches the activity in the hotel lobby—

the people checking in and readying for their evenings of business or pleasure. She taps her front tooth with the end of her pen. She knows the people in front of her have their own problems and challenges, but as they laugh and scowl and chatter and stride, she's envious of each and every one of them. Sometimes, she wishes she weren't so…*her*.

She's about to respond to Olivia when her phone beeps with an incoming call.

She holds the device away from her face and is shocked to see Weston Moss's number displayed across her screen.

"Olivia, I'll call you right back."

Without waiting for a response, she switches to her uncle's call.

"Hi. I'm in DC. What can I help you with?"

"Candace," he says warmly with his slow, low country drawl. "How's the conference?"

Candace doesn't work directly for Mosswood Development. She consults for the company, but she has other clients and non-competing interests. The fact that her Aunt Josephine's husband is calling means that someone reminded him of the purpose of her visit to the nation's capital.

"Oh, you know. These things are all about the connections…and the drinks. But I've got some good meetings set up tomorrow on the hill. I'm meeting with Senator Clayton," she says, name-dropping the elected official from their district.

"Good, good," says Weston, but his tone is distracted.

She pictures Weston standing in his office, his steel-gray hair brushed back from his broad forehead. Weston Moss is a large and powerful man—personally, professionally, and politically. The fact that Candace is meeting with Senator James Clayton on behalf of Mosswood is somewhat laughable, considering her uncle likely played a round of golf with him last weekend.

But that's how the political game is played.

Weston hesitates, then says, "Kelly tells me you're close with Dahlia Reed. That true?"

Candace hesitates. This call is not so unexpected after all, she thinks. This call is about Dahli. But why on earth would Weston be asking Candace about Dahli? The man is so wrapped up in his own life, money, and success—Candace is sure he's never taken the time to connect Dahli to Candace.

"I know her. Sure." Candace's voice is cautious. "Why?"

"Funny thing. Dahlia didn't show up to work today. In my experience, that's not like her. Thought I'd check in with you to see if you had any insight."

It's not a question, and Candace knows Weston has carefully chosen his words.

"I—I haven't spoken with Dahlia since late last

week," says Candace. This is a lie, but a small one. "Perhaps she's ill," she says, borrowing Olivia's rationale.

"Perhaps," Weston repeats. His tone is doubtful.

There's another pause. Longer. She waits it out. She has become comfortable with awkward silences. Often, those silences bear the truth.

"When you spoke to Dahlia last, did she indicate any…cause for concern?"

"Concern about what?"

"Anything that might be going on in her life. Issues…developments."

"Developments," Candace repeats slowly. She blinks as the last conversation she'd had with Dahli returns to her. Dahli's eyes shining over weekend mimosas. Her friend had mentioned someone. A man. She'd said she wasn't ready yet to give details. Candace's heart had fallen. Then she'd gotten angry.

It hadn't been the right reaction, and for the past week, Candace has felt the frequent pull of regret, trying to find the best way to apologize. Trying to find the best way to explain her own hastily blurted admission.

And now…

Her heart squeezes as a new alarm sounds in her mind.

Surely the man to whom Dahli had been referring was not Candace's uncle, Weston Moss? Impossible,

Candace assures herself. There's no way Dahli is sleeping with Weston.

Is there?

Candace goes silent as she tries to puzzle it out. But Weston says her name again. Clearly he's worried.

Perhaps he's worried for the same reasons Candace is worried.

She remembers Dahli's breathless excitement. Is it possible Weston had produced that excitement? Her heart thrums as her mouth goes dry.

"Dahli hasn't said anything out of the ordinary to me. We mostly talked about work, but she didn't mention any concerns with her family. Kids are fine. Husband is great."

She waits for a reaction.

Weston's breath is heavy. "Happy to hear that," he finally says. If you do hear from her, could you tell her to please give me a call? We've got some things to discuss. Work-related," he adds.

"Sure, Uncle Wes." It's a designation she rarely uses with her uncle through marriage. "I'll try to give her a call right now."

"You do that. Perhaps you'll have better luck than the rest of us."

Candace says her goodbyes and stares at her phone.

There is something Dahlia Reed hasn't shared with her, and it makes her incredibly sad and increasingly hopeless.

In spite of what she'd told Weston, she doesn't try Dahli's number again. She's already tried her friend's mobile over twenty times. It's gone to voicemail every time. She's sent at least that many unanswered text messages.

Instead, she calls Olivia back. When Olivia answers, Candace says, "That was Weston Moss."

"He's been over here a few times today," says Olivia.

"Over where?"

"At my desk, checking Dahlia's office."

What the hell does he think he's doing?

"Enough is enough. We need to call the police."

"I just feel like it's not our place. Not yet."

Candace considers her own life as a single woman—how long it might take a concerned acquaintance to notice she hasn't been returning calls and texts. A successful professional woman at thirty, she is expected to take care of herself. And she does. But should the unthinkable happen, she's not sure anyone would consider checking up on her.

Olivia continues, "Maybe her husband—"

"Fuck her husband," Candace interrupts.

A shocked silence meets her on the phone, as a woman holding a small child scowls from the chair to Candace's right.

Candace shifts away from the woman and lowers her voice. "Look, I'd rather look foolish in front of the police and Jeremy Reed than find out later she was in danger." *Or worse*, she thinks.

Olivia seems to be considering this. She says, "How about if I wait until the end of the day and check in with Mr. Reed one more time? If Dahlia hasn't surfaced by then, I'll call the police."

Candace wishes she were home. She'd call the damn police herself. But she agrees to Olivia's proposal and disconnects.

She stares again, unseeing, at the rush of foot traffic in the hotel lobby.

Then she lifts her phone and dials again. The next call is gentler, kinder.

"Hey, Aiden. How are you?"

"Hi, Candace," the young man says. His voice sounds tense, stressed. "You always know just when to call."

She isn't sure the comment is meant as a compliment. "Is something going on?" she asks her youngest cousin. While Candace might not be close with Weston, or even Josephine, she's always had a soft spot for their son, Aiden. When she could, Candace was a refuge for the boy from the overbearing, suffocating attention of his mother, whose love for Aiden bordered on obsession.

A memory flashes into Candace's mind: Aiden hiding from his mother in the chicken coop of the family cabin during a birthday party in the rural town of Jamestown over a decade earlier. Candace had found him huddled in the coop as Josephine called his name, frantic at the thought of her son wandering away into the dense forest surrounding their home. *What if he'd fallen into the salt marsh or a tidal waterway?*

But he'd just been looking to escape from his mother. Her attention was fierce, but Aiden was ultimately obedient. He'd always do as his mother asked. He seemed to think he had no choice.

She supposes it is that complicated maternal pull that has drawn Aiden to Dahli as well. Dahli is over a decade older than Aiden, but when he'd begun to help out at Mosswood as a teenager, he'd become obsessed with her. And Dahli, too nice to turn the boy away, had unwittingly encouraged his attention just by being kind to him.

Now that he's a young man in college, Dahli continues to think Aiden's attention is harmless.

It probably is.

And Candace certainly doesn't think Aiden will have any information about Dahli's whereabouts, but with the Moss family…you just never know.

"It's always something with this family," he mumbles into the phone, his comment mirroring Candace's thoughts.

Candace hesitates then asks, "Everything okay at school?"

Aiden studies business with a minor in political

science at Clemson. The plan is for him to take over Mosswood Development, but Candace knows Aiden isn't as interested in this path as his parents like to pretend. Aiden wants to enter politics. And someday, he likely will. But first, he'll do as he's told.

"I'm actually home."

"Home, as in Charleston? For what?" Candace frowns. It's October. The semester is not yet over. "Are you missing a meet?" she asks, referring to his cross-country schedule. "Prep for your finals?"

"Nah," he says. "All good. Where are you?"

She repeats her location for her cousin, then says, "I'll be home tomorrow."

"Maybe…" His words trail off and he hesitates before finishing. "…maybe we can meet."

"Aiden, is everything all right?" She contemplates bringing up Dahli's name but decides against it.

He doesn't mention Dahli or her absence, and so neither will Candace. Not yet.

Aiden is silent for a long time before he answers. When he does, he says, "Let's talk when you get back."

There are a million questions she wants to ask, but she's not sure she's ready to hear the answers. She nods and says, "Sure, Aiden."

Why does it feel like Dahli's name is hanging unspoken between them?

Candace ends the call and considers calling her aunt, but thinks better of it. There's a larger family dynamic at play which Candace is not privy to, nor does she want to be.

Candace's mother, before she passed away, had been Josephine's older, less successful sister. The two of them had grown up in the same house, but once Josephine had set her sights on Weston Moss, she'd shot forward in society and never looked back.

Her mother had never spoken an ill word against her younger sister, but Candace knows how much Josephine's judgment had hurt her.

And when her younger sister had died, Josephine had been so busy with her boutique, she hadn't bothered to come to the service.

Though she'd sent the most beautiful bouquet of Juliet roses.

Participants begin to emerge from the conference center through the far end of the hotel lobby, each adorned with a lanyard and burdened with briefcases, notepads, and business cards. It's not long before a flood of bodies flows into the lobby.

A handsome man with sandy brown hair and blue eyes stands in the throng and glances around. He looks down and types something into his phone. A second later, Candace's phone pulses with a short vibration.

Where'd you go?

The right corner of her mouth quirks as she watches him. *To your left*, she responds.

He lifts his head and scans the lobby.

Joel, from Chicago, is a real estate developer. They'd met yesterday morning when reaching for the same dry dinner roll during the lunch buffet. There had been a connection, and what he wants from Candace has nothing to do with real estate, government affairs, or business. It also has nothing to do with the Moss family, and that is appealing in itself.

She raises her hand, and he spots her, smiles, and heads in her direction.

Candace sighs inwardly. They will make their rounds this evening, attending the conference reception, then heading to a few hospitality suites set up by vendor companies and suppliers wooing the big-name developers and brokers.

While Mosswood Development isn't massive, it's large enough to be a target for some of the smaller suppliers. Candace, as the Mosswood representative, has been popular this week for a number of reasons.

So, she will do her duty and her job. She will listen politely and say all the right things. Then, she will take this handsome man to her hotel room and her bed, and she will attempt to forget all about politics and construction. She will forget about the Moss family.

And for just a little while, she will try to put out of her mind her beautiful and complicated best friend Dahli Reed. And her own equally complex feelings for the missing woman.

CHAPTER 6

Jeremy Reed sits at a sticky vinyl booth in the corner of the Bolthole Lounge. He huddles over his glass, barely noticing the other patrons in the restaurant. As the afternoon wears on, the increase in ambient noise surrounds him like a cocoon.

There's a country song playing. Like the male singer, Jeremy feels like his world is also on fire. The flames feel like they're going to consume him.

He takes another swallow of the amber-colored medicine from the cloudy glass in front of him.

He's made so many bad choices. Choices he can never escape.

He's not sure how much time has passed since he walked out of his office. The sun had sunk low in the sky then disappeared. In sync with the planetary movement, Jeremy graduated from light beer to bourbon.

Now he's bleary-eyed and cotton-headed.

A sudden hush falls over the crowd, leaving only the sound of the song—*flames getting higher.*

Jeremy looks up as two uniformed police officers

walk toward him. He eyes them, and only when they stop next to his table does he think to straighten.

"Jeremy Reed?" the larger of the two asks. His nametag reads 'Parker'. He is young and lean, and has a round face that hasn't yet lost its boyishness.

Despite the man's youth, Jeremy lifts his head up a notch. These men cannot be there for him, can they? He searches his memory, but his thoughts swim together. The only memory that surfaces is a long-ago recollection of the small-town sheriffs who'd visited his home back in Ohio when he and Sammy were young. He remembers the panic he'd felt when he realized they could take them away. Put them in strange homes. Split them up.

Jeremy shifts his shoulders back. "That's me." In his inebriated state, the words sound forced and unnatural to his own ears. "What seems to be the trouble, sir?" This second attempt sounds even worse—nasal and high-pitched. He clears his throat as if his voice may be the problem.

The officers exchange a glance. The other officer, whose nametag reads 'Lucero', says, "You're a hard man to track down."

"Not trying to hide."

"Really? You checked your phone lately?"

Jeremy makes a show of looking around, but he knows he's left his phone in the car.

Lucero—a short, stocky, muscled man at least a

decade Jeremy's senior—eyes the empty bottles and the glass in front of him. "How long have you been here?"

Because Jeremy had just been contemplating this very question and doesn't have a good answer, he says, "An hour or so."

Parker sucks on his front teeth. "How long do you plan on staying?"

"As long as it takes, I guess." This means absolutely nothing, but Jeremy thinks it sounds good, and he's pleased with himself. He grins.

Lucero leans forward, his hands on the table. Though his expression is mild enough, the movement is vaguely threatening, and Jeremy leans back.

"Did you forget about something this afternoon, Mr. Reed?"

He scrambles back through his foggy memory. Was he forgetting something? The events of the day assault him in violent flashes. His palms begin to sweat.

He manages to summon a self-righteous sense of anger. As far as these two clowns are aware, he hasn't done anything wrong. He's a grown man, and he's allowed to have a drink. Or two. Or even three.

"I don't have anywhere to be but right here." To drive home his point, he takes the last swallow from the glass of whiskey. He drinks it too fast, and it threatens to come back up again. He belches but swallows it back, keeping the liquid in his stomach.

Parker's face hardens. "I think your children would

beg to differ. Luke and Maeve, isn't that right?"

Jeremy's mind goes blank for a few seconds. Then, for the first time since the officers walked in, fear rushes in. "What do my children have to do with anything?"

"Luke's teacher called us when he couldn't get in touch with you or your wife. Maeve's principal called us separately."

Jeremy opens his mouth to respond, but no words came out.

"They're at the station," Lucero continues.

"That makes no sense. Dahli would have picked them up." He drops his head in his hands and rubs his temples as if he can massage some clarity back into his mind.

"Your wife, Dahlia Reed?"

Who the fuck else would he be talking about?

"She picks them up every day. If she wasn't able to pick them up, she would have let me know."

"And where is your phone?"

Shit, Jeremy thinks.

The officers are waiting for an answer. "It's—it's in my car," says Jeremy. "If Dahli hasn't gotten them, I'll pick them up now."

He moves as if to stand, but Parker holds up a hand. "You won't be driving anywhere, sir. Not in your state."

"But if Dahli isn't home—"

"We'll drive you, and I'll radio for someone to bring the kids," Lucero answers. "Maybe by then your wife will have arrived home, too. You'll likely get a call from Children and Youth Services over the next couple of days, but if this is the first issue you've had—and it's indeed a miscommunication—it shouldn't be much more than an inconvenience for you."

"Kids are a hell of an inconvenience," says Parker with a smirk.

His words unleash an anger in Jeremy. Perhaps it's because of his own childhood, when his mother decided that getting high was preferable to parenting.

Jeremy is not his mother, and he wants to punch the young cop in the face. The kid knows nothing.

The eyes of both cops are judging him, trying to decide what caliber of man he is. What kind of father.

One thing's for sure—he loves his kids more than anything on earth. He would never do anything to hurt them or place them in danger. And that will never change. No matter how he feels about his wife.

He abruptly raises his hand, and the cops startle and take a step forward. But he only intends to signal the server for the check.

The bartender—who's also the owner of the Bolt-hole Lounge—is hovering close by, and Jeremy notices that every one of the customers in the bar is looking in their direction with a mixture of interest, amusement, and disgust.

When Parker and Lucero also look around, the owner hurries over. He doesn't look at Jeremy.

"Everything all right here, officers?"

Jeremy pulls out his wallet and credit card.

"Nothing to worry about, Rick," Lucero says. "Personal situation, that's all."

"You know I don't want any trouble here. I run a clean place."

"No trouble from us," Lucero says. "If we have any other questions, we'll be sure to be back though."

Jeremy tries to hand Rick his credit card, but the bartender just scowls at it. "Your money is no good here," he says.

It's clear Jeremy won't be welcome in the Bolthole again.

As he rises and leaves the lounge, accompanied by the police, the people who'd been staring moments earlier avert their eyes. Jeremy feels like a criminal, even though, as far as they know, he hasn't done a damn thing wrong.

They pass through the doors into the cool night air, and Parker says, "You're going to want to call your mother."

Jeremy glares at him. "Excuse me?"

"When the school couldn't get in touch with you or your wife, the receptionist started to call other numbers on file. Your mother is concerned and has called the department a number of times for an update.

She wants to know if she should fly in."

"My mother is dead." This isn't technically true, but it may as well be.

What *is* true is that there's no way in hell Jeremy's mother's phone number has been listed on either of the children's school contact forms.

Parker is unbothered. "Your wife's mother then."

That makes much more sense. Sherri Darling never hesitates to stick her nose where it didn't belong. Jeremy would not be calling the woman back. But to Parker, he says, "We'll get in touch with her." He feels mostly sober now, and impossibly tired. All he wants to do is climb in bed, drift off, and never wake up.

But that is not an option. Luke and Maeve need him, even if his wife doesn't anymore.

Lucero helps him duck into the back seat of the Hanahan police cruiser. He reminds himself this is just a ride, and tries to ignore the people in the parking lot watching. It doesn't matter that he's not cuffed. He imagines the photos they're likely posting on social media, his identity clearly visible for the world to see.

Is this going to get back to his company? he wonders. If he thought he was in trouble with Carter before, things might get a whole lot worse for him.

Another wave of anger rises up at the memory of the day's events: at Dahli's blatant dismissal of him that morning; of Carter's pronouncement of his demotion; of his children, abandoned at the police station. Of the darker thoughts that had overtaken him.

Jeremy pushes back against the pressure of Lucero's hand guiding him into the rear of the vehicle. "My phone," he says, hitching his head toward his SUV.

The older cop sighs and nods, and Parker accompanies him to his black Toyota, not trusting that he might not get in and take off. Where they think he might go is beyond him.

He uses his fob to unlock the doors and leans over the console where he'd stashed his mobile out of sight of thieving eyes.

He grabs the device, and when his thumb brushes the screen, the phone activates. Jeremy balks at the number of notifications on his screen. Dozens and dozens of missed calls and text messages overlap the family photo on his screensaver. The notifications are from everyone—his wife's coworkers to his in-laws, along with a host of numbers that aren't familiar to him.

He scrolls through them, noting that many are from contacts asking about arrangements for the children, but just as many are demanding Dahli's location.

He remembers the call he'd received from his wife's assistant as he was in the middle of his demotion. What was her name? *Allison? Andrea?*

He glances down at the phone.

Olivia. Olivia Mitchell.

A thin quiver of fear pulses through him.

Leave it to Dahli to fuck him over once again, one last time. This time, with her absence.

Lucero peers at him, trying to get a look at his phone. Jeremy huddles away.

"Everything okay? Looks like a lot of people have been trying to get in touch with you. Not just the police."

"Some missed calls," Jeremy mumbles.

"I imagine there'd be quite a few."

Jeremy glances at him to see if there's a hidden meaning behind his words, but Parker has looked away as the pair walk back to the police cruiser.

The darkened scenery of the town passes by as he looks out the window from the back seat of the car. And when they pull up in front of his home, the residence is just as dark as the scenery.

He frowns deeply, glancing around at the inert piles of untouched dirt on the front lawn and the windows staring at him like black malevolent eyes.

Both Parker and Lucero seem to feel the need to walk him to the front door, which he unlocks.

He steps inside, then turns and pastes on a smile for the officers. Whatever buzz remaining from the alcohol is long gone.

"Thanks so much for your help this evening."

The officers stare at him.

"Wife still isn't here?" Parker asks. He glances around Jeremy to the interior of his home.

The wattage of Jeremy's fake smile dims. He blocks the officer's view with his body and digs the short nails of his left hand into his palm. "What about my kids?"

"Someone from the Youth Services Division will be by shortly."

Jeremy nods, mumbles a thank you, and shuts the door on Officers Parker and Lucero. He hopes he never sees either of them again.

He flips on the lights and moves around the house.

The kitchen is exactly as he left it. Same dishes in the sink basin. Dahli's empty water bottle still stands sentinel on the countertop. The rooms feel empty. They smell empty.

He moves into the master suite. The bed is the same—unmade and sleep-rumpled. He visualizes Dahli's slim body under those covers. Her dark hair fanned out over the pillowcase. In his mind, her eyes are open. Can she see him, too?

He's not sure how long he stands in the room, staring at the bed.

The chime of the doorbell startles him, and he rubs his face with his hands. He must put on a show for the children. They must not worry.

But when he throws open the door, it's not the children.

It's a man and a woman staring at him with unsmiling faces. They're both dressed in drab unshapely slacks and dark button-down shirts. They carry with them the scent of stale coffee.

"Mr. Reed?" the woman asks.

He answers in the affirmative, and she holds up a slim leather portfolio with a photograph and small gold badge. "My name is Detective Miriam Ballard. This is my colleague, Detective Arthur Hill."

Jeremy stares at the pair of them without reacting, though inside, his stomach is roiling.

The woman's eyebrows lift, pulling her expression upward. It makes her look younger, and Jeremy thinks he may have seen her somewhere before. "Can we come in, ask you a few questions?"

"Is this about the children?" he asks. "Because the other two told me they'd be dropped off."

Detective Ballard glances briefly at her partner, whose expression doesn't change. "Children?" No one speaks, and Ballard finally says, "Mr. Reed, we're here about your wife."

The air squeezes from Jeremy's chest, but after a moment, he stands back and allows the pair to step past him into the small foyer.

Ballard glances around the living room, but the other one—Hill—keeps his eyes trained on Jeremy's face.

"Nice house," the woman comments, surveying the decor.

Her eyes land on the wedding photo of Jeremy and Dahli displayed prominently on the mantel. Dahli is looking straight ahead at the camera—at the observer—a soft, secret smile on her face. Jeremy is gazing with a serious expression at his wife. Though it is a photo of both of them, the subject here is clearly Dahli. Jeremy has been relegated to the background.

Jeremy waits for the commentary on Dahli's beauty—the typical reaction to the photo—but Ballard remains silent. Instead, she shifts her attention to Jeremy, who looks back at her.

She's in her mid-forties. Her hair is a dusty brown color, darker at the ends and graying at the roots. She was probably attractive once upon a time, but she seems to have stopped trying.

"Mind if we sit for a minute?"

He gestures toward the sofa, where the detectives settle side by side. Reluctantly, he perches on the edge of an armchair.

"You play?" Detective Ballard asks, nodding toward the piano on the other side of the room.

He shakes his head. "My wife does."

"I've always wanted to learn but never got around to it. What does she play?" At his blank expression, she holds out her hands. "Classical, blues, jazz…" she suggests. "You know, what genre?"

Jeremy blinks. He opens his mouth, then shuts it before clearing his throat. "I should amend—she *used* to play. She doesn't have much time anymore." A note of bitterness has crept into his tone. He attempts to mask it by offering, "She's talked about trying to teach our daughter, though."

Ballard nods. "Well, I hope your daughter learns. Not enough art in the world if you ask me."

"Why are you here?" Jeremy asks after a pause.

"You don't know?" Hill asks.

Again, Jeremy hesitates. They may be trying to trap him. He says carefully, "You said you had some questions about my wife?"

"And you mentioned your children," says the woman.

There's another brief silent standoff before Jeremy responds. "It's why the other officers tracked me down." At their blank looks, Jeremy says, "Lucero and Parker. They said the kids were down at the station."

Ballard and Hill do not look at each other, but their postures straighten. Then, Ballard smiles and shrugs. She says in a breezy voice, "Just when I think our department is small, I'm surprised again. You work in an office, don't you, Mr. Reed? You know how it is. Not much communication between divisions." She shakes her head. "I guess we're not going to solve that tonight."

He doesn't smile back, and Ballard's expression hardens almost imperceptibly. But Jeremy is watching her.

Hill consults a notepad that he's pulled from his pocket. "Dahlia Reed. That's your wife?"

Jeremy nods.

"When is the last time you saw Dahlia?" Ballard asks.

Again, he's silent.

"Mr. Reed?"

"Dahli," he clarifies. "I-I think it was this morning." Of course, he knows exactly the last time he saw her. He'd just been considering that very thing before they showed up. His heart pounds. "Has something happened?"

"You tell us, Mr. Reed."

Jeremy wishes they'd stop using his last name. He holds his hands out in front of him, helplessly.

The situation has just turned real.

He has nothing to say, and his mouth tastes terrible. He really needs a drink of water. But he doesn't dare get up.

Finally, Detective Ballard leans forward. "The Charleston Police Department received a call, Mr. Reed. From Mosswood Development. Your wife's place of employment. She didn't show up for work today. Are you aware of that?"

His palms are damp. He swallows and his throat bobs with the effort. "No. I mean I..." His words trail off, and he clears his throat and tries again. "Her assistant called me today. I just assumed she had an offsite meeting. She has those often."

Ballard looks down at her notes while Hill stares at him.

"According to the call, her coworkers are extremely concerned. Aren't you?"

He gets the implication. If his wife were missing, he should have been the one to report it.

"Is Dahlia's car here?" Hill asks.

It takes Jeremy a second to process the question. "No, I don't think so." But he looks toward the interior door leading to the garage. He has no idea if Dahli's car is in its bay.

"Mind if we take a look?"

Jeremy stands and leads them to the door. The detectives follow. With every step, he feels as if he's walking in quicksand. His body is numb as he turns the knob and pushes the door open, pressing a button for the overhead light.

In the glow of the fluorescent lighting, Dahli's dark blue Lexus sits like a portent in the pristine bay of the garage. Jeremy walks toward it and peers in the windows. It's empty. The interior is littered with Dahli's usual clutter—bottles of water, sunglasses, and a notebook on the front passenger seat embossed with the Mosswood logo.

In the back is Maeve's booster seat and a pair of Luke's soccer cleats. A half-empty box of crayons sits in the middle console, and a foil candy bar wrapper lies discarded on the floor mat.

The car is just a car.

From inside the house, the doorbell chimes again.

Ballard and Hill, who are watching him from just inside the interior garage door, glance over sharply.

Jeremy brushes past them and hurries down the hallway. He can hear Maeve's voice chattering outside, and he throws open the door.

Another female uniformed officer holds Maeve's hand. When his daughter sees him, she rushes forward and wraps her arms tightly around his leg. "Daddy!"

He places a hand on her back and leans down to kiss the top of her head.

Luke hangs back, looking sullen, embarrassed, and angry.

Detectives Ballard and Hill have followed him, and the female officer who has delivered the children stares at the pair. "Oh!" she exclaims. "I didn't expect to see you here."

Though neither Ballard nor Hill answer, there's an entire unspoken conversation between the officer and the detectives. If the officer had planned to say more, she abandons those plans. She offers a quick goodbye to the children, who don't respond, and a tight nod to Jeremy. She tells him he'll be receiving a follow-up phone call from someone, but Jeremy isn't listening. He nods distractedly and shuts the door.

"I got to see a real jail today," Maeve says, unbothered by the presence of the two strangers in the house. "They showed me where the prisoners go, and they let me do my fingerprints." She holds up her hands which are stained with ink.

"That's great, honey. Why don't you go get your pajamas on and I'll get you something to eat in a minute."

"We had hamburgers already."

"Then get ready for bed and brush your teeth. I'm just finishing up with these nice people."

Luke looks from Jeremy to the detectives and back to Jeremy again. "Where's Mom?"

"She isn't home yet. We're hoping she gets here soon."

"Why didn't you pick us up?"

"I am really sorry, bud. There was just a miscommunication."

"Why weren't you answering your phone? I called you, like, a million times."

"It's a long story." He tries not to let his irritation or his embarrassment show. "Please just help your sister and get ready for bed. I'll come in as soon as I finish up here. Do you have any homework to do?"

"I did it in jail."

If the detectives hadn't been there, Jeremy would have had something to say about his son's attitude. But to his relief, Luke says, "Come on, Maeve." They shuffle to their bedrooms.

Jeremy turns back to the detectives still standing behind him.

"We have just a few more questions then we'll be out of your hair." Ballard actually guides him to the living room, and despite his incredulity, he has no choice but to follow the woman around his own house.

They settle back into their original seats. Jeremy can hear Maeve's high-pitched voice, and Luke's lower one in response.

"Look," Hill says. "We don't want to be here any more than you want us here. Do you have any idea where your wife might be?"

Jeremy recalls his conversations with Dahli over the past few days. There haven't been many of them lately. He shakes his head. "I don't recall her saying anything to me. As far as I know, she planned to go to work today, like normal."

"Did you see her this morning before you left for work?"

"She went out for a run. She's training for a marathon."

Ballard stares at him. Hill makes a note in his notebook. "What time was that?" he asks.

Jeremy thinks back. "Around five."

"And you didn't see her again?"

"No," he says. "I went to the gym. When I got home, she wasn't back, so I got the kids ready. I thought maybe she decided to go for a longer run and just didn't tell me." He tries, but he knows he hasn't completely erased the irritation from his voice.

Hill makes another note.

"When is the marathon?" Ballard asks.

Jeremy's sure Dahli must have told him, but he can't remember. Maybe she hadn't told him. God knew he hadn't been invited along on the trip. He shrugs at the detective.

"You're not a runner, Mr. Reed?"

He shakes his head. He hates running. "I go to the gym when I can."

"You said you went to the gym this morning," says Ballard. "You leave the kids home alone?"

Jeremy feels defensive, just like Dahli had made him feel that morning. "Luke is twelve. I don't think that's too young to stay home for an hour or so in the morning. Both he and Maeve were still sleeping, and the door was locked."

"I'm only trying to establish the timeline." She holds up a hand and drops it back into her lap. "So, you go to the gym, your wife goes out for a run. You get home and she's not here. You don't think that's terribly out of the ordinary because she often goes for a longer run. Is that something she does often? Leaves the kids so she can train?"

Jeremy tries to work out what the detective is implying. He says, "She would never do anything to harm the kids. Neither would I."

Hill and Ballard shift in their seats, and he knows what they're thinking—an officer had to drop the kids off at the house because no one picked them up from school.

No one acknowledges this out loud, but Ballard says, "No one called you about your wife or the kids? I'm just trying to understand how you didn't know."

His hackles rise, and he grinds his teeth together, the muscles in his jaw working. "I'd left my phone in the car."

"All afternoon?" Hill's voice is skeptical. "What were you doing?"

God. They were going to make him say it. "I stopped to have a drink."

Hill's expression doesn't quite devolve into cynicism, but it comes close. "In the middle of the day. Without your phone."

"You can check with Officers Parker and Lucero if you don't believe me. They picked me up at the Bolthole." Even to his own ears, it sounded pathetic. They must think he's a complete loser.

Ballard continues to stare at him.

Hill snaps his notebooks shut and Jeremy slides to the front of the chair, hopeful they'll be leaving in a minute.

"What route does your wife take?" Ballard asks.

"Excuse me?"

"Dahlia's running route. Does she run the same

path every day?"

"I'm not sure," Jeremy says. "It depends on the length of her run. She's very safe, though. She carries an alarm, and I think she has mace or pepper spray or something."

Hill nods, but Ballard stares at him and gives a small shake of her head. She looks toward the front door. "We're going to need to see the footage from your security camera."

"Why?"

"Why do you think, Mr. Reed?" Her voice is strained. "We're trying to find your wife. And I'm finding it really curious that we seem more concerned about locating her than you do. Or is there something you're not telling us?"

He opens his mouth and considers telling them about the frequent text messages Dahli receives. About her meetings that seem to take place later and later in the day. About the quiet phone calls she takes with her home office door shut, or about the times he's come across her smiling at her phone then immediately locking her screen and wiping the emotion from her face.

He considers telling them he suspects she may be with someone else right now.

Instead, he says, "I'll get you the footage."

Ballard sighs. "Can you think of anywhere your wife might be? And anyone she might have gone with, either willingly or unwillingly?"

Jeremy can think of a few people…in both scenarios. But he shakes his head. "Dahli was very careful. I'm sure she'll turn up."

"Mr. Reed. Your wife went for a run this morning, and no one has seen her since."

Jeremy understands the implication, and he realizes they want him to panic. They can't understand his reaction, and he can't explain it to them. All he can do is say, "I'm sure Dahli is safe."

Finally, both detectives stand and walk to the door. Jeremy follows so he can lock the house behind them.

Ballard turns around and hands him a card with her contact information. "If your wife comes home, contact us immediately. In the meantime, we'll start to make some inquiries. If, as you said, she'd do nothing to hurt her kids, her continued absence is unusual, to say the least. Wouldn't you agree?"

Jeremy can do nothing but shrug.

He's about to shut the door when Ballard says over her shoulder, "Who's doing your landscaping?"

Jeremy frowns at the change in topic. "Uh…a place called First Shot."

"It looks like they've been hard at work on it." She surveys the yard from the top step. Jeremy waits. "I'm looking to have some landscaping done myself. Always nice to have a reference."

Jeremy doesn't respond.

"We'll be back in touch tomorrow morning. Hopefully Dahli gets back home safe and sound before then."

He shuts the door and leans his head against the smooth wood, sick to his stomach. Deep down, he knows nothing will ever be the same again.

CHAPTER 7

Miriam Ballard gazes at the lawn of the Reed home as she and her partner, Arthur Hill, walk back to their nondescript city-issued black sedan.

"You really thinking about doing some landscaping?" Hill asks.

"Sure," mumbles Miriam, but she doesn't offer any more.

She climbs behind the wheel. She and Hill have been together for five years now and have investigated some mildly interesting cases together. But most cases handled by the Criminal Investigations Division tended to be administrative. Embezzlement. Fraud. Forgery. They've investigated a few sexual assaults and two missing persons cases during which both persons turned up a few days later.

Hanahan is a small town, and the majority of crime tends to happen closer to the city. They're lucky, and Miriam knows it.

But it's a case from a decade earlier—before Hill had joined the team—that's on Miriam's mind. It's a case she will not discuss with her partner, though she knows he's aware of it. She suspects it's on his mind, too.

Erica Abington was a missing single mother whose body was found deep in the Francis Marion National Forest. Miriam has no idea if the circumstances surrounding Dahlia Reed's current absence are anything like Erica's situation. Given how the Abington case ended, she hopes the circumstances are different. But it's hard not to think about it. And it's hard not to dwell on the fateful mistakes Miriam herself made during that case that damaged the course of lives forever. Her own included.

Guilt and shame barrel through her like a train, and she stuffs it down deep, thinking instead of those solemn-eyed children—Luke and Maeve. She keeps their names in her mind like an invocation, and offers a prayer that Dahlia Reed will come home soon.

"Let's take a drive," she says to Hill. He's been with her long enough that he doesn't question the suggestion. When she turns toward Goose Creek, he says, "You really think she would've run this way alone?"

Miriam herself hasn't run for years—not since Erica Abington. Not since her own daughter was a teenager who still loved her.

"Yeah, I do. Her husband said she carried pepper spray and an alarm, remember?" She says this sarcastically, and it's a subtle dig at Dahlia's husband, who'd seemed woefully unconcerned about his absent wife.

But despite the sarcasm, Miriam very much believes Dahlia may have taken this route. Miriam knows from experience that women who run sometimes discount the predatory dangers that can lurk in the shadows. It shouldn't have to be that way. Unfortunately, it is.

She turns onto Henry Brown Boulevard then stops at an intersection.

"She could have gone anywhere," Hill comments.

Miriam nods, but looks toward Red Bank Road which leads toward the Naval Command Station. Beyond are the scenic wetlands surrounding Foster Creek and the Black River. If Miriam were training for a marathon, she'd want a little beauty along her run. And if there'd been problems in the marriage—and something about Jeremy Reed had set off alarm bells—maybe his wife had wanted some serenity, too.

Miriam is careful not to assign premature suspicion to Jeremy, however. She knows from experience it's not always the husband.

Beyond that, they don't even know if a crime has been committed.

She glances up at the stop lights and peers through the window at the stores along their route. "If Dahli doesn't turn up tonight, I want to pull the security footage from these businesses," she mumbles.

Hill doesn't answer.

"What's that app called?" she asked.

"What app?"

"The running one—it tracks your progress and allows you to share with other people. Like social media for your workouts."

Arthur Hill dips his head and looks at her from below his thick eyebrows. He pats his ample midsection. "Do I look like I'd have any clue what you're talking about?"

In his late thirties, Hill isn't obese, but he's not in shape either. He sports a belly made prominent from too much weekend beer, barbequed meat, and fast-food dinners. Hill's wife, Trish, is a real estate agent, and Miriam knows that when Hill isn't eating something unhealthy at the station, he and his wife, along with their two young teenagers, are eating out. What saves Hill is being out in the field. At least he's on his feet.

As she steers back in the direction of the station, Hill says, "It's mighty interesting that her co-workers are the ones who called the cops. Not the husband."

Miriam makes a noncommittal noise and blinks at the road in front of her.

"I mean, who doesn't check their phone all damn day? I've got kids—I'd never leave my house without my phone. And if I somehow forgot it, I'd go back for it. Imagine purposely leaving it behind."

Miriam remembers the days before cell phones. She remembers the days of pagers. She remembers the days when if you were out, you were *gone*— incommunicado. Those days don't exist anymore.

But she's also careful not to get ahead of herself. She's done that before. She wants to do it the right way this time.

"We need to talk to Lucero and Parker," Hill continues.

Miriam nods. Her partner is a verbal processor, and she is cerebral. "Maybe she'll come home tonight," she says aloud, mirroring her earlier thoughts. But she thinks again of Maeve and Luke. Something would have to be awfully important for Dahlia Reed to go 'no contact' for an entire day and leave those children to their own devices.

"We can't assume she will."

There's a warning note in Hill's tone; her partner doesn't want to lose an entire night's worth of searching. She understands. If Dahlia Reed had disappeared that morning, they've already lost a full day of the investigation.

She pulls into the designated parking spot behind the station, and they walk into the building which is bustling with activity, though it is a relatively quiet night.

Miriam nods acknowledgments to a few people and glances toward the closed office door of her boss— Chief Vincent Manning—before heading to her desk. Uneasy, she kneads the tender, stress-tightened back of her neck with her fingers.

She wants to listen to the initial emergency call from Mosswood Development that reported Dahlia Reed missing. She also wants to look at the report from the officers who'd done the first welfare check. Obviously they hadn't found anything, but she wants to find out what they'd observed, regardless.

Hill follows her to his desk next to hers. She looks at her partner. He has an eager look that she recognizes because she feels it herself. She also recognizes the danger of reacting in a situation like this one. She's done it before. Driven and rabid, she'd pursued what she thought was the truth with abandon. And also with revenge.

It had backfired spectacularly.

They must be slow and methodical about their path here, and she says as much to Arthur Hill.

He shakes his head. "You know, I don't understand you, Ballard. We finally get a juicy case—something we might be able to sink our teeth into. And here you are, pissing the opportunity away."

"Dahlia Reed is not an *opportunity*."

"You know what I mean."

"You know what else I know? We fuck this up, and Charleston PD will be in here faster than you can turn your head. You saw the pictures of the woman's headshot on Mosswood's website—the photos of her with her children on social media. That wedding photo…" Dahlia Reed seems to have the kind of timeless beauty the camera loves. "Do you know what happens when photogenic young mothers go missing?"

Miriam thinks of Lacey Peterson, Jennifer Dulos, Suzanne Morphew, Shanann Watts. *Erica Abington.*

"Yeah, I do," Hill shoots back. "I also think about Mollie Tibbits and Eliza Fletcher, and I say *fuck protocol.*" He leans back. "What if it was Samantha?"

It's a low blow, and Hill knows it. He looks guilty as soon as he says it.

But it gives Miriam the opportunity to get angry. "I don't want some TV lawyer, or a bunch of inexperienced online sleuths on social media picking apart everything we do." She's already been there, and she's very aware that as soon as the press get ahold of this case, she'll be there again. "So we need to do this right. Got it?"

She pulls her phone out of her back pocket and types 'popular apps for runners' into the search engine.

Four results appear at the top. She chooses the first—'RunKeeper'. There's a free version, which she downloads, using a throwaway email account that's in no way related to her actual name or existence. When she opens the application, she uses her online searching pseudonym—Elyse Masterson. Then she clicks on the magnifying glass in the search bar and types in 'Dahlia Reed'.

Two results appear—one athlete from Maryland

who has no profile picture or activities on file. The second result has a thumbnail photo of a pretty, fresh-faced runner from Hanahan, South Carolina. She has a public account.

"Gotcha," mumbles Miriam.

Miriam clicks on the link. Dahlia has logged seven runs. Each appears to begin at her house and take varying paths around Goose Creek Park and the Naval Command Station.

"Check this out," Miriam says to Hill, and he moves to stand over her shoulder. "This is what we're looking for."

He peers at a simple map titled 'Morning Run'.

"Is that from this morning?" he asks.

Miriam uses her thumb and finger to zoom in on the map in the system. "Looks like it's from last week," she says and chooses a few of the other runs. "Dahlia doesn't seem to post consistently, but all of the routes seem to follow the same path."

Hill nods, pressing his lips together. "It would be real easy for someone to track her then."

"Sure would."

Hill straightens and runs a hand through his hair. "This change anything for you?"

She bristles. "I still think we need to be cautious. But let's send a team out there to check it out."

"On it," he says, looking just the slightest bit self-satisfied. He picks up the phone, and Miriam glances back down at the app.

She notices the tab titled 'Social Stats' under which are two options: 'Following' and 'Followers'. Miriam clicks on 'Following' and four names appear: Bernadette Murphy, Rachel Burcik, Carter Brooks, Aiden Moss.

Aiden Moss.

She clicks on 'Followers'. Aiden Moss is missing from that list, but a few others are included. She scans the additional names: Stephanie Finch, Jane Vance, Robert Nickloff, Tara Massey. None of those names mean anything to her, but she takes a screenshot of both groups and sends them to herself.

When she looks up, Parker and Lucero are sauntering toward them.

"Heard we got something in common," says Parker.

Miriam regards the young officer. He has the swagger of youth about him, and an arrogant look on his face.

She turns to Lucero. "Where'd you pick up Jeremy Reed?"

"At the Bolthole."

"He was crying in his glass," adds Parker.

"Do you know why?" she asks Lucero.

The more seasoned officer shakes his head. "Didn't ask. We just wanted to get him home with his kids."

"Do you think he has something to do with his

wife's disappearance?" Parker's voice is eager and excited. The tone borders on gleeful.

Miriam regards the young officer, who she knows has designs on bigger and better things in his career. She knits her brow. "We don't know anything about Dahlia Reed. Got it? We don't know she's missing. And so, at this point, we have no suspects, because we have no crime." She leans closer. "And I don't want to hear one word about you running your fucking mouth to the contrary. Got it, Peter?"

Parker's round cheeks redden, and Lucero hides a smile. Hill looks down.

Parker's first name isn't actually 'Peter'. Miriam has no idea what it is. But the fact that she's invoked the mildly pejorative nickname referencing Spiderman's human alter ego is enough to shut the kid up.

She turns back to Lucero. "I'd like to see a copy of your report after you write it."

"Ten-four, boss," he says.

She's not his boss, but in this case, she's going to act like she is. Because what she really wants to do is make sure Dahli Reed comes home.

And she's not going to let a bunch of amateurs get in the way of that.

CHAPTER 8

Josephine is glaring at him. Weston should have realized he held no high ground in this discussion-turned-argument. He'd only been looking for a reasonable conversation. But there were no reasonable conversations. Not anymore.

His wife wears a set of lilac-colored loungewear, and her carefully colored silver hair gleams, hanging loosely around her shoulders. She smells of expensive lavender and vanilla lotion. She is a handsome woman in a cool, cultivated, regal way.

But Josephine doesn't hold a candle to Dahli. Dahli, with her long brown waves, warm eyes, and infectious laugh.

When he's with Dahli, she looks at him as if he's the only man in the world.

"You're so preoccupied," his wife quips. "I'm shocked that you actually noticed, let alone care. Besides, we both know what this argument is really about."

Weston has no idea what the last part of her comment means; only that it's meant to entrap him, drawing him into a fight he can't win.

He doesn't fall for it. "I just don't understand why he needed to come home. In the middle of the semester."

"Pardon me for wanting my children around me after I've found out their father was a philandering fool," she says and walks into the ensuite bathroom. He can see her in the mirror's reflection, applying a clear serum to her well-preserved face, over the thin, loose skin of her neck, and onto her freckled décolletage.

Weston looks away and stands in place, halfway between the king-sized bed and the door. He's unsure what to do with his hands and if he should stay where he is or follow his wife.

When Josephine returns to the bedroom, Weston says in an accusing tone, "Adeline is not here," referring to their errant daughter. "*She* is not around you." Their daughter is god-knows-where. Perhaps at one of the other Vamoose locations. Likely not. Her precious Aidan is the child she wants. They both know that.

After a moment, Josephine stares at him, her fists balled at her hips. "What did you think was going to happen, Weston? Did you think you'd just get to keep fucking her? Did you think you might tuck her away somewhere for your own pleasure? Living two different lives?"

He is silent. It won't matter what he says. His wife

will not believe him anyway.

She waves a breezy hand in front of her. She is just warming up, taking pleasure in the fantasy she's weaving. "A little late afternoon delight, then come home to South of Broad where you play the dutiful family man while I twirl about you as if you're the lord himself."

"We're talking about Aiden."

"No, *you're* talking about Aiden. I'm talking about my *life*."

At the very least, she doesn't seem to expect any actual answers to her rhetorical musings.

But Weston is still concerned about Aiden's sudden presence. The last thing he wants is his son coming into the office and catching wind of the drama around Dahli's apparent disappearance.

Aiden knows Dahli. His son has spent the past four years interning at Mosswood during his summers and holiday breaks. Dahli has watched Aiden grow from an awkward teenager to a man.

"I just think we can deal with this on our own. It's inappropriate for Aiden to be involved in this situation—which involves you and me. Not our children."

"You don't get to decide how I deal with this, Weston. You don't get to decide how I *feel*. And you don't get to decide who I tell."

"So you're going to tell the children?"

"I haven't yet. But I might. I haven't decided." She

makes a show of looking into the air as if she might receive some divine advice from the spirits. Then, without another word, she slips off the silk robe and lays it carefully on the ivory-cushioned bench at the end of the bed before moving to her side of the mattress. She turns down the corner of the comforter.

Weston pauses before moving to his side of the bed.

"What do you think you're doing?"

"I'm going to bed."

"Not in here you're not."

He levels a look at her. "Josephine, you haven't wanted me to touch you for the past two years. I'm certainly not going to try tonight."

His wife's eyes flash. "Is that how long you've been fucking her?"

Weston hasn't admitted to an affair, nor will he. Because anything he admits now will lead to other questions regarding past indiscretions. And while Weston had been sure to insist on an air-tight prenuptial agreement, Josephine had agreed to sign the document only with an infidelity clause.

When they'd been twenty-seven and twenty-five, that hadn't seemed like a problem. A lot has taken place over the past thirty years.

Josephine has accused him of infidelity based on an eyewitness report by a gleeful acquaintance. There wasn't much he could say about it, and he didn't try to defend himself. The woman had seen what she'd seen. No matter that there was more to the story.

In this case, he knows what he needs to do. He's already paved the path for it. The question is—can he carry it out? His wife is correct about one thing. He is in love with Dahlia Reed.

"Don't be ridiculous," he says.

Josephine rears back. "*Don't be ridiculous?*" she repeats, her voice high and strident. "Are you really trying to gaslight me into thinking *I'm* the crazy one here?"

He holds his hands out in front of him, patting the air. "I'm not trying to gaslight you." His voice becomes soft to compensate for her volume. "I'm just..." He stops. Swallows. "You've got this all wrong."

"Pray tell, what do I have wrong?"

He takes a deep breath, trying to decide the best way to approach the subject. He should have called his lawyer immediately. Graham Fowler would have had helpful advice. But he'd thought he could contain this thing on his own. Quietly. Discreetly. Without public knowledge.

He may have underestimated his abilities.

Weston exhales. "I was at the hotel with Dahli last week. We had a meeting at Gabrielle with Stephen Saylor, the new editor-in-chief at the *Post and Couri-er.*"

"Elaine Lagare did not see you at Gabrielle," Josephine says, referring to the hotel's restaurant. "She saw you walking into a room with the slut. She said you had your hands on her ass."

This swearing is not in Josephine's nature, and each vulgar word that escapes her lips jars Weston to the bone. He doesn't mind it when women use coarse language. In the construction world, women as well as men tell it like it is. But from Josephine, it's unbecoming. It's embarrassing for her.

Dahli is not a slut. Despite the fact that she's currently missing, he imagines her wild in the bedroom—completely uninhibited, untamed. She is comfortable with her own body, and relaxed while enjoying Weston's body—doing to him as she wishes…

"You're not even fucking listening!" Josephine shrieks.

"I am," he assures her and again smooths the air with his hands. "What Elaine Lagare saw—"

A knock on the door startles him, but before he can move to open it, Aiden pokes his head into the room. He looks from his mother still standing at her side of the bed to Weston, now halfway to the door.

Their son shifts his gaze back to Josephine. "Everything okay in here?"

Josephine gives the boy a tight smile. "Yes, sweetie. I'm sorry to have bothered you."

Weston sees his chance. "Aiden, son, you don't need to come into the office tomorrow. I know your mother asked you to come home, but there's no need for you to work while you're on break. Especially if your mother needs you." *There*, he thinks. He'll use her own reasoning against her.

"It's no problem, Dad. I'm happy to come in."

Josephine smiles indulgently at Aiden—her precious boy. "Honey, I'm just happy to have you under my roof again. But I'm not holding you hostage. You go on, if you'd like to go."

Weston grits his teeth. He's not sure if Josephine is doing this on purpose just to goad him. Perhaps his wife is using Aiden as a mole at the office. Was that her original intent in asking him to come home?

Weston's face flushes with anger. "Really, Aiden," he says, his voice more aggressive now. "I think you ought to go back to your classes, truth be told. There's no reason to be hanging around Mosswood when you've got a meet against Central Florida next weekend and finals to think about."

Aiden appears unconcerned. "I've got weeks before finals, and UCF isn't that good this year. I've spoken with my professors. If Mom needs me here, I can spare the time."

Josephine simpers at him. "That's my boy," she says, beaming.

Weston struggles to keep his temper in check. There's too much at stake to fuck this up. "I must insist—"

But Aiden's voice is harder than Weston's when his son says, "Dad, it's fine. I'm staying. I'll be in the office tomorrow."

With a smile for his mother, Aiden closes the door behind him, leaving Weston enraged and impotent.

He takes three deep breaths. "Jesus Christ, Jo," he mumbles. "What do you think you're doing?"

"I'm getting into bed." She slides between the sheets and moves to switch off the lamp on the nightstand.

Muttering under his breath, Weston also moves to the bed.

"Oh, no you don't," his wife says. But he ignores her, climbing onto his side of the mattress and punching down the pillow.

"I paid for this bed," he mumbles. "And this is my house."

He can feel her staring daggers at his back in the dark. With a huff, she flops back onto the mattress, tugging the comforter off his body.

"Not for long," she announces.

Weston rises early and heads into the office before Aiden and Josephine are awake.

Kelly is at her desk, and she mumbles a good morning and doesn't say anything else. Weston takes that as a good sign. He doesn't ask about Dahli. He'll head to her office himself in a few minutes.

He visualizes her at her desk. She'll smile up at him and say, "Good morning, Mr. Moss." Because that's what she calls him when others are around. When they're alone together, she calls him 'Wes'.

His pulse begins to thrum as he prepares his coffee. He forces himself to move slowly, methodically. He adds one packet of sugar and two small thimbles of cream. He stirs until the dark liquid lightens.

His chief financial officer, Tom Gerard, enters the executive kitchen area and says, "Weston, we need to discuss—"

Weston holds up a hand. "Set up a meeting through Kelly."

"I will, but regarding the quarterly—"

He waves the man away. "It's not a good time, Tom." Weston turns around and walks out of the kitchen.

He fixes a scowl on his face that is partly for show but partly due to anxiety, and heads to the other side of the building where Dahli's office is located. As soon as he rounds the corner, he sees it is still dark. Olivia is at her desk. He catches the woman's eye—a silent question. She shakes her head.

As he approaches, Olivia says, "We called the police yesterday afternoon."

His eyebrows lift in surprise. "What did they say?"

"They took a statement and told me they'd look into it. They didn't seem overly concerned, since her family hadn't reported her missing. They said they may pass it to Hanahan PD since that's where she lives."

Given what Dahli has shared with him about her husband, he isn't exactly surprised the man wouldn't have reported her missing. To Weston, he sounds like a real dud.

"Did they ask for any other information from you?" Weston notices the man in the cubicle next to Olivia shift toward them, eavesdropping. The man from yesterday. The man who'd stunk.

"No, not really. They just requested that we call back if we had any updates. I haven't spoken to Candace yet today."

"Candace?"

"Candace Witten, sir. She and Dahli are friends."

He had just discovered this information yesterday from Kelly. Apparently, though, the friendship is common knowledge. "And you spoke with her yesterday." It is more of a confirmation than a question.

"A few times, yes. She's the one who insisted I notify the police."

Weston hesitates. When he'd spoken with Candace the day before, she'd seemed unconcerned. Blasé, even. What kind of game was she playing? He wonders if Josephine has spoken with her niece. If so, what had

Josephine told her? And what had Candace told Josephine?

He changes the subject. "Who on Dahli's team can cover her work? We've got some high-profile issues that we need to address."

"Uh…" Olivia seems taken aback by the abrupt change to business. "Laura Anderson or Todd McElroy should be able to pick anything up."

"Have they been informed Dahli is out of the office?"

"I sent a general message to the team yesterday, but I'll send another note and ask them to cover until further notice."

"They'll likely have questions."

"We all have questions," Olivia quips.

Weston opens his mouth to respond, to tell her she needs to toe the party line. But he's not sure what exactly that is.

His phone buzzes, and he half expects to see Josephine's number flash across his screen. But it's Kelly. He answers it with a brusque, "Yes?"

"There are some detectives here to see you."

"Detectives?" The question bursts from his lips before he can censor himself. "What do they want?"

Kelly's voice is quiet. "They'd like to ask you some questions about Dahlia Reed."

He inhales. "I'll be right there." He walks away from Olivia without a word, aware that he has just a few minutes to pull himself together.

CHAPTER 9

Miriam and Hill are quickly ushered into a conference room by a harried-looking assistant with a frenetic energy about her. The woman doesn't offer them water or coffee—not that Miriam wants any—but she notices the oversight anyway.

She takes a seat in a plush gray swivel chair at the gleaming conference room table, rich mahogany in color, while Hill wanders around the room studying the large black and white photos of various construction projects affixed to the walls. The room is open and airy, and there's plenty of natural light filtering in through the windows.

Miriam pulls out her notebook and studies the details she's captured. There aren't many. This, she regrets.

Jeremy Reed had finally called them back at five that morning to report that his wife hadn't returned, but in the hours leading up to his phone call, she and Hill had dedicated minimal effort to the case.

Immediately after Jeremy contacted them, Miriam instructed their eager junior detective—Kristie

Kaylor—to start tracking down footage from security cameras in the area.

But now they are behind the eight ball, and Miriam is feeling rudderless. She doesn't like that feeling. It makes her feel desperate. And desperation is a dangerous place.

Hill has turned from the photos and is peering through a window overlooking the Mosswood parking lot. "We've lost some time," he says, verbalizing her thoughts.

She isn't sure if the comment is directed at her. She's well aware of her decision to proceed cautiously. She'd been trying to protect her own ass, but it probably hasn't done Dahlia Reed any favors.

She taps the tip of her pen against the polished surface of the table and jiggles her knee. They have better things to do than languish in a conference room. They need to start talking to people now.

Just as Miriam is about to rise to track down the harried assistant, the door opens and a tall, ramrod-straight man with steel-gray hair appears. Miriam recognizes the man as Weston Moss, the founder and chief executive officer of Mosswood Development. He is intimidating and handsome, dressed in tailored slacks that hang perfectly from his lean frame. He wears a designer button-down shirt and no tie; an energy of power and money radiates from his core.

Miriam has met the man before. On more than one

occasion, actually. He doesn't appear to recognize her, and she won't remind him of their long-ago meetings.

Much has changed over the past decade.

Weston offers them a smooth smile, though his eyes remain sharp and watchful. "Detectives. Apologies for keeping you waiting." He looks at the empty table in front of them. "I'm so sorry—we should have offered you some refreshments. Coffee? Water?"

Miriam shakes her head, but Hill says, "I'll have a coffee, thanks. Black."

Weston Moss nods and steps out of the room for a second before reappearing. "Kelly will have that for you in just a moment." He sits at the head of the table and steeples his hands. Hill takes a seat opposite Miriam.

"What can I do for you?"

Miriam opens her mouth, but the assistant enters the room with a mug of coffee bearing the Mosswood logo. She sets it on a coaster in front of Hill before hurrying out again.

When the door is shut behind her, Miriam clears her throat and says, "Mr. Moss, I'm Detective Miriam Ballard and this is my partner, Detective Arthur Hill. We're hoping to ask some questions about Dahlia Reed."

"Why are you asking those questions *here*? I'd think you'd be better off concentrating on…" His words trail off as he gestures with a small wave.

"On what?" Hill prompts.

"On wherever she was last seen. That wasn't at Mosswood."

"How do you know that?" Hill asks.

Miriam interjects. "Since your employees were the first to report her missing, we thought perhaps they might have some valuable information and insights for us."

He rests his chin on his fingers, his brows drawn together. "Ms. Reed didn't come in yesterday. Do we even know she's missing?"

"Your employees seem to think so." Miriam consults her notes. "A woman named Olivia Mitchell is the person who made the call. Do you know Ms. Mitchell?"

Weston Moss's throat bobs, but his voice is smooth when he says, "I do."

"She was worried enough to call the police during work hours. Were you aware of that?"

Weston recovers after a brief pause. "Look, Detective…" His words trail off as if he's searching for her name.

"Ballard," Miriam offers.

He nods, his eyes glazing over. He doesn't care about her name, and he doesn't remember her face.

She bristles. It's not that she wants him to recognize her, but a part of her vanity has taken a hit. Once upon a time, she'd moved in the same circles as Weston Moss. Back when she'd had a different last name and a higher social status. Before she'd methodically, recklessly, destroyed her own existence.

She tells herself that the anonymity is valuable. She knows a few things about Weston Moss. He's not the perfect, stand-up family man he'd have everyone believe.

"Look, you're free to ask all the questions you like. I'd just ask that you perform your interviews in here, to minimize any distractions. I can make this room available for as long as you need today."

"We won't need all day," says Hill and follows with a loud slurp of his coffee.

Weston stands. "Kelly can get you access to anyone you'd like to interview."

"We'd like to start with you," Miriam says quickly.

She clocks the smallest flash of annoyance—and some other unidentified emotion—on his face before he quickly smooths out his expression and settles back into his seat. "I don't see what I could possibly tell you, but I'm happy to answer any questions you have."

He lays his hands flat on the surface in front of him. He wears no wedding ring, though she knows Weston Moss is married to Josephine who owns the high-end clothing boutique Vamoose on King Street. Miriam has a few items of clothing from the store. She rarely wears them nowadays.

Miriam doubts Josephine would recognize Miriam now either, though she's been to the woman's house for cocktails.

"Dahlia Reed works for you, is that correct?"

"Yes. As my vice president of public relations, she reports to me. Image and reputation management are very important at Mosswood."

"So I've heard. How long has she worked for the company?"

"Over ten years. I'd be happy to get you her records from our human resources department."

Hill says, "We'd like to see those."

"How long has she held her current position, reporting directly to you?"

Weston looks into the distance. "It must be a little over a year now."

"She's young for a vice president." Miriam doesn't phrase it as a question, but Weston answers anyway.

"She's good."

His reply comes quick, and Miriam looks up. "She must be," Miriam responds in what she hopes is an equivocal tone. Does she imagine the color in his face?

Weston continues, "What I mean is, Dahli's worked hard to get where she is. Her work ethic is second to none, and she does what it takes to get the job done. I've come to rely on her as much as I rely on any of my senior staff members." His tone has shifted from defensive to impassioned, and Miriam thinks carefully about her next question.

"When did you notice that Mrs. Reed was missing?"

"I noticed she wasn't in the office yesterday morning. We'd been scheduled to attend a meeting together in the afternoon, and I walked over to her office to talk to her about it. It was unusual that she hadn't come in yet, and no one seemed to know where she was."

"What was the meeting about?"

He cocks his head. "Excuse me?"

"The one you were supposed to have with her yesterday afternoon?"

"It was…" He shifts back in his seat. "We were having some difficulties on the permitting for one of our projects and it had caught the attention of the press. She and I were scheduled to strategize a response."

"Is that normally something you do?"

"Is *what* normally something I do?"

"Spend time crafting the narrative with the executive you've placed in charge of that function." In the pause that follows, Miriam shrugs. "I would think she'd craft the response on her own or with her team. It's a task that seems rather 'in the weeds' for the CEO."

"As I've already told you, reputation management is important to Mosswood and it's important to me. I'm a hands-on leader."

The man meets her eye and then looks away quickly. This time, Miriam knows she isn't imagining the slight rush of color in his neck. She glances over at Hill, whose eyebrows are ever-so-slightly raised.

She doesn't want to push her luck with this subject, but she thinks she can get just a few more details out of him.

"So this meeting to strategize," she says as sincerely as she can. "This would have been something important to Ms. Reed? Something she wouldn't have wanted to miss?"

"Dahlia knew that the matter was important," says Moss. "If she hadn't been able to make it, she would have let me know."

"How did she communicate with you? Did she email? Call? Text?"

"However was convenient. If it was a day-to-day issue, she usually emailed. But if it was urgent or after hours, she would call. As you know, the press doesn't always keep bankers' hours."

"Right," says Miriam. "I'm used to that." She laughs, and he chuckles too. *Good*, she thinks. *Loosen up, Weston.* "What about text?" she asks.

His laughter fades. "What about it?"

"Does Dahlia ever text you?"

"On occasion, yes. All of my leaders have my mobile number. My chief operating officer texts me more than my wife."

"And does *Dahli* text you more than your wife?" Her question is asked softly, and there is no mistaking her meaning.

A weighty silence fills the room.

But Weston Moss's face becomes hard. "Dahlia Reed was my employee, Detective Ballard. Nothing more." He stands and straightens the sleeves of his shirt in a crisp motion. "I have work to do."

He opens the door, and Miriam catches sight of a younger man standing at Weston's assistant's desk. He is just as tall as Weston, and he shares the same chiseled cheekbones, wide mouth, and heavy brow. But the young man's hair is dark—nearly black—and he must be three decades younger.

Weston's movements are abrupt as he speaks to him then gestures him away to a door on the opposite side of the hallway. Before the young man follows Mr. Moss, he looks over and locks eyes with Miriam. She can't quite read the look he gives her.

"What do you think?" asks Hill after they've walked away.

"I'm sure I think the same as you," answers Ballard. "Dahlia Reed just became a bit more interesting."

Miriam notes Olivia Mitchell's pasty white coloring when the younger woman is ushered into the room.

Olivia is plump and her skirt and blouse cling to her midsection as if she'd recently outgrown the clothing. She pulls on her skirt as she walks into the room and adjusts the collar of her rumpled blouse around her bosom as she sits in the seat at the head of the table—the one Weston Moss had vacated moments earlier.

She brushes a piece of non-existent hair from her face with her left hand, which sports no jewelry. She wears no earrings, no bracelet, and no necklace, either. What she does have with her is a notebook and a pen, which she taps unconsciously against the table.

"Why don't you start by telling us a little bit about Dahlia Reed," Hill says. His voice is more aggressive than normal, probably because he's sensed Miriam's softening toward the nervous woman who'd been the one to report Dahli missing. Her partner knows how to compensate for her shortcomings, as she does with his.

Olivia clears her throat. Still, her voice wobbles. "Dahlia is great. A bright spot around here."

"Bright spot," repeats Hill. "Say a bit more about that."

Olivia shifts, then purses her lips before speaking again. "It's just that construction and development firms like Mosswood tend to be filled with a certain type of employee."

"Men?" prompts Miriam.

"Yes, but a certain type of man. Hard-driving and rough. Even the executives."

"And Dahlia isn't like that?"

"Oh, no. Not at all. She's kind and funny. And helpful and responsive."

"Have you worked for construction firms other than Mosswood?" Hill asks.

"Yes." She names two other firms that sound vaguely familiar to Miriam, and Miriam makes a note.

"Those places didn't have female executives?"

"I've come across a few, but they were focused on climbing the ladder or getting ahead."

"And Dahlia isn't interested in that?"

"I don't think she needs to be. She's advanced at a comparably young age."

Olivia drops the pen and clasps her hands together tightly. Miriam waits, but the woman doesn't say more, though two splotches of color appear on her cheeks.

"Dahlia has been working for Mosswood for quite some time."

"From what I understand. She was here two years ago when I started. But she wasn't in her current position."

"What position was she in?" Hill asks.

"Internal communications. She wrote a lot of the messages that go out from leadership—appointment announcements, health and benefit information…HR sorts of things."

"And she jumped into an executive role from that one?" Miriam asks.

Olivia considers that. "She started doing a customer newsletter, which was a short monthly publication that was distributed to all of our clients and partners."

"What kinds of things were included in that?"

"Project updates, company successes, awards we'd won." She knits her brow. "It also includes an introduction from Weston Moss."

"So Dahlia worked pretty closely with Mr. Moss on this project?"

The red splotches deepen as Olivia nods.

"How long after she started this company newsletter was she promoted into her current position?"

Olivia shifts again. "I couldn't say exactly. I don't think it was long."

Miriam could feel Hill's energy crackle. She understood, but she also knew an alleged relationship between Dahli and Weston was only one piece of a potential puzzle—if a puzzle even existed. Besides, an affair was rarely the end of the story. Oftentimes, it was just the beginning.

"Does Dahlia have any other friends at Mosswood?" asked Miriam.

"I mean, everyone likes her. But as far as friends go, Candace Witten is the only person I'd put into that category."

"Who is Candace Witten?"

"She's a consultant who helps with government affairs and relationships with elected officials. She and Dahli partner closely. She doesn't work directly for Mosswood, but she's always around." Olivia glances at the door and leans closer. She looks both terrified and something else. She looks thrilled, Miriam realizes. Olivia is nervous, but she's enjoying the drama. "Candace is Mr. Moss's niece," she whispers, though the door is shut. "Not many people know that, but I do. She was the one who wanted to call the police yesterday."

"Why didn't she call the police herself?"

"She's at a conference in DC."

"How did she know Dahlia was missing?"

"I called her. When Dahli didn't come in, I thought she might know where she was."

"And *you* didn't want to call the police yourself?" asked Hill.

Olivia looks as if she hadn't been expecting the question. "I just wasn't sure if it was my place. I'd spoken to Dahli's husband, and he didn't seem concerned." Olivia picks her pen back up again and clicks it. "It seemed strange that Dahli's place of work would be the one making a police report when her own husband wasn't worried."

Hill sighs. "Let's go over the timeline of your involvement." He sounds exasperated, and Olivia shrinks back. The excited expression vanishes.

"Dahlia didn't show up yesterday…you called her husband…and then you called Candace Witten, before you made the police report? Is that right?"

Olivia's brow knits; Miriam can tell she's trying to remember the order of events. "I-I noticed she wasn't in her office, obviously, but I didn't think too much about it at first. Sometimes she has offsite meetings…" Her words trail off. "Or I thought maybe one of her children was sick or something and she was running late."

"Would that have been like her?"

"No, but life gets in the way sometimes, and Dahli is busy."

There is a pause, and Miriam says, "Please, go on, Ms. Mitchell."

"Then Mr. Moss came over and started asking questions."

"Does Mr. Moss often visit your side of the building?" Miriam thinks of Weston's commanding presence. He appears to be a man driven by hierarchy, not someone who'd socialize with the common folk in the office.

She knows she's assigning to him her own attributes, and those assumptions are based on decades-old interactions with him. But Miriam also knows that people don't change. Not really.

Olivia confirms her assumptions. "I rarely see Mr. Moss in person," she admits. "But he hadn't heard from her either, and they had a meeting scheduled for yesterday afternoon."

"What was the meeting for?" Hill asks.

Olivia squirms. "I'm not sure. It was an offsite meeting."

There was the word again...*offsite.* It seemed to be code for something, and Miriam was fairly certain she knew what it was.

Miriam's ex-husband had taken a lot of 'offsite' meetings. Many of those had been with a young constituent named Erica Abington.

"Was that a normal occurrence?" Hill asks. "Offsite meetings between Mr. Moss and Ms. Reed?"

Olivia's voice quavers when she whispers, "Yes." The excitement returns.

Hill opens his mouth, but Miriam doesn't want to dwell on the potential affair. Not yet, at least. They were sidetracking themselves and confusing their interview subject. "What happened next?" Miriam asks.

"That's when I called Candace. I hadn't really been concerned until Candace was concerned. I thought maybe she knew something I didn't about Dahli."

"Like what?"

Olivia leans back and wraps her arms around herself—a protective gesture. "When I called Jeremy Reed, he basically told me to go f—" she stops herself. "To mind my own business," she amends. "He was mean, and not interested in talking about his wife. He didn't want to hear what I had to say. It just seemed like strange behavior to me. Especially considering how sweet and nice Dahli was." She blinks. "I thought maybe Candace knew something about their relationship, or had some suspicions about her husband." She leans forward. "Everyone knows it's always the husband." Her voice is conspiratorial.

Both Hill and Miriam are quiet. It's true it was often the husband. But not always.

"Candace wanted me to call the police right away, but that didn't seem quite right either, so Eugene and I drove to her house, just in case we might find something there."

At that, Miriam and Hill look at each other. "You went to the house?" Hill asks at the same time Miriam says, "Who is Eugene?"

At Olivia's widened eyes, Hill motions toward Miriam, signaling Olivia to answer her question first.

"Eugene Ryan," Olivia responds. "He sits in the cubicle next to me, so he could hear everything that was happening. He's creepy, but harmless. Smells a bit," she says, almost apologetically.

Miriam jots down, *Creepy but harmless?* She underlines the word 'harmless'.

"Creepy?" Hill asks.

"Just a little…" Olivia looks to her left. "…I don't know. *Off*, maybe." She shrugs. "I've heard he lives with his mother who's morbidly obese or something. There's a rumor they're hoarders—like the ones on that show…" She shivers and the corners of her mouth pull down. "I don't want to speak badly of anyone."

"And you invited him to go with you?"

"No." Her tone is adamant. "He offered to ride along, and I wasn't sure what I was going to find." She shrugs. "It seemed safer to go with someone else."

"Does Eugene know Dahlia?"

"Everyone knows Dahli." She pauses. "Dahli had a meeting on her calendar with Eugene. An appointment," Olivia adds. "Eugene said he didn't know what it was for, but it was strange. I can't think of any reason Dahli would've had to talk to Eugene."

Miriam makes a note to talk to this Eugene person.

"What did you find when you got to the Reed home?" asks Hill.

"We didn't find anything. She wasn't there. We rang the bell…looked in the windows…looked in the backyard."

"Nothing out of the ordinary at all?"

Olivia shakes her head. "There was a car in the garage, but we couldn't tell the make or model. It may have been Dahli's Lexus. I don't know how many cars the Reeds own—it could've been someone else's car for all I know."

"Anything else?" Miriam asks. She's thinking about the Reeds' doorbell camera. They'd asked for that footage from Jeremy Reed. It would be interesting to see if he'd come through without a warrant.

"When I got back to the office from Dahi's house, I called Candace. She told me to call the police, but I convinced her to wait until the end of the day. I tried

Jeremy Reed a few more times, but didn't get any answer and then decided I shouldn't wait any longer."

Miriam is aware Olivia didn't get an answer from Jeremy because he was drowning his sorrow at the Bolthole Lounge.

She looks at Hill and notices the twitch below his left eye that tends to happen when he's focused.

"You mentioned Dahlia's rise through the ranks of Mosswood at a young age. Was that out of the ordinary?" Hill asks.

"I've only been at Mosswood two years," Olivia says, rather evasively.

"In your opinion, was Dahli's promotion a deserved promotion?"

"Like I said, Dahli is quite capable."

"That doesn't answer my question."

"Look, I don't want to speak out of turn. Dahli is good at her job. But she's *my* age. Though much, much more beautiful than I am." While her words are delivered flatly, Miriam detects the hint of bitterness beneath them.

Hill nods once. "Were Dahlia Reed and Weston Moss having an affair, Ms. Mitchell?"

Miriam nearly stops this line of questioning. It's clear to her there's some sort of attraction between the boss and his employee, but she doesn't want to get caught up in that. She knows all too well the danger of continuing down the wrong path with blinders to the other roads.

Olivia's eyes shine, but she says carefully, "There were some rumors, which I will not repeat. And you can draw your own conclusions from that."

Hill opens his mouth, and Miriam interjects, "Thank you, Ms. Mitchell. If we have any other questions, we know where to find you." She slides a business card across the table. "If you think of anything else, give us a call."

Olivia stares at the card for a moment before picking it up and rising with her notepad and pen. She spares them one backward glance and walks out of the office, her sloped shoulders slumped forward.

After she's gone, Hill says, "Why'd you do that? We were just getting somewhere with her."

"You were in the weeds."

"What do you mean?"

"You know what I mean."

"Yeah, I do, Ballard. Believe me, I do." He shakes his head.

"Don't turn this around on me."

"I don't have to. You're turning it around on yourself. I know for damn certain the Abington case is on your mind. But Weston Moss isn't Senator Mark Edwards, and even if he were, that doesn't mean you don't ask the right questions."

Miriam shoots him a disgusted look then glances away.

"Hey..." His voice softens. "...I don't mean to

bring up the past. I know I wasn't here then—I wasn't your partner. But I can imagine how hard it must have been."

Miriam shuts her eyes for just a moment, and flashbacks from the case assault her memory—Mark in handcuffs while she'd read him his rights. Samantha's tear-stained face, begging. Pleading. And then, a week later, the discovery of Erica's body, the suicide note clutched in her decomposing left hand.

Hill continues, "I know it hurts, but I'm going to do what I need to do to solve this case." It's a warning.

Miriam ignores it. She blinks away the memories. "Let's find Eugene Ryan."

CHAPTER 10

Eugene's breathing is shallow, and his body itches.

The police have summoned Olivia. He assumes this is about Dahli, who hasn't shown up to work again.

Why aren't they interrogating Dahli's piece-of-garbage husband? The guy doesn't deserve her. A woman like Dahli deserves to be cherished. She deserves to be watched over.

His palms sweat, and he rubs them on his thighs. He knows they're coming for him.

You haven't done anything wrong, he reminds himself, as he blankly stares at the inspection report on his screen. At least, nothing they know of.

Glenda's rotten smile floats across his mind. *They know*, she cackles at him.

"Shut up," he whispers under his breath. He looks around to see if anyone has heard him.

They *don't* know, but they might start poking around. They might realize who he is. They might discover his secrets.

He stares at the wall of his cubicle and listens to the

low static of the white noise pumped through the sound-masking speakers. The system was supposed to have been designed so the employees didn't notice it. But Eugene notices.

He wishes it hadn't been Olivia who'd reported Dahlia missing. And what had he been thinking, riding with her to the Reed house? He'd thought he was being clever. He'd thought it was ironic.

It was more *moronic* than ironic, he now realizes.

Stupid Eugene, his mother says. This time her voice is different. Younger. It's the voice she'd used as a child when he'd done something wrong. *Stupid, stupid, stupid.* She lifts a hand and closes her fist.

Eugene squeezes his eyes shut against the memory.

When he opens them again, he sees Olivia's fawn-colored head approach over the partition. She slips back into her space opposite him.

The energy changes when she's there. It vibrates and crackles.

Despite the white noise, he can hear her breathing. He hears her shift her mouse over the smooth surface of the mouse pad. He hears the clacking of the keyboard.

He waits to see if she'll call anyone: Candace; Weston Moss.

She doesn't.

When Eugene can't stand it anymore, he rises and looks over the wall.

He sees her frown in silhouette.

When she notices his presence, she minimizes whatever image she's looking at on the desktop monitor.

"What?" Her tone is hostile.

"What happened?"

She looks up at him. Her eyes are narrowed, but he sees alarm in her expression.

"Nothing happened."

"What did they tell you?"

"They didn't *tell* me anything. They asked questions." She looks back at the Mosswood logo screensaver on her monitor.

"What kind of questions?"

Her shoulders rise and fall on a sigh. "Questions about Dahli," she says with exaggerated patience.

Eugene waits, but she is silent. He's about to sit back down when she adds, "They asked a lot of questions about Dahli and Weston Moss."

Eugene's jaw clenches at the mention of Weston's name. He knows how the man looks at Dahli—like she's a prize to be conquered.

"What did you tell them?"

Her eyes dart away, avoiding his gaze. "I may have mentioned the rumors," she admits with a guilty tone.

Eugene feels a familiar anger start to boil inside of him. He tugs at the collar of his shirt, trying to calm himself down. "What rumors?"

Olivia meets his gaze again, silently assessing his reaction before answering. "The ones about Dahli and Weston. The ones about how she got her job."

Eugene's skin prickles. He knows what those implications mean—that Dahli slept her way to the top. But he refuses to believe it. She's too good—too pure—to do something like that. And she's too smart to be manipulated by Weston.

"I didn't mean to say anything," she adds quickly. "I don't even know how it happened." She's talking more to herself than to him.

Eugene's hands shake.

Olivia apologizes—he's not sure for what—but he barely registers it as he sinks back into his seat.

As he sits there, seething with anger and frustration, he can't help but wonder who else has heard these rumors and believes them to be true. It makes him sick to think that anyone could doubt Dahli's hard work and dedication to her career.

His desk phone rings. No one ever calls his desk phone. On the ID screen, the name Kelly Murry is displayed. There can only be one reason Weston's assistant is calling. The cops want to talk to Eugene, too.

The phone's strident trill chases him as he hurries to the restroom around the corner. The sound reverberates through his mind as he pushes open the heavy door of the men's room.

The lavatory is mercifully empty, and Eugene ducks into a stall, latching the door behind him. He sits down on the toilet and leans forward, his head resting in his palms. After a few seconds, his pounding heart begins to slow. Another minute passes before he's able to think clearly.

Olivia must have told the detectives about him—that he'd accompanied her to Dahli's house. How else would they've known about him?

He considers this development. It's not necessarily a bad thing, is it, to be concerned for a colleague's safety? Dahli was well known and well liked. Of course Eugene would be worried. He *is* worried, in fact.

He rubs his palms down the legs of his pants. He does it again, harder. Then he rocks forward and back, over and over again.

The main lavatory door opens and footsteps squeak lightly on the tiled floor. They come closer until a pair of brown loafers become visible and stop briefly outside of Eugene's stall. He holds his breath and glances at the thin crack of the stall's door.

The form continues on and enters the space next to his.

Barely breathing, he keeps an eye on the shoes, the cuffs of the tan slacks.

The occupant does his business, flushes, and exits the stall, taking his time at the sink washing his hands.

Eugene listens to the whirring sound of the paper

towel dispenser and waits. There is silence, but he hasn't heard the person exit the room.

Eugene doesn't dare make a sound.

A few seconds later, the shoes squeak away. The main door opens then clicks resolutely shut.

Eugene is alone again, and he fills his lungs with air.

His legs have started to tingle with pins and needles from his sitting position. He wishes he'd have thought to grab his keys and leave the building. But in his panic, he's trapped himself in the restroom.

He can't sit here forever.

He thinks—plans—deciding to rush back to his desk, grab his keys, then head out without a word. He will disappear. And he knows exactly where he'll go.

He exits the stall and washes his hands, hesitating for just a minute and staring at himself in the mirror, his face illuminated by the sallow lighting.

His skin is pale and waxy; his thinning brown hair is tussled. He needs a shave.

The pupils in the center of his hazel eyes are wider than they should be.

He looks down at his hands, away from the reflection. It's no wonder women like Dahli overlook him. They barely notice his existence. Even Dahli had been mostly oblivious to him. Until recently, that is.

Then, she couldn't ignore him, could she?

An inadvertent sneer lifts the corner of his mouth.

He smooths it away. Dahli doesn't deserve his contempt.

She'll never love you, Glenda whispers. *No one loves you.*

His mother is right.

He dries his hands quickly, inhales, then exits the lavatory, turning right down the hallway toward his desk.

When he rounds the corner, he catches site of a middle-aged man and woman standing next to Olivia's desk, facing him.

He clocks the bulge on the woman's hip under her coffee-colored blazer. The detectives.

Immediately, he doubles back in the direction from which he'd come.

A woman's voice calls out. "Eugene? Eugene Ryan?"

Despite his best intentions, he reacts. Then Olivia is standing, too, facing him.

"Eugene, the detectives want to talk to you," she says.

The interaction is loud enough that a few heads poke up over their partitions. Familiar faces look curiously at the detectives, then at Eugene.

He considers running. But that would be stupid. There's nothing to run from, he reminds himself.

He does his best to assume a casual expression and walks slowly back toward his desk and the trio waiting for him.

The woman detective is older than Eugene by at least a decade, maybe more. Deep lines are etched into the grooves of her mouth, and two vertical lines run prominently between close-set brown eyes as she frowns.

He hates her immediately.

The male detective has an easy-going expression and a quick smile. Eugene fastens his attention to the man, who says, "Just want to ask you a few questions."

"I can't really help you with anything. I didn't work directly with Dahli."

"Word travels fast," the detective quips. "Olivia…" He nods to Dahli's assistant. "…says you went with her yesterday to check out the Reed house. Is that right?"

Even though he'd assumed Olivia had mentioned him, he silently curses her again. Why couldn't women keep their goddamn mouths shut?

"I won't be able to add anything more than what she's probably already told you."

"You never know what you might remember differently. What small detail you may have picked up that Ms. Mitchell may have missed."

The woman detective speaks. "We're also trying to get a sense of who Dahlia Reed was in the workplace."

"She didn't disappear from here," says Eugene, but still, he doesn't look at her.

"Do you know that for a fact, Mr. Ryan?" In the

silence that follows, she says, "And are you sure she's disappeared?"

He knows what they're trying to trap him. "I'm afraid I can't help you."

The male detective leans forward, as if they're buddies sharing a joke. "This is a pain in the ass, I know. You're probably a busy guy. I'll make sure we don't take up too much of your time." He flicks a quick glance in the direction of his female partner, then shares a quick, conspiratorial look with Eugene.

Eugene almost falls for it. But he's not an idiot, and he won't be patronized or manipulated. He glances at the woman who wears the ghost of a smile.

They're laughing at him.

"Fuck off," he says, and sits down. His heart is pounding. It was a stupid thing to say to cops. They won't arrest him for it, but they might start looking into him more closely.

Stupid, stupid, stupid.

He hears the woman let out a long, slow sigh. As if he's an obstinate child. The two detectives appear over the wall of his space, staring down at him. They have the high ground, and he does his best to ignore them.

The woman now leads the conversation. Her voice is curt when she says, "Ms. Mitchell tells us Dahlia Reed had a meeting scheduled with you yesterday—the day she went missing. Is that true, Mr. Ryan?"

"I don't know anything about that."

"It doesn't seem strange? A vice president talking to a low-level employee like you?"

Again, he knows what she's trying to do. He tries not to fall for it, but it irks him all the same. His eye spasms, and he blinks.

"She must have had something to say to you, Mr. Ryan. What could it have been?"

"I didn't see Dahli's calendar, and I have no idea what she wanted."

"You work on inspection reports, is that right?"

He doesn't answer. It doesn't matter.

"Were there any problems with your contractors?"

A slow smile slides across Eugene's face, and he relaxes. He likes this new path they're following. This feels safe and manageable. And it might present an opportunity. "There are always problems with contractors," he answers.

"Like what?" the woman says.

"Cost overruns, scheduling issues, quality concerns. You name it."

"Any of those causing any public relations issues at the moment? Anything Dahlia may have been concerned about?"

A thrill of joy flickers in Eugene. He tries to seize on this opportunity to steer their attention in a different direction. "Maybe," he says quickly. "We just recently had to cut loose one of our biggest contractors for falsifying records related to their quality assurance training," says Eugene. "It's a big deal."

The woman makes a note. "The decision to sever ties with this company," she says, looking down. "Would that have been your responsibility, Eugene?"

"No, that would have been Weston Moss or Tom Gerard, the chief operating officer."

She returns her gaze to him. "So…why would Ms. Reed have wanted to talk about the situation to you?"

Eugene opens his mouth and shuts it again. The truth is, Dahli rarely talked to him about anything. But she smiled at him. She was kind to him. That one day, when he'd emerged from his manager's office, embarrassed and angry after a poor performance rating, Dahli had passed him and noticed his anguish. She'd placed a hand on his arm and regarded him with concern. "Are you okay, Eugene?" she'd asked, her voice gentle and quiet.

She'd known his name. And with that soft touch and tender question, she'd shifted his world.

You're a fool, Glenda says, the familiar disgusted look on his mother's face.

"Mr. Ryan?" the woman detective asks, and Eugene blinks up at her.

The two detectives glance at each other, and the man says, "Ms. Reed is a beautiful woman. I've seen the pictures." He makes a modified fanning motion with his right hand, indicating Dahli's desirability.

Eugene feels the heat creeping up his neck.

"I can imagine what she must look like in person."

Eugene keeps his mouth clamped shut.

"The rumors about her are probably true."

"What rumors?" Eugene spits. But he knows what the detective is going to say. He's going to start asking about Weston Moss. Eugene is ready for it.

But instead, the man says, "About all the men."

Eugene looks up sharply.

The man leans closer. They're buddies again. His voice is quiet. "The men she'd been sleeping with."

Eugene rears back. "Dahli was not sleeping with any of the losers at Mosswood."

"How do you know?" the woman asks.

Eugene clenches and unclenches his jaw. "Because she wouldn't do that."

"Were *you* sleeping with her?"

Eugene is temporarily stunned. Could it have been a serious question? He wants to laugh, but the larger part of him wants it to be true—both the question and the answer. What would it have taken for someone like Dahli to be interested in sleeping with him?

A miracle, that's what.

The male detective's face breaks into a grin. "I'm just joking around with you."

The high that Eugene had just felt—the hope—comes crashing down in a pool of fury. He hates these detectives. He stares down at his desk.

Now it's the woman's turn to ask questions. "Did

you know Dahlia Reed was a runner, Mr. Ryan?"

The change in subject confuses Eugene. "I-I'm not sure."

"You're not sure?"

"She may have mentioned it." Why are they asking him that question? Do they know something? Has someone seen him?

He's been careful, the times he's watched her. He's made attempts to hide his face, wearing a baseball cap and a turned-up collar so she didn't notice or recognize him.

But he's never attempted to conceal his route or his vehicle from the security cameras. There hadn't been any need. No one had been watching him watching her.

He sucks in a breath and then lets it out quickly. He does this a few more times.

Other people around the cubicle farm are probably watching and listening. The white noise pumped through the hallways can only conceal so much of the sound.

"Can we go to a conference room or something?" he asks. He feels as though he might faint.

The woman raises her eyebrows. "I thought you didn't have anything to say."

His head is fuzzy. "I-I don't. But you shouldn't be talking about her like that, out in the open."

"Right," the man says. "Let's go to the conference

room for a private conversation."

Eugene stands and steadies himself before following the pair down the hallway. They pass by Weston Moss's assistant who watches him suspiciously.

Eugene glances at Weston's door. It's shut.

The detectives do not acknowledge the woman outside Weston's office but lead Eugene into the executive conference room—a place he has never been invited. It's an expensive-looking area where Eugene imagines Weston pounds his fist against the polished table, or leans back into the leather chair at the table's head, steepling his hands while minions appeal to his conscience, his money, and his power.

Eugene takes a seat in that very chair. Even the act of sitting in it makes him feel formidable and in control.

As the detectives sit across from him, he says, "What do you want from me?"

"The same thing you want from us, I imagine," the man says. He slides two business cards toward Eugene. "To help locate Dahlia Reed."

Eugene looks at the cards. 'Detective Arthur Hill' and 'Detective Miriam Ballard'. He's never heard of them.

"I don't know where she is," says Eugene.

"Of course you don't," says the woman. "But you may know something that can help us to, if not find her, at least narrow down her movements. Thank you, by the way, for helping us."

Eugene sits up a little straighter in Weston's chair. In *his* chair.

"Let's go back to yesterday," the woman—Ballard—says. "Did it strike you as odd that Weston Moss would have been over in your area of the office?"

"Most people go to Weston. Weston doesn't go to other people. Especially his employees."

"Not even Dahlia Reed?"

He lifts a shoulder. It's easier to talk in the conference room. "Dahli wouldn't have been interested in Weston. Not the way you're implying."

"Why not?" Hill asks. "All that money? All that power. He's a good-looking guy. Seems like *exactly* the type of person a beautiful, intelligent woman like Dahlia would be interested in."

Eugene shakes his head firmly. "Dahli was…" His words trail off as he tries to summon the word for her. *Magical. Enchanting. Mesmerizing…*

"Was what, Mr. Ryan?"

"She was amazing," Eugene says, but his tone carries all of the other descriptions with it.

"Do you know her husband?"

"She never talked about him."

Ballard looks up and eyes him closely. "I thought you didn't talk to Ms. Reed."

"I didn't," answers Eugene. "But my desk was right outside her office, and next to Olivia. I overheard things."

He can tell Ballard doesn't believe him.

The other detective—Hill—says, "Let's talk about Dahlia's house. Had you ever been there before, Eugene?"

Eugene swallows hard. "No," he says quickly.

Hill leans forward and smiles—just a few men shooting the breeze. "You didn't drive past even once just to get a sense of where she lived?"

His throat bobs again. "Not before yesterday."

"What did you do when you got to the Reed home?" asks Ballard.

It was a stupid question. What does this woman think he did? "We rang the doorbell." He doesn't bother trying to keep the contempt from his tone.

"I mean, did you look around before you went to the door? Did you notice anything out of the ordinary?"

"No one answered the door, and the house appeared to be empty."

"Did you go in?"

"We didn't have a key."

"Did you look under the mat or a flowerpot or something?" Hill asks.

"No, and it was one of those keyless entry displays attached to a doorbell camera. Seemed fairly high-tech, like a key wouldn't be necessary."

Ballard makes a note. "That's an interesting observation," she says. "I didn't notice that myself when we were there last night. Did you, Hill?"

Hill shakes his head. "I don't think I did."

Eugene's chest puffs slightly. Looks like he's not such an idiot after all, he thinks with a smirk.

"Anything else you may have picked up about the house?" Ballard asks. "Anything else Olivia might not have seen or that we might have missed?"

Eugene thinks back, this time in earnest. "I looked in the backyard. Everything seemed in order. And when I talked to the neighbor…" He searches his memory for a name but comes up empty. "He didn't notice anything either."

"Neighbor?" asks Ballard. "What neighbor?"

Eugene raises his eyebrows. Something else they didn't know. He gives them a brief description of the guy. "Said his name was Bob, I think." Eugene frowns. "No, Bill. He claimed he worked from home and didn't see anything strange." He leaves out the part about Bill recognizing Eugene from bingo with his mother at the senior center. He doesn't want them digging into his life.

"Did he seem suspicious?"

Eugene sees another opportunity. "He knew exactly when Dahli's husband left with their children. You never can tell with people."

"That's an understatement," says Hill. "We'll be sure to check out this neighbor guy. Bill you said?"

Eugene nods, then adds. "I looked in Dahli's garage. There was a car parked inside."

"Was it Dahli's car?" Ballard asks.

"I couldn't tell. It was dark. I could only make out the outline."

"What kind of car does Dahli drive?" Ballard asks.

"A 2023 Lexus GX. Midnight blue."

Ballard's hand hovers above her notepad for a second before she makes a note. "Good to know," she mumbles.

"Did you and Olivia come straight back to the office?" Hill asks.

He nods. "I went back to work. Olivia made some phone calls, and eventually she called the police. I guess they told her they'd send somebody out to the house to do a well-being check. And that was it."

After a short pause, Ballard extends a hand. "You've been extremely helpful, Mr. Ryan. Thanks for taking the time to help us and to help Dahlia."

He blinks, waiting for the other shoe to drop, but nothing else happens.

He starts to rise, thinking he'd like to stay in that chair just a moment longer, but then he remembers something.

"There is one other thing."

Both Ballard and Hill look at him, waiting.

"It struck me when I looked at the pristine back yard… The front yard was all torn up."

"I understand they'd contracted to have some landscaping work completed. Tends to get messy with that type of project."

"That's the thing," says Eugene. "It was beautiful weather yesterday. Sunny and pleasant. But where were the landscapers? They weren't around, and it didn't look like anything had been touched."

Ballard opens her mouth as if she's going to say something, then she shuts it again. She makes a note. "Another helpful observation, Mr. Ryan," she says. "Thank you for your help." She nods down at the cards in front of him. "If you think of anything else, feel free to give us a call."

This time, Eugene does stand. He picks up the cards and slides them into his pocket. "I will," he says. And he walks out of the room, his posture straight and his head lifted.

He feels better than he has all week.

CHAPTER 11

Aiden Moss sits in the windowless corner office and watches people come and go from the conference room. It hadn't been clear what was going on, at least at first.

But now he gets it and knows why his father wanted him to stay home.

It has been discovered that Dahlia Reed is missing.

Three years earlier, Aiden, fresh from his first year at Clemson, had started an official internship at Mosswood. He'd been around the company when he was younger, but this assignment was real.

Dahli had been the one to take him under her wing.

Just over a decade older than Aiden, she was the most beautiful woman he'd ever seen, or has seen since.

Her long, brown hair falling in a sleek curtain down her back. Her wide eyes watching him—seeing *him*. It hadn't mattered that she was married or even that she had children. When Dahli looked at Aiden, she was all that existed on earth.

His breath constricts in his chest with the emotion

he feels when he thinks about her.

His father emerges from the large office in the opposite corner. Unlike the tiny closet where Aiden is stashed, his father's office takes up nearly the entire length of the front of the building. In it, there is a bathroom, sitting area, and full kitchen along with Weston's workspace. A person could comfortably live in Weston's office.

His father looks at the door to the conference room which has been commandeered by two average-looking detectives—a man and a woman with bad haircuts and cheap clothing. Right now, they're holed up with the weird-ass guy from the other side of the building. Aiden's seen the guy before but doesn't know his name.

Aiden watches as Weston leans forward and says something to his assistant, Kelly. Then his father glances around. He catches sight of Aiden watching him and pastes on a big, bright, phony smile.

Aiden doesn't smile back. He hates his father. He's *always* hated his father—a man with a big, arrogant laugh, and even bigger egotistical temper. The whole world revolves around Weston Moss.

His father is the reason his mother is the way she is, and this is also why Aiden cannot say no to his mother.

He hasn't been able to say no to either of them, if he's being honest.

He's never been given a choice about what he

wants to do with his life. Weston Moss has it all figured out for his son.

The only thing Weston can't completely control is his wife. Josephine Moss is the reason Aiden's name is Aiden and not Weston, the fifth. Thank God for small miracles.

Weston has no idea why Aiden is really back home, and Aiden isn't about to tell him.

Aiden's cell phone vibrates on the desk; 'Candace Witten' flashes on the screen.

He snatches up the phone and rises. Weston is still looking at him when Aiden shuts the door of the tiny office in his father's face.

"Hey," Candace says when he accepts the call. Her voice is warm and liquid. It flows through him like thick honey and helps to calm his pounding pulse. But still, he's angry with her.

He says, "Hi," but beyond that, words fail him.

"Where are you?"

"I'm at Mosswood."

"The police are there?" she asks, then adds quickly, "Olivia called me."

"Why didn't you say something yesterday?" He can't keep the petulance from his tone.

Candace lets out a small audible sigh. "I didn't know what was going on, Aid. And I didn't want to worry you."

"Of course I'm worried."

"But you *shouldn't* be," she says emphatically. "You should be at school right now, having fun with girls your own age. *People* your own age. This obsession with Dahli isn't doing anyone any good."

"And now she's missing," Aiden reinforces.

"We don't know that."

"You're the one that wanted to call the police," he blurts out. He's heard things in his tiny anonymous office when they hadn't realized he'd been listening.

Candace is silent on the other end of the line.

He immediately feels guilty. "Sorry. I know you're probably worried, too."

His cousin does not confirm this. "Who are they talking to?"

"Right now, the weird guy from the other side of the building. They've already talked to Weston, of course. And Dahli's secretary."

"Have they asked to talk to you?"

Aiden's breath constricts again. "Why would they?"

"They shouldn't," says Candace. "But that doesn't mean they won't." There's a hesitation in her voice. Unspoken words hang heavy between them. *What is it that she's not saying?* he wonders. *What is it she might know?* He doesn't ask because there are things he's not telling her, too.

Aiden swallows. "Even if they do ask, I have nothing to tell them."

"No, you were at school."

"I was at school," he affirms.

"Why again are you home?" she asks. "You said Aunt Josephine asked you to come?"

Aiden considers how much to tell Candace.

Of all the people in the world, he probably trusts her the most. But still… These are family secrets and she's not a part of his immediate family.

Finally, he says, "Mom found out Weston is cheating on her."

A long silence stretches out between them before Candace asks, "Is it confirmed? Does she have proof?"

"Apparently."

Candace does not sound surprised. Hell, no one would be surprised. Weston is the picture of posh, casual arrogance. He probably thinks the world owes him a pretty young thing on the side, like an accessory, in addition to his solid, faithful wife. It's what the universe promises to men like Weston.

Aiden doesn't give two shits that Weston is fucking someone else. But he does care who that person is rumored to be.

He notes that Candace doesn't ask. He's not sure if this is because she's guessed, or because she knows.

"What does your mother think you could possibly do about it?"

Aiden isn't sure how to answer. He's always been the substitute for any affection his father failed to show Josephine during their marriage. Aiden knows it's sick and toxic. But he doesn't know how to untangle it.

"You know how she is. She just needs someone around." He hopes his voice sounds normal.

"Adeline didn't fit the bill?"

Aiden scoffs at the mention of his sister. "God knows where she is right now." New York? Los Angeles? Hell, she might not even be in the country.

"Well, you can't stay home forever. You need to get back to school."

But he wonders how he's supposed to make his exit with everything else going on. Everything else he needs to take care of.

"What are you working on for Mosswood while you're home?"

"Nothing. Weston didn't want me to come in. He practically begged me to stay home. But he couldn't say anything—not in front of my mother. And he certainly doesn't want me to know what's going on. He thinks I'm an idiot."

"He thinks you're a kid," Candace amends.

Aiden is immediately defensive. "I'm nearly twenty-two."

"I know." She exhales then inhales deeply. "And I love you, but you've made some fucked up choices in the past couple of years."

He wants to argue that he isn't the only one, but he remains silent.

"I'm telling you right now, Aiden, as your cousin,

as your big sister, but mostly as your friend—you need to get out of there. Nothing good will come from you being home."

To assuage her, he agrees, then tells her he loves her and disconnects the call.

But it's a little too late to heed Candace's warning.

He rises from the desk again and pulls open the door. His father is gone, but he watches as the creepy little man exits the conference room looking pleased with himself. He waits to see if the detectives will emerge again, but they don't, so he goes back to the desk and begins scrolling through the video app on his phone. The clips are mindless and distracting, which is exactly what he needs right now to keep his mind off Dahli and what she must be going through.

After a few minutes, he feels a presence in the doorway. Thinking it might be Kelly asking him for his lunch order, he glances up.

It's the female detective.

Aiden's heart quickens, and he glances behind her to signal to Kelly. But Kelly is not at her desk.

Shit, he thinks.

"Yeah?" he says rudely, while noting the outline of the gun at her hip.

"Mind if we ask you just a few questions? It won't take long."

"I don't think my father would like me to speak with you."

"Your father is Weston Moss?"

He presses the inside of his cheek with the tip of his tongue and doesn't respond. He needs to learn to keep his mouth shut.

The detective assesses him, then she says, "Your father tells you what to do? Seems to me you're old enough to be making your own decisions."

"Okay then. It's *my* decision not to talk to you."

"We're trying to find one of your father's employees."

He tries to keep his face passive, but from the suddenly interested look on the detective's face, he knows he's failed.

"Do you know Dahlia Reed?"

"I've interned here for the past few summers."

"I'll take that as a yes. I assume you're aware she missed work yesterday and didn't come home last night?"

"I'm aware you're looking for her," he answers. "I don't think you're going to find her here."

The woman's eyes are kind, but she sees too much. He looks down.

"You have any idea where we might be able to find her?"

He mumbles, "No," and the woman leans against the doorjamb.

"You said you've interned here. Where did you go to school?"

This seems safe enough to answer. "I go to Clemson."

"Ooh." She draws out the sound. "I won't hold it against you, I guess. My daughter went to USC for a while." She looks as if she'll continue to address the schools' well-known rivalry. Then she frowns. "It's not fall break, is it?"

He doesn't answer and she shrugs. "Easy enough to check. It should be on their website."

He clenches his jaw. "It's not fall break."

She nods once, but doesn't ask a follow-up question, and he doesn't offer any information. It's none of her business.

"When did you get home?" She asks this innocently enough, but he knows she's waiting for the answer.

"Yesterday afternoon," he says. He prepares himself for more questions about his whereabouts and his movements. That's not a problem. His mother will vouch for his location. So will his father. So would Candace, if he asked her.

But the detective doesn't ask for that information. Instead, she says, "Tell me about Dahli."

The sudden change in subject catches him off guard, and he doesn't have time to mask his expression. His mouth goes slack and his eyes a little glazed. He lifts a shoulder as a fire licks at his belly. Finally, he ekes out a lame, "She was nice."

She tilts her head to one side. "Do you work with

her often?"

"Not really. But she was around a lot."

"Around you? Or around your dad?"

Before Aiden can respond, Weston's voice bellows through the foyer. "What the hell do you think you're doing?"

The detective turns around, but Aiden can see the smallest hint of a smile on her profile. "Just asking your son some questions, Mr. Moss." Her voice is calm and smooth.

"He doesn't know anything. He wasn't here." Weston appears in the doorway. "Son, you don't have to answer anything they ask you."

The detective cocks her head. "Mr. Moss, no one is under arrest here, or even a suspect in the disappearance of Dahlia Reed. We're just trying to paint a picture of her life and understand what may have led to the circumstances we find ourselves in today. Surely, you can't object to that."

"Of course I don't object to it. But Aiden wasn't here, and he didn't know Dahlia. There's no need to bother the boy with this." His father's neck is red above his white dress shirt. "And speaking of understanding the circumstances, why aren't you talking to the husband?"

The detective nods. "We're talking to Jeremy, too." Then she looks at Aiden and assumes a perplexed expression. "But you did say you knew Ms. Reed, correct, Aiden? I just want to make sure I get all my facts straight.”

Aiden can feel his father's stare. He doesn't answer the detective's question, and she doesn't seem to expect one.

The other detective comes out of the conference room. He holds his phone up at the woman. “The security footage is in,” he says.

She looks between Aiden and Weston, then says to Weston, “Thanks for your help today. It'll go a long way in helping us locate Mrs. Reed. And if we need anything else from you or your employees—emails, cell phone records, text messages—we'll be sure to let you know.”

Aiden notices the pull of his father's mouth.

The detective reaches into the pocket of her blazer and pulls out a small white card. She hands it to Aiden and gives him a meaningful look. “If anything else should occur to you, don't hesitate to reach out.”

He nods and throws the card on the desk without looking at it.

The detective nods once to Weston. “Talk soon, Mr. Moss.” The words have an ominous ring to them.

Then they're gone. With them goes some of the charge in the air.

Weston rubs a hand over his mouth. He looks at Aiden and says, “Not a word to your mother about any of this.”

He leaves the foyer, opens the door to his office, and closes it firmly behind him. But Aiden doesn't have to tell his mother about any of this. Because Josephine Moss already knows.

CHAPTER 12

Candace waits in the terminal of Reagan International Airport for her flight to board. She tries Dahli's cell phone for the thousandth time in the past two days, but it goes straight to voicemail. Her friend's perky voice reaches her ears.

Hi, you've reached Dahlia...or Dahli, if you'd prefer. I can't take your call, though I'd love nothing more than to ring you back. Leave me a message, and we'll connect later.

Dahli's voice is warm and inviting, and Candace feels tears prick at the back of her eyelids. She ends the call on the tone and blinks hard.

"Where are you, Dahli?" she mumbles, and the elderly woman next to her says, "Excuse me?"

Candace shakes her head. "Sorry. I was just talking to myself."

The woman grins. "Don't make a habit of it. They'll put you in the looney bin."

Candace manages a half smile, then shifts her body away from her fellow passenger. No danger of anyone having her committed. There's no one in Candace's life right now to care enough about her mental state to take any action anyway. No one except Dahli.

But even if Dahli *were* taking her calls, after the last interaction Candace had with her, she's not sure Dahli would care enough either.

Candace feels the woman studying her.

"Are you sure you're all right, dear?"

"I'm fine, thanks." The smile is gone, and her voice is clipped.

"I'm sure it's lonely traveling alone." The woman glances down at Candace's bare left ring finger. "No one waiting for you at home, either."

Candace stiffens. She doesn't respond as she fishes her earbuds out of her laptop bag and connects to a music app, choosing Tchaikovsky. She shuts her eyes and loses herself in his joy, love, sorrow, and pain.

A few minutes later, her phone pings, and the AI-generated voice of her earbuds announces a new message from an unknown sender.

Candace immediately thinks of Joel, from Chicago, whose number she hadn't bothered to assign a contact name. Last night, he'd consumed far too many drinks before they'd returned to his hotel room. Once in his bed, the alcohol had caught up with him; there'd been a lot of panting, perspiring, and exertion with very little result.

Her heart hadn't been in it anyway, but the effort had done nothing to distract her from her life. Instead, it simply reminded her of her empty existence.

She doesn't bother looking at the message. She'll never see Joel again, even if she does find herself in Chicago in the future.

Another message chimes, and then a third.

She's going to have to block him, she thinks, unlocking her phone and glancing down at the new string.

But this is a Charleston area code, and the first message reads:

—I know what you've been saying to Dahli, you stupid bitch.

Candace blinks, startled. She's been called worse, but it's jarring to see the words spelled out, especially accompanied by the 'Romeo and Juliet Fantasy Overture' playing through her earbuds.

The second message identifies the sender.

—I know you've been trying to convince my wife to leave me.

Jeremy Reed, she thinks.

She shakes her head. He's a fool.

The third message sends a chill down her spine.

—You will not succeed. I will never let her go.

As she's reading, an ellipsis appears at the bottom of her screen. The instantaneous intrusion across time and space causes a foreboding in her belly. She holds the phone lightly in her palm, and the message appears.

—Cunt.

The word makes her suck in a breath, though part of her wants to laugh. Name-calling is the lowest form of insult. She expects nothing more from the man Dahli described. A man she's never actually met in person. The word itself doesn't bother her. What bothers her is, she doesn't know what game Jeremy is playing. The detectives are, at this moment, searching for his wife, and he's texting Candace ugly, accusatory messages.

She's probably giving the man too much credit for having a strategy. Though she *is* impressed he's found her number. It wouldn't take much more than a simple internet search, but even that means he's put effort into tracking her down. The question is…*why*.

Candace debates not answering the texts. But she assumes the police will eventually want to look at Jeremy's phone.

She types back:

—*Where is Dahli, Jeremy?*

Less than a few seconds later, the ellipsis appears, and Candace finds that her palms are damp.

—*Tell me who she was fucking.*

—*I know nothing about that.*

—*Bullshit. She changed when she became friends with you. Not for the better.*

Candace's thumbs hover above the screen as she considers what to text back. The ellipses appear again, followed by another message.

—*I think you know where she is.*

This gives Candace pause. Why would he say this? And what did it mean?

She knows she should end the interaction. She should text Olivia for the detectives' contact information and send them these messages. Instead, she types:

—*She was afraid of you. She told me you might hurt her. Did you hurt your wife, Jeremy?*

The ellipsis appears and then disappears. She stares down at the phone, and just when she thinks he's abandoned the conversation, the three dots appear again. She waits.

—*If anyone should be afraid, it's you.*

Candace smiles to herself. Gotcha.

The woman next to her makes a *tsk*ing sound with her tongue and says something. Candace glances over to find her looking through her reading glasses at Candace's phone. Candace immediately closes the messaging app.

The woman's mouth moves, but her words are masked by the sound of Tchaikovsky still playing in her ears. Candace takes an earbud out so she can hear the woman. "Excuse me?" she says abruptly, making it clear whatever advice the woman wants to give her is not needed or welcome.

But if the old lady notices Candace's irritation, she pays no mind. "You should be careful, honey. You don't want to stir up trouble where you don't belong."

For a split second, Candace thinks she's talking about something else. Then the woman says, "Just when you think you know what a man is going to do, they do something stupider than you would have thought possible."

Ain't that the truth, Candace thinks. But she doesn't respond. Instead, she replaces the earbud, gathers her things and moves to another seat, settling back into the music. As the 'Fantasy Overture' plays on, Candace ponders Dahli's situation and wonders what she should do about it.

The gate attendant's voice cuts through the music to announce instructions for the boarding process to Charleston, and Candace goes through the routine— she and her fellow passengers are herded onto the plane, single file.

In her window seat, Candace switches her phone to airplane mode, ignoring the new text messages. She shuts the window covering and closes her eyes to her surroundings for the next hour and a half.

Candace rouses when the plane's public address system announces the plane's descent into Charleston. She manages to get through the remainder of the flight and deplane without making small talk with anyone.

Her plan is to return home and run the lone errand that will take her the rest of the afternoon.

Then, she will still herself to face whatever it is that

awaits her.

It takes her nearly an hour to navigate the process of deplaning, working her way through the tourist crowds, and retrieving her car. When she finally steers through the midday traffic and pulls into her gated community off Ben Sawyer Boulevard, a familiar bright red Maserati is parked on the road in front of her unit. The license plate reads VAMOOSE.

Candace sighs as she drives into the garage bay and shuts down the engine.

She exits the garage with her suitcase in tow to find her aunt Josephine standing on the street waiting. The woman is impeccably put together in a blue and white striped button-down shirt with a popped collar and wide-legged white trousers. Her silver-blonde hair is voluminous and arranged neatly around her shoulders.

Candace considers her own rumpled slacks and blouse, wrinkled and worn from travel. Her dark hair has long since gone flat and she'd not bothered with makeup. Next to her aunt, Candace looks like the help. Worse, she thinks. She looks like her mother—Josephine's sister. From the way Josephine is eyeing her, she knows her aunt is thinking the same thing.

"Aunt Josephine," she says, as brightly as she can manage. "How did you get in the gate?"

Josephine waves her hand toward the security entrance of the upscale community, and the silver bracelets jangle on her wrists. "The man let me in. We need to talk, Candace. It's about Mosswood."

Candace motions for Josephine to follow her as she climbs the stairs to the front door of her condo. Once inside, she nods to the living area at the far end of the hallway. "I'm just going to put my suitcase upstairs. Help yourself to anything in the kitchen."

Her aunt has never been in her condo, and Josephine doesn't remark on the space—the Brazilian Rosewood flooring, sapele wood kitchen countertops, and stunning marsh-front views over the deck. But Josephine would not be impressed by Candace's modest condo in comparison to her spacious southern mansion.

Candace moves quickly to stow her suitcase in the closet, then hurries back down the stairs.

When she enters the living room, Josephine is sipping from a small green bottle of sparkling water. There's not much else in the refrigerator.

"Can I get you a glass?" she asks.

Josephine shakes her head. "I don't mind being a commoner every once in a while."

The woman lets out a brittle laugh, and Candace grits her teeth and sits down on the sofa opposite her aunt. "What can I help you with?"

"Tell me what you know about Dahlia Reed."

Candace glances at Josephine's bottle of water and longs for something stronger. From her conversation with Aiden, she knows that her aunt suspects, at the very least, an affair between Dahli and her husband. But Candace certainly isn't going to own up to that. Hell, Candace doesn't even *know* what's going on between Dahli and Weston.

She has no idea if Josephine knows Dahli is missing, and she decides the safest strategy is an ignorant strategy. "Dahlia Reed, the vice president for public relations at Mosswood?"

"Is there more than one?" Josephine's voice is dry.

"I suppose not," Candace admits. "What would you like to know?"

"I've heard a rumor that you and she are friends. Is that true?"

Candace considers lying, then decides there would be more risk than benefit. "We are friendly, yes. We work together regularly on issues at Mosswood."

"She's fucking my husband."

Candace makes a show of appearing surprised. "Are you sure?"

"You can stop the theatrics." Her voice is flat. "You didn't know? Her *friend*?"

Candace shakes her head. "Dahli is married, but not happily." She remembers those text messages from Jeremy Reed and shudders. "I knew there was someone else in her life, but she didn't tell me who it was."

Josephine arches a brow, deciding whether or not to believe Candace.

Candace doesn't owe this woman anything. After

Candace's mother passed away five years earlier from ovarian cancer, Candace barely heard a peep from her aunt beyond the standard obligatory invitations for holiday parties or family gatherings.

Candace hadn't needed financial support, but she sure could've used some emotional support. She didn't get it from Josephine. And she hadn't gotten it from Weston or their daughter, Adeline. Shockingly enough, she'd received a measure of sympathy from Aiden, who was only a teenager. Likely because he'd needed support from her just as much.

"Frankly," says Candace, "I have a hard time believing Dahli is sleeping with Weston."

Josephine settles back into the sofa, allowing her silver hair to fan over the back of the cushion. "Dahli." She draws out the name. "Well hello, Dahli," she says in a sing-song voice, then laughs toward the ceiling. "Find her an empty lap, fellas."

It's a reference to the song lyrics, but Josephine's eyes have a crazed, haunted look, and Candace wonders if her aunt is experiencing a break from reality.

Josephine raises her head and fixes Candace with a dark stare. "The thing is," her aunt says, "Weston's lap wasn't empty. Weston is mine. And so is Mosswood."

Candace presses her lips together then blurts out, "Dahlia Reed is missing."

"Oh, I've heard," Josephine responds. Her voice is

suddenly light and breezy. "I've gotten plenty of calls about that today. None from my husband, of course. *He* hasn't told me a goddamn thing."

Josephine takes a long sip of the carbonated water and stares out the window at the afternoon sun sparkling off the water in the marshland. Candace glances at the time on the clock opposite her fireplace. It's getting late, and she has things to do.

"What is it you want from me?"

Her aunt replaces the cap on the small green bottle. "I came here to find out what she was like. Why, after all these years, Weston has chosen this woman for his most public of *indiscretions*." She scoffs. "He's had affairs before—I know he has. They all have them. *Pigs*," she adds under her breath. "But what is it about *this* woman that has made him become careless? What about this woman has made him risk everything?"

Candace considers her friend—lovely, lively, lithe, and lambent. She's surprised when a sob bubbles up from her heart.

"Jesus," Josephine sneers. "I can see I have no allies."

"It's not a war."

"Oh, honey, you better believe this is a war. And I won't rest until I've taken every last one of the spoils. Every last dollar, dime, and dick. I don't care who I have to take down with me."

CHAPTER 13

Back and forth…back and forth.

Fueled by caffeine and adrenaline, Jeremy Reed paces between his living room and kitchen for what feels like hours.

The detectives told him to go about his day as normal. Take the kids to school, make them feel settled and secure. Call off work and stay home in case Dahli showed up.

He knows that isn't going to happen.

And yet he's been in this house all goddamn day, waiting and pacing.

The detectives have supposedly increased their efforts to find his wife. That's likely true. He wonders if he should have acted differently. Should he have waited until this morning to officially express his concern? He's not sure. He doesn't think there's a blueprint for what to do—how to behave—when your wife goes missing.

He can't stop thinking about Dahli in the good years, when her million-watt smile lit up a room. When her supple body melted against his side. He's got the photographic evidence to prove she loved him, once upon a time. She'd smiled up at him as if he'd been the only man in the world—her light and her anchor.

He wants that back. He knows he will get that back. He has to.

After a sleepless night, he'd waited until five a.m. to call Detective Ballard, and she'd been infuriatingly nonchalant about the situation.

Oh, he'd known what they must have been thinking—he should've been more concerned yesterday. And perhaps that's true. But yesterday he'd had other concerns. Selfish concerns. Today his only concern was making this right.

Ballard and Hill hadn't even returned to the house. They'd told him to 'hang tight'. And he'd been trapped all day, trying to pretend, for his children's sake, that their entire world wasn't falling apart.

Luke knows, though. His son's solemn, all-seeing eyes recognize something is very, very wrong. Jeremy's lame and frantic attempts at jokes while making a less-than-mediocre breakfast were met with accusatory stares by his son. Maeve had been easier to distract, but it is only a matter of time before she realizes her mother isn't coming home. And once that happens, the meltdown will ensue.

For now, the house is quiet. And that may be worse than chaos. Because in the quiet, all there is left to do is wait—Jeremy stewing inside his own head. Pondering all the decisions he's ever made. Especially the ones he's made in the past two days.

He knows what they say about the husbands of missing wives and mothers.

It's *always* the husband. Hasn't every crime podcast, made-for-television movie, popular novel, and primetime news magazine, literally banked on that certainty?

If Dahli doesn't come home, Jeremy will be the next subject of the news media's vitriol.

The thought makes his breath catch. He will become a punchline. He will become a meme. He will become a target.

He debates how to paint the picture for the detectives. There was a time Jeremy would've sworn Dahli would never leave her children. But the way she's been acting this past year, his certainty is gone.

They'd married early—had children early—but after Dahli had been promoted and tasted a hint of success, she seemed to give up on him and their marriage. Why not the children too?

Back and forth, he paces.

He shouldn't have texted that bitch, Candace. But he wasn't able to help himself. He'd needed a target, and without Dahli here, Candace was the only target he could find. He doesn't know her, but he imagines a condescending smile and old-money arrogance.

Candace has the life that Dahli wanted—the life Jeremy hadn't been able to give her.

He also suspects Candace is covering for Dahli's affair. Had she really been with Candace for all those late dinners and Sunday brunches? He doubts it.

His phone chimes with a message, but this time it's only Sherri Darling asking how Dahli's feeling.

—*Her messages still aren't going through*, his mother-in-law texts.

No shit, Jeremy wants to type back.

Instead, he types:

—*She's still under the weather. Will be in touch soon.*

He feels mildly guilty lying to his mother-in-law. It's inevitable he'll eventually have to tell the woman the truth. And when he does, more drama will fill his existence. Sherri is nothing if not addicted to chaos and attention. And the tragedy that surrounds a missing daughter? It will be Sherri Darling's dream come true.

Jeremy runs his hand through oily hair and over his unshaven face. He looks like a rogue, and not the good kind. In his dirty sweatpants and stained T-shirt, he fits the profile of a criminal. It will work nicely into the narrative.

He fully expects to be fired. He's told neither Carter Brooks nor Alan Powell what's happening—only that he wouldn't be in the office. And he sure as hell hadn't told his new child-boss, Kara, even though she'd texted him 'just to check in'. More like checking up on him.

He hadn't responded.

If Dahli doesn't reappear soon, there'll be no need for Jeremy to explain his circumstances to Alan and Carter. The news will do that for him. He tries to think of one scenario in which he doesn't look like the villain.

He can't.

"Fuck!" he screams at the top of his lungs. It feels good, so he does it again. There's no one there to hear him or to stop him.

Of all the times he's messed up in life, this might just be the worst. If he still talked to his mother, she'd laugh and tell him you can't take the loser hick out of the mountains, no matter how far you manage to run away.

And she'd be right.

There's a knock on the front door, and he moves quickly to answer it. The two detectives stand there with deadpan faces.

"It's about fucking time," Jeremy says.

"Afternoon, Mr. Reed," Hill responds evenly, as if Jeremy had greeted them with a pleasantry.

"May we come in?" Ballard asks.

Get a grip, he warns himself silently, and he holds the door open as they walk over the threshold.

They sit down in the living area—the same seats they'd occupied the night before. The detectives stare at him as if waiting for him to speak.

"Have you heard anything?" Jeremy finally asks, impatient.

Ballard speaks first. "We haven't heard anything from your wife, if that's what you're asking. But we have learned a few things. Some of those things we need to discuss with you."

He holds out his hands in front of him, hoping to portray an open and cooperative attitude. "Anything to get Dahli home."

Hill gives him a look that could be construed as sympathy. But Ballard doesn't look as if she believes him. *Typical woman*, he thinks.

"We were able to gain access to security footage from yesterday morning. Starting with your doorbell camera, and working through the neighborhood, we were able to place your wife on a run through Goose Creek."

He shrugs. "I think she's mentioned that route. She didn't say anything yesterday, but it's possible."

"We have officers out searching areas along that potential path."

"Searching for what?"

Hill says, "Evidence, Mr. Reed."

But in Ballard's pointed look, Jeremy can see her unspoken words.

A chill runs through him at the thought of his wife, alone and abandoned.

"We need to ask you some other questions. Potentially…delicate questions," Ballard says.

Jeremy steels himself. He doesn't know how much they know, but clearly they know something.

"How is your marriage?"

Jeremy lets out a long exhale. "Like any marriage, we've had our ups and downs." He makes a wave motion with his hand and ends on a down trough.

"How long have you been married?" asks Hill.

"Thirteen years." Ballard's brow knits, and he knows what she's thinking. "Luke's twelve. Dahli got pregnant on our wedding night. Or around there."

"Was that the plan?"

Of course it wasn't the fucking plan, he thinks. But he says, "You know how it goes. We'd just graduated from college. We would've liked a few years to establish ourselves. But life rarely goes according to plan." He was aware of how ironic that statement sounded given the current circumstances. "We made it work. We both wanted children."

"So your wife put her career on hold when she had your son?"

"For a little while. But she didn't mind. I may have been more upset when she found out she was pregnant."

"You were upset?" Ballard asks.

Jeremy can feel her building a case against him. "Upset is the wrong word. We were young—there was still fun to be had. That type of fun came to an end when Dahli got pregnant. But we adapted, and after a few years, Dahli started working at Mosswood."

"What about when Maeve came along?"

"That was harder for Dahli. She'd just started to establish herself when she found out she was expecting, and it set her career back. But again, we made it work. And the plan was always for Dahli to be able to stay home. If that's what she wanted," he added.

"Given she seems to be the main breadwinner in the family, it doesn't seem like being a stay-at-home mom is what she wanted," Ballard quips.

Other than a small tick of the muscle in his jaw, Jeremy does not react to her dig. "As I said…life doesn't always go according to plan."

Hill shoots Ballard a look that the female detective does not seem to notice, then he says, "Mr. Reed, we discovered some sensitive information at your wife's place of work today—information that could potentially affect how we approach your wife's absence. So, we want to ask you some questions with the understanding that we have no proof of wrongdoing on anyone's part."

Jeremy nods.

"Did you have any indication that your wife may be having an affair?"

Heat creeps into Jeremy's neck and cheeks. He becomes warm as he thinks about the best way to answer. "I've suspected she was having an affair for a while now."

"How long?" asks Ballard.

Jeremy thinks back to when Dahli went cold. "A few months," he says. "Maybe longer."

"And what were the signs?"

Jeremy tries to answer, but suddenly his throat is very dry. He feels like he's choking on the words. "I-I need some water." He stands quickly and moves to the kitchen, where he rests his hands against the counter. He doesn't know if he can do this.

But he must. He has no choice. And anger with his wife fills him completely, venomously. He isn't a monster, but sometimes he feels like one.

He fills a glass with water from the tap and takes a long drink before walking back to the waiting detectives.

When Jeremy is settled, Ballard stares straight at him, not missing a beat. "You were saying that there were some indicators of an affair."

"I-I couldn't tell you exactly when it started. I probably don't even know. I remember picking up on little things over the past year, I guess." He thinks back, and his anger rises. So does his shame. "Dahli was promoted into her executive position about a year ago. It wasn't uncommon for her to get work emails, messages, texts, well into the evening. If there were any issues, she was usually one of the first to know, so she was tied to her phone."

He pauses to take another drink, and Ballard says, "That must have bothered you. To have your wife at the beck and call of another man."

"It wasn't another man," Jeremy says. "It was her job. I understood. And I was proud of her."

He takes a breath. A pressure settles in his chest, but he presses on. "I started to notice other things. She would respond to messages away from me with a small smile on her face. Sometimes, she returned from business dinners smelling faintly like cologne. Not her normal perfume. Something deeper and more pungent. Masculine."

"Did you ask her about these things?"

He shakes his head. "I thought—hoped—it was my imagination. I'd almost convinced myself that was the case. And there was probably a part that didn't want to know. After a while, it was clear our love life wasn't quite as…vibrant. But we were both tired, and after all those years…I'd accepted that's how it was going to be. It wasn't really an issue. But for the past few months, Dahli has seemed repulsed by my touch. More than that, she's seemed repulsed by *me*."

Ballard is looking at a framed photo of Dahli and the kids on the end table. Dahli's mouth is wide with laughter. Her eyes are laughing, too. It is a photo taken by a professional, but the joy on his wife's face is not manufactured.

"And still, you didn't say anything."

It's a statement, and he's aware they think he's a weak, impotent man.

"It must have made you angry."

"If I didn't know anything, there was nothing to be angry about." He stares at Ballard, and she stares back. A visual standoff.

"Do you know who it is?" Hill's voice is gentler.

"Do *you*?"

"They're just rumors," says Hill.

That's not true, and they all know it. Jeremy shrugs. He'd rather hear it from these strangers. It may have killed him to hear it from his wife.

"Weston Moss."

Hill's words come out in slow motion, and Jeremy is momentarily stunned. Dahli's boss, Weston Moss—community leader, paragon of industry, well-known philanthropist, married to elegant socialite, Josephine Moss. Sleeping with his wife?

It seems outside the realm of possibility, though Jeremy isn't sure why.

He knows the man has money and power, but he must be over twenty years older than Dahli.

Jeremy's hands have begun to perspire and he nearly drops his water glass.

He sets it on an end table beside the loveseat.

Ballard watches him. "You look surprised."

The late nights, the business trips, the messages… Like pieces of a puzzle, they form an image of Weston

Moss in his mind.

"I thought I was ready to hear it."

"Is Weston Moss a runner?"

He glances up sharply. "I have no idea. Why would you ask that?"

"You said she was training for a marathon."

He nods. "That's right."

"Has she run a marathon before?"

Jeremy shakes his head. "She did a few half marathons in her twenties. She started running again in earnest this past spring."

"About the time she took this job?"

He thinks about that. "No," he says. "It was after." He's not sure what connection they're trying to make.

"Dahlia is a thirty-five-year-old woman having an affair." Ballard shrugs. "It just seems odd to me that a woman in her situation would randomly decide to become a runner again after a decade away from the activity. But I could be wrong."

He thinks about Weston Moss—the times he's met the man and the photos he's seen of him in the newspaper and online. The guy appears to be fit, but he doesn't have that lean, taut look of a man who competes in that sort of race.

Then again, what did Jeremy know?

Ballard makes a note and says, "We'll check it out."

"What about you?" asks Hill.

Jeremy shakes his head. "I told you. I've never been

much for the endurance it takes, and Dahli had never welcomed my company. Not even when we were young."

"No, Mr. Reed. Are you having an affair?"

Jeremy's mouth goes slack, and he rubs his hands against the knees of his pants. "Of course not," he finally says and mumbles, "Ridiculous."

Ballard raises an eyebrow. "Is it ridiculous? Your wife was cheating on you. Maybe you decided to have an affair to get back at her." She holds out her hands. "It's not so uncommon."

"If I were going to get back at my wife, I wouldn't do it by cheating on her."

A heavy silence hangs in the air as Jeremy realizes what he's just said.

"How *would* you get back at her?" Hill asks.

"I-I wouldn't. I just meant… I just meant I wouldn't cheat. That's all."

"Have you ever cheated on her?"

"No, detective. I have not."

Ballard's phone makes a noise and she glances down at it. Her manner shifts and becomes more abrupt. More impatient. "We've been operating under the premise that Dahlia disappeared while jogging. But is it possible she left on her own? I know you said she wouldn't leave the children, but maybe she felt like she needed to get away. A break from life. It happens more often than you think."

Jeremy shakes his head. "She would've told her mother, and her mother has no idea where she is."

"You've told Dahlia's family she's missing? I'm surprised they're not here."

He studies his hands. "Not exactly. Yesterday, during the miscommunication with the kids, Luke's principal called Dahli's mother. Her number is on the contact list. I called Sherri to let her know there'd been a mix-up, but I hadn't wanted her to worry yet."

"When do you think she should worry?"

Jeremy leans his head back against the cushion and conjures an image of Sherri Darling. If he calls her, she will fly here and make the entire situation about herself. Jeremy can't deal with that on top of everything else.

He's still looking at the ceiling when he hears Detective Ballard exhale. "Okay, Mr. Reed. We're going to have our officers take a look around the house. Do you have any issues with that?"

He shakes his head and rubs his hands over his face. "Whatever you want."

"We'll need to search Dahlia's car and her personal laptop, if she has one. We'll need access to her cell phone records to see who she was talking to—texting and calling. If she has a desk she uses at home, we'll want to look through that, too."

He waves his hand in front of him. He is very tired.

"Our next step is an appeal to the public—a press

release and a press conference. We'll ask the public for any tips. If Dahlia did leave on her own, knowing that we're looking for her should flush her out. If someone's taken her, it might appeal to their humanity. If someone's harmed her, we might get a tip from an informant. People can't keep their mouths shut. Which is good for us."

His head begins to spin. This is all becoming too real. "Then everyone will know."

It's not a question, but Ballard nods grimly. "Things will change quickly once Dahlia's disappearance goes public."

"What am I supposed to tell the kids?" He thinks of Maeve's innocent face. He thinks of Luke's solemn eyes.

"I suggest you consider that now, and have the conversation soon," says Ballard. "This afternoon. If you need help, we can put you in touch with a social worker to give you guidance on what to say to each of them. They'll view the situation differently based on age and personality."

Jeremy sits up and presses the heels of his palms into his eye sockets until tiny sparks of color fill the blackness.

"You need to call your wife's parents. They absolutely cannot learn about their daughter's disappearance from a news report. And there will be a news report."

"Many news reports," adds Hill.

"They live in Ohio," Jeremy says. "They won't see Charleston news coverage."

Hill leans forward. "Mr. Reed, your wife is successful, she's beautiful, and most importantly, she's a mother. Her case will get national attention. Her parents *will* see the coverage. It will be all over the internet."

Jeremy lets out a long groan. He wants to take a drive, clear his head.

Ballard continues, "You're going to need help dealing with this. And your children are going to need support. If you have to make amends with your in-laws, do that now. I suggest you also call your own parents—"

"They're not part of the equation," he interrupts.

"Okay. If there's anyone else you need to support you—family friends, Dahlia's friends, neighbors, co-workers—call them, too. It'll be better if they hear it from you."

"I…I just need more time to prepare myself."

"Unfortunately, one of the things we do not have is time."

In the unspoken void, he knows what they're thinking. The other thing they do not have is Dahli.

"What time…?" he starts and pauses. "What time is all this happening?"

Ballard pulls out her phone and glances down at it.

"We'll send out the press release at four-thirty and plan for the press conference at five. We'll do it here, in front of the house, to humanize Dahlia. Remind viewers—and any potential perpetrators—that your wife is a respectable woman and an upstanding member of the community."

"Our house will be on the news?" He doesn't like that one bit.

Ballard presses her lips together before she speaks. "We could do it at the station, but I'd rather not give the public an image of you standing in front of a police department."

Jeremy stares at her. "You think I had something to do with this?"

"I didn't say that."

He notices the stern look Hill shoots in his partner's direction but neither of them offer more words of either comfort or condemnation.

"Do I... do I have to speak?" Jeremy thinks about the media events he's seen in the past. Some sad-sack husband in front of a bunch of cameras, either standing in the background or reading canned and stilted remarks. Inevitably, in the following days, he's announced as a suspect, imprisoned, and condemned in the court of public opinion.

Another rise of anger emerges. It's directed toward his wife.

"You don't have to," Detective Ballard answers, but

her tone says otherwise. Then she continues, "If we don't find Dahlia—Dahli," she amends, "this won't be our only plea to the public. We'll likely hold another press conference with all her family and friends present to keep the case in the news. Our goal today is simply to gain attention. We've wasted too much time already."

He glances at the time. It's early afternoon. He needs to shower, shave, make some phone calls, pick up the kids, tell them their mom is missing. Act normal. *Jesus.* He cannot *do* this.

Hill says, "Mr. Reed, I'd advise you to try and control your emotions, especially if you're on camera."

Jeremy feels the scowl that has overtaken his expression and does his best to neutralize it. These detectives are watching him; judging him. They are finding him wanting—and perhaps finding him guilty.

"Do I...?" He stops, swallows. "Am I going to need a lawyer?"

The detectives don't look at each other, but their postures straighten, almost imperceptibly. Hill leans forward and opens his hand. "You're not a suspect." His voice is quiet. Careful.

"But am I going to be?"

This time, it's Ballard who answers. Her tone is not nearly as friendly. "Not if you haven't done anything wrong, Mr. Reed."

CHAPTER 14

The man across from Miriam Ballard is tired. He's angry. But he's not broken. And she's not sure he's done anything to his wife.

Jeremy Reed reminds her of her ex-husband both physically and emotionally. Mark Edwards had also been a blandly attractive man, disappointed one too many times. Approaching midlife, and despite his professional success, he'd become detached and frustrated. His defeat had very little to do with Miriam, until he destroyed her world.

And then she destroyed his.

Miriam feels restless. She wants to get back to the station and talk to the officers who conducted the initial canvas of Dahlia's last suspected route. She wants to review the security footage herself. She wants to prepare for the press conference. She feels the familiar rush of adrenaline, fast and feral. The one she'd quashed yesterday. The one that has gotten her into trouble before.

She needs this boost of chemical energy, but she must use it wisely if she wants to help Dahlia Reed.

But first, she wants to once again drive the route she thinks Dahlia may have last taken.

They leave Jeremy Reed in his living room looking shellshocked.

As they climb into the car, Hill looks over at her. "What do you think?"

"You first," she says.

Her partner exhales. "He's not a likable guy."

Miriam nods.

"But I'm not sure he's either smart enough or ambitious enough to plan for the disappearance of his wife. He seems unprepared to deal with the consequences."

While Miriam generally agrees with this statement, she also knows that when it comes to love, betrayal, and revenge, no possibility can be excluded.

"And…" Hill continues, staring out the window as Miriam turns from Pulaski Street onto Red Bank Road, "…there's the possibility that Dahlia disappeared on her own. Beautiful woman, rich and powerful suitor. Family tying her down. They could have planned it together."

"A married suitor," Miriam reminds him. "Besides, she wouldn't leave the kids willingly. Not like this."

She feels Hill leveling a look at her, and she sets her jaw.

"You're speaking like a woman, and not like a cop."

"You'd leave your kids, Art?"

"We're not talking about me."

"No, we're not. We're talking about Dahli." She's starting to feel as if she knows this woman through the perceptions of the people they've spoken with.

"All I'm saying is we need to keep an open mind."

He flicks her another quick glance, and she knows he's referring to the Abington case. He's warning her about her ex-husband.

She doesn't respond, instead staring at the entrance to the Naval Command Station. Prominent cameras point to the driveway, but Miriam knows that the road will be partially visible in their field of capture. She wants to see what cars may have passed this way around the time Dahli went missing.

She glances to the right. Perhaps Dahli is also in that footage.

Before Miriam can ask if the officers had accessed the footage from the agency, Hill answers her question. "Kaylor has already placed the request. We don't have the files. We also don't know if she came this way at all. There are no cameras beyond this point."

They turn onto Marrington Avenue and Miriam notices the signs for the Marrington Plantation Trailhead. She pulls into the area and looks around. Two cars are parked in the lot—probably birders out for an afternoon hike in the marshlands. A wooden latrine is positioned in the corner of the lot, with a camera affixed to the roof of the shanty. *Jackpot,*

Miriam thinks.

Noticing the direction of her stare, Hill says, "It's broken. I talked to Franklin." He's referring to the lieutenant for the Uniformed Patrol Division whose officers conducted the initial search of the area. "They walked this whole perimeter and did a pretty thorough exploration of the woods and salt marshes beyond."

Miriam exits the car and walks around the parking lot, her eye on the empty vehicles, which had likely not been there the day before. Just innocent birdwatchers and hikers, out on a pleasant autumn afternoon, having no idea that a woman may have gone missing from the area. That danger might be lurking in the quiet beyond.

Or perhaps those vehicles held the key to the investigation, she thinks. There were so many possibilities, and they had wasted too much time already.

Miriam moves to the edge of the parking area where the grasses are tramped down and the weeds bent back, likely from the officers' search. She sighs. They've been taught to find a person—perhaps a body—not preserve evidence.

Her phone buzzes, and she glances at the display before quickly lifting it to her ear. "Chief," she says, then moves toward her car for some privacy. Hill wanders to the edge of the lot.

"Ballard," he greets her back. "Sergeant Lance tells me there'll be a press release and conference on the

Reed case later today?"

"Yes," says Miriam, silently cursing Public Information Officer Tony Lance. The guy isn't quite a snake—he's not smart enough to be given that kind of credit. But Lance uses knowledge as his weak attempt at power. The guy is always looking for information to put him ahead. Sharing the news of the press conference with Chief of Police Manning before Miriam does it herself is on brand for him. *Asshole.*

"You weren't going to let me know?"

"Of course I was, sir. We just left an interview with Jeremy Reed—the husband—and stopped out at Goose Creek, at the Marrington Plantation Trailhead."

"What are you doing out there?"

"I had a hunch."

"A hunch." He repeats the phrase slowly.

She feels him weighing his words on the other end of the line. Chief of Police Vincent Manning is tall, imposing, and direct. When he goes silent, his next words could be profoundly impactful or an explosion of vitriol.

He begins carefully. "Ballard, please tell me this isn't going to be a repeat—or some kind of redemption—for what happened with Erica Abington and the rest of that shitshow."

Chief Manning hadn't been with the department a decade earlier. He'd been in Pittsburgh, and had probably heard very little about Erica Abington until he'd come to Hanahan.

The case had faded from the public's mind, but people in the department had long memories, especially when it came to Miriam's role in the investigation.

"This isn't the same situation." Her voice is tight.

"I would hope not," he responds. "And if it were, I'd throw your ass off this case."

Miriam recognizes this as a dig at the prior chief of police. It was true the man hadn't been paying enough attention, but Miriam had also purposely withheld information from him. From everyone, in fact. And no one had realized what she was doing until it was too late.

"You got that, Ballard?" Manning asks.

"I got it, Chief."

"So you're gonna take this one nice and slow, and you're gonna do it right."

She grinds her teeth together. "That's what I'm trying to do."

"Tell me about the husband. How's he looking?"

She does her best to ignore her wounded ego and concentrates on the case. "I'm not sure yet. He's acting out of the ordinary—waiting to report his wife missing, not wanting to call his in-laws. He's cagey and detached. But he has no problem with us looking around and taking things from the house."

"He got a girlfriend?" Manning asks.

Miriam looks at Hill who's crouched in the parking

lot studying something on the ground.

"He claims he doesn't, and we haven't found evidence to the contrary." Not that they'd explored that yet. "But," she says slowly, "Dahlia Reed, it seems, is having an affair."

Manning's breath whooshes into her earpiece. "That's not going to garner any sympathy with the public," he muses, half to himself. "The husband knows about it?"

"Yes," says Miriam. "He's suspected it for some time."

"Gives him motive," Manning says.

She hesitates, then continues. "Sir, there's something else you need to know…"

He waits for her to speak again without prompting.

"The man we think she's been sleeping with is Weston Moss."

"You've got to be fucking kidding me," he says quietly, nearly to himself.

She waits.

"How sure are you?"

"We haven't confirmed it, but the co-workers seem certain. And he was cagey with us himself."

"Does he know about the press conference?"

"No, sir. We're treating him as a regular co-worker. No special treatment. No inside information. As I said, we haven't confirmed the affair, and we're early in the investigation. Nothing so far indicates he had anything to do with Dahlia's disappearance."

"His wife is Josephine Moss," says Manning.

"Yes."

"You think a woman like that is going to take kindly to sharing her husband with a beautiful, accomplished younger woman?"

Miriam knows Manning is speculating about potential perpetrators, just in case Dahli doesn't come home. And now that they're in day two of the woman's absence, Miriam has begun to speculate herself. But she hasn't said any of these things out loud yet. "No sir," says Ballard. "I don't expect she will be."

"You'd know, wouldn't you, Ballard?"

Miriam presses her lips together and stares out the window. She watches a middle-aged couple in colorful, outdated tracksuits come down the path and eye Hill suspiciously as they walk toward one of the parked vehicles. Hill is dressed in plain clothes, but he's still easily identifiable as an officer of the law.

"Can you be objective on this case, Miriam? After everything else?" Chief Manning asks.

"Sir, with all due respect, Erica Abington was ten years ago. It's not fair that I'm being judged on what happened a decade earlier."

"This isn't about fair. This is about the fact that your husband, a state senator, was sleeping with a younger woman who went missing. And you destroyed an innocent man."

Miriam runs her teeth over her tongue. *He wasn't completely innocent*, she thinks.

While the case is now rarely mentioned, the articles are still widely available through an internet search. Anyone in the public can search 'Erica Abington' or 'Former South Carolina Senator Mark Edwards', and the search would result in a flood of information.

A search of 'Miriam Ballard' would produce fewer results. Because that was not her name a decade ago.

Back then, she'd had a husband who she thought had loved her and a daughter who looked up to her.

The eye of that husband had wandered to a pretty younger woman, and when that woman went missing, Detective Miri Edwards had picked up the case. Miri Edwards's investigation revealed the affair. It revealed Senator Edwards' motive. It revealed Senator Edwards' opportunity. And Miri Edwards had gone after the senator hard, fast, and very publicly.

If there were questions about the propriety surrounding her involvement, she'd paid no attention. All she could hear was the sound of revenge and punishment. She didn't much care that a really good defense attorney would likely rip the investigation to shreds. She'd been focused on retribution, but not for Erica Abington.

Two months later, when Erica's body was found not far off a hiking trail in the Francis Marion National Forest—one single shot with her brother's gun to the side of her head and a suicide note in her hand—Senator Mark Edwards had been cleared of suspicion. But not before he'd been ostracized by his family, his colleagues, and the community.

When it was revealed that Erica was pregnant with Mark's baby and had been attempting to save the life, reputation, and political career of her lover, Mark was belatedly cleared of all suspicion. But the damage had been done, and Mark was destroyed. Erica Abington couldn't have known that Mark's own wife would have been the one to participate so readily in that destruction.

"Ballard?" Chief Manning asks.

Miriam pulls herself back to her current reality. "Yeah…"

"Am I making a mistake by not pulling you off this case now?"

She takes a breath and sits up straighter. "No sir. I won't let you down."

"It's not me I'm worried about. It's Dahlia Reed."

Miriam swallows. "I need to do this."

Chief Manning doesn't ask any more questions. Maybe he knows what she means. More than likely, he's had a similar case of personal retribution. Personal forgiveness. Personal redemption. For herself, but also for Erica Abington, who for all her sins did not deserve the end that befell her. And neither, Miriam knows, did her ex-husband.

"I need to make this right," says Miriam.

There's a long pause. "Okay, detective. But you should know—I'm watching you. Because your career may have survived your actions a decade ago, but it won't survive another failure as big as that one. Got it?"

Miriam nods and says into the phone, "Understood, sir."

"Good. Now go find Dahlia Reed. Preferably alive."

PART 2

CHAPTER 15

The silence is deafening; the darkness, absolute. Dahli thinks she must be dead.

After a split second of consciousness, she realizes this is not the case. She is alive, and she is trapped.

She can't move her arms or legs. Something is tied into her mouth, and cloth obscures her vision. She blinks and her eyelashes drag against the material. She thinks she can see shadows through the fabric, but her mind might be playing tricks on her.

Her head pounds from an unidentified pain.

Struggling against her binding, the most she can do is writhe against the hard surface under her body.

Dahli begins to panic; tries to scream, but the sound is muffled. Her breathing intensifies then constricts. Every movement is agony.

Stop moving, a voice inside her head commands, and despite the urge to fight, she obeys.

She slows her breathing and lies still, attempting to assess her situation.

She listens. The only sound seems to be intermittent birdsong. When she strains, she can make out the steady whir of a distant fan or compressor. It seems she's alone. There are no voices or footfalls. No rustling of clothing or clinking of tools or utensils. No sound of traffic or outside activity.

The air is artificially cool and dry. Wherever she's located seems securely protected from the elements.

Her arms are fastened behind her back. She runs her exposed fingertips against the floor beneath her. It's cool, smooth, and waxy to the touch—hardwood flooring, she realizes.

With some effort, struggling against the pain, she manages to twist her body and propel herself a short distance across the floor. She backs into a wall and touches the surface. The wall is also smooth and finished.

Dahli may be in someone's house.

She tries not to cry, knowing that the gag in her mouth could make her suffocate.

But whoever has placed her here has not meant to kill her. At least not yet.

Despite the murky shapes through the cloth over her eyes, it's impossible to make out any discernable objects. The only thing she's sure of is the presence of light in the room. Her world is nothing but a shadowed haze.

Giving up on the present, she struggles to recall the past. The last thing she remembers is running her normal route along the Goose Creek loop.

Hadn't she?

Like her vision, her memories are shifting and malleable. Her brain is foggy, and she doesn't trust her recall. Perhaps her run was just a dream or a distant memory.

The harder she strains to remember, the more intense the throbbing in her head becomes. The pain reverberates into her eyes, her face, her body.

She lies still and considers her body. She is clad in shorts and a short-sleeved top. She feels air on her bare legs and arms. She runs the tips of her fingers against the cloth of her shirt on her back. Nylon… Her running top? That would coincide with what she believes are her last memories.

Has she been violated? Raped?

She tries to assess pain in other parts of her body, but the throbbing in her head doesn't allow it.

She shuts her eyes and tries to shut out her reality.

Luke and Maeve.

Thoughts of her children fill her mind and fill her eyes with tears. A well of sorrow and fear bubbles up from deep in her chest and lodges in her throat. It's nearly as painful as the pulsing ache in her head.

Where are her children? Are they safe? Have they been kidnapped, too? Are they as terrified as she is?

More questions roar through her mind—an avalanche of demands with no answers.

Again, the voice in her head orders, *Remain calm!*

She tries to breathe slowly through this new round of panic.

She *must* believe that Luke and Maeve are safe. Otherwise, there's no point in going on.

And where is Jeremy?

A thought makes her blood run cold. Could her husband have done this to her?

The image of Jeremy's face occupies her mind. As it always does, the thought of him fills her first with hope, then doubt, and finally with resentment and anger. She blames him for her plight, perhaps irrationally. But he'd allowed this to happen. If he'd been more attentive, more focused on something—*anything*—besides himself and his victimhood, Dahli knows she would not be lying on this floor.

Others from her life encroach upon the blackness of her mind, but she pushes them away. They are useless characters to her. They cannot—will not—help her.

And then…the one face she can't ignore.

Her pulse begins to race.

She was going to tell him. She didn't get to tell him…

A cold sweat breaks out on her skin, and her body begins to shake.

She must escape.

Dahli isn't sure how long she lies there, alternating between panic, planning, and grief, before she hears a noise—a break in the monotony of the silence.

The sound of an engine. Her body tenses. The sound of tires crunching on gravel.

The engine stops and a door thuds.

Heavy footsteps, first on gravel, then thumping onto a solid surface. The footsteps become louder. A door opens then shuts, and Dahli feels the slam of it in time with her heart against her ribcage.

The person is now in the dwelling with her.

Footfalls on stairs—loud, heavy. Closer...*closer*.

The quiet squeak of a door, then another creak with a rush of air.

She feels the energy of another human. She senses the attention of that presence, that vibration of existence.

She holds her breath. She does not dare move.

It is watching her, she thinks. It is trying to determine if she's awake or asleep. Dead or alive.

Then it comes closer. It moves slowly.

Dahli's breath comes in quick, shallow puffs.

It leans down close, and she can feel its panting on her face, smelling its humanness.

But it is not human. It is a monster.

It touches her face, and she instinctively jerks her head. It makes a noise. A chuckle? A sneer? It's hard to hear over the pounding of her heart in her ears.

It stands and moves away, toward the door and down the stairs.

As much as she'd wanted it to leave her alone, she's terrified it will abandon her again and leave her there to die.

But it is still in the house.

She listens to its movements—cabinet doors opening and shutting. The rush of water and the creak of pipes.

Then, footfalls on the stairs. It returns to the room.

It crouches down beside her and places a hand over the cloth in her mouth.

Dahli barely breathes. It leaves its hand in place for a few seconds, brushing its fingers over her covered lips. She strains her head backward.

It feels male, this energy.

Finally, clumsy fingers work at the cloth. As soon as the gag has been removed, Dahli screams, ignoring the pain stabbing in her brain.

The hand slaps her face, hard. She's shocked into silence.

It places its hand on her cheek, the movement gentle. She realizes it's communicating with her. It does not speak.

And she doesn't scream again.

A second later, cool glass rests against Dahli's lips, then liquid touches her mouth. She is thirsty, and despite her fear, she opens her lips. Water drizzles into her mouth and she gulps at it. She chokes on the liquid and air.

It moves the glass away and hauls Dahli into a slumped seated position against the wall. It again pours water into her mouth, and she drinks greedily, wondering exactly how long she's been unconscious.

After she drinks, she feels something else brush against her lips. It's soft and slightly spongy. Bread. She bites down, chews, and swallows. It repeats this process five times, then offers her the water again.

When she finishes drinking, she whispers, "I need to use the toilet." Her voice is hoarse and rusty, and the words come out in a croak.

It pauses, then leaves the room, shutting the door behind it. But it comes back, and she can feel it at her feet.

A moment later, her legs are free.

It hauls her to her feet and her legs give out under her.

Any plans Dahli may have had to run for her life are quickly dashed; she wouldn't make it far anyway, with her eyes still covered and no use of her arms.

It half carries, half drags her out of the room.

This is a man; she's sure of it.

She tries to make out the shape of the body or a familiarity of touch. He doesn't have a recognizable essence, but no one she knows would do this to her.

And if this *is* someone she knows, the individual has been a traitor to her all along.

They are in a smaller space now—presumably a

bathroom. The figure forces her to stand on shaking legs while it works her shorts down over her hips.

Dahli wants to cry.

But other than to guide her down on the toilet, it doesn't touch her. And once she empties her bladder, it hauls her back to her feet and roughly hikes up her shorts.

The abrupt movements and low grunting seem angry.

He yanks her from the room by her arm, ignoring her cries of pain, then pushes her back to the floor. She falls forward hard, and without the use of her arms, thuds heavily to the ground. A pain shoots through her shoulder.

He's back at her feet, fastening her legs. Plastic slides against plastic and her ankles press tight together—bone on bone.

"Please," she whispers. "Why are you doing this?" She begins to cry, and once the tears begin, she can't control her emotions. Her tears dampen the cloth over her eyes and sobs wrack her body.

He hits her again, harder, and stars burst into her head and across her eyes.

In the shock of the blow, she stops crying, and the figure stuffs the cloth back into her mouth and fastens it behind her head. She gags against it.

He leaves her there, slamming the door to her prison. A toilet flushes. Heavy footfalls on the stairs and fast steps retreating.

The slam of a heavy door, then a car door followed by the soft roar of an engine. Tires on gravel.

Finally, silence.

Dahli lies quietly. Despite the blow, her head is clearer now. She thinks.

While the figure's touch had been rough, the hands had felt smooth against her skin. She detected no odor. No cologne and no sour smell of an unwashed body.

Whatever this place is, it has working plumbing, and is at least stocked with drinking glasses. She doubts the person would've brought a tumbler with him.

Again, she notes the lack of traffic noise. The location must be remote.

The only thing she thinks she knows about the purring engine she's heard is that it seems to be a relatively late-model vehicle. Where she'd grown up in rural Ohio, her father and neighbors had driven old-model pickup trucks and cars badly in need of repair. The vehicles had sputtered and knocked around noisily as they'd puttered down their country roads.

The engine or transmission of the vehicle her captor had been driving did not fit that description.

Something else is clear—her captor does not want her dead. At least not yet.

He had not violated her or touched her inappropriately.

She thinks of her children and prays they are safe.

If it would guarantee their safety and their health, Dahli would gladly trade her body and her life to her abductor.

Yet, he had not asked anything of her.

Which begs the question—what is it that he wants?

CHAPTER 16

Candace stands apart from the small scrum of bystanders and reporters who've gathered in front of the Reed home.

A light drizzle is falling, but no one in the crowd complains.

She peeks out from under the substantial hood of her waterproof jacket, thankful for the anonymity it provides.

She isn't supposed to be here. She *wouldn't* be here if it hadn't been for Dale Soltis, a reporter from the Courier with whom she'd shared the briefest of affairs a few years earlier. Just a half hour earlier, Dale had let her know the press conference was happening. Of course, the event is not for entertainment purposes—the police are trying to get the word out about a missing young mother—but Candace feels slighted. Dahli is her best friend, after all.

There's been no acknowledgment by the leadership of Mosswood of the news surrounding one of its most high-profile employees. No email signed by Weston Moss, no town hall, not even an anonymous message from Human Resources.

Candace can't help but think her uncle is hiding something. Aunt Josephine had certainly thought so.

Under her hood, she shifts and glances over at her fellow group of nosey bystanders. The clump of bodies murmurs and speculates, armed with even less information than Candace. They seem to have gathered simply because there are news crews on their quiet street.

A tall man with ramrod straight posture and closely cropped spikey hair says to a small frumpy woman next to him, "You were home all day. You didn't see anything?"

The woman wears a tight grey sweatshirt and holds an umbrella screen printed with oversized, jewel-colored flowers. "I already told you. The police were here a few times, and a car was parked out front earlier. I didn't see Dahli or Jeremy." She pauses. "No, that's not right. Jeremy went out. At least, I think it was him. It was his car that backed out of the garage."

Another woman, a few years older than Candace, balances a slobbery baby on her hip and holds a frayed umbrella with one of its metal ribs exposed. The baby grabs the stem of the umbrella and the instrument sways, threatening to impale the other bystanders. "Did you see the kids with him?" she asks.

"I couldn't see anything. Those windows in his SUV are dark."

Another woman says, "I haven't seen Dahli out running in a few days. Do you think something might've happened to her?"

The frumpy woman says, "I doubt it. She's always so put together." The tone is high and judgmental. "How someone hits the genetic jackpot like that is just beyond me."

A middle-aged man in a dark blue baseball cap with pants hitched over a distended belly grunts in what could have been agreement or dissention. He says, "I seen Jeremy with the kids not a few hours ago. They all looked fine to me."

"Did anyone ask the reporters?" The woman with the baby glances over at the scrum.

"I don't want to end up on the news," the well-postured man says.

Distended-belly agrees. "Can't trust that lot of vultures anyway."

There are various murmurs of assent. None of them seem to notice Candace, a stranger, in their midst.

Candace stops listening and considers her own set of circumstances. She'd tried to call Aiden, but her cousin hadn't answered. She looks around, half-expecting to see him, but he isn't there. Nor does she see Weston. Given Weston's connection to the city's leaders and government officials, there isn't a chance in hell he hasn't been informed about the press conference. *Someone* would have called him, just as someone had called her.

As if on cue, the Courier reporter Dale turns around and catches her eye. Likely he's expecting some sort of repayment for the information. She raises her hand a few inches in greeting and thanks, but like the other members of her adopted group, she also has no intention of making it onto the evening news, nor does she particularly trust the media.

Two uniformed police officers stand off to one side of Dahli's yard, close to the garage. They talk with a middle-aged man and woman in all-purpose, ill-fitting suits. They look like cops, Candace thinks. The woman—looking weary and rumpled even from a distance—points to a spot on the lawn, then says something to the man beside her, who nods and climbs the stairs to the porch.

A few minutes later, a sleek black sedan pulls up to the curb and parks to the side of the driveway, behind a marked Hanahan police cruiser.

The man who emerges is tall and commanding. Though he's dressed in plain clothes, his suit is impeccable, and he carries an air of importance. The cops—both uniformed and suited—stand straighter as he approaches.

The group of bystanders around Candace stop chattering and pay attention. "Now who is this?" the frumpy woman wonders aloud.

"FBI," says Distended-belly.

"Nah," says the tall man with the cropped hair. "Wouldn't be FBI." He doesn't offer another explanation, but the group seems to accept that he's correct.

Candace knows who the imposing man is. Chief of Police Vincent Manning. She's met him on more than one occasion, and he'd recognize her if he spotted her.

She tucks her chin into her jacket.

A few additional news vans pull up and fresh reporters join the growing fray on Dahli's front lawn.

From the house to the left of the Reed home, a youngish man and woman exit, glancing at the commotion. They cross the lawn and join the group of neighbors around Candace.

The woman looks at Candace with a friendly curiosity, as if she wants to introduce herself. She doesn't have the chance before the frumpy woman says, "Bill, Susan… Do you have any idea what's happening?"

"It must be about Dahli," the man—Bill—answers.

The woman with the baby says, "I knew it. Too damn pretty for her own good."

The frumpy woman nods. "Any young mother that looks like that is on the market for trouble."

Candace bristles. Women were the worst to other women.

The tall man waves the two of them away. "What about Dahli? Has something happened?"

"There were some people here yesterday asking questions."

"What people?"

Bill shrugs. "They said they were from her office, and she didn't show up. I didn't think too much about it, and I didn't ask many questions, but now I feel like I should have."

The woman with him—Candace assumes this is Susan—says, "You never ask questions. You always only have half the story."

"Well, how the hell was I supposed to know what was going on?"

"You *ask*," Susan says with an exasperated sigh.

The other women make noises of agreement.

The men stay silent.

Candace watches Chief Manning, who has pulled the woman in the ill-fitting suit aside. He's standing very close to the woman and leaning forward. She nods briskly, and opens her mouth as if she's trying to say something. He continues to talk, and she continues to nod.

Finally she gestures toward the house.

He has stopped talking, but looks impatient. He almost, but not quite, points a finger at her.

The woman appears to snap back at him; the Chief shakes his head and walks away. He calls something over his shoulder and the woman stalks up the porch steps.

"Who did you talk to?" Distended-belly is asking Bill. "I mean, were they men, women? Are you sure they weren't FBI?"

"A man and a woman," says Bill. "They weren't FBI. I recognized the guy. Takes his obese mother to bingo on occasion at the senior center." He shakes his head. "Once I recognized him, I felt bad for the poor bastard. The mother is a tyrant. Talks to him like he's a five-year-old. I hadn't seen them around in a while, so I thought maybe the old woman had died."

Susan says, "I'm surprised you didn't invite them in for a drink. You know Bill. Never met a person that wasn't a friend. Won't ask them any questions, of course," she adds. Then a look of horror crosses her face. "What if they were the ones who hurt Dahli? What if you interrupted a crime and you didn't even know it because you didn't think to ask one damn question?"

Before anyone can react to this new theory, the front door of the Reed house opens and the man in the suit emerges with a man she assumes is Dahli's husband, Jeremy. He looks tired and shell-shocked. The hair on one side of his head spikes up, but he's wearing a button-down shirt and a pair of dress slacks. The outfit doesn't match his persona.

"What did you do with Dahli?" Candace asks very quietly under her breath.

The reporters' cameras begin to click, and a hush falls over the crowd.

Jeremy and the two middle-aged suits, along with

another plain-clothed man, are clumped together. Chief Manning steps up to a portable podium emblazoned with the Hanahan Police Department insignia. The rain begins to fall harder, and one of the uniformed officers holds an umbrella over Manning's head.

Someone holds out an umbrella to Jeremy Reed. He looks at it like it's a foreign object. The woman grabs it, pops it open, and hands it to Jeremy. He holds it up obediently.

She doesn't seem to notice that she's soaked.

"Good afternoon." Manning's deep voice booms across the lawn. "We'll keep this brief. You've all received the press release from our public information officer, Sergeant Lance. I think you all know, I'm Vincent Manning, Chief of Police for the Hanahan Police Department. With me are lead detectives Miriam Ballard and Arthur Hill. We're here today to inform the public of a situation and ask for help in locating a missing woman."

He pauses, perhaps for dramatic effect. The frumpy woman says, "Oh, my." It seems she's finally realized that Dahli is a human in trouble, rather than just a pretty face for her to judge.

Chief Manning continues. "Mrs. Dahlia Reed—Dahli, as she's known—is a loving wife and the devoted mother of two young children. She's a professional woman, who some of the members of the media may know through their own work with her."

Candace knows Manning is attempting to make a connection with the press so they're more likely to push the story far and wide and keep it in the headlines.

"Late yesterday, we were informed that she didn't show up for work, and she didn't come home. While Dahli is certainly an adult, this is out of character for her. She's a valued member of her workplace in the position of vice president of public relations for Mosswood Development."

The other uniformed officer holds up Dahli's enlarged headshot—the one from the Mosswood website. It's a stunning photo, if overly posed. Her dark waves are perfectly styled, and the photo has been retouched so that her face is flawless and her teeth are a bright white.

Dahli would hate that they're using that photo, Candace thinks. While beautiful, it holds no soul, and none of Dahli's essence. It doesn't show her kindness or the mischievous twinkle in her eye. It doesn't show her heart.

Jeremy Reed should know that.

"She's beautiful," says Distended-belly.

Candace hears a "Harumph" from the woman holding the baby, who has somehow fallen into a damp sleep against his mother's shoulder despite the pouring rain.

Chief Manning goes on. "We're asking anyone with any information at all to call or text our tip line." He reads the numbers, and Candace knows the broadcast news stations will run those numbers like a ticker at the bottom of their news segments. Likely every news station in Charleston will lead with the story of Dahli's disappearance.

If the leadership at Mosswood wanted to keep this quiet, it's now too late.

Candace wonders what her aunt is thinking. She imagines Josephine with a glass of good Sauvignon Blanc, spitting insults at the screen. She imagines Aiden beside her, staring at the images of his workplace obsession, torn between his obedience to his mother and his passion for Dahli. She imagines Weston holed up in his home office, a glass of scotch in front of him and anger and regret coloring his dark mood.

"No tip is too small or insignificant," Manning says. "If you think you've seen something or know something, we want to hear about it. If you live in the area, we may be reaching out to gather more information. Thank you in advance for your cooperation."

There's a shuffling of the main players, and some of the reporters begin shouting.

Manning says, "Just one moment, and we'll get to your questions."

"I wonder if they want the footage from our security camera," the tall man with the cropped hair muses.

"Good thought," says Distended-belly. "I'm going to call them, too. Did anyone catch the number?"

"They'll print it in the story," says Candace, and the group turns to stare at her as if they've just noticed her existence. She silently chides herself for speaking.

Chief Manning says, "And now I'd like to introduce Detective Ballard, who's going to walk through some of the specifics of the case for you."

The weary-looking woman in the wrinkled suit steps up to the podium. "Thank you Chief Manning. Good afternoon, and thank you for joining us. As Chief Manning told you, today we're appealing to the public to help us in our search for Dahlia Reed." She gestures toward the photograph of Dahli. "Dahli is thirty-five years old, approximately five feet, four inches tall. She was last seen by her husband yesterday morning at five o'clock in the morning when she left the house to go out for a jog. The security footage we've received so far indicates that she may have followed the Goose Creek Loop along the Red Bank Road."

This is correct, Candace thinks, though no one had bothered to talk to her.

Dahli has been running the same trail for a few months. Candace knows this because she'd cautioned Dahli against running the same route every day. But Dahli insisted she was safe, with her industrial-strength pepper spray and her screeching alarm.

"We don't have much more information than that. As Chief Manning mentioned, if you live on this route, and we haven't already contacted you, we'll likely be reaching out to see if you've seen anything. We'd rather sift through a lot of information than miss something because a neighbor didn't want to bother us." She pauses.

"Are you sure she disappeared while running?" Dale Soltis yells.

Detective Ballard frowns and opens her mouth like she's going to chide him. Instead she says, "No, we're not. But it's the best theory we have right now."

Another reporter shouts a question, but Ballard ignores her. Instead, she turns around to say something to the other plain-clothes officer who Candace assumes is the public information officer.

Detective Ballard shifts toward Jeremy Reed, who stands silent and dazed, his gaze fixated on some unknown object in the distance.

"Mr. Reed?" Ballard prompts, her voice gentle.

Jeremy steps up to the podium, and the sky opens up. A nearly simultaneous bolt of lightning and crack of thunder shock the group. The newspeople do their best to hold up umbrellas, but they stay put. Candace wonders what possessed the officer to hold an outdoor press conference with rain forecasted. If they were going for hopeless and foreboding, she supposes they've accomplished their goal.

The woman with the baby and the tall man with the cropped hair make their exit. The others stay put, hunched against the rain.

Candace can barely hear Jeremy's words above the rain and the rumbling of thunder. He doesn't react to the rain.

"I'm Dahli's husband, Jeremy," he says. "Dahlia is…" He pauses as if he's gathering his thoughts. "Dahli is my world." His voice gives out, and Candace can't tell if it's from emotion or from nerves.

"Our kids—Luke and Maeve—and I just want her home. So if you know where she is, please just come forward." There's another pause as the rain beats down. "And Dahli," he continues, addressing his wife directly, "if you can hear me… I love you. I miss you. There's nothing we can't make it through. It doesn't matter what you've done. Just come home to us. I forgive you."

If he were going to say more, he doesn't get the opportunity. The other plain-clothes detective whisks him away, back onto the porch and into the house.

One of the reporters shouts, "What has Dahlia Reed done?"

Another follows with, "Mr. Reed, do you think she's run away?"

Ballard steps back up to the podium. Her hair is drenched and hangs forward like oily snakes around her chin. She's pulled the big hood of her parka around her head. "We'll take just a few questions and then let you get out of this rain."

The first reporter repeats his question. Candace recognizes him as a WCIV News 4 reporter. "Has Dahlia Reed done something wrong?"

Ballard shifts. "No, she has not. And we have no indication she disappeared willingly."

"But the husband—"

"We have no indication she went willingly," Ballard says more firmly this time.

"Is your assumption that she's dead?" a female reporter from Live 5 News asks.

"Obviously we're hoping that isn't the case."

Soltis asks, "Are you planning on conducting a search if you think she disappeared out at Goose Creek?"

"We've already had teams out there, and we'll continue to search the area."

"What about a public search?"

Ballard consults with the other wrinkled-looking officer then says, "If Dahli isn't located by tomorrow, we'll announce plans for a public search."

Candace knows that plenty of locals will conduct their own searches, livestreaming their activities every step of the way. A search open to the public will be more for publicity for the police department than for the hope of yielding any usable results.

"Have any suspects been identified?"

"We don't know that any crime has been committed. But there are people we're interested in talking to."

"Persons of interest?" someone yells.

"Persons who have information that may be useful," replies Ballard cagily, irritated.

"Are you exploring the possibility that Dahli Reed left on her own?"

"We're pursuing all possibilities, but as I've said twice before, we have no indication that she left willingly," says Ballard.

"Do *you* believe she left on her own?"

"No," says Ballard. Her voice is flat. "I do not."

"And yet her husband does. Interesting."

Ballard doesn't comment.

Another voice rises above the others. "I have a question," it announces, the tone high-pitched and slightly slurred.

Candace freezes. She knows this voice.

"I happen to know that Dahlia Reed is having an affair. Have you explored that avenue yet?"

Ballard squints, momentarily speechless, then says, "We can't comment on Ms. Reed's personal life, nor do we think it's relevant to the case. At this time, we're ending the press conference. Thank you all for coming."

Ballard starts to turn away, but the woman's voice says, "Really? I would think an affair would give a bunch of people a whole host of motives."

The press have trained their cameras on the woman in the long tan trench coat clutching a Burberry-plaid beige umbrella that sways above her head.

Ballard says something to the public information officer then whirls back around on the woman. "What outlet did you say you were with?"

"I'm with the outfit of the Moss household," Josephine Moss announces. "It's my husband the little slut has seduced," she says. "*Dahlia Reed.*" She draws the name out in a sing-song way. "And now she's missing?" Josephine begins to laugh as one of the uniformed officers emerges in the rain to escort Candace's aunt away.

"This is just too good," Josephine says as the officer drags her by her arm. But the officer is no match for the will of Josephine, as she addresses the reporters directly. "The police are wasting their time on searches. You all need to focus your attention on Dahlia's boss— Weston Moss, the fourth. Because he knows more than he's saying. He always does."

CHAPTER 17

Dahli has fallen into an unsettled sleep. She dreams of Luke and Maeve. And she dreams of Jeremy. Not the Jeremy of today, but the man she married—kind, sweet, and caring. He leans over her and caresses her hair, cups her cheek with his hand.

She wakes to a clap of thunder and the sound of rain. It pounds on the roof steadily, drowning out the silence of the house.

Her body aches and she fights the urge to strain against the plastic that binds her. She feels as if she's going crazy. She feels as if she might die from the inability to move.

Her head still pounds, but she tries to think logically. Why can't she remember anything? If it's her body's way of protecting her, it's doing the opposite. She needs to know who's keeping her hostage. And why.

She tries to remember details about the man who'd come earlier. How long had it been? Hours? Days?

She's not sure if he was familiar. She of course remembers the last time a man touched her. But that contact had been soft and gentle. Not the rough, impersonal handling of her captor.

On occasion, Jeremy had been rough with her. She'd never felt it had risen to the level of physical abuse, but of course it *had* been. If a man ever touched Maeve the way Jeremy had touched Dahli, she'd demand that her daughter leave him. *Why hadn't she done that for herself?* she wonders. Why had she assumed she deserved to be treated that way?

That line of thinking is useless. And none of it matters now. Unless it's Jeremy who's holding her. But he doesn't have access to another house. And if her husband were going to take the time to kidnap her, wouldn't he have just gone ahead and killed her?

She thinks of other possibilities. Aiden?

No. No chance. Despite her discouragement, Aiden loves her. And while his love is young, eager, and intense, the boy is too cocky and brash to risk his future by harming her. Isn't he?

Weston? Too much to lose. Too much to risk. He wouldn't get his hands dirty, either. Though he might pay someone to get their hands dirty *for* him.

She thinks about their last dinner together. Weston had been livid after Dahli's rejection. Would he have gone so far as to kidnap her to teach her a lesson? To keep her for himself?

Eugene Ryan. Despite her restraints, Dahli shivers. Eugene had seemed harmless to her, even when he'd watched her a little too closely and lingered too long outside her office door. She'd tried to be kind to him.

But she'd seen him on more than one occasion—downtown on King Street, at the Hotel Bennett. He'd been in the shadows, but she was sure it was him.

He'd been following her. Watching her. Stalking her.

She'd planned to confront him about his behavior the day she'd been taken…

A flash of memory—quick and fleeting. A black car, the hint of a smile.

Who was it? she demands of herself.

Dahli wants to scream at her inability to remember. She *must* remember.

She searches the blackness of her mind until she's exhausted. Then she gags against the cloth in her mouth.

She's not sure how much longer she can lay here before she loses her mind.

She must keep her wits. She needs to escape so she can get to Luke and Maeve. So she can put all of her plans in place. There were so many plans.

She wonders if she's being punished for falling in love with someone else while she's still married. She's being punished for not being the good girl she's supposed to be.

She starts to weep, but forces herself to stop so she doesn't choke.

The rain continues to pound, loud and steady. And

perhaps in a token of mercy from her mind and her body, she drifts back into unconsciousness.

When she wakes again, Dahli can feel the quiet pulse of a person's energy in the room with her.

The presence must sense the shift in Dahli, because after a moment, footsteps cross the floor. Dahli stiffens as they near.

"I'm going to take the cloth out of your mouth."

The man's voice is very quiet, falsely deep, and distorted as if he's trying to disguise it. She thinks she knows this voice, but she can't be certain.

"If you scream, I will leave you here to die. Nod if you understand."

Dahli hesitates. Then she nods.

He unfastens the cloth around the back of her head; she swallows and opens and shuts her mouth. "Thank you," she croaks. Maybe if she ingratiates herself to him, he'll…

He'll what? Let her go?

There's no chance of that.

A second later, water is being poured into her mouth. She drinks, lapping up as much as she can. It runs down her chin and neck.

Small pieces of bread are fed to her. She wonders if she'll only be fed bread and water in captivity.

Her body and soul deflate. She will not leave this prison alive. She has no idea why he's keeping her alive now.

"Why are you doing this?" she whispers.

There's a long pause before he finally whispers, "You know why, Dahli."

She feels him at her feet—the soft swish of the knife—and her legs are free. The sudden ability to move is painful, and she moans in agony.

He grabs her by one shoulder, hauling her to her feet. He drags her across the room roughly.

She's made him angry, though she has no idea what she's done.

They're in the bathroom again. She has not consumed enough liquid for her bladder to be full, but she manages to relieve what little fluid is there.

He doesn't bother replacing her clothing this time. With her shorts around her knees, he drags her back to the room and pushes her back down onto the floor.

In the stillness of the moment that follows, Dahli is aware of what will happen next. Women must have an intuition about this type of unpredictable, feral danger. Women must sense the moment their will is completely overpowered by someone bigger, stronger, and savage.

She hears the unmistakable sound of a zipper, then the friction of denim fabric sliding against skin.

He has not replaced the gag in her mouth, but she

doesn't scream. Instead, her teeth chatter uncontrollably even before his hands are on her again.

She lies on her back, her arms pinned painfully behind her, against the wooden floor.

He removes her shorts and forces her legs apart with his knee.

Though she tries to prepare herself for what will come next, she is still shocked when he enters her in one quick, powerful thrust.

Her teeth chatter so hard, she thinks they might clatter right out of her mouth. She tries to press her jaws together, but it's no use. She can't stop her body's uncontrollable shaking.

His movements are rough and painful. Even though she can't see anything through the blindfold, she turns her head to the side and squeezes her eyes shut. She rises above herself—out of her shaking body. Out of the pain.

She floats on a cloud of blackness, imagining flames licking their way around her. *Just consume me,* she thinks. *Let me die.*

Vaguely, she's aware of the monster climaxing inside her with animal grunts. Her eyes leak tears down her face, wetting the cloth.

Finally, there is stillness. His weight is heavy against her, pressing the bones of her shoulders, elbows, and wrists against the floor.

Finally, he uncouples from her, his breath still

coming in quick pants.

Fluid oozes down her inner thigh, and as she reenters her own body, she realizes she's still shaking. She rolls onto her side and vomits onto the floor. The scant food and water in her stomach regurgitate in a puddle of sick.

She retches over and over again, her stomach in a spasm.

"Stop it," he orders, his words floating around her ears.

But she can't stop the violent heaving of her body.

His hand reaches around her throat and squeezes lightly at first, and then harder until she gasps against the pressure. He tightens his grip. Blood pulses in her head, in her eyes.

Bright pricks of light burst through the blackness. They swirl into her field of vision—brighter, brighter like a swarm of fireflies.

The harder she struggles, the more brilliant the lights.

The pressure is too strong.

Her soul becomes the light and begins to merge with the darkness. Relief is within her grasp. She succumbs…

Suddenly, the pressure is gone, and her breath whooshes back into her lungs. She gasps and coughs.

His hand has not left her throat. His breath is hot against her ear. He drags a knuckle up her cheek, then replaces it with his tongue.

She wants to tear a chunk out of his flesh with her teeth, but she lacks both the speed and the energy to fight.

Her body goes limp as he reaches down and tugs at her shorts, hiking them up crookedly over her hips. She is damp between her legs, but at least the cloth absorbs what he has left behind on her.

Her stomach roils and her head pounds.

He walks away, shutting the door of the room behind him.

There will be no more food. Not tonight.

She makes out the sound of the front door closing and the heavy hollow footsteps on outdoor stairs. There is the crunch of shoes on gravel, the thud of a car door, and the soft rumble of an engine.

She lies still for a long while. Then she makes a shocking discovery.

Her legs are free.

Carefully, she comes to her knees. With her weakened muscles, the movement is painful, but she maneuvers to the wall and pushes herself into a standing position.

She touches the wall with her fingers. It is smooth—painted—with regularly spaced grooves. Finished wood.

Carefully, she makes her way around the room, examining each obstacle that she encounters. A chest of drawers. A wooden chair. A doorknob. A bookcase.

Dahli nearly weeps when she reaches a narrow bed.

Here, she backs herself onto the mattress, which is covered with a blanket.

She isn't sure if he'd meant to leave her legs unrestrained, or if after he'd raped her and nearly killed her, he'd simply forgotten to bind her again.

She will not question it.

In spite of everything, she's still alive and a bright spot has presented itself. She has more hope than many people in this world, and gives thanks. Real thanks.

She lies down on her side. Compared to the floor, she feels as if she's lying on a bed of clouds. Her body is wrecked and ravaged, and she is exhausted. She will not make it out alive, but at least her last sleep will be soft.

CHAPTER 18

"What the hell were you thinking, Ballard?"

Chief Manning's voice is loud enough to carry through the closed door of his office. Miriam cringes inwardly, careful to control her facial expressions which remain stoic and rigid.

"I told you it was a bad idea to hold the press conference at the home. I told you I wanted to be careful about how we handled this case. You didn't listen. And isn't your inability to listen exactly what fucked everything up the last time? Isn't that how you arrested your own husband for a crime he didn't commit?"

Manning goes silent, and he paces in the space behind his desk.

His question doesn't require an answer, so Miriam remains silent. But her head is raised, and her chin is defiant. In her periphery, she can see them through the glass walls—officers who have no reason to be in the hallway milling about. Listening.

Most of them weren't even there for Erica Abington and Mark Edwards. They wouldn't even recognize the names.

Miriam is a spectator sport. And it isn't malicious. It's human.

"What the fuck am I supposed to say to Weston Moss?" Manning says.

This, too, is rhetorical, but she answers anyway. "I would think that should be up to his wife."

Manning's eyes shoot fire at her. "You're off this case."

Miriam blinks. It takes her longer than it should to process his words. "You… You can't do that."

"I can. And I should've done it immediately. I know I wasn't here when Erica Abington went missing, but I sure as shit would have booted your ass then. I had hoped, with maturity and distance, you'd have better sense this time. I'd hoped you'd learned your lesson."

"Chief," Miriam says, her hands in front of her, "you know what happened out there wasn't my fault. Maybe we should have held the press conference in a more controlled setting. But even then, there's no guarantee Mrs. Moss wouldn't have interrupted. You *know* that," she repeats. She has sense enough not to point out that Sergeant Lance had been responsible for securing the scene. Because of her past, she's catching flack for his mistake, and it isn't fair.

Manning blows out a long breath, and Miriam holds hers. She needs to be on this case. She needs to be the one to find out what happened to Dahlia Reed. She needs it as much for herself as she does for the young mother.

When Manning speaks again, his voice is softer.

"Miriam…"

Her name an invitation, he motions for her to sit across from him. The fire has been extinguished from his voice. She sits, and Manning runs his hands over his ruddy cheeks, then over his head.

"When I took this job, of course I'd done my homework. I knew all about you. All about what happened with Mark Edwards and Erica. How you broke protocol to investigate your own husband. If he *had* been guilty, any defense attorney worth their salt would have gotten him off."

Miriam shifts in her seat. Even though she'd been driven by emotion on the case, she still thinks her detective work was solid. It's true she'd gone after Mark harder than she would have a random man, but her viciousness had been warranted. A jury would've appreciated that the man's *wife* went to the lengths she did to assure he'd never hurt any woman again.

The discovery that Erica had taken her own life to protect her older, successful, married lover was beside the point.

Clearly Manning doesn't think it is, because he says, "And any defense attorney hired to represent the suspects on the Dahlia Reed case is going to raise the issue of your credibility, too."

"This case is nothing like Mark's investigation."

Manning stares at her. "Young mother goes missing. Husband seems good for it, but so does the older, prominent, married lover. And now you've got the lover's wife accusing him. It's damn well close enough." He leans forward. "You're a good detective, Ballard. But you're compromised."

"Chief," she says. Her palms are raised on the desk between them. "I have nothing personally invested in this case. I don't know Dahlia and Jeremy Reed. I don't know the Moss family. I'm about as objective as you can get."

"But you're not, Ballard. You're using this case to make up for *that* one."

Miriam sits back.

"You're off the case," he says again. This time his words are quiet. Gentle. Final.

To Miriam's mortification, her throat tightens painfully. "Come on, Chief," she says, and her voice is husky. She swallows. "That's not fair, and you know it."

"This isn't about fair."

"What's it about then?"

"This is about finding Dahlia Reed."

"I can do that better than anyone."

Manning holds out his hands across the desk. It is a gesture of helplessness, and something inside Miriam's chest shifts and lights the slow burn of her anger. Manning isn't helpless in this situation. It's his call who to put in charge of the investigation.

Unless it isn't…

"Who got to you?" she asks.

"What are you talking about?"

"Was it Moss? His lawyer?" Miriam blinks. It could have been anyone.

Her husband had lost a lot of friends and colleagues in the Abington investigation. When he was finally cleared, they didn't come crawling back. Mark had still been radioactive.

But there are plenty of his government cronies still in power.

It's equally possible this is their belated, indirect attempt to assuage their guilt for turning their backs on Mark in his time of need. God knows they'd all seen how Miriam decimated the man's reputation. It's a distinct possibility they're now considering Weston's plight, realizing it could happen to any one of them who couldn't keep his dick in his pants.

"Who owns you, Manning?" she sneers.

The chief draws himself up. "No one owns me, Ballard."

"You sure about that?"

"Check yourself," he says, his eyes narrowing.

"I don't have to check myself. I *know* myself."

How dare he act as though she's in the wrong when they both know he's not protecting her *or* the investigation. He's protecting his own ass. Even that is beside the point. A woman is missing. And Manning is worried about nothing but his reputation.

He opens his mouth as if he's going to offer a retort. Instead, he closes it and runs his tongue over his teeth before saying, "How is Mark these days, Miriam? Still in rehab? Or is it the mental health facility his government pension is paying for?"

Miriam glares at him.

"And Samantha? How's your daughter?"

She doesn't know what Manning knows of her estranged family. If he's heard Mark moved back to his native Florida and Samantha had gone with him.

It's been over two years since Miriam has spoken to her daughter, much less seen her.

She doesn't answer Manning.

"How do you think they'd feel about you taking this case? What do you think they'd say if I called them?"

"It doesn't matter what they'd say, nor what they think. It's not them who's missing and endangered. It's Dahli Reed." Why must she continue to remind people what this case is really about?

"So you're doing this for Dahli Reed?"

"Of course I am."

"Just like all those years ago, you were doing it for Erica Abington…"

Again, she doesn't answer.

Manning rests his fists on the desk. "You asked

who owns me. I'm asking you the same question, Miriam. Who owns you? Because your intentions are not as pure as you're making them out to be. Are they?"

Miriam does not want to explore her motivations. And she does not need to. Not here. Not with her boss.

Manning picks up a folder at the corner of his desk. "You're off the Reed case, Ballard," he says for the third time.

She starts to argue again but stops when he looks at her with blank round eyes. "Hill will take over with assistance from Detective Kaylor."

"Kaylor!" The name bursts from Miriam's mouth. "The girl has been in the position for less than a year." Kristie Kaylor is young and eager, but she's not capable of helping Hill solve this case. She's too green.

"She'll learn," says Manning. "Hill will teach her."

Miriam doesn't think Hill will be able to handle the case, either. He doesn't have the fire that she does. He doesn't think strategically. *He thinks like a man*, is what she wants to say. But she doesn't.

"You're making a mistake," she says instead.

Manning lets out a long, heavy sigh. "Maybe I am. But I'm not going to repeat the mistakes made in the Abington case. You should have been removed then, and you know it. More than one life was ruined because of *that* error in judgment."

He's talking about her family. And she can't even argue with him.

He closes the folder and taps it on the desk before holding it to her. "The trustees at Hope Presbyterian Church think their treasurer may be embezzling money. I want you to look into it."

She stares at the folder, then at Manning. "Embezzlement? At a church?"

"You're not to go near the Reed case. I've already informed Hill he's taking over. He's setting up a search out at Goose Creek. We need to show the public we're actually doing something, even if we won't find anything. You're not to show up, nor are you to contact anyone on the case. No family of Dahlia Reed. No witnesses. Is that clear?"

Miriam's mind is racing. She thinks of her next tack. She's tried arguments, insults. Begging is not her style, but she leans forward, and is mortified when the words come out thin and reedy. "Please, Vince. I need this." Tears color the words.

Manning seems to pause and consider. Maybe this might work after all.

But finally, he shakes his head. "This isn't what you need, Miriam. Solving this case isn't going to undo what you did in the past. And we both know that's what you're attempting."

He holds the Hope Presbyterian folder out again, and Miriam deflates. He's not going to budge. She takes a breath and snatches the folder from his hands. She doesn't look at it.

"You're making a mistake," she repeats. Then she turns on her heel and strides out of Manning's office, past all the curious glances and knowing smirks.

Assholes, she thinks.

When she gets to her desk, she slaps the folder down and glares at Hill, who's standing at the desk across from her with Kristie Kaylor, young enough to be Miriam's daughter.

Hill holds up his hands. "I didn't ask for this."

"But you didn't turn it down, either. And you didn't go to bat for me."

"We were all there. We all saw what happened during the press conference."

"That wasn't my fault. Lance was responsible for securing the area."

"Come on. This isn't about the press conference." Hill's low voice makes her cringe. Then it makes her boil.

"I don't need your sympathy, Hill," Miriam spits. "After two years of being your partner, I hoped you'd know that about me." She moves closer to him, out of Kaylor's earshot. "You know why I have to do this."

Hill glances around. After the confrontation in Manning's office, others continue to pay attention to the drama, and Hill doesn't want to feed that. "There's nothing I can do, Miriam," he says softly.

They look into each other's eyes for a moment, then she steps back and swallows. "I never took you for a ladder climber."

He isn't offended by her low blow. "That isn't what this is about, and you know it."

She raises her hands and pushes the hair back from her face. She looks from Hill to Kaylor and drops her hands. "This isn't about either of us, Hill. This is about Dahlia Reed, who's missing and in danger. With each passing moment, the chances become better that she's dead." Miriam opens her mouth and closes it again. She swallows. "I've been in this situation before, and I forgot the goal. I just want to find Dahli Reed, alive. For the sake of her children."

Hill nods. "I know you do."

A flash of understanding passes between them, and Miriam exhales. She breaks eye contact and moves to her desk. "I guess I'll start working on this Hope Presbyterian case." Her voice is loud enough for anyone around them to hear, including Kaylor.

Hill's voice is quiet. "Just…be careful."

"I will," she says. Then she says quietly, "Let's find Dahli."

CHAPTER 19

Jeremy peers out from behind the sheer curtains in the living room window to the line of news vans parked on both sides of Linden Lane. He shifts his attention from the media to the two marked Hanahan police cars in his driveway. The morning sun glints off the windshield of the second car, and he's blind to who's stationed inside.

His phone is silenced because the press has somehow obtained his number. He doesn't answer even the calls attached to his contacts. He can't bear to address what happened during the press conference. Now, not only has the public decided he's the main suspect in the disappearance of his wife, but the spectacle made by that Moss woman has also given him a very strong, very public, motive.

Jeremy moves from the window and paces around the living room. He hasn't showered, and his odor is rank.

Luke appears in the opening to the living room wearing a University of South Carolina Gamecocks T-shirt and boxers. His thin arms poke out from the oversized sleeves like twigs.

"Are we going to school?" he asks.

Luke and Maeve had been in the house with a county social worker while the press conference took place the prior evening. Luke is astute enough to know that something has happened; he just doesn't know what it is.

"No school today," says Jeremy. *No school for a while*, he thinks. He'll ask the detectives if someone can collect the kids' schoolwork until this thing resolves itself.

A wave of despair and guilt washes over him. Whatever happens, his son's life will never be the same.

Jeremy takes a shaky breath, blinks, and studies Luke, who looks so much like Jeremy had at that age, except with Dahli's eyes—eyes that always saw too much.

He motions for his son to sit at the dining table, and Jeremy sits next to him. He isn't sure how to start, and in the expanded silence, Luke says, "Mom isn't coming home, is she?"

Jeremy's breath catches in his chest. "The police are working really hard to find her."

Luke appears to process this development. His next question surprises Jeremy. "Who was that woman last night? The one on the lawn?"

"How do you know about that?"

Luke shrugs. "I watched the news later on my tablet."

Shit. Jeremy hadn't even considered Luke might be viewing coverage of the situation.

"Who was the man she was talking about?"

Jeremy exhales. Twelve was too young for this conversation. But twelve was also too young for everything else that was going on. "She was talking about Mom's boss—Weston Moss. But the woman was…a little unhinged. We don't know that anything she was saying was true. We don't know what's true right now."

"But we don't know what's not true, either."

Jeremy lays his hands flat on the table. "We don't," he admits.

"They're saying it was you," says Luke. "They're saying you, like…did something to Mom."

Jeremy can barely breathe. He's done a lot to his wife, but his microaggressions—those are not what the pundits and commentators and social media warriors and armchair quarterbacks mean. They mean he killed his wife.

"I loved your mom very much," he says to his son.

"But you don't anymore?" Luke asks, picking up on Jeremy's use of the past tense.

"Of course I do. Always." He tries to correct himself, but from the look on Luke's face, it seems to be falling flat. He exhales. "Everything you hear online… There will be a lot of rumors and opinions. But people don't know. They don't know your mom. They don't know me. They don't know our family."

Luke stares at the table.

"I think we should take away the tablet for now."

At that, Luke's head snaps up. His face has started, just recently, to lean out. To show signs of the man he will one day be. He shakes his head.

"Look, everyone is going to have something to say about this situation. Even people you think are your friends. We just have to… We just have to hunker down for a little bit. You, Maeve, and me. We need to let the police do their work, and we need to trust in that process."

After Jeremy's finished speaking, he sits back. He doesn't trust the police himself, but Luke doesn't need to know that. Luke doesn't need to know that his father is scared shitless.

"How will I know what they're saying?" Luke asks.

"You don't need to know what's being said about us. Most of it is garbage."

"What if it's true?"

"What if *what* is true?"

"That Mom is dead. And you killed her."

Jeremy's stomach drops. He rubs his hands over his face. When he's calmed himself enough to speak, he says, "That's ridiculous, Luke. I would never intentionally hurt your mother. And I wouldn't hurt you." He leans forward to place his hand on Luke's thin arm, but his son pulls it back.

Jeremy sees the shadow of fear that passes over Luke's expression, quickly replaced by an expression of shame or guilt.

He's never raised a hand to either of his children, and yet now his son can barely stand sitting next to him.

Another wave of hatred for Dahli wells up in his chest, and he attempts to clamp down on it. As the situation escalates, it's becoming harder and harder to do. How could she have allowed this to happen? How has she done this to her family?

Had she really been sleeping with her boss? The wife had thought so, just as the police had.

Dahli, with her infectious laugh, beautiful face, carefully toned body—Jeremy has a hard time believing Weston Moss had been her choice of romantic partner.

But for money and power, perhaps Dahli would have done anything. Jeremy had long ago concluded he didn't really know his wife. Maybe he had once, but not anymore.

He can't help despising her for that. He knows it might not be fair, but he feels the way he feels. All he can do now is try not to let it show.

"Luke, we're going to get through this, one way or another. And we're going to get through it as a family."

"A family without a mother."

Jeremy couldn't argue with that. But his anger was

beginning to bleed from mother to son. "Go get your tablet. You'll get it back when this nonsense is over."

Luke blinks up at him with his big, brown eyes. Again, Jeremy sees that flash of what he'll be as an adult.

"No," says his son.

"This isn't a negotiation." Jeremy's words are very quiet and deliberate. "Get the fucking tablet. Now."

Luke looks as if he might argue, but in the end, fear and uncertainty win out. He shoves his chair away from the table, his face grim and mouth set in a straight slash. The chair topples backward; Jeremy catches it before it crashes to the floor. He resists the urge to scold his son.

On the kitchen counter behind him, he catches sight of his silenced phone. The screen continues to light up with notifications. He snatches it up and scrolls through the messages. Most of them are unfamiliar numbers, but a few are from Dahli's extended family, trying to reach him and get information. He doesn't feel bad about ignoring them. Dahli's family has been ignoring his existence for their entire marriage.

Besides, Sherri and Leo Darling are on their way to Hanahan now. They can keep their own family informed. That's one thing they'd be good for, at least.

He's about to put his phone down when the screen illuminates with an incoming call. It's Carter Brooks, his boss. He wants to ignore it, but something makes him press the accept button.

"Carter," he says.

"Jesus Christ! What the fuck, man?" Carter's words punch through the device into Jeremy's ear.

Luke has returned with his tablet, but instead of putting it on the table or the counter, he smashes it down onto the tile floor of the kitchen. Jeremy jumps at the violent crash as the fragile screen explodes into a web of cracks. The screensaver of the block figure and dog—an image from Luke's favorite video game—flickers and pixelates. Colors flash across the face of the device.

Luke stomps back out of the room without waiting for Jeremy's reaction.

"What was that?" Carter demands through the phone's earpiece.

"Nothing," Jeremy responds. "It's… It's just chaotic around here."

"Why didn't you call me? I had to hear about Dahli from a press conference?" Carter sounds more distraught than Jeremy thinks the man has any reason to be.

"I called human resources and told them I'd be out for a few days. They didn't let you know?"

"They did, but…come on, Jeremy. Dahli is missing? How could you not let me know?"

"I'd been hoping there wasn't reason for concern.

Once the police got involved, all hell broke loose."

"But where is she?"

"If I could tell you that, obviously we wouldn't be talking on the phone, Carter," Jeremy says dryly. For maybe the first time since meeting Carter, Jeremy doesn't feel intimidated by the more successful man.

"She's having an affair?" Carter asks. "It's all over social media that she's sleeping with Weston Moss." When Jeremy doesn't respond, Carter says, "Is it true?"

It's an odd and insensitive question, and Jeremy isn't sure what to say. He's always known Carter to be smooth and thoughtful. The man is on the fast track for the C-suite at the company, and Jeremy doesn't doubt he'll be the CEO someday. To hear the man ask about his missing wife's sex life is not only insulting, it's unnerving.

"I have no idea what's true and what's false anymore," he murmurs.

"I just can't believe Dahli would be with someone like Weston. The man's an arrogant blowhard. Surely she can see that."

"Yeah, I'm not really concerned about Weston. I'm concerned she's not here. I'm concerned the police think I had something to do with her disappearance. I'm concerned they think she might be dead."

Carter is silent, then he says, "Of course." Another pause. "Yes, of course. I'm sorry. I just…" Carter's voice is long and slow through the phone. "Dahli is just so damn…good. You know?" Jeremy hears Carter exhale. Then a low, plaintive, "Jesus… Dahli." He says this to himself. "How could this have happened?"

Even though Jeremy is almost certain it's a rhetorical question, he says, "The detectives are trying to figure that out."

"Yeah," comes the whispered response. A long silence follows. "Is there anything I can do? I think they said she'd disappeared while running. I know that area well. I've run there myself many, many times."

Jeremy stares at the broken tablet on the floor of the kitchen. "You've run at Goose Creek?"

"It's a beautiful, peaceful place."

"But you live in Folly Beach."

"I…I've trained all around the Charleston area."

Folly Beach is about forty-five miles from Goose Creek. And Carter isn't from Charleston originally. He'd relocated to the area from the Pacific Northwest within the past five years. That he's been running in Goose Creek is coincidental, to say the least.

Something clicks in Jeremy's mind, which begins to buzz with a disquieting energy.

"You're a marathoner, aren't you?"

"I try to run one a year."

"Dahli was training for a marathon, too. She was heading up to Virginia in a few months for the race."

Carter doesn't immediately answer. When he finally speaks, his voice is tentative. "I seem to recall talking to her about it during the Christmas party."

"No," Jeremy says. "She hadn't made the commitment at Christmas. She started training after the party. After she'd talked to you."

"Maybe we'd discussed her getting back into it. It was a while ago. And I think we'd all had a few too many glasses of wine." Carter lets out a misplaced chuckle. "A lot has happened between then and now."

"Has it?" Jeremy asks. "Like what?"

"Well, the obvious, of course."

The obvious. The fact that his wife is missing, and he is now being examined with suspicion by the world. "What else?" he asks Carter through a clenched jaw.

"You know. Just…life. The months pass and the world changes. People change."

Jeremy thinks back on how Dahli has changed since Carter's Christmas party. It had been a while since their marriage could be described as romantic. The decline in the affection between them had been years in the making. But looking back—if Jeremy had to pinpoint an occurrence coinciding with Dahli's disgust, it was close to the time of Carter's party at his serene Asian-inspired bungalow that overlooked the flat marshes.

It was after that party Dahli first talked about moving from Hanahan—now that he thinks about it—closer to Folly Beach. He thought she'd been enamored with the area. Was the area all she'd been enamored with?

"So, is there a search planned?" Carter asks. "I thought I saw something on Facebook…"

Jeremy draws himself up. He doesn't use social media, and he's aware both Luke and Carter likely know more about the efforts of the police than he does at this point. But he says, "They're apparently planning for one at Goose Creek. They haven't given me all the details, yet."

"I'll drive up then…if you don't mind."

The buzzing in Jeremy's head gets louder. His boss is asking his permission. He's never considered Jeremy's thoughts or feelings before.

"I'm sure the police will be happy with all the help they can get."

A commotion outside interrupts Jeremy's suspicions. The reporters shout from the street as a uniformed officer enters through the front door with Sherri Darling.

"I just can't believe this debacle," Sherri is saying. "Can you remove them? Tell them they can't park on the street and harass private citizens? This isn't a trending topic on social media. This is my daughter's life." Her voice breaks on the word 'life'.

"I'm sorry, ma'am," the officer says. "They're on public property, and they have the right to report from it."

"But it's causing a safety issue. My grandchildren are here."

She catches sight of Jeremy. There is contempt in her eyes. It isn't unlike the expression which crossed Luke's face earlier.

"I have to go," he says into the phone, then presses the end button without waiting for a response from Carter.

Jeremy shuffles toward the door.

His mother-in-law is a force of a woman. Shorter than Dahli's five feet, four inches, Sherri Darling makes her presence known by speaking in a loud, nasal, unapologetic voice. Her dark curls are threaded through with a caramel color, and they bounce around her plump, overly made-up face. Tears have streaked mascara in black rivulets through the powder on her cheeks. She smells of sweet, stale perfume and lightly of sweat.

A large pink suitcase is hauled in by a second officer. Jeremy stares at it as the cop places it on the floor in the entryway.

"Sherri," he says and leans in to hug her, even though it's the last thing he wants to do.

She sidesteps his greeting and demands instead, "Where are my grandchildren?"

Luke, who must have heard the commotion, has appeared in the doorway. Luke has never spoken an unkind word about his grandmother, but Jeremy knows her frenzied energy and tendency for dramatic behavior overwhelms his son. It has always overwhelmed Jeremy, too.

Today though, Luke hurries to her and buries his face in the black knit fabric of her blouse. As he settles into her body, his shoulders begin to shake with sobs.

"Oh, honey," Sherri says, gathering him close. "It's okay. We're going to find her. We're going to find your mom. I promise you that."

The officer motions to Jeremy, who follows him to the door. "Detective Hill is on his way over to talk to you about the search out at Goose Creek tomorrow morning."

"What if someone has taken her from the area?" he asks.

The officer furrows his brow. "Do you know something you're not saying?"

He shakes his head. "No, I…" He cuts himself off and considers that he needs a lawyer. But…that will make him look even guiltier. "Goose Creek. Got it," he finishes, then asks, "Can I leave?" He points at the door.

"Where would you go?"

"To the grocery store, for starters." They have food in the house, but they're running low on staples—milk, bread, coffee. And coffee is something he's going to need.

"You'll have to talk with Hill about that. We can have someone bring you what you need."

"Are you telling me I'm trapped here? The last I

checked, I wasn't under arrest."

"I'm not telling you anything other than you have to talk to Hill." The guy looks at Jeremy with disgust. "I would think you'd have other things to worry about."

Jeremy's blood pressure spikes, and his words come out in a shout. "You don't think I'm worried about other things?"

At his raised voice, Sherri says, "Jeremy," in a chiding tone that is so like Dahli's that Jeremy rears around.

"Stay out of this."

Her chin rises a notch, and she glares at him briefly before turning back to Luke. "Come on. Let's check on your sister."

The officer shakes his head and walks out the front door, closing it behind him.

Jeremy stands in the entryway and closes his eyes, taking deep breaths. He needs to deal with Sherri's arrival, he knows, but for the moment, he's glad she's preoccupied with the kids. He moves to the kitchen and picks up Luke's broken electronic device. He places it into the junk drawer in case it can be salvaged later.

Then he brews a fresh pot of coffee. He and Sherri have never been close. Sherri and Leo had always thought Dahli—their only precious daughter—should have married someone more accomplished, more attractive, more established, more affluent than

Appalachian trash like Jeremy Reed. And despite a marriage that has lasted over a decade and produced two beautiful, healthy children, their opinion of him hasn't changed much since they first met him.

To them, he'd always be the flawed product of his drug-addicted mother, unknown father, and dead brother.

He pours himself a cup of black coffee and scowls at the world.

A few minutes later, he hears a bedroom door latch lightly. He can sense and smell Sherri's strong presence enter the kitchen area even before her physical form rounds the corner. Despite the perfect hair and the careful attempt at her now ruined makeup, her clothes are rumpled from the early-morning flight and deep hollows underneath her eyes make dark craters.

He pours her a cup of coffee—black—and she accepts it, taking a scalding sip.

They both seem at a loss for what to say.

Sherri speaks first. "I said hello to Maeve. She's gone back to sleep, which is a good thing. Luke is playing a video game in his room."

Jeremy nods.

"He told me you took his tablet away."

"He doesn't need to be reading everything that's being said right now."

She nods and takes another swallow of coffee. "I agree. It was the right thing to do."

Even this small moment of harmony with his mother-in-law brings him such a rush of relief it nearly brings him to his knees. But it doesn't last. He knew it wouldn't.

"Do you know where she is, Jeremy?" Sherri's voice is quiet. She's not looking at him.

"Of course I don't know where she is."

"Because if you do—no matter what has happened—it would be best for everyone…" A sob bubbles up from somewhere in her soul, as a swell of anger rises up in him.

She continues, "It would be best for everyone if you just told us. At least we'd have a place to come back from, instead of this untethered murkiness."

"I didn't hurt my wife, Sherri."

She glances up at him and then back down. "Your kids are hurting."

He slams the mug down on the counter, and Sherri jumps. Brown liquid sloshes over the mug's edge. "I loved her. I didn't fucking kill her. And if you think I did, what the fuck are you doing here now?"

Jeremy doesn't know how long Maeve has been standing in the doorway. She begins to keen, and Sherri goes to her. His daughter is inconsolable, and while Jeremy knows it's exactly the wrong reaction, he rolls his eyes. The women in this family are so goddamn dramatic.

Sherri cradles Maeve's head against her ample

midsection and discreetly covers the girl's ears. She seethes between her teeth, "I'm here for my daughter, you good-for-nothing piece of shit. And I'm here for my grandchildren. They may not have enough evidence to arrest you, but I'll be damned if I leave these children in the house alone with you."

She turns to guide Maeve away, and Jeremy calls after her, "If I'm so fucking terrible, where's Leo? Why didn't he come along to save the world from the evil Jeremy Reed?"

"I told him to stay home." She stops and glares at him, then she leans down and says something to Maeve, who runs down the hallway to her bedroom.

Sherri watches her go and then faces Jeremy, her eyes flashing. "If he'd stepped foot in this house, he would have killed you. And as much as I'd like to see you dead, I'm not willing to lose my husband *and* my daughter because of you. I wouldn't give you the satisfaction."

The woman walks away, leaving Jeremy speechless. Despite the tense relationship he's had with Dahli's parents over the years, he'd certainly never thought they hated him quite as much as they clearly do. And he wouldn't have expected the realization to be such a punch to his gut.

He grabs his keys and cell phone, then heads to the garage and climbs into his SUV. He starts the engine, pushing the button for the garage door opener. He catches sight of the officers' shocked expressions as he begins to back out, coming dangerously close to the front bumper of the patrol car. His back-up alarm screeches at him—one long, obnoxious tone.

One of the nameless officers rushes to his door, and Jeremy reluctantly powers down the window. It's the same guy who'd accompanied Sherri into the house.

"Where are you heading, Mr. Reed?" the officer asks. He's trying to play it cool, but Jeremy can hear the tension in the words.

"None of your fucking business. Move the car."

"Sir, I've been advised to watch the house."

"No one's stopping you from doing that job."

"It would be best for your safety if you stayed here. There's nothing preventing the press from following you to your destination."

Jeremy laughs. There's no way in hell any of these reporters are going to be able to keep up with him. He'd love to see them try.

To the police officer, Jeremy says, "I'm going to the grocery store. Not much interesting to see there."

"But, Mr. Reed, it would be in your best interest—"

"Stop with the condescension. It's insulting to both of us. Either move the car or arrest me. It's that simple."

The officer glances back toward his partner, and Jeremy knows they're trying to decide what to do. The guy in the car is probably on the radio with the police chief.

Jeremy takes his foot off the brake and lightly taps the bumper of the cruiser.

The officer steps away from the car, and the other cruiser begins to back out of the driveway. Jeremy powers the window back up.

The reporters close in around him. He backs through the bodies slowly and without eye contact, but at no point does he stop. They shout questions through the glass.

"Where is Dahli?"

"Did you kill your wife?"

"Did you know your wife was having an affair?"

He ignores them all, and once he is out of the driveway, he punches the gas and accelerates down Linden Lane. The tires squeal as he turns down one side street, then another. He loops back on himself twice, taking the long way through the streets of Hanahan, before steering south toward the grocery store.

When he pulls into the parking lot, there's no one behind him. He parks in the far row of cars between two oversized empty pickup trucks and cuts the engine. He sits for at least ten minutes. When he's sure no one has followed him, he backs out of the space and heads southeast toward North Charleston, until he sees the signs for Highway 41.

CHAPTER 20

Candace is in her home office responding to client emails when she hears a knock on the front door. She glances at the time on her phone and sighs. It's hard to concentrate on anything, but the world keeps functioning even when the lives of others are falling apart.

She presses 'Send' on her reply, then runs down the stairs and throws open the door, expecting to see a delivery driver. Instead, it's a familiar-looking middle-aged woman. It takes a moment to place her, but when Candace realizes the woman's identity, her eyebrows shoot up. It's the detective from the press conference.

"Can I help you?"

"I'm sorry to bother you, Ms. Witten. My name is Miriam Ballard, and I was wondering if I might ask you a few questions." She quickly flashes a badge then tucks the portfolio back into her pocket.

Candace hesitates before moving to the side and gesturing this woman into her home.

Candace looks her up and down. The woman is wearing a burgundy blouse that doesn't fit quite right across the shoulders and chest. The top is tucked into a pair of black slacks, and a gray belt is fastened tightly at her waist, creating an unnecessary bulge at the top of her hips.

After stepping in, Miriam begins to slide off her heavy black ankle boots that don't match the rest of the outfit.

"You don't have to…" Candace begins, but by the time the words are out, Detective Ballard is already out of the boots.

Worn pea-green trouser socks cover her long feet. "I'd rather guests in my home take their shoes off," she says. "I don't mind."

Candace ushers her inside. "Would you like some coffee, tea, water?"

"Water would be great."

Candace moves into the kitchen, and Ballard follows. The detective perches awkwardly on the end of a barstool while Candace fills a glass with ice and filtered water.

"I'd offer you sparkling water, but I'm fresh out."

Ballard doesn't comment. She takes a drink and looks around. "Lovely place." She looks down the hallway to the views of the lowlands beyond. "Beautiful views."

Candace doesn't answer. They can skip the small talk. Detective Ballard is here because of Dahli. She'd been expecting a call, of course, but she thought it might come with an invitation for an interview or with a conversation at the office. She knows the detectives had spent much of the prior morning at Mosswood. "What can I help you with?" she asks.

Ballard shifts her gaze back to Candace, and suddenly she's all business. Candace likes that.

"You were the one who encouraged Olivia to call the police and report Dahli missing."

"I was. It's not like Dahli to miss work."

"But you were out of the office. Out of town, I believe?"

Something about the way Ballard asks the question sets Candace on edge. Her spine stiffens, and she moves away to fill a glass of water.

"Yes, I was attending a conference in DC," she answers.

"When was the last time you'd heard from her?"

"The previous weekend. We'd met for brunch."

"Not for a run?"

Candace shoots the detective a quick glance and frowns. "I'm not a runner."

"What about Weston?"

Candace doesn't answer immediately. *Where is this going?*

"He's your uncle, isn't he?"

"Through marriage, yes."

"And Josephine is your aunt. Your mother's sister."

It isn't a question, but Candace nods anyway. Of

course the detectives would have this information. Though Candace doesn't publicize her ties to the Moss family, it's no secret. Anyone with an internet connection could easily discover it.

"And neither of them runs either?"

Again, Candace pauses. "I'm not sure what that has to do with anything. But, no. Neither Weston nor Josephine are runners. At least not at this point in their lives."

"Are you aware Dahli may have been sleeping with your uncle?"

It takes Candace a moment to adjust to the change in subject. She stiffens. She knew this question would come up, and it makes her uncomfortable. Dahli was beautiful and bright and enthusiastic. Even given Weston's money and power, Candace could not wrap her mind around the possibility Dahli might be sleeping with the man.

It makes the memory of her last conversation with Dahli that much more painful.

Ballard picks up on her wariness and says, "You don't believe the rumors?"

Candace takes a sip of water. It is cool sliding down her throat. When she answers, she says, "If she was sleeping with Weston, she didn't share it with me." It occurs to her that she'd used the past tense. She doesn't correct herself and the detective doesn't remark on it.

Instead, Ballard says, "But she does work for your

uncle, and he'd promoted her quickly and at a young age."

"Because she's good at what she does." Candace has always hated the assumption that intelligent, attractive women may have been promoted based on looks rather than competence. She especially hates it coming from other women.

And this female detective looks skeptical.

Candace lets out a slow breath. "Dahli is a knock-out. Maybe Weston has feelings for her. Or maybe he feels paternal toward her. She has that kind of evocative quality, and it goes way beyond her looks. Men want to take care of her." That isn't quite accurate. "*People* want to take care of her," she clarifies.

"Is that why you wanted Olivia to call the police?"

When Candace frowns, Ballard says, "Because you want to take care of her, too?"

A flutter of panic seizes Candace's chest, and she shifts from one foot to the other. She doesn't immediately answer.

"Or is it something else?" Ballard is studying Candace, seeing things Candace would prefer she not see.

"Do you have a specific question for me about Dahli? Because if not, I'd like to get back to work and keep my mind off other things."

Ballad looks at her a beat longer. "The last time you saw her, did she talk about the problems in her marriage?"

"Of course. She wasn't in love with Jeremy, and he wasn't in love with her. Not anymore. She didn't keep that a secret."

"And Jeremy knew?"

She pulls out her phone, unlocks it, and shows Detective Ballard the text messages she'd received from Jeremy Reed. The ugly words accusing Candace of taking Dahli away from him.

Ballard scrolls through them without reacting.

When the woman looks up, Candace says, "According to Dahli, they hadn't had sex in months. I'd say that's a pretty big indicator of a problem. If he didn't know, it's because he didn't want to know."

Ballard runs her finger down the condensation on the outside of the glass. "And she wasn't intimate with anyone else?"

Candace swallows, aware that Dahli would not be comfortable with Candace sharing Dahli's personal information with this stranger. And Candace has her own interests to protect. But Dahli isn't here right now, so Candace finally responds, "She talked about someone the last time we were together."

"Someone," Ballard repeats.

Candace lifts a shoulder.

"You don't know who it was?"

"I… I didn't ask."

"Why not?"

"I didn't want to know."

Candace thinks back to Dahli's face, which had glowed that bright, blue Sunday morning. She'd looked radiant and excited. She'd talked about new beginnings. Candace had tried to appear happy for Dahli, but all she'd been able to think about was her friend moving on without her.

There'd been something in the way Dahli's face had shone; in the way she was even more dazzling than normal. It had hurt Candace's heart.

"So if it wasn't Weston, who could it have been?"

Candace shrugs. Her thoughts inadvertently slide to Aiden before she pushes that possibility from her mind. There's no way Dahli was planning to leave her family for a twenty-two-year-old kid.

Aiden is a runner, Candace realizes. He'd run both cross-country and track in high school and was on the university cross-country team.

An unease creeps up her spine.

Aiden has had a crush on Dahli for years. The intensity of his feelings spiked each time he came home for Christmas, but it was still just a crush. He'd never hurt Dahli.

"Have you looked into Eugene Ryan?" Candace asks suddenly. She wrinkles her nose, thinking of the creepy man with the off-putting odor who's always lurking about the office. She swears she's seen him following her on occasion. In fact, the last time she'd been with Dahli at Camellias, she thought she'd seen him across the street.

"We've met with him. Do you have new information?"

"Not really. He's just…weird. Always skulking about. I'm pretty sure I've seen him following us in the past. Dahli always poo-pooed it and said he was harmless. He gives me the creeps."

"Any reason he might have had to harm her?"

Candace thinks about this. She opens her mouth and then shuts it again. Then she says, "Dahli is…" She shuts her eyes. "That protectiveness that people feel for Dahli—it's easy for that to transform into…" Her words trail off again.

When she doesn't speak, Ballard says, "Into what?"

"Into obsession," Candace whispers. She doesn't mean it to sound like an admission, but she's aware her words are exactly that.

She turns away from the detective and busies herself at the sink, rinsing a coffee mug. She wants Ballard to go away. She blinks away the tears that have sprung into her eyes and rolls her head from side to side as the water runs.

When she shuts the water off, Ballard says, "How long have you been in love with her?"

Candace's breath catches in her chest. No one has ever said the words aloud, and Candace has never directly admitted it to herself, though she knows it's true.

"I guess since I've known her," Candace says quietly, not turning around.

"But she doesn't love you back. Not like that."

"There have been glimmers." Candace's eyes brim with tears, and she lets them spill down her cheeks. "I just miss her so fucking much," she whispers.

There is a long silence. "We're going to find her. I promise."

Candace nods, but she doesn't respond. Because she isn't so sure that's true.

CHAPTER 21

Dahli opens her eyes. Through the cloth covering her face, she sees light and thinks it must be morning. She shifts on the mattress, and the frame creaks. She's aware she should feel something physical—pain, thirst, hunger. But there's nothing. She seems to have detached from her physical body.

She thinks of her spirited Maeve and her soulful Luke. Are they okay? Do they miss her? She hopes Jeremy is easing their concerns. She hopes he is sensitive to Luke's introspection. She hopes he's patient with Maeve's emotions.

They are such a miracle, her children.

Despite her soul's fragile connection to her body, her emotions are fully intact. The sense of devastation and despair is so strong it threatens to cripple her.

She takes long, slow breaths. She must not lose control.

She eases herself from the bed and inches in the direction of the door. Despite her careful movements, her body jolts against a solid obstacle. When Dahli recovers, she turns so the wall is behind her, and she runs the fingertips of her bound hands over the surface.

After a moment, she detects the doorframe. Her heart pounds with excitement. She moves her body up and down, feeling for a doorknob or handle. With her back, she encounters the rounded knob. She stands on her tiptoes, trying to reach the object with her fingers.

It's no use. She's too short to do anything but lightly swipe her fingers against the metal.

She slumps to the floor, exhausted and spent.

A wave of nausea passes over her, and she gags against the cloth in her mouth. She must not throw up, not even bile.

She's not sure how long she lies on the floor, floating in and out of an ephemeral dream. At one point, she swears Luke is beside her, his small hand against her cheek.

But when she turns her head, she's still in captivity.

Her fate appears more and more grim.

After what might be minutes, or hours, Dahli inches her way back to the bed and lies on her side. She tries to keep her mind off the growing pressure to urinate.

Again, her mind moves to her children, but she pushes those thoughts away, too. She must devote her remaining energy to thoughts that can help her. Grief over her children will not help anyone.

Instead, she tries to remember those last moments.

Her morning run. The Marrington Plantation Trailhead. Vetr Road. The path is a familiar one.

A vehicle had come up behind her. It was black. It was familiar. Still, she can't quite remember the details of the day. Her memories are nothing but hazy, abstract concepts.

The pain in her head has faded along with most of the sense of her body. Perhaps she'd been hit in the head.

Or she could have been drugged. That may explain the memory loss and the fogginess. The nausea.

Think, she demands of herself. There must be something—some detail—she can conjure from her forgotten memories.

She remembers cool air on her face. She remembers water hitting her lips. She remembers uncertainty, and then fear.

She catches the edge of a memory. The fight with Jeremy. She'd been thinking of the future and how her life was going to change—she was full of anticipation and joy.

But the vehicle that had approached her had not been a welcome one.

Think.

The fog in her mind swirls.

She breathes in on a count of four, pauses her breath at the top of the inhale, then breathes out on the count of five. She repeats the cycle, and suddenly she's back there on Marrington Road.

The morning light is soft, and the marshes are misty. A tri-colored heron takes flight in front of her. She raises a hand to a couple with binoculars hiking off the path.

Dahli smells the brine and the acrid scent of the swamp's decay. Thick and humid, it fills her nose and her mouth.

Her legs pump and her calves burn. She should have stretched more before she'd left that morning. She would have if it hadn't been for Jeremy. She feels just the beginning of a stitch in her side when she hears the engine.

The brown van, she thinks.

She increases her speed and controls her breathing. The stitch in her side is sharper, the lactic acid in her legs burning.

She wills the vehicle to go around her.

It slows, and she glances over.

A sleek, black SUV. She knows this vehicle. She's been *in* this vehicle.

Weston, she thinks.

Her shock jolts her out of the meditation.

Cold perspiration blossoms over her as she remembers the violation of her body. She tries to reconcile the violence and invasion with her boss.

Weston is a man used to getting the things he wants. He'd made it clear one of those things was

Dahli. She'd navigated his not-so-veiled insinuations and had even delicately extricated herself from a recent situation where he'd convinced her to join him in a hotel room.

Perhaps she'd not extricated herself as well as she'd thought. Perhaps she is now the sole property of Weston Moss; tucked away in a remote property where no one can hear her or find her.

Her body begins to shake. She draws her knees into her belly on the bed.

She sucks in a breath.

The sudden jerk of her body jars something loose in her brain…an image of a face in the car window.

Dahli knows she can't trust herself or her memory. But the reflection that enters her mind is not a man. It's the hazy image of a woman.

The woman smiles at her and beckons her forward. Dahli floats toward the outstretched hand.

The face becomes clearer; it is the face of her mother.

Stay here with me, Dahli, her mother says. Maeve is beside her in the passenger seat. She reaches for Dahli, and Dahli smiles.

"Take care of her," Dahli whispers to the woman who had given her life.

She feels herself floating away, breaking apart, coming undone. She drifts into unconsciousness.

CHAPTER 22

Weston Moss wants to kill his wife.

If he could get away with it, he would place one hand around her windpipe and squeeze. Slowly at first. He'd watch her eyes widen as she realized what was happening. Then he'd increase the pressure as her delicately manicured pink fingernails clawed at his hand.

The image stays with him while he peers behind the blinds at the news crews on the cobblestone street in front of the South of Broad mansion he'd purchased for his bride nearly forty years ago.

The police are here as well, keeping the media from encroaching on the property and clearing the way for the sparse traffic on the normally quiet, bucolic street.

He suspects Manning—that useless piece of shit—has sent in the police to offer protection as a kind of peace offering after the disaster of a press conference. It was Manning who'd alerted Weston of the press conference in the first place.

He blames Manning for this entire situation. The man should have had his press conference secured and those damn detectives in check.

Weston called his lawyer who revealed there wasn't much he could do about the police department, and who instead talked about the need for Weston to protect himself from his wife's false allegations. J. Graham Fowler had encouraged Weston to stay right where he was—in his house with his wife. Avoid the external world until this thing blew over. "Hopefully they'll find the woman's body soon so we can put this thing to bed," he'd said. Weston's heart had lurched in his chest, but he hadn't said a word. "We'll deal with the divorce later."

Divorce, Weston thinks. He shudders to think what Josephine will try to squeeze out of him. Surely she remembers the details of their prenup and the infidelity clause. She'll get very little unless she can prove he's had an affair.

Fowler had assured Weston that an allegation of unfaithfulness would not be enough. "She's got to have concrete, irrefutable proof—photos or video," he'd said. "Even a witness we can discredit."

A witness like Elaine Lagare, he thinks. The woman who claims to have seen Weston with Dahli, walking into a hotel room.

But an arrest for Dahlia Reed's murder? All bets were off when it came to Weston's money. Josephine would take it all.

His imagination returns to his hand on his wife's throat.

He can hear her in the kitchen moving around—banging pots and pans, running water. Humming—fucking *humming*—to some upbeat music. He thinks it might be Sinatra. Or perhaps Bobby Darin.

He listens more closely as the scent of bacon wafts through the air. It *is* Bobby Darin, he realizes. The smooth lyrics are familiar. 'Hello, Dolly', the singer croons through the speakers.

Weston freezes. His wife is taunting him.

He glances toward the grand stairway. Aiden is home, still upstairs sleeping. He does his best to ignore the music.

If Josephine gets her way, Weston will rot in prison. And with her precious boy, she will live in the home he has provided, playing the victim while spending his money. As he's beginning to suspect she'd always wanted.

He itches to check his phone, but Graham advised him to turn it off to avoid the onslaught of calls and texts from friends and enemies alike. Weston had listened to that piece of advice. The number of people who'd been able to obtain his cell number frightens him. There is no privacy—no anonymity—anymore.

He mops blooming beads of perspiration from his forehead with the back of his hand.

His wife appears from the kitchen doorway at the back of the house. She wears form-fitting tan slacks and a low-cut navy-blue tunic top with white embroidery around the neck. The tendons in her mature throat are taut and pronounced.

After the spectacle of last night, he can't believe they're still in the same house together. But he'll be damned if he is the one to leave.

She looks him up and down with contempt; he fights the urge to pull his robe closer together over his lounge pants. What's the point of dressing if he can't leave?

This captivity poses a problem, but he pushes that out of his mind. He needs to sit quietly and develop a plan. Preferably with a glass of good bourbon.

"You should probably dress," she says and glances at the silver antique watch on her wrist. "They should be here soon."

"Who?" he asks.

"The police." She waves her hand toward the door. "Not the patrolmen on the street. The real ones. The ones who will arrest you."

"I haven't done a goddamn thing wrong, and you know it."

"I know you were fucking your pretty, young employee, who is now missing. She's probably dead, buried somewhere in a shallow grave in the woods." Her voice is plummy and pleasant. She smiles.

"You're sick."

Her laugh is bright as it echoes off the high ceiling of the living room. "Oh, Weston. You always did take yourself too seriously. It's a fatal flaw, you know. No one else thinks you are as important as you do."

She comes into the room and moves past him closer than she needs to be.

Weston flinches, looking at her elegant throat. *It would be so easy.* He clenches and unclenches his fists.

She pulls the cord to open the blinds wide, exposing the living room to the photographers outside. There is a swell of noise as they notice the movement and start shouting. In the light of morning, he can still make out the flash of cameras.

"Shut the fucking blinds!" he yells, and before she can turn, he is in front of the windows, yanking the cord until the blinds slide back to their original position.

"I've never known you to be shy," Josephine coos.

His nostrils flair, and he fixes his arms to his sides. The woman standing next to him is a far different woman from the one who'd confronted him about Dahli two days earlier. She's also different from the woman who'd just last night drunkenly accused him of murder on live television, in front of the world.

If he didn't know her better, he'd think she was crazy.

But Josephine Vance Moss is anything but insane. In fact, the precision with which she conducts her life has, at times, made him envious. So he can't help but wonder what the hell she's up to.

He can hear the chorus from 'Call Me Irresponsible' coming from the kitchen.

She gazes past him, into the distance. "I never thought I'd be the pathetic stereotype of the scorned wife whose husband abandons her for a younger woman." She shakes her head slowly. "I've watched my friends go through it, and I've pitied them. No one is going to pity me like that," she says, and something flickers in her eyes. Then the look is gone, replaced by a cool stare. "Whatever happens, Weston—you caused it. Remember that."

Weston clenches his jaw, but he does not respond. He has not slept with Dahlia Reed. But his wife isn't all that far off.

He and Dahli had developed a friendship, at first. Her radical vulnerability had opened something within him. She'd made him laugh without meaning to. She'd brought joy into his life.

She'd shared with him her hopes, dreams, disappointments, and fears. And he'd opened himself up to her, too. She'd listened to him with kindness and compassion long after Josephine had stopped seeing him for the man he truly was.

And though he'd never slept with Dahli, he'd certainly wanted to. He'd imagined what she would feel like moving beneath him. He'd envisioned those liquid brown eyes locked with his as he joined with her. He'd imagined her slim, lithe body, with soft skin and toned muscles. Her gentle moans and tender whispers.

He hardens and turns away from his wife.

But despite their connection and his desire, Dahli hadn't felt the same way. She'd been painfully clear about that. Especially that last time…

"You have it all wrong, Josephine."

She is quiet, and he can feel her studying him—feel her sharp gaze probing into him.

"Save your defense for the courtroom, Weston."

She turns and heads back to the kitchen, leaving Weston feeling depleted. She's good at that, his wife.

A moment later, the Westminster chime of the doorbell reverberates through the room.

Weston freezes. The only visitors able to make it past the police line would be the police themselves.

His eyes move to the landline phone on its antique stand in the corner of the room. He must contact Graham again.

Josephine calls from the kitchen, "It's time to face the music, Weston." Her disembodied voice resonates through the air.

The doorbell chimes again. Weston swears under his breath. He pads through the living room in his slippered feet and stands to the side as he cracks open the door.

He recognizes the face of the detective he'd met two days ago at the Mosswood offices. The man. Weston can't remember his name. Beside him is not the tired-looking middle-aged woman. Instead, a fresh-faced younger woman gives Weston a severe look.

"Mr. Moss, may we have a minute of your time?" the man asks.

Weston hesitates before opening the door just enough to allow the two bodies to pass through. He stays out of sight of the reporters, whose voices have joined into an indecipherable cacophony.

Weston scowls and draws himself up with a confidence he doesn't feel. "Can't you do something about that?" he demands.

The young woman fixes him with a stare that Weston supposes is meant to intimidate him. She reminds him of his daughter when she doesn't get her way, and he turns instead to the man who says, "They're on public property."

"Mr. Moss, we're here to ask you some questions," the younger woman says. She's wearing a sharp, citrusy perfume, and the scent makes Weston's nose twitch.

The man steps in. "This is my colleague, Detective Kaylor."

"Where's the other one?"

The man shifts. "Detective Ballard was needed on another case."

Ballard. He frowns at the memory of the smug woman who'd tried to question Aiden yesterday.

Ballard, he thinks again, and the name triggers something in his memory. "What was your name again?" he asks.

"Hill," the detective says. "Arthur Hill."

"Mr. Moss," Detective Kaylor interjects, "we have some questions about your wife's allegations last evening. We need you to come down to the station."

"You're arresting me?"

Weston catches Hill's annoyed glance at his younger partner.

"No, sir. We're not," he says. "We just have some questions."

"Well, I'm not leaving this house. Not with all of that going on." He points to the door, indicating the vultures outside. "And beyond that, I'm not talking to you without my lawyer."

Detective Kaylor draws herself up. She's ready for a fight. Hill discreetly motions in a downward manner with his hand behind his back. The fact that Vince Manning has installed someone this inexperienced to investigate the disappearance of Dahli is both insulting and encouraging. They'll certainly give his attorney something to work with, if it comes down to that.

Hill says, "It's certainly your prerogative to have your attorney present. But I can assure you, I won't be taking you out of here in handcuffs, if that's your concern. I believe you know Chief Manning well."

Weston sees this for what it is—an attempt at collaboration. An attempt to assuage his concerns. And it works. Weston has no intention of answering difficult questions from these two Keystone Cops who have probably never investigated anything more serious than stolen office supplies.

Again, something scratches the recesses of his memory. *Ballard*, he thinks. And then it comes rushing back to him—the female detective's face, but younger, harder, more determined.

Ballard hadn't always been her name. She'd been the wife of Mark Edwards, the former senator who was falsely accused of killing his mistress. In the end, the poor bastard had been exonerated, but not before his career and life had been decimated by the woman he'd married.

Vince Manning had been an idiot to allow Edwards's ex-wife to take Dahli's case at all, but at least the chief seems to have had the sense to remove her.

Weston imagines the way the woman had likely been planning to go after him. The circumstances must remind her of her own experience—successful older man allegedly sleeping with a younger woman. With Ballard, it would have been personal.

He looks at Hill and his silly young partner and feels in control of the situation. "You can ask the questions, and I'll decide if I want to answer them." He'll take his chances.

Detective Kaylor starts to say, "That's not how this—"

Hill interrupts her. "That's perfectly fine." He steps

slightly in front of the woman, and she huffs in response. "Can we sit?" He looks around as if searching for a seat.

"Right here is fine."

A clattering sound emanates from the kitchen.

Hill glances up sharply. "You're not alone?"

"No."

Hill raises his eyebrows and lowers his voice slightly. "I imagine you know what took place at the press conference last evening and are aware of the allegations your wife made." It wasn't quite a question.

"I am."

"What do you have to say about that?" the younger detective asks.

This time, Hill turns to face his partner. "Kaylor, I'll handle this one, if you don't mind."

Before she can answer, Hill turns back to Weston. "Mr. Moss, some of your employees indicated you might be having an affair with Dahlia Reed. I don't need to tell you a relationship with her could potentially give you motive to harm her. That combined with your wife's allegations puts you at the forefront of the..." He glances toward the door. "...of the now national discussion," he finishes.

Weston doesn't react to this stark statement of reality.

Hill continues. "In the past twelve hours, a number of other women have come forward to allege affairs with you."

Weston's blood pressure increases. He can feel the heat in his face. He hadn't heard that, and it shouldn't surprise him, but it does. There hadn't been many women over the years, but there had been enough.

He hears the sound of the oven opening and closing from the other room.

Surely Josephine is aware of these recent developments.

"It would help us to know the nature of your relationship with Ms. Reed."

Weston clears his throat. "I don't make it a practice of sleeping with my employees, detective. It's bad for business."

"Let me try again. Were you sleeping with Dahlia Reed?"

"No."

"What would make your wife think you were?"

"Dahlia is an attractive woman who, because of the nature of her job, spends a lot of time with me. Josephine heard rumors and chose to believe them. The rumors are not true."

Detective Kaylor openly scoffs. Hill's reaction is more nuanced, but Weston knows the man doesn't believe him, either.

"What rumors did your wife hear?"

Weston hesitates, considering whether Graham would advise him to answer the question. He decides there's no harm in telling the truth. Especially a partial truth that can vindicate him. For the affair, at least.

Weston lowers his voice. "An acquaintance of Josephine's claims to have seen me at a hotel with Ms. Reed." He still cringes when he thinks about the meeting in question. It's true he'd been at the Hotel Bennett with Dahli. They'd dined at Gabrielle, and Weston had, indeed, booked a room. He'd thought finally the time had been right.

He'd been wrong.

She'd very kindly, very gently, let him down, admitting she was in love with someone else.

Weston tried to play it off, but he'd been hurt. And he doesn't like to think about the anger that had swelled up from a deep, primal place within him.

Even now, the fervor of his humiliation threatens to swallow him up. He, of course, doesn't admit any of *this* to the detectives.

"And you'd been there with Dahli?"

"Yes, detective. Ms. Reed and I were there to meet with the head of a community group."

"Which one?"

He blinks. "Excuse me?"

"Which community group?"

Weston flounders, then recovers. "You can't possibly expect me to recall every meeting I take. I'll have to have Kelly get you that information."

Detective Hill stares at him before nodding slowly.

"All right, Mr. Moss. If you were there for a business meeting, why would your wife's acquaintance think it was something else?"

This, Weston should not answer. He can hear Graham's voice in his ear. But ending the conversation now would just make him appear guilty. And he hadn't done anything wrong. At least not anything to Dahli. Not that night.

"I had…booked a room," he admits. Then adds, "Just for myself. Things weren't…good here. They haven't been for a long time." Surely, after what his wife had tried to do last night, Hill would understand Weston's plight.

The detective waits. He doesn't nod or otherwise acknowledge Weston's words.

Weston's gaze slides to the portrait of his great-grandfather hanging above the mantelpiece in the living room. The first Weston Moss looks regal and hard in silhouette in the painting. Weston often wonders what the man would think of his distant offspring.

He clears his throat. "After dinner, I asked Dahlia to accompany me to the room, and she did." His face burns. "But we'd only had some business to discuss."

"In your room," Hill says. Again, not a question.

"She wasn't there for more than five minutes." That's all the time it had taken to break Weston's heart. It's pathetic that he'd fallen in love with a woman half his age. It's embarrassing that he'd allowed himself to become so weak. The simmer of anger boils up again. "You can check the cameras," he says. He knows they will.

"Did you explain this to your wife?"

Weston had not bothered. "She's not interested in hearing the truth."

"Mr. Moss, did you kill Dahlia Reed?" Detective Kaylor asks suddenly.

Weston borrows the stern look from the painting of his ancestor and trains a hard gaze on the woman.

She stops herself from flinching, but he can see the almost imperceptible lift of her head.

"No, Detective Taylor. I did not."

"*Kaylor*," she corrects him with a hint of indignation. "Did you have anything to do with her disappearance?"

At that, he moves toward the door and opens it. "That's all the questions I'll answer." His voice is calm, but there's no mistaking his meaning. "If you want to know anything else, you'll need to contact my lawyer, J. Graham Fowler."

Hill, at least, would know Graham's name. The man had successfully defended some of the state's most high-profile criminal suspects.

Hill sighs and nods. "Thank you for your time, Mr. Moss."

Mercifully, they make an exit without additional

questions or games. Weston rests his head against the heavy wooden door when they're gone.

He stands there listening to the hum of voices outside. An engine rumbles to life, likely Hill's dark sedan.

Then his wife's voice breaks his meditation. "You're still here," she says.

He doesn't look at her. "Sorry to disappoint you."

"Don't worry, Weston. I'm used to it." There is a smile in her voice that makes him turn in her direction.

They stare at each other before Weston says, "I have some errands to run."

She laughs. "Where could you possibly have to go?" She gestures toward the front of their home.

"You don't get to ask me that question, Josephine. Not anymore."

Before he climbs the stairs to the second-floor bedroom, his wife says, "You won't get away with this."

"Get away with what, exactly?" He dares her to say it.

"You know what I'm talking about."

He looks back at his wife. She is a beautiful, accomplished, terrifying woman. His pulse quickens. She may suspect him of his misdeeds, but she'll never be able to prove them.

He turns without another word and almost collides with his son, who is dressed in running attire. Weston nearly chides him for planning to leave the house with all the media attention, but as he's about to do the same thing, he keeps his mouth shut.

It's Josephine who says, "Aiden, sweetie, I've kept your breakfast warm."

"I can't."

Weston hears the strain in Aiden's voice.

"You need your strength, baby." When Josephine talks to Aiden, her trained southern debutant's voice lifts an octave. She doesn't quite engage in baby talk, but it's close. It makes Weston want to roll his eyes…and squeeze that refined windpipe.

"I have some things to do," Aiden mumbles. He heads for the side entrance where his vehicle is parked in the enclosed courtyard. Before Josephine can get her next sentence out, the door slams, and Josephine sighs.

"It looks like everyone is trying to get away from you," Weston quips from halfway up the stairs.

His wife flips him off, and he smiles.

In the end, she'll see. It's Weston Moss who holds the power. And he's not going down without a fight.

CHAPTER 23

Eugene stands in the space that should be the small galley kitchen of his mother's house. Since he's never lived anywhere else, he supposes this is his house too, but he never thinks of it that way, nor would he want to. It will always be his mother's, even after she's dead and gone.

He surveys the debris piled high around him—boxes, bags, trash, and other unidentifiable mounds of junk. His lip curls in disgust.

Four frozen breakfast sandwiches rotate on the turntable in the microwave. He stares through the food-spattered window at the hazy biscuit mounds pirouetting on their paper plate, then he glances at the time on his phone. He taps his fingers against a small bare space on the countertop littered with snack foods, crackers, cans of soup, haphazard stacks of paperwork, unopened mail, and cardboard boxes that contain various gadgets and god-knows-what else.

Bags overflowing from cupboards and boxes stacked around the kitchen floor are piled high on the kitchen table. Most of the time, Eugene is able to overlook the objects that surround him, though he always knows they exist.

The house hasn't always been this way, but it's become progressively worse over the past few years. Now, it seems too overwhelming to consider trying to remedy it.

There had been signs, he supposes, as he thinks back. He remembers his mother's aversion to throwing out a perfectly good cardboard box, and her tendency to collect any magazines or random catalogs that found their way into her mailbox. "You never know when these might come in handy," she'd mumble and stack them in the corner.

Then, she'd started to save used bits of aluminum foil, any type of plastic container, the empty rolls that had once held toilet paper and plastic wrap.

Even used paper towels had joined the collection.

He sighs. It would take weeks of hard labor to clean out the place.

The really hardcore hoarding behavior had started when Eugene was thirteen. And only Eugene knew *why* it started. It had been all his fault.

"Eugene!" his mother yells from the living room where the TV blares at full volume. He can hear the angry morning talk show hosts arguing with each other. So much rage and dissention.

"Where's my breakfast?" Glenda Ryan bellows.

Eugene doesn't respond.

He imagines a fire sweeping through it all, taking the house and its contents—inanimate and otherwise.

"Eugene!" The bellow is louder this time.

The microwave beeps loudly and Eugene tugs open the door.

While the biscuits encasing the sandwiches look overdone and hard, he suspects the processed ham, cheese, and egg inside are still half frozen.

He pulls the plate from the microwave anyway, then fills a dirty mug with burnt coffee. He holds the food and beverage carefully and picks his way via a narrow path into what had once been a dining room. He enters the living room where Glenda is settled in the one massive human-shaped clear spot on the sofa, a TV tray already set up in front of her.

Next to her are heaps of clothing, bags of what Eugene suspects are actual trash, moldy books, napkins, and other paper products.

Glenda glances up at him from the television set; her small piggy eyes are slits behind the pockets of fleshy cheeks. She turns back to the television set and pants, "What the hell took you so long?" Her breath wheezes. Even the act of existing seems to exhaust her these days.

Eugene sets the plate and the mug on the TV tray. "I'm going to have to get going, Ma."

She sniffs at one of the sandwiches, lifting the tough biscuit with the tip of her finger. "It's cold inside," she complains then pushes the plate away. "I want McDonald's."

"I have somewhere to be this morning." The search for Dahli would be starting shortly.

Dahli would be appalled at the way he lives in his mother's home. She'd look at him with pity. He doesn't want that. Which is why he needs to take care of things.

"You've had a lot of places to be lately," Glenda grumbles. "I need you more than anything else you could possibly have going on. I'm the one who gave you life. A roof over your head. You wouldn't even exist without me."

Glenda is a taker and a victim. She thinks the world—not just Eugene—owes her. He tries not to take it personally.

She'd been an attractive woman once upon a time, and plenty of men had been happy to give themselves to her, at least for a little while. But they hadn't been good men. And they hadn't been good to her awkward, inept son.

There was one man, though, who Glenda had especially liked. That man had also done things for Eugene. When Eugene had been a young impressionable teenager, the man had taken Eugene into the deep wooded forest to his remote cabin and taught Eugene how to shoot. He'd taught Eugene how to hunt. And he'd taught Eugene other unthinkable things that

Eugene tries hard to forget. Things that lurk in the shadows at the back of his mind.

One day, that man had disappeared, and as far as Eugene knows, no one ever noticed or came looking for him.

But he'd left some things behind. Things that had proven useful to Eugene, even now, all these years later.

Glenda takes a bite of the sandwich then hurls it back onto the plate. "I can't eat this," she cries and leans back heavily. She waves her hand in front of her, her corpulent arm wobbling beneath her nightgown. "Just get me some cereal."

He doesn't bother picking up the plate. It will join the other trash on the sofa where Glenda eats and sleeps and exists.

Eugene studies his mother. It's been weeks since she's bathed, and her long red-gray hair hangs in stringy clumps over her shoulders. He is certain she smells terrible—that the house reeks of garbage and decay and body odor and fluids. He is nose-blind to it.

He picks his way back through the trash to the kitchen where he fills a semi-clean mixing bowl with a box of sugar-coated flakes and pours the remainder of the nearly expired milk over the cereal. He locates a soup spoon and returns to the family room.

Glenda's eyes light up at the site of the large bowl. "That's my boy," she says.

He sets it in front of her. She leans forward and grasps the spoon, slurping up the mess.

Eugene glances at the screen. A commercial for an impossibly expensive set of pots and pans gives way to a preview of the next local newscast. A plastic-looking blonde wears a concerned frown and announces, "A local woman is missing, and a community is on the lookout." Half the screen fills with Dahli's face; Eugene's heart leaps into his throat. "Dahlia Reed didn't return from a morning run three days ago, and now the town of Hanahan is asking for the public's help in locating her. A search will take place at ten a.m. at the Marrington Plantation Trailhead in Goose Creek Park. Our crews will be there live. Join us at noon for that story and more from Hanahan."

Eugene's heart is pounding.

Dahli's face disappears, replaced by the hosts of a morning show who immediately begin to argue about something the president has said, but Eugene's mind is still reeling from the shock of seeing his beloved Dahli's face in his living room.

He thinks back to last night's press conference where he'd been watching from afar.

He'd studied Dahli's pussy of a husband, who wasn't even trying to act sad about the fact his precious wife was missing. Jeremy Reed had stood back, huddled into himself with his hands in his pockets as if he'd rather have been anywhere else.

Eugene had watched Jeremy Reed, his hand on the cold smooth metal of the Sig Sauer pistol buried in the deep pocket of his sweatshirt, the hood of which hung low over his face. No one had paid him any mind.

Eugene does his best to forgive Dahli for having married the loser to begin with. She'd probably thought he was different. He'd probably tricked her when they were young. Still, she should've known.

But when Weston Moss's wife stumbled forward and accused her husband of sleeping with Dahli, implying that Weston may have murdered her—well, Eugene couldn't abide that at all.

The Mosses were liars in all situations, even the tragic ones.

What's more, it had confused Eugene. Dahli would never have sex with someone as corrupt and awful as Weston. If she had, that meant he'd had her all wrong. And he didn't want to rethink his perception of Dahli. He cannot fathom her flaws. Not his beautiful, sweet Dahli.

The desperation fills him again. It makes him want to claw off his skin.

He thinks about Dahli's lovely, slim body. Her melodic voice. Her kind smile.

Then, an image of Weston fills his imagination. The man looming over Dahli. It defiles his daydream, and rage rises into Eugene's chest.

He tries to tamp it down. He tries to get her back.

"What the hell is wrong with you?"

Glenda's voice causes his eyes to fly open—back to the filthy house. Back to the flickering screen with the shrill, unpleasant women still arguing about something meaningless.

Milk dribbles down Glenda's chin and onto the bosom of her nightgown.

He looks away.

A pretty young brunette on the TV screen points and yells at an older woman with auburn hair and a taut unnatural-looking face. Eugene hates them both.

A thought occurs to him. If Weston Moss goes to jail, what will become of Mosswood? Will Eugene lose his job?

Another sharp pang of desperation rises up in him. He can't take care of his mother on her monthly social security checks. He can barely afford the groceries she needs to survive as it is. And he's just bought a new car. He won't be able to make the payments.

His world feels as if it's closing in around him.

Nothing is going as he'd hoped.

"Did you hear me?"

Glenda is glaring at him.

"What?"

"You never could fucking listen," she mutters. She reaches forward as if she wants to strike him. But he's too far away, and she is far too feeble to do any damage. Not like in the old days. But the movement brings up a hidden memory, and he flinches anyway.

"Little sissy boy," she says laughing. Then she continues, with emphasis, "I said, I want to go to bingo tonight."

"We've talked about this. It's too hard to get you in and out of the car."

"Maybe if you weren't such a sissy boy."

Eugene turns to leave the room, and she says quickly, "You've got that nice new car. There's plenty of space for me."

"You refuse to use your walker or let me get you a wheelchair. If you fall, I won't be able to get you back up. You don't want to end up in the hospital, do you?"

Frankly, Eugene doesn't care what his mother wants. *He* doesn't want this. He doesn't want the inquiries, the complications. There's just no point.

"I want to see Sharon," Glenda says.

Eugene doesn't have any clue who Sharon might be, or if Sharon even exists.

The alarm he'd set on his phone begins to trill, and he looks down at the time. "I need to go, Ma."

"Will you take me to bingo?" She blinks rapidly, and he assumes she's attempting to bat her eyelashes as she must've done when she was younger to get her way. Back when she'd talked men into doing things for her. It's an odd attempt, and one she doesn't normally try on him. Usually, she just bullies him until he finally gives in.

"Sure," he sighs, to shut her up.

She nods and picks up the bowl, slurping the remainder of its remnants from the container.

He's halfway to the front door when she says, "I have to use the toilet."

Eugene lets his head fall back and looks toward the water-stained ceiling, exhaling fully.

He turns back around. "Can't you try using the walker?"

"I wiped your ass until you were twelve. You live in my house. The least you can do is help me to the bathroom."

Eugene hesitates a beat longer before he steels himself for the task. He should be glad she's still asking to use the toilet, he supposes. It won't be long until this physical task is impossible, and she'll have to soil herself where she sits.

The bubble of desperation again floats to the surface.

He pushes the TV tray out of the way. The leg catches on a box, and the tray lists to the side, against a mound of clothing and atop an ancient dog crate. The mixing bowl tumbles off of the mound, splashing the rest of the milk over the trash. Eugene pushes the tray out of the way with his foot, then plants both feet before leaning in and grasping his mother's massive arms.

He strains and manages to pull her to her feet,

keeping her upright.

Though she's done very little of the work, she wheezes with the effort, and they begin a slow shuffle to the home's one bathroom. She leans heavily on him, and he somehow bears her colossal weight.

Because Eugene must use the shower, this room is less littered than the others. The appliances are pink and outdated, and the ancient flowered wallpaper peels at its seams. The toilet bowl is rust-stained and the walls are damp. But for now, the plumbing works and the water runs.

Glenda barely fits into the space between the toilet and the sink, but Eugene wedges his mother inside. As she clutches at her chest and wheezes, Eugene fixes his gaze on the bathtub and gathers up the folds of her nightgown until the fabric bunches at her waist.

"Okay," he says, breathing nearly as heavily as his mother. "You need to lower yourself down slowly."

She nods, but instead of sitting, she falls back. The toilet tank clatters against the wall and the bowl and piping creak.

He winces, wondering how much longer the commode will last.

"Get out," she pants, and he backs out of the room, pulling the door shut behind him.

He glances at the time on his phone as his mother's intestines loosen, groan, and release.

The search for Dahli will already be underway.

His heart, already beating heavily with the effort, continues to pound in his chest.

A few minutes later, Glenda calls, "Done!"

Eugene opens the door and gags. He attempts to breathe through his mouth.

He hates this part.

The toilet is lower than the sofa, and he has no leverage with which to hoist his mother to her feet. He maneuvers himself into the room, squeezing around her flesh so she can grab onto his arms. With his back against the sink, he pulls her weight and lifts with all his strength.

On the first try, she falls back heavily onto the toilet. "Fuck," he swears loudly.

"Don't you dare speak like that," she yells back.

Ignoring her, he plants his feet again and focuses. This time, when he pulls, she makes it to her feet. She pitches forward and he pitches backward, until she's pinning him against the sink.

He can't breathe. For a moment, he believes he might suffocate.

Then, somehow, he manages to heave her upright, and they both miraculously stay on their feet.

This routine, he knows, is not sustainable.

They shuffle back to the family room, where she falls back against the cushions. The sofa creaks too under her weight.

She leans her head back and shuts her eyes.

Eugene has made a decision. Without a word, he goes to his room—neat as a pin compared to the rest of the house. He finds a backpack and fills it with the things he will need. From under his mattress, he takes a roll of cash he's been saving. He's not sure he will need it, but he doesn't want to leave it in this house.

When he comes back, his mother's eyes are still closed. He watches her chest to see if it moves.

She must sense his presence, because she says, "Get my snacks before you go."

He brings back a block of processed cheese, a pound of lunchmeat, four sleeves of crackers, a vat of cheesy-puffed snacks, two packages of chocolate chip cookies, and a gallon of sweet tea.

Glenda opens one eye and says, "You've actually brought me enough for once." She opens the vat of cheese puffs. "Bingo tonight," she reminds him.

"Bingo tonight," he agrees.

She fixes her gaze on the television, and he stares at her, trying to conjure some happy memories of the mother she'd once been. But there are no happy memories. He mourns his lost childhood.

He quickly walks out the front door. He doesn't lock it behind him, and he doesn't look back.

He climbs into his SUV and throws his backpack on the seat next to him.

He drives the familiar route out to Goose Creek.

On Marrington Plantation Road, he parks behind a

long line of cars he assumes are there for the same reason he is. He walks nearly a quarter of a mile to the trailhead where the search party was instructed to meet.

There's a table manned by a few self-important-looking women, set up with snacks, water, and bug spray.

A middle-aged man dressed in a pair of khaki chinos and a polo emblazoned with the call sign of a news station leans against a water fountain and chats with a man with a camera. They don't look in his direction.

At another table, a young cop in a uniform holds an electronic tablet and looks Eugene up and down.

Eugene swallows and approaches the kid. "I'm here for the search," he says.

The cop nods. A nametag on his chest reads 'Parker'. "They've already gone out."

"Can I still help?"

The cop—Parker—shrugs. "I'm not sure how much any of this will help us."

"It might help Dahli." Eugene's voice has gone high and reedy, and the officer squints.

"You know her?"

He clears his throat. "Not really." He's perspiring, finding it highly ironic that he *wants* the cops to remember him for once.

"Are you one of those sick freaks who likes to get their rocks off to women in trouble?"

Eugene doesn't feel the need to answer.

Parker looks down at the tablet. "Name?"

"Eugene," he says.

The officer smirks. "Last name?"

"Ryan." He sighs and swallows. As the officer is typing in Eugene's name with fat thumbs, Eugene says, "Weird situation, huh? The way she disappeared?"

Parker looks up and studies him—really looks at him. "Not so weird, if you ask me. Plenty of people seem to have had motive."

"Do you think someone she knew did it?"

Parker looks as if he might answer the question, then thinks better of it. "Why don't you just get out there with the other ghouls?" he says instead.

Eugene nods once and points to the trail behind the cop. "Back there?"

"Yeah."

"Is there, like, a group? A grid we're searching?"

Parker snorts. "You watch too much 'Law and Order'." He hands Eugene a handful of small red flags. "You see something strange or unusual, don't touch it. Put a flag in the ground next to it, raise your hand in the air, and call out 'assistance'." Someone will come and help."

"What would qualify as strange or unusual?"

"Could be anything at all. A scrap of clothing, a cigarette butt, a cup or a wrapper, foil from a piece of gum. If you'd been here when the search started, we went over all this," Parker chides.

"Sorry," Eugene mumbles. But he's not sorry at all.

The officer studies him closely one last time, then waves him on. "Good luck," he says.

Eugene bows his head in acknowledgment. He has a feeling he's going to need it to accomplish what he needs to do.

CHAPTER 24

Miriam's phone rings through to the car's Bluetooth system. The number flashing on the display of the dashboard causes her to startle and steer into the rumble strips on the side of Interstate 526.

Samantha.

With a shaking hand, she accepts the call.

"Samantha?" Miriam asks tentatively. She tries to keep her voice neutral and not allow the eagerness, the hunger for connection, to flow outwardly.

"What the hell is going on, *Detective*?" Her daughter's voice is filled with scorn.

Miriam grips the steering wheel. She should've known this wouldn't be a social call. "I take it you've seen the coverage."

"Of course I've seen the coverage. It's all over the news."

Miriam thinks back to the news crews, the flashes of bulbs, the cacophony of questions. She blows out a breath.

"Why are you even investigating this case? Why are you allowed to be involved after what you did to Dad?"

Over the past decade, every time the subject has come up with her daughter, Miriam resists the urge to remind Samantha that Mark Edwards is not completely innocent.

But the emotions flowing through her now are too abundant to sort through. Not on a brief, unexpected phone call. She says evenly, "Dahlia Reed has nothing to do with what happened back then."

"We're talking about a missing young mother who is allegedly having an affair with a powerful, older man. That sounds pretty close to me."

Miriam lets the word 'allegedly' slide. There was nothing *alleged* about Mark's relationship with Erica Abington. He may not have pulled the trigger, but he'd been involved, all right.

She takes the next exit and eases to the side of the road with her flashers on. Her palms are damp on the wheel. She says to her daughter, "You were sixteen. There's a lot you didn't understand about that time."

Samantha barks out a humorless laugh. "I understand more than you know."

Miriam rests her head back against the seat. She has no idea what Mark has since told their daughter. After their very public divorce, Samantha had elected to live with Mark even before they'd moved south to Florida to be close to his parents.

Miriam hadn't fought him for custody—not when neither Mark nor Samantha had wanted that. She'd learned to live with increasingly infrequent visits with her child. It had broken her heart. It still does.

"How do you think this makes us feel—watching all of this again?" Samantha's voice is softer now.

Miriam clears the emotion from her throat. "I've been removed from the Dahlia Reed case. I'm investigating an embezzlement at the moment." This is officially true, even though Miriam has no intention of abandoning Dahli.

There's a pause; Miriam imagines Samantha is deciding what to do with her anger. Finally, slightly deflated, her daughter says, "Well, good. I assume your debacle of a press conference reminded your superiors of your failures. Dad said he knew Weston Moss. I'm glad you won't be able to ruin that man's life, too."

"I'm actually more concerned about Dahli Reed's life." Miriam is unable to keep the bite out of her voice. But in the space that follows, Miriam realizes she's in danger of losing the opportunity to prolong the conversation with her child.

Before Samantha can disconnect, Miriam says, "How are you?"

"I'm fine."

"And Tyler?" Miriam asks, referring to Samantha's husband of two years. Miriam hadn't been invited to the ceremony, but she'd seen photos on social media of the couple's beach wedding. Samantha had been a beautiful, radiant bride.

"He's fine, too. Busy with work," Samantha adds, and Miriam's heart swells with this small piece of inconsequential conversation.

Then Samantha offers, "We're expecting a baby next month," and Miriam can't help the audible sigh that escapes. A new swell of emotion fills her. She is temporarily stunned.

I'll be a grandmother, she thinks.

"Next month," she whispers. It doesn't escape her that her daughter has been pregnant for eight months, and Miriam has had no idea.

She'd not been there to take her daughter to doctor's appointments. She'd not been there to help her decorate the nursery. She'd not been there to offer motherly advice or soothe hormonal emotions. She'd not been there because she'd not been wanted.

Miriam will not be wanted in this child's life, either. She must mourn the relationship before it even begins.

She steadies her voice and attempts to keep her tone neutral. "That's wonderful news," she says. Her voice is tight. "Do you know what you're having?"

"It's a girl."

Miriam thinks back to the earliest days with Samantha. She wishes she'd taken more time to enjoy early motherhood. She wishes she'd taken the time to enjoy the full experience of motherhood, in fact. Chaos and all. But there was always so much work to be done. Much of that work had meant nothing in the end.

If she could travel backward, she'd do things differently.

In a normal world, a granddaughter might allow her that opportunity.

Miriam swipes away tears that have leaked from the corners of her eyes and swallows down hard. "I'm happy for you. Having a daughter is a…blessing." Her voice breaks on the last word.

She wants to keep talking. She wants to ask how Samantha is feeling. She wants to know if they've chosen names. But she doesn't want to overwhelm her daughter with questions. Especially given the reason for Samantha's phone call.

And so, she's not sure what else to say. She feels the shift in energy and knows Samantha is about to end the call.

"Take care of yourself," her daughter says. "I do hope they find Dahli Reed."

"Me too," answers Miriam. She waits, and there's another pause before her daughter disconnects.

Miriam sits at the side of the road in silence as the flow of traffic rushes past her. She stares, unseeing out the windshield, considering her life and her decisions. After a few moments, she feels as if she's able to join the world of the living again. When she does, she's surprised to discover she feels determined.

Perhaps her instincts are wrong, but despite Samantha's anger toward Miriam, she knows she can't allow her granddaughter to grow up in a world unsafe for women. If there's something she can do about it, she'll be damned if she won't do everything in her power to change things. Maybe Miriam's daughter will never meet the woman named Dahlia Reed, but Miriam is not going to let this case go. If it means she's ruined her professional career forever, she'll make that sacrifice.

Something bigger is at stake.

Miriam eases her way back onto the highway where she heads first toward the Hope Presbyterian Church to talk with the pastor about his treasurer.

She would much rather be at the Marrington Plantation Trailhead where the search for Dahli Reed is taking place. If she weren't certain she'd be caught on camera, she'd attend anyway. But she doesn't want to risk suspension before this case is solved.

She can play it cool for now, she decides. But she's not going to give up.

When she finally reaches the station over an hour later, she walks in with purpose and makes a beeline for her desk. She'd been hoping to talk with Hill without Kaylor, but neither is around.

Chief Manning walks out of his office with two men in dark suits. They lock eyes before he turns back to the men and says something. Both men nod in response.

Miriam can't be certain, but she'd swear those men

are FBI. That makes no sense, though. This case isn't multi-jurisdictional, and no federal laws or statutes have been impacted. The only reason the FBI would be here is if there were a request for assistance, and that would have to come from Vince Manning himself.

Of course, if they *are* FBI, they may be at the station for an entirely different matter.

But Miriam knows better than that.

The chief's expression is unreadable, just like those of the two stone-faced men. They don't look in her direction, but Miriam senses their awareness of her.

She waits until they move down the hallway to the conference room, go inside, and shut the door. Only then does she deliberately, casually, sidle to Arthur Hill's side of the desk.

She shuffles through the paperwork on the cluttered surface, not sure what she's searching for.

A deep voice from behind her says, "Last time I checked, your desk was on the other side of the wall."

Miriam slows her movements and turns, letting out a slow breath. *Parker.* She turns to the young officer and says, "Hill is well aware I'm here."

He narrows his eyes. "Really? So if I just called him…" He makes a show of pulling out his phone.

She snorts. "How is this any of your business?"

He lowers the mobile device. "Last I heard, you were off the Reed case. Doesn't seem to be any of your business, either."

Parker is young, with an arrogant swagger and designs on a bigger career. He'll probably get it, too. She can already see he's ready to stab backs, step on shoulders, burn relationships to get what he wants. Miriam certainly doesn't condone that behavior, but she remembers what it was like to be young and hungry. She remembers the struggle and the chances you had to risk to inch just one step forward. Her experience certainly would've been much different than Parker's, but at the end of the day, he wants the same thing they all do. For a number of reasons, she decides to make nice with her young colleague.

"Hill attends Hope Presbyterian. He left me the church bulletins from the last few months. For the case I've been assigned," she adds.

"You can't find those online?"

She has no idea. But she says, "You know how these churches are." She doesn't know how they are at all. But the words make Parker nod.

He backs down, but he doesn't leave. "Interesting turnout during the search party for Dahli Reed."

Miriam's pulse picks up, but she stays calm. "I didn't realize you were involved."

"A number of us from Patrol were out there this morning."

"So what are you doing back here?"

"Kaylor took my spot when she finally decided to show up." Resentment has crept into Parker's voice at the mention of Kristie Kaylor. She briefly wonders if Kaylor had spurned Parker's advances, or if his bitterness was just run-of-the-mill professional jealousy.

"What was interesting about the list?" Miriam asks.

"Want to see it?"

She hesitates. She knows she should decline his offer. Instead, she taps her fingernail against the surface of Hill's desk. "You have it?"

"All online," he responds. "Hanahan PD has moved into the twenty-first century, a mere twenty-five years later."

"Why would you think I'd want to see it?"

Parker smiles. "Come on, Ballard. I'm not stupid." He gestures toward Hill's desk. "I know you're not snooping around here for some church bulletin. I see you," he adds, and Miriam knows the phrase is more figurative than literal. Parker may be over twenty years her junior, but they're not so different.

"I guess the better question is, why would you give it to me?"

"Because I've done my homework. I know what happened with the Erica Abington case. Your daughter was a year ahead of me in school, you know."

Miriam *hadn't* known that. She doesn't say anything.

He leans closer. "I didn't think what they said about you was fair, and I don't think it's fair to take you off the Reed case because of what happened back then." He doesn't seem to expect a response. He straightens and continues, "I know you're still working this case. And if you come through, maybe you'll be in a position to help me, too."

"Help you with what?"

"Kristie Kaylor isn't the only one who wants to play detective."

"So this is a game to you?"

One side of his mouth lifts in a grin. "It's *all* a game."

She opens her mouth to argue, then she realizes he might be right. If she takes Parker up on his help, she'd owe him something. But wasn't that how this went? How many favors had she traded over the years to get to where she was? Along the way, she'd lost count. But she disagreed with his metaphor. It wasn't a game. It was more like a dance—an intricate, complicated dance.

She nods at the younger officer. "Let's see it."

She follows him to his shared desk on the other side of the station. No one pays attention to them while he logs into his laptop and opens an application.

She leans forward, looking closely at a color-coded spreadsheet. As she watches, a name appears in real-time, as if by some ghostly hand. "Who is typing that?" she asks.

"Someone at the park," he says. "Maybe Kaylor."

"Can she see we're looking at it?"

"She can tell I'm logged in," he says and hands her the mouse, "but as long as you don't type or change anything, she won't know anyone is looking at the data."

Miriam hesitates, then takes the mouse and starts to scroll through the names. There are nearly one hundred names on the list. She recognizes some of them: Candace Witten, Kelly Murry, Eugene Ryan. She sees the names of neighbors, business owners, and other co-workers they'd interviewed.

She does not see either Aiden or Weston Moss on the list, which doesn't surprise her. They're likely laying low.

Then she notices a name that catches something in the back of her mind. *Carter Brooks.* Where has she seen that name before? She searches her memory for a moment, to no avail.

Finally, she straightens. She wishes she could've been there to observe the behavior of the participants. Criminals often return to the scene of the crime or the act to revisit the psychological thrill. Without the observation, she fears that the list of names doesn't mean much for her search.

Still, she says, "Thanks, Parker," before she turns to leave. "I owe you one."

"I'll remember that," he says.

She doesn't acknowledge his comment as she walks away. No doubt he won't forget.

CHAPTER 25

A woman in slim black pants, a tight pink top, and a white visor skirts the edge of a briny pond. Jeremy watches her gaze into the shallow pool which is murky and crowded with muskgrass and lily pads.

She keeps her head turned to the water, where the morning mist has burned off. He realizes she's likely scouring the surface for a sign of Dahli. Jeremy shivers at the thought of his wife's body alone and decomposing, her dark hair tangled in spike-rush and primrose.

He looks away from the pond and tramps through the rushes toward the trail. A group of chattering women he doesn't recognize approaches. When they spot him, the chatter stops. He averts his eyes as they squeeze to the other side of the path, far away from him.

He's at least fifteen feet away when their whispered voices reach his ears in a rush of inaudible words.

Despite the fiasco of a press conference—despite that crazy Moss woman accusing her husband of abducting Dahli—everyone thinks it's Jeremy who's done something to his wife.

They have no proof, but that won't matter. He's the husband. The husband is always guilty.

Another figure walks toward him—this one male—intently looking down as he wends his way slowly through the trees. This figure, Jeremy recognizes.

"Carter?"

The man looks up, mild surprise on his puffy and exhausted face. He stares at Jeremy as if in a fog before he finally says, "I didn't think I'd see you out here."

"Where else would I be?"

"At home with Luke and Maeve."

The answer comes quick, and the man says his children's names with a misplaced familiarity. His boss has never met his children.

"Dahli's mother is at the house," Jeremy responds after a pause. He regards his boss, who's wearing a pair of tactical pants and a blue T-shirt with 'Boston 26.2' emblazoned in gold letters.

"What are *you* doing out here, Carter?"

In the shade of the tupelo and oak trees, Carter pushes his sunglasses on top of his head. His eyes are swollen and red. "I'm here for Dahli," he says.

The two men stare at each other.

Dahli's early morning texts; her soft, secret smiles; unexpected evening runs…

Jeremy opens his mouth, then shuts it again, not sure of what he should say. What emerges is not what he'd planned. "Did you do something to my wife, Carter?"

"No." The response is quick, emphatic. "I would never—" He pushes a hand through his hair, knocking off the sunglasses. He bends to pick them up, and when he rises, his face is pale, as if he might pass out. He places a hand against the trunk of a sweetgum tree.

Jeremy watches and waits. His heart beats a heavy tattoo.

"I would never hurt her," Carter says after a minute. His eyes turn red and shiny. "Dahli was—" He clears his throat. "She shouldn't be gone."

This is who she'd been sleeping with, Jeremy thinks, and everything else falls into place. The added pressure at work. The demotion. It had all been by design. A slow dismantling of his psyche while his boss courted his wife.

Dahli was in love with Carter, he realizes.

Jeremy doesn't expect the rush of desperation in his chest. The utter hopelessness as he realizes Dahli is lost to him forever, and not just physically.

"What did you do with her?"

Jeremy looks up sharply. His boss's hands are extended, and his face is pleading.

There are many things Jeremy wants to say, but none of the words come. Just as he does at work, he feels small and lacking in front of Carter, and he finds himself searching for an excuse. A defense.

He tips his head back and stares up through the canopy of branches and golden leaves. The sky is a clear blue.

In the distance, a female voice calls, "Assistance!" Some do-gooder who thinks she's found something. She hasn't. Dahli is not here.

"Jeremy!"

Both men look toward the path as Detective Arthur Hill lumbers toward them, his breath coming in puffs. "It's getting warm," he says breathlessly as he reaches them.

If he notices the tension between the two men, he doesn't give any indication. He barely seems to notice Carter Brooks. "I need to talk to you," he says to Jeremy. Carter hesitates before he wanders away to continue his pilgrimage in the trees.

Hill's breath slowly returns to normal. "I didn't know if you'd show up today."

"My wife is missing," Jeremy answers in an irritated retort. It's the second time he's had to answer the same question in the last few minutes.

Hill ignores this. "Your mother-in-law told me you'd left early. Looks like she was giving the kids lunch."

Jeremy wipes his mouth with his hand. He's still trying to process the revelation about his wife and his boss. He doesn't have time for nonsense right now. And he doesn't want to play games.

"After last night," Hill is saying, "I thought you'd want to lay low."

Jeremy doesn't know if Hill is trying to trick him

into saying something incriminating. Hill had seemed like the more reasonable of the two detectives. It was the woman—Ballard—who had it in for him. But he knows enough not to trust either of them.

Hill puts his hands on his hips and looks around as if he's never been in nature before. The man is overweight and soft. He probably prefers drinking beer and watching football in front of the television more than he does hiking, biking, or fishing.

Jeremy has a flash of memory from the early days of his marriage to Dahli, when they'd first moved to Hanahan. They'd hiked these very trails together, and talked about getting a little cabin in the woods somewhere. That had almost happened, but they'd never quite gotten there. At least not together. Not really.

"We have a team at your house now," says Hill.

"A team?"

Hill quickly adds, "Don't worry—we're doing everything we can not to alarm the kids."

"A team for what?"

"They've taken in Dahli's car and laptop for processing. And yours. Gathering some other potential evidence."

"Evidence," Jeremy repeats. It's coming together now. He should've known it would happen quickly.

"We have a warrant."

Jeremy doesn't respond. He'd already given them

permission to search his home. A warrant meant they were covering their bases and ensuring any charges would stick.

"Sherri has been extremely helpful in letting us know what state of mind Dahli may have been in," Hill says, and it feels like an accusation. He's not sure what Dahli shared with her mother. God knows she'd stopped sharing things with him.

He imagines his wife's comments about him over the past few months. Complaints about his mood and his anger. His distance. When all the while, it had been Dahli pulling away. Trying to gaslight *him* into thinking he'd been the problem.

He considers telling Hill about Carter, but he thinks better of it. They already think Dahli's alleged affair with Weston Moss has given Jeremy reason to harm his wife. Best not to give them the real motive.

"We're taking in your car, too," says Hill. There is something in his look.

Jeremy's black Toyota is parked just down the road near Menriv Park. "My car is *here*," he says.

"Not anymore."

"You can't take my car." Jeremy's voice is slightly raised. "I need it."

"We'll give you a ride back." Hill's tone is placating.

"No, you don't understand. I can't—" He runs a hand through his hair. "I need the car. It's important."

Hill cocks his head, frowning. "You have somewhere to be, Jeremy?" His voice is lower, a direct contradiction to Jeremy's raised pitch.

"I… I can't be trapped in that house," he tries again. Sweat blossoms and his skin prickles.

Hill nods slowly. "As soon as your car is processed, we'll get it back to you."

"You don't understand…" Jeremy cuts off his comment abruptly. How could the detective understand? He'd never been in a situation like this one. "How long will it take?"

"Not long. Not long at all."

Jeremy inhales and exhales slowly, trying to think.

The detective says, "If you have somewhere to be, I can arrange one of the patrolmen—"

"You don't understand," snaps Jeremy again. "Look, am I under arrest?"

Hill's pause tells Jeremy all he needs to know. "If you were under arrest, you'd be in custody." His voice is conciliatory, condescending. "We're trying to find your wife. We want her back as much as you do."

Jeremy can hear the innuendo in that sentence.

"Have you looked at anyone else?" Jeremy gestures wildly at the wooded area around them. "We're wasting time out here. For what? A photo op for the press? Have you looked at the Naval Command Station? Anyone working at the water treatment plant?" Even out here in nature, he can hear the hum of the compressors close by. "Anyone could have picked Dahli up. A crime of opportunity," he adds. But he doesn't believe that for a second, and his voice belies him.

Hill sucks his teeth with his tongue. "The thing is, we couldn't find one person at those locations who have any connection to Dahlia," Hill says evenly. "Even so, we're looking into that, too."

"Too," Jeremy repeats, and the lump in the detective's throat bobs.

Hill has shown his hand, but he doubles down. "That's right, Mr. Reed. *Too.* There are certainly other theories—a crime of opportunity. Some random man saw a beautiful woman out jogging and decided to take his chances. Someone else that she knows who had evil designs on her. Of course those are theories we're pursuing. But if you take everything together, the facts seem to be adding up to something else.

You didn't call the police when your wife failed to come home. *You* didn't pick up your kids that evening. *You* insisted your wife was fine, even though you didn't know that. Not for certain. And *you* knew she was having an affair, giving you motive."

Another group of volunteers pass by with curious glances. His life and his wife have become a sideshow. Entertainment. A juicy drama for the news stations and the social media warriors. One of the younger women in the group seems to think she's being stealthy as she holds her phone at her hip and records. Jeremy angles his body so that his face is hidden from their sick reels.

If Hill notices, he doesn't comment, nor does he seem to care. "We need you at home, Jeremy."

Jeremy doesn't want to be home. Not with Sherri there, and not when Sherri believes Jeremy is guilty. He can't bear her sideways glances and the way she huddles his children away from him. It doesn't matter that there are plenty of other suspects, including Weston Moss—the man who was publicly accused of harming Dahli. Sherri will never believe her daughter—her only precious child—could have done anything that may have led to her disappearance.

Hill presses his mouth into a tight line and looks off into the distance. Finally, he says, "I shouldn't be telling you this, but we viewed all the surveillance video from the morning of Dahli's disappearance. One of the tapes shows an SUV that looks remarkably like yours driving down the Red Bank Road."

Jeremy blinks and a misplaced quiet comes over him. Time seems to slow. "My car is surprisingly common," he says.

"Yes, it is. The most common vehicle sold in the year you bought it, in fact." Hill says this like an accusation. As if Jeremy had purchased the vehicle for the purpose of committing a crime three years later.

"So you can't be sure it's mine."

Hill stares at him, waiting. When Jeremy doesn't

say anything else, Hill says, "Huh."

"What?"

"It's just that I thought you'd ask about the license plate."

Jeremy is mystified. "What about it?"

"You aren't worried about your license plate on that footage?"

Jeremy exhales loudly. He doesn't know where this discussion is going, and he just doesn't have the energy for Hill's riddles. "Where's your partner?" Jeremy asks. "The woman." She'd been more intimidating, but she also seemed smarter.

Hill stiffens but ignores the question, shifting the topic back to the car. "I just find it odd you wouldn't ask," Hill says, instead. "Because the license plate of this car was covered in something. And we didn't get a good look at the driver because he was hunched forward, wearing a ballcap pulled down low. Almost as if he'd known he might be on camera."

"What are you trying to say?"

"If you didn't know your plate and your face were hidden, I think you'd be much more worried than you are."

Hill's voice is friendly, like they're old pals. Jeremy prefers the formal tone of the other detective—'Ballard', he remembers. At least he'd known where he stood with her.

"Not if I wasn't there," Jeremy says. His voice is

calm. The air around him slows, as if the atmosphere had begun to vibrate at a different frequency. "I did not kill my wife." And that is the truth.

But this detective doesn't care about the truth. They'd begun to build the slow, steady case against Jeremy, and Hill is no longer trying to pretend that they haven't.

Jeremy knows how this will go. More and more pieces of circumstantial evidence will be pieced together to build a precarious assemblance for an indictment. They will have no concrete proof of wrongdoing, but it won't matter. Propped up by the court of public opinion, the shaky case will stand.

Jeremy pushes all other thoughts from his mind and focuses on himself. "I think I might need a lawyer," he says to Hill.

The detective lifts a shoulder. "That's up to you. We'll get the evidence we need. Don't you worry."

Jeremy doesn't answer. He knows there is evidence they will purposely omit. And there's nothing he can do about it.

He throws out a Hail Mary. "Are you at least looking at Weston Moss?"

"We're considering everyone, Jeremy. But we're looking at *you*."

Before Jeremy can respond, there's a commotion in the trees. A young woman dressed in plain clothes rushes toward them. Hill looks up, his slouching posture suddenly straight and alert. With a glance at Jeremy, he moves toward the woman and out of Jeremy's earshot. The woman talks fast and close into Hill's ear.

Jeremy notices two other officers in the trees behind them.

A number of searchers alerted to the noise have stopped their exploration. They stare at Jeremy. The woman in the pink top and white visor has moved away from the pond. He can't see her eyes behind her dark sunglasses.

Jeremy's heart pounds so hard that his hearing is muffled.

Then Hill and the woman stop talking. They stare at him for a moment before they head back in his direction. The cops behind them have their hands on their hips, each with a palm near their holsters.

Hill's mouth moves in slow motion and his words come out deep and distorted. Jeremy struggles to process the words.

Physical evidence of your wife in your trunk…Suspicious searches on your laptop…Reports of threatening text messages…

Jeremy's world is spinning, and he doesn't resist when Hill grabs his arms and forces them behind his back.

"You have the right to remain silent. Anything you say can and will be used against you in a court of law.

You have the right to an attorney. If you cannot afford an attorney, one will be provided for you…"

Jeremy looks at the smug faces of the audience that has gathered. They point their phones at him. They call out to him, jeer at him.

A news crew appears on the path, and someone shoves a microphone in front of his mouth.

Where is Dahli, Jeremy? What did you do with her body?

They start leading him away. Jeremy looks around wildly. He sees Carter, whose eyes are wide, his mouth slack.

The woman with the white visor has taken off her sunglasses. Her dark eyes, too, are wide. Jeremy's gaze locks with hers, and he doesn't know why, but he tries to transmit his panic through that one, desperate look. "Please," he mouths to her.

Her mouth falls open while her hand moves to her throat.

He will be all over the news, guilty in the court of public opinion before a trial can take place.

Jeremy thinks of Dahli. He thinks of his children, who are losing not one, but two parents.

"Oh, God," he cries. "I'm so sorry, Dahli."

He nearly falls to his knees, but Hill pulls him up.

"Save the theatrics," the detective says evenly. "No amount of acting is going to get you out of this one."

Jeremy knows the man is right. There is no going back.

CHAPTER 26

Candace removes her sunglasses and watches with equal parts fascination and horror as Dahli Reed's husband is taken into police custody. People cheer as the handcuffs click over his wrists. They shout, as if this is an occasion for celebration. And they record on their phones, as if the game has been won.

But Dahli is still not here.

Jeremy Reed looks back at her. Their gazes lock. Candace cannot look away from the desperation in the man's eyes. She feels sorry for him.

He seems to be communicating with her. His lips form a single word: *Please.*

The detectives drag him forward. He nearly falls. Candace looks around at the gleeful crowd who appear to be excited for the downfall of this man.

She wonders if she, too, should be joining in the celebration.

Perhaps Jeremy will tell the cops where they can find Dahli. Perhaps her friend will come home, one way or another.

He doesn't look back again.

The trees sway on a sudden breeze, and Candace looks up. The midday sun is warm on her face, and the world should be filled with promise and hope. Instead, it feels bleak.

Jeremy's arrest brings a sense that the search has ended. Groups of volunteers chatter excitedly and head back toward the trailhead, as if the fact that Dahli has not been found is irrelevant.

At the edge of the pond, two officers stand and point. Candace follows their attention to the shallow, murky water. She sees nothing but alligator weed and pennywort with its clusters of white flowers.

She looks around for Detective Ballard, the one to whom she'd admitted her deepest secret. But Ballard isn't here, and Candace feels very alone.

A man in his mid-forties stands nearby, his hands on the hips of his Patagonia jacket. Like Candace, he is solitary and staring into the distance. She holds up a hand to get his attention; when he notices, he straightens.

She heads in his direction, intending to find out if, like her, he feels unsettled by this disorganized search and the dramatic public nature of Jeremy's arrest. She wants to find out how he knows Dahli, and if there's a part of him that has fallen in love with her, too. Like the rest of the world.

Like Candace.

Before she can reach him, however, he hurries away

through the grasses. He moves in the direction of the trailhead, abandoning the search. Abandoning Dahli.

Truthfully, Dahli could be anywhere. And the detectives wouldn't have arrested the husband without a strong case.

Still, those haunted eyes. That whispered 'Please'.

Jeremy Reed has no idea who Candace is. To him, she's just a stranger in the Lowcountry. And that makes his desperation all the more unnerving.

She sighs and looks around one last time. But she doesn't feel Dahli here. So, like the others, she heads toward the trailhead where the news correspondents talk in excited tones in front of cameras.

As she passes, a woman thrusts a microphone in her face. "Excuse me, ma'am. You were here for the stunning arrest of Jeremy Reed. What do you make of this new development?"

Candace is temporarily shocked into silence. She glances from the correspondent—artificially dressed in hiking gear as if she too were helping to search for Dahli—to the camera that's now trained on her face.

She swallows and says, "There's nothing to make of the arrest without information on Dahli's whereabouts."

"Do you think the husband killed her because she was having an affair with her boss?"

Candace isn't sure what comes over her, but she says, "Her children could see this, you know. You should be ashamed of yourself." She turns to walk away, but undeterred, the woman calls, "So you don't think Jeremy Reed did it, even though he's in police custody right now?"

Candace opens her mouth, then snaps it shut again.

"Where do you think he's hidden her body?"

Something about the way the question is phrased—*hidden her body*—sparks an errant thought.

Candace keeps walking past the news crews and the remaining police officers. She ignores the young men and women filming themselves furiously for their social media channels, trying to turn tragedy into clicks, likes, and followers.

She reaches her car, parked on the edge of the road, and climbs in.

Hidden her body.

Jeremy's pleading eyes.

She starts her car and hits a button on her phone. A dial tone trills. Aiden answers.

"Hi, Candace. Can I call you back?" he asks. His voice is muffled. He has answered her on Bluetooth.

She looks behind her and pulls out onto Marrington Avenue. "It won't take long. I just had a quick question," she says. "Does your family still own that house out in Jamestown?"

There's a long pause, but she can hear the car noises from Aiden's speaker. After a moment, she says, "Aiden? Did you cut out?"

"Uh, no. I'm here. I don't think I caught what you said."

"Your dad used to own a house in Jamestown, up near the Santee River. It's been years, but I was wondering if he still owned it."

Another pause. "Why?" Aiden asks.

The engine noise shifts in his car and the background sounds soften.

Candace turns left onto Red Bank Road. "It's probably silly. I know the police have placed a great deal of emphasis on this running route of Dahli's, but I just don't think she's here."

"And you think she might be at my family's country home?" Aiden says slowly.

"Well, no." Candace lets out a breath. "I have no idea where she is."

"Then why are you asking about the cabin? What would our cabin have to do with anything?"

His voice is cautious, and there's something just beneath the surface. A nervousness that is unlike the stoic Aiden. Candace frowns. The hair on the back of her neck prickles. She chooses her next words carefully. "I just wondered if maybe you'd ever mentioned the house to Dahli."

"You think she's hiding out there or something?" He scoffs. "That's the stupidest shit I've ever heard."

The sound of his engine becomes audible again. She hears him shift gears; the roar of the engine increases in volume.

Candace takes a left on Bushy Park Road. As she drives, she types 'Jamestown, South Carolina' into her GPS.

"Yes, you're probably right. Stupid," she repeats, glancing down at the route highlighted on her phone.

Without an address, she'll never find the Moss country house tucked away near the Francis Marion National Forest.

She passes over the Black River, knowing full well that if someone had wanted to harm Dahli, they likely wouldn't be hiding her in a house in the middle of the forest. She'd be caught in the current of the Black or Cooper Rivers. She'd be stuck in the brush in one of the remote tributaries. Or perhaps her body has already floated out to sea.

She tries to imagine Dahli's wide brown eyes staring up, unseeing, at a cloudless sky.

She can't conjure the image. In Candace's mind, Dahli is not dead.

She can't explain it, but she knows she's right.

Suddenly, something is telling her Aiden might hold at least part of the answer.

"So," she continues brightly. "Are you on your way back to school?" She hopes she sounds friendly and perky rather than frantic and alarmed.

"Yeah, I am shortly. There's no need for me to stick around. Looks like they got their guy. And thank God it's not my dad."

"Word travels fast," murmurs Candace, and she can't help adding, "Must be a relief for your mom, too. She seemed pretty certain your father was guilty."

"You know how dramatic she can be."

Candace continues driving north. She presses her accelerator, passing the chemical plant and the manufacturing facility built near the remote marshes decades ago, far away from the city's zoning.

Candace is traveling well above the posted speed on this rural road. She pushes the limit, flying around a curve at nearly sixty.

"Where are you?" Aiden demands.

"I… I just left the search. Guess I'll head home now." She gives a little laugh that she hopes doesn't sound forced. But nothing about this situation is funny.

Another pause. "So, what do you think happened to Dahli?"

He'd just said he had to go. And yet here he was, asking questions.

"I have no clue. None at all. Just throwing ideas out. Trying to see what might stick."

"It sounds like you might have a theory. One that might involve my family."

After the manufacturing plant, the road through the swampy land is isolated. There are no businesses or homes. Just brown terrain and a rusty railroad track paralleling the remote road.

She turns left—her tires squealing—and crosses Chicken Creek. She laughs again, keeps it light. It sounds forced and unnatural to her ears.

"I thought *I* was your family, Aiden."

"The *Moss* family," he says with emphasis, and the response stuns Candace. Her laughter fades quickly. As close as she'd thought she and Aiden were, he would always pick his nuclear family over her.

She imagines she hears another swell in the sound of Aiden's engine.

Where is he going?

Where is she *going?*

Candace doesn't have the answer to either of those questions.

"So, what's your theory?" he asks again. There's a new harshness to his voice.

"Like I said…no theory. I don't know what I'm talking about. Clearly."

"Clearly," he agrees.

Candace turns onto Old Highway 52 in the silence that follows.

"Maybe I can stop by your place," says Aiden.

Heat flames in Candace's cheeks. "I… I thought you were headed back to school."

"I can wait another day. We didn't even get to see each other this trip home. You'd wanted to talk, right?"

"Yes, I had," Candace says. She increases her speed.

"How about if you stop over in about an hour?" she suggests. She knows she won't be home, but it will buy her some time. For what, she has no idea.

"How about sooner? I'm near your place now."

Candace briefly shuts her eyes. "Yeah, sure," she says. "I'll be there shortly."

"I'm counting on it."

After his ominous statement, she disconnects and considers her next move. If Aiden goes to her place and she's not there, he'll likely head to the cabin she'd asked about. Any time advantage she has will be erased by her lack of direction.

Her mind races as the speed of her car barrels down the forested road. The marshy terrain has given way to a thick stand of longleaf pines.

She has nearly twenty miles to go before she reaches Jamestown, which isn't much of a town at all. It's more of a common address for the houses scattered throughout the forest. Like most rural places, Candace assumes the residents keep to themselves, and they won't be eager to share information with a stranger asking after a fellow homeowner. Even if that homeowner couldn't be more different from them.

Candace considers turning around. This is starting to feel like a lost cause, and she's acting on nothing more than a hunch.

She thinks of Detective Miriam Ballard and the woman's business card, which Candace had left on her kitchen countertop.

She presses the voice-recognition button on the side of her phone. "Call the Hanahan Police Department," she directs, and her phone does what she requests.

A few seconds later, a woman answers. "Hanahan P.D. How may I direct your call?"

"I'm trying to reach Detective Miriam Ballard."

"What's this pertaining to?"

"I may have information about the Dahlia Reed case."

There is a pause. "Detective Ballard is no longer on that case. I can transfer you to the tip line."

Despite her surprise, Candace says quickly, "No. Please. I… Detective Ballard, please. It's urgent."

There is another pause. "Name?"

Candace exhales. "Candace Witten. Please hurry."

There must be something in Candace's voice because the officer mutters a grudging, "Hold please."

After a minute, a tired-sounding voice answers. "Ballard. Can I help you?"

Relief surges through Candace. "It's Candace Witten," she says, in case the dispatch officer hadn't provided her identity. "I think I know where Dahli Reed might be. I need the address for a property owned by Weston Moss in Jamestown, somewhere out in the forest."

Detective Ballard's voice sounds decidedly less tired

when she says, "Whoa, slow down. What's this about?"

Candace repeats her words slower, then adds, "I don't think there's much time. Aiden Moss is aware of my suspicions, and I think he may be—I don't know." She blows out a breath. "Maybe I'm going crazy. But if Aiden is worried, then maybe there's something to worry about."

She hears the clacking of fingers on a keyboard. "Where did you say this property is located?"

"Jamestown, I think. Somewhere near the Francis Marion Forest. It's been years since I've been there."

"And what makes you think Dahli might be at this property?"

Candace is forced to admit she has no earthly idea. "A hunch, I guess," she says weakly. "It was Aiden's reaction…" Instinctually, she looks behind her, but there are no vehicles trailing her on this remote road.

"Where are you now?"

Candace checks her location on her dash's display. "I'm a few miles from Route 17."

"The property is on Chicken Creek Road," Ballard says, and gives Candace the house number. She hears the detective shuffling things on her desk. "The address is Jamestown, but it's near a small town called Shuler-ville off of French Santee Road. I'm on my way."

"You're coming?"

"I don't think Jeremy Reed is guilty, but right now, I have nothing else to go on. It can't hurt to check this out. Wait for me there. Do not go in. Just in case."

Candace shivers as the call disconnects. She punches the new address into the GPS.

A few minutes later, her ringtone belts through the silence in the car. *Aiden.* She lets the call ring through. There's nothing more to say. She's got nearly forty minutes on him, if he's planning on following her to the remote property. But she still looks in her rearview mirror.

Nothing but empty road and a long, slow finger of fear running down her spine.

CHAPTER 27

Eugene glances in the rearview mirror and sees nothing but barren gray road behind him.

Despite the emptiness in his wake, he can't shake the feeling he's being followed. He knows it's an illusion. No one is interested enough to follow him. He's invisible.

How has it taken him this long to figure that out?

Even in the midst of the crowd at the trailhead, no one had noticed him.

But he'd noticed all of them. Candace Witten with her sad, simpering misery, looking out over the reeds and marsh like some kind of lady-in-mourning. It would've been laughable if it hadn't been so pathetic.

As if she had any right to mourn Dahli.

The last interaction between Candace and Dahli was not friendly—Candace stormed off in a huff leaving Dahli looking like she'd been slapped.

Candace could pretend all she wanted that she'd suffered a loss, but Eugene had seen the look of confusion and betrayal on Dahli's face as he watched the two women from across the street. They'd eaten beignets and sipped mimosas on the patio of the trendy restaurant along King Street. Then Dahli had said something Candace didn't like. Her face clouded over, and she gulped her alcohol instead of sipping.

Eugene had been watching so intently he'd nearly forgotten to hide in the doorway of the office building across the street from the restaurant.

Candace then said something that caused Dahli's head to snap back. Candace stood abruptly and thundered down the street, leaving Dahli shocked and alone.

Eugene had nearly stepped out of the shadows and gone to her.

Then her head had swiveled around, and her eyes seemed to meet his. He'd frozen for less than a second before he'd shoved his hands in his jacket pockets and scurried away, his heart hammering.

He'd been a coward. He should have gone to her. Rescued her.

Perhaps if he had, they wouldn't all be in the situation they were in right now.

He swipes at his face and presses the accelerator, speeding down the remote road. He's tired, but soon that won't matter anymore.

A tractor-trailer appears from around a bend up ahead. It roars toward him on the two-lane road, and he swerves to his right, hitting the rumble strips on the side of the lane. He jerks the wheel and overcorrects.

The rear of his car fishtails, and he panics, nearly driving into the path of the truck.

The driver lays on the horn, and Eugene jerks the wheel back to the right, managing to straighten his path as the trailer rushes past.

His palms are slick on the wheel, and when he gets his bearings, he glances over the seat at his backpack and the worn black case that has slid to the back seat.

He eases off the accelerator in an odd moment of self-preservation. There are things he must do, and they must be done the right way.

He glances in the rearview mirror again, watching the truck disappear into the distance until he's alone on the road. He wipes first one palm, then the other, on the leg of his pants and blows out a long breath.

This road is a familiar one, and each time he drives the route, it feels like fate. He hates the journey, but he can't seem to escape it.

The first time he'd traveled this road when he was twelve years old, he'd done so with anticipation and excitement. Over time, it had become his hell.

He blinks rapidly and chuckles. The chuckle deepens and builds, erupting into full-blown laughter. The guffaws belch out of his chest and fill the space of the car. Tears slide down his cheeks. He wipes them away with the back of his hand and shakes his head as he calms.

They'll never know.

None of them at the trailhead—Candace, the handsome man with the expensive hiking gear, the clumps of do-gooders, the social media warriors, the police and detectives—suspect what Eugene has done or what he's about to do.

Before he'd met Dahli, the only person who'd ever truly seen him was Carl. That hasn't changed.

Whatever leftover frantic amusement he feels seeps away, leaving Eugene deflated. The memory of Carl has that kind of power over him. Once Carl anchors himself in Eugene's mind, he burrows in deep.

Eugene hits the side of his temple with the heel of his hand.

Carl laughs inside his brain.

Eugene is twelve again in the living room of his mother's house. The room is relatively clean and neat, and Glenda is slim and pretty, and mean as a snake. Her hair is buttercup bottle blonde, and her lips are red. She beams at Carl as she presents her scrawny, awkward son. The red of her lipstick has leeched onto her nicotine-stained front teeth.

Carl doesn't seem to mind. He puts a heavy hand on Eugene's shoulder and squeezes hard.

Eugene tries not to flinch, but the vice grip hurts, and a noise escapes his lips. His narrow shoulder crumples under the weight of the hand.

"We need to toughen you up, boy," Carl says, letting him go.

Glenda sneers, but Carl levels a gaze at him, looking deeply into Eugene's eyes. Eugene forces himself to maintain eye contact.

Carl smiles. It seems sincere.

Eugene smiles back.

Born from that moment of eye contact is something Eugene has never experienced—a father figure.

Within weeks, Carl moves his scant belongings into his mother's house, and he shows an interest in Eugene. Their interactions are superficial at first. Carl takes Eugene to the hardware store to pick up new hinges for the hanging kitchen cupboard. He invites Eugene to help him repair the busted screen door. He shows Eugene how to use the weed-eater while he mows the lawn, a cigarette hanging precariously from his lower lip as he pushes the mower in a stained white T-shirt and ratty old jeans.

Carl is of medium height and well-muscled. He claims to have a vague job as a maintenance man at an apartment complex in the city, but he is mostly around. Neither Eugene nor Glenda questions his schedule.

Eugene can tell Glenda doesn't like the attention Carl pays to him, but she doesn't complain outwardly; she just pouts and scowls at Eugene. Unlike her other boyfriends, Carl doesn't hit either of them, and Glenda doesn't hit Eugene nearly as much as she had in the past. At least not when Carl is in the house. His mother seems almost happy for the first time.

Eugene lets his guard down. He allows himself to hope. And then he settles in.

After two months in Glenda's home, Carl tells Eugene he has a surprise for him. When Glenda is at her job as a nurse's aide at the Summerville Residential Care nursing home, Eugene climbs into the passenger seat of Carl's white 1995 Ford Mustang and they rumble their way deep into the Lowcountry.

As he follows that same route now, Eugene thinks that fateful ride may have been the happiest he'd ever been in his entire life.

He hits the side of his head again and lets out a howl, but Carl is still lodged inside his brain. The man isn't done with him yet. It's Carl's retribution, and Eugene is powerless to fight him.

Carl takes Eugene to a rundown cabin that sits on a swamp where bald cypress and tupelos rise out of water as black as tea. He leaves Eugene in the front yard, and from the cabin, Carl retrieves the black case that now slides around in Eugene's back seat.

He lifts out the Sig Sauer pistol and hands it to Eugene. It's heavy in his young hands, but Carl places his large palms over Eugene's small ones.

Then he follows Carl across the lawn and into the trees. At the edge of the swamp, they watch and wait. When the water ripples, Carl's hands tighten over Eugene's. "Stay still," he whispers at Eugene's ear.

Eugene shivers.

The smooth head and eyes of an alligator are visible just above the dark water.

Eugene holds his breath.

When the creature is in front of them, Carl guides Eugene's arms up and places his pointer finger over his.

He aims the gun at the water and pulls the trigger.

Eugene's body bounces back into Carl's coincident with the crack of the gun. There's a wild thrashing and a terrible commotion, accompanied by Carl's whoop of laughter.

Eugene is terrified. His bladder lets loose, and the urine warms his pants. Tears wet his cheeks as fear, shame, and embarrassment cause his body to quake.

Carl's laughter subsides as he looks down at Eugene, who cowers away. This is the end. Carl will use his fists on him now, just like Glenda does.

He stares down at Eugene's wet pants for a long while, and something shifts in his expression.

Eugene shuts his eyes. But Carl just says, "Come on. Let's get you cleaned up." His voice is low and thick.

Carl grabs the gun and walks the short path from the swamp to the cabin, up the rickety front porch stairs, then disappears inside.

Eugene keeps his eye on that silver weapon held loosely in the man's right hand. He hesitates, but in his wet pants, which have gone cold, he has no choice but to follow.

When he walks through the front door, the light disappears, and he's swallowed up by shadows, and thick, oppressive air. The air is musty-sweet—old wood and decay.

It's hard to breathe.

Still holding the gun, Carl says, "Well, come on, boy," and leads him up a short flight of creaky stairs to the second floor. Eugene peers into a bathroom, but Carl waits for him inside the doorway of another room. A bedroom.

Eugene's chest feels tight. He glances behind him, back down the stairs.

"Eugene," Carl says. His voice is tense. He is silhouetted in the backlit bedroom, his face in shadow.

Eugene moves forward slowly, and when he gets close, Carl puts his left hand on Eugene's shoulder and guides him inside.

A filthy window filters a stream of sallow light inside, and Eugene looks around. A small bed frame and yellow-stained mattress are pushed against the wall, and an old chest of drawers leans against another wall.

Carl sets the gun on the chest and rummages through the top drawer. He pulls out a pair of old sweatpants and turns around, flicking a glance at Eugene's soiled jeans.

"Take 'em off," he orders.

Eugene's hands move to his fly. He hesitates, hoping Carl will turn around. He doesn't.

Finally, Eugene does what he's told and pulls the wet pants down where they get stuck on his sneakers. He nearly falls forward, and Carl laughs. "Dumb kid," he says, but there's no malice in the words.

He moves forward to help Eugene, and Eugene can smell his stale cigarette breath as the man comes close.

He pulls off Eugene's shoes and then his pants, and then his drawers...

Then it happens.

Eugene blinks.

He pushes the rest of the memory deep down, but it's always there. It's a part of him. An open wound that will never scab over.

After that day, Carl takes Eugene to the cabin regularly.

They shoot the gun at objects—tin cans, bottles, ancient, twisted cypress trees. Afterward, Carl leads Eugene to that bedroom with its stained mattress, and every time, Eugene tries not to cry.

At home in his mother's house, Eugene grows quieter. No one notices. Glenda is caught up in her new, better life, with the man who hasn't yet left her. At school, his teachers ignore him as they do with so many of the white trash kids from the wrong side of town. No one cares about him.

At night, in his bedroom, Eugene listens to the sound of his mother's moans joined with Carl's low grunts.

For over a year, he is sad. He is angry. He is trapped. He is desperate.

Then a plan forms in his mind.

Carl has taught him to become a good shot. When he pretends those objects are Carl, he becomes a *better* shot.

And when he turns thirteen, he knows it's time.

On a cloudy, oppressive summer day, Eugene is silent as they drive to the remote cabin near the town of Kingstree. Eugene doesn't know who the closest neighbor is, but he knows the way to town from the cabin. And he knows he can probably get a ride south with one of the truck drivers who uses the rural highway to avoid the interstate to Charleston.

If he can't get a ride, he'll have to walk. It will take him the whole day, but it won't matter. No one will miss him, and no one will ask where he's been.

Carl is in a good mood, like he is on most of their trips to the cabin.

At home, Carl's mood has begun to sour toward Glenda. Eugene isn't sure if his mother has noticed, but Eugene detects the curt replies and sarcastic comments. Carl never behaves that way with Eugene, and there are many days when Eugene thinks he might be able to tolerate the other things.

But when Eugene side-eyes Carl singing along to a song about taking three steps toward the door, and he sees the stiff wind blowing in the window of the Mustang through Carl's feathery brown hair, Eugene's resolve deepens.

He has no choice.

They pass through the town of Kingstree—past the corner gas station where the cab of a tractor-trailer is filling up on diesel—and Eugene's blood begins to course through his veins.

Ten more minutes and they'll reach their destination. His armpits sting with a blossom of perspiration.

Even though he's familiar with the route, he watches the scenery whizz by, noting the trailer homes along the way—the deep cuts in the forest where an all-terrain vehicle may have made a path. He notices good places to duck off the back road should someone hear the shots and finally decide to investigate.

When they reach the cabin, everything is as it always is. Carl pulls the case from the back of the car and sets it on the ground near the porch. He takes the porch steps two at a time and bangs into the house, coming back with a can of cheap beer for himself and a knock-off brand soda for Eugene.

The can fizzes open with a whoosh, and Carl takes a long pull of the brew before he says to Eugene, "Let's go down to the swamp and see if any gators'll come to play." He pulls out the gun and loads the magazine before pushing it into the grip.

Eugene swallows. "Can I go first?" he asks. His voice cracks.

Carl lets out a howl of laughter. "My boy is finally growin' some hair on his peaches," he bellows, laughing. He claps Eugene on his shoulder. "I knew I could make a man outta you."

Eugene's smile is shy and unsure. Again, his resolve wavers.

Is it really so bad? Carl is the only one who cares about him.

Then Carl's hand slides from Eugene's shoulder and snakes down his back to his rearend.

Eugene holds his breath.

But the man removes his hand. "Time for that later," Carl growls more to himself than to Eugene. "Let's shoot."

Eugene lets the air leak out from between clenched teeth.

Carl hands Eugene the gun, and they head to the edge of the swamp. Eugene pulls the slide forward, chambering the bullet, then pulls back. When the slide clicks into place, a wave of nausea washes over him and he gags. His hands are shaking.

"You okay, boy?" Carl asks and steps forward.

Eugene levels the barrel of the pistol at the other man, whose eyes go wide.

"Whoa, there…" His hands instinctively go up,

palms forward. "Water's that way." He tilts his head toward the swamp, but he doesn't take his eyes off the pistol.

Eugene doesn't budge either. He is frozen in place.

There's a splash in the black water to his left. Momentarily distracted by the fat body of the gator on the opposite shore, Eugene's gaze darts to the water as Carl lunges forward.

He doesn't remember pulling the trigger. He doesn't remember hearing the crack of the shot. But he remembers Carl looking down at his torso where a circle of blood seeps through the white cotton of his sleeveless T-shirt. He remembers the sound the man makes—the croak of his voice when he whispers, "Eugene…"

Carl stumbles forward as Eugene takes a step back. The man lurches sideways and staggers a few steps before tripping on an exposed root. His voice doesn't make a sound when he splashes into the shallow water.

The ripples are wide, and Carl emerges only once to try to suck in a last breath. Eugene watches, the gun dangling limply from his hand. He is suspended in time and space.

Then there is silence.

Carl is face-down and still.

Eugene isn't sure what to do. He stares at his tormentor, waiting for him to move. Willing him to move.

He's not sure how long he stands there, but when

the same fat alligator emerges from the other bank to investigate Carl's body, Eugene finally backs away. He lifts the gun to shoot the creature before realizing the alligators are his friends here. They will dispose of Carl's flesh and scatter his bones.

Eugene looks around, making sure no prying neighbor or passerby has come looking for the source of the commotion. But there are no witnesses.

Eugene returns to the cabin and picks up the soda from the step where he'd left it. He drinks it down quickly and belches. Then he removes the clip from the pistol and packs it neatly back into its case. He contemplates setting the cabin ablaze, but realizes the smoke and flames will alert the neighbors and passersby.

Eugene does not enter the cabin that day. His body will no longer be violated.

But he'd been unprepared for the memories of what had been done to him, and the flashbacks of what he'd done in turn.

Now, as Eugene drives north, he realizes tears are running down his cheeks. He angrily swipes them away and continues through town, passing by the scattered neighbors along the rural road. People here keep to themselves, and if anyone wondered what happened to the lean man with the loud Mustang, no one had ever said a word. Nor had they remarked when, three years later, Eugene had started driving through town to take possession of the rotting cabin.

Aside from Eugene, Glenda seemed to have been the only other person to notice Carl's absence, and Eugene had witnessed his mother's fast descent into madness. She'd called the police, hospitals, the apartment complex where Carl had supposedly worked. No one had any information on Carl, and it turned out he'd never worked at the apartment complex at all. The police hadn't been interested in some homeless man who wasn't on their radar. His disappearance was of no consequence to them.

Eventually, Glenda accepted Carl's abandonment, but afterward, she wasn't the same. She'd spent so much time searching for the man, she lost her job. The only thing she gained was her appetite—filling the void of Carl with food and junk. Since Eugene was responsible for Carl's disappearance, he figured he was also responsible for his mother's addiction. He figured he was now responsible for *her*, too.

Eugene pulls up the long drive leading to the cabin. The tires of his SUV crunch on the gravel outside, and he gazes at Carl's old home. It's a far cry from the ramshackle house it once was. After Carl had been gone for nearly a decade, an investor took possession of the abandoned property then rebuilt a new structure around the bones of the old one.

Eugene, who'd claimed the old place as his own—a consolation prize for his suffering—had been livid. But he'd never stopped visiting. The family didn't live here full-time, of course. They were much too good for that. So, Eugene continued to let himself in when the place was empty, careful to leave the home in pristine order when he left.

Then, the family stopped coming entirely, and once again, he had the property to himself.

The day he'd met Dahli Reed, he dreamed of bringing her here. Making a home here with her. He'd wanted it so much that his imaginings felt real. He couldn't think of any better way to overcome what Carl had done to him here—what he'd done to Carl—than by filling the place with love. With Dahli.

He swallows down a lump in his throat.

When Dahli looks at him, she *sees* him. All the hurt and pain and regret and shame. Without him needing to say a word, she'd taken it all in, and she'd accepted it. She'd accepted him. With that acceptance, she'd helped absolve him of his sin.

He stares up at the cabin, at the upstairs window.

But now, it is too late. Eugene has fucked it all up. Just like he always does.

Dahli is lost to him.

Beside him, the ghost of Carl laughs, his teeth protruding over his bottom lip. *You can never outrun me, boy*, Carl says and shakes his head slowly.

"You're right about that," Eugene says aloud.

He cuts the engine and twists around, grabbing the

worn black case from the back seat. With the case of the Sig Sauer banging against his thigh, he walks heavily up the stairs, then unlocks and pulls open the door to the place of his final torment.

CHAPTER 28

Candace's eyes dart to her rearview mirror. She's traveling well over the speed limit, but still, a lifted white pick-up truck has roared up behind her. She tenses. But the two young men occupying the truck's cab don't glance in her direction as they speed past.

She reaches rural Jamestown and drives as fast as she dares through the heart of town. The GPS software guides her down another country road dotted with infrequent homes, a church, and a small cemetery.

Finally, Candace turns onto the heavily forested Chicken Creek Road, struggling to recall a past visit to this area. There is very little development along the pastoral thoroughfare, and it's likely her mother had driven the same route the last time she'd been in the area. Yet these surroundings aren't at all familiar to Candace.

When the female voice on her GPS indicates she's arrived, she is mystified. There is nothing but trees.

By the time she makes out the cut of the driveway through the growth of loblolly pine on her right,

Candace has rolled past the lane. She shifts her car into reverse, then makes the turn down the passage.

This driveway, she vaguely remembers; she had marveled at the remoteness of the property and wondered why anyone would be interested in a home so far removed from civilization.

She recalls remarking as much to her mother, who'd responded with a wry twist of her lips. "I'm sure the purchase was Weston's attempt to be outdoorsy and Josephine's to be trendy. They'll sell it off in a year when they get bored with it."

Clearly, the Mosses hadn't sold the property, though the gravel is washed away, and weeds cover the path.

Ahead of her, the grass has been recently flattened by the tires of a vehicle.

This disturbance doesn't prove anything, she reminds herself. Nor did Aiden's reaction to her questions about the property proven anything. Right now, she's operating on a blind instinct that's likely to prove fruitless. And she's bringing a detective right along with her.

She rolls slowly down the lane, keeping her eye out for security cameras. A security system seems to her like something Weston would insist on, but judging by the lack of landscaping, she's not sure the Mosses would've maintained the equipment.

Candace doesn't want to leave anything to chance.

When she notices a clearing to her left where branches hang low, she drives in, wincing at the sound of twigs screeching against the paint of her car.

The vehicle isn't completely obscured, but it would be adequately hidden from the view of a distracted interloper.

She cuts the engine and climbs out, heading for the house through the clearing ahead.

The only sound is the rustle of wind high in the treetops; the silence envelops her like a blanket. It should be peaceful, she thinks, but instead the lack of noise raises her anxiety levels until her pulse roars in her ears.

You're being ridiculous, she chides herself. The likelihood of Dahli's presence is extremely low.

It's infinitely more likely Dahli's husband had discovered his wife's interest in another man and taken revenge than it was that Dahli is being kept in this remote location, dead or alive.

The police have arrested the man. They must have some proof of guilt.

Besides, isn't it always the husband, after all?

Yet, Dahli herself hadn't appeared afraid of Jeremy. Had her friend misjudged the man she'd married so spectacularly?

That kind of blindness happens all the time, Candace knows. She feels a wave of desperation. She should've paid more attention to what had been happening in Dahli's life. She'd been so caught up in her own perspective of her relationship with her friend, she'd given very little thought to who Dahli was as a wife and mother.

Aware she might never know the fate of her best friend, Candace trudges on.

She'd been horrible to Dahli during their last interaction. It's that guilt which makes her continue moving in spite of her self-doubt. She needs to do *something*. So, she continues up the lane until the house comes into view.

Josephine had called the place a cabin, but the structure is not rustic. A flight of wide, wooden stairs leads to a wraparound porch, and the house is constructed of faded slate-gray cement siding. The windows have been reinforced, and solar panels have been installed on the roof.

There are also signs of neglect. The lawn is overgrown, and the paint on the porch is peeling. Moss grows on the roof between the panels.

She remembers a long-ago conversation during which Weston had bragged about the ability to live off the grid here. If necessary, the house and property could be completely powered by solar and two large propane generators hidden behind the home.

Still scanning for cameras, Candace skirts the edge of the clearing near the forest and makes her way around to the rear of the property where she surveilles the back yard.

A dilapidated chicken coop sags in the corner of the land next to a large dirt parcel that looks as though it once held a garden. A large shed looms beside the garden patch.

Two deer graze on the opposite side of the acreage. As Candace moves forward, they turn their big, black eyes upon her, momentarily frozen. After a pause, the animals seem to decide she is far enough away to continue their meal.

Candace turns her attention to the house. She can see no cameras on the back deck, but that doesn't mean they aren't there.

She crosses the length of the yard at an angle, where a security system would be less likely to capture movement. Then she crouches as she climbs the back stairs to a massive deck that spans the length of the house.

Ten years ago, the family had gathered on this deck where Weston had barbecued on an industrial-sized grill, and guests had lounged on comfortable outdoor furniture. Someone had erected a volleyball net in the yard where friends of Adeline and Aiden had laughed and called to each other.

Despite her mother's resentment of Josephine's lifestyle and good fortune, they'd all had a good time that day. Candace holds the memory tenderly. There are not many instances of the entire family together.

Now, the deck is empty, and the grill is gone. There is no laughter. There is no movement.

She tries the back door, which is locked. She thinks of Aiden's reaction to her mention of this property—of what she'd thought had been her cousin's suspicion and panic.

Perhaps what Aiden had really been transmitting was a very reasonable annoyance at Candace's thinly veiled accusations against his family.

She feels foolish. She cups her hands together and peers through the glass panes in the back door. The window looks into an empty kitchen outfitted with white appliances and butcherblock countertop. She expects the kitchen to be as empty as the rest of the property, but Candace stares at two plastic bags, branded with the Harris Teeter logo, placed in the middle of the counter.

She frowns at the unexpected sight. To her knowledge, the closest Harris Teeter supermarket is in Charleston. She doubts any of the upscale chain's franchises have been built out here, in the middle of nowhere.

Her ears begin to ring with alarm. Someone has been here recently.

Still, that doesn't mean anything, other than per-haps one of the Moss family had visited the location. There would have been nothing unusual about a member of the family checking on the property they owned. Certainly nothing illegal.

But Candace can't ignore those alarm bells.

She jiggles the doorknob; the door doesn't budge.

Candace scans the house for another way in. The windows are higher than reasonable to attempt climbing.

Her gaze returns to the door. Breaking the glass pane might be her only option if she's determined to search the interior.

She places her hands on her hips, considering. She hasn't yet tried the front entrance, but if a security system exists—and she's increasingly doubtful it does—she isn't about to call attention to herself.

She turns, about to make her way to the shed to find an object to shatter the glass, when she notices a black bag slumped in the far corner of the deck. She walks over and kicks it gingerly with the toe of her sneaker. It makes a dull metallic sound.

When she looks inside, she discovers handheld gardening tools. The tools are high-quality and well-made. She examines a trowel, rake, and transplanter, but finally chooses the sharp, heavy pruners for her task and returns to the back entrance.

Placing the sharp end of the tool against the bottom left pane, Candace thrusts the beak solidly into the glass, which shatters with a crack. She holds her breath for the sound of an alarm, but nothing happens.

Sharp, jagged shards remain in the window, and

Candace retrieves heavy gloves from the gardening bag. She slides her hand into the dark fabric and gingerly reaches through the broken pane to unlock the door from the inside.

Pushing the door open, she steps carefully over the glass.

At the kitchen counter, she peers into the grocery bag and discovers fresh bread and peanut butter, along with other staples: cans of soup, a box of crackers, two rolls of toilet paper. There are crumbs on the counter-top and a lone glass tumbler in the basin of the sink.

She looks around. There's also a hum of energy here, and it is human.

She makes her way through the kitchen into the living area.

The odor is close and musty. The house is shaded from the sun by the large trees on the property, and even in the middle of the day, shadows darken the room. Ghostly drop-cloths drape the furniture.

Candace listens, but doesn't hear a sound.

She heads for the interior staircase.

She's nearly halfway up the flight when she hears an engine and the crunch of tires on gravel at the front of the house.

She freezes as the engine stalls.

A car door opens then thuds closed.

Candace scrabbles back down the stairs and into the dark living room. She ducks behind the covered sofa and makes herself small and invisible as heavy footfalls sound on the wooden stairs outside. There's a jangle of keys, followed by a click and the turning of the lock.

The intruder enters.

Candace holds her breath as the person pauses.

She is well hidden, but she has no idea if her car has been spotted. She has no idea if she's being pursued.

She feels the person's presence filling the room, and wonders if they can feel hers, too. Do they sense her panic? Her fear? She screws her eyes tightly shut as if that might help hide her.

After a long pause, the individual continues through the small foyer and moves toward the staircase.

Candace exhales a slow, quiet breath, and risks lifting her head above the sofa. All she can make out is a shadowy figure silhouetted in the dim light from the shaded windows.

It disappears from her line of vision, and then the stairs creak.

Another pause, and Candace presses her forehead against the dusty fabric.

The footfalls sound again, but the steps echo differently. The person is moving down the steps toward the kitchen, she realizes.

Shit. The broken glass pane would be visible from the foot of the stairs. In her haste, she hadn't thought to conceal her vandalism or discard the broken glass.

Candace peers around her hiding spot, frantically considering her options. She glances around for something to use as a weapon. Seeing nothing, she realizes she must bet on her own speed—on being faster than her pursuer.

She calculates the distance to the door.

But the individual doesn't come looking for her, and instead bounds fast and heavily up the stairs.

With a wave of relief, Candace darts out from behind the sofa and reaches her exit. Her hand is on the door handle when she stops short.

Why had the person sprinted up those stairs…unless there was something worth defending on the second floor? Something worth guarding. Something worth securing…

The footfalls echo on the ceiling above her, and the blood rushes to her head.

Dahli is in this house.

CHAPTER 29

ahli's hope has faded. She drifts in and out of a dreamlike consciousness, teetering between life and death. Yet she's still in her body. If she concentrates, she can sense her feet, her legs, her hands.

The effort is exhausting.

In this fog-like state, she thinks she may have called out, but the sound of her voice turns into the voices of her children. Maeve's call. Luke's soft whisper in her ear.

Her own voice is nothing but a hiss in her throat. Her cries have gone unanswered.

She's too depleted to walk. The scant amount of bread and water her captor has given her is not enough to sustain her. Her body is rapidly drying out. Dying.

In her dark visions, she floats out of her body and walks unfettered down the stairs and out the door into the cool fall air. She dances under red-golden leaves and breathes in the scent of pine.

Are these visions real? Has her spirit floated free from her body? She can't tell if she has died. Maybe she's turned into a ghost herself...

But then a sound jolts her back into consciousness, and she's thrust again into the prison of her bound body.

Even if she were to somehow summon the strength and the will to escape, how is she supposed to find help when she's blind and shackled? She has no idea where she is or how close she is to civilization.

In the lucid moments, she thinks of her children. She hopes they know how much she loves them. Maeve will be fine without Dahli in her life. Her daughter is young and spirited. The girl will be confused and sad, but she will adapt to a world without Dahli.

Luke, on the other hand… Her sweet, sensitive son. She wishes she were strong enough to hold on for him. Her only hope is that Jeremy will keep him close and protect him.

Jeremy…

Her husband's image drifts across the blackness of her mind.

Inexplicably, she feels closer to him than she has in a very long time.

She knows the tenderness is a result of her slowly diminishing mind and reality. But before she drifts from the earth, she feels compelled to revisit her past. To remember simpler times, when there'd been nothing but the two of them and their dreams for the future.

In one of those memories, she swears she and Jeremy had sat together in a house she imagines this one is like—tucked away in the trees. A place that reminds them of home. Up until just a few years ago, they'd still talked about purchasing their home in the forest near Lake Moultrie, where they could walk hand-in-hand through the foliage and drive a short distance to DeBordieu, where they'd dine in the tiny coastal town on fresh flounder and sea trout.

Dahli laughs up at a younger version of her husband, who smiles down at her youthful form.

But his smile twists and becomes mournful. *He knows*, she thinks. He knows what she's done, and he taunts her with his knowledge. He will not allow her to escape.

She turns away, embarrassed. Filled with shame.

It's all Dahli's fault. She'd become restless, and Jeremy had become complacent. Maybe they'd married too young.

She gives up. It is too late now.

Jeremy stares down at her on the bed. When she reaches for his hand, his face pixelates, and the molecules rearrange themselves into the image of Weston Moss.

Weston doesn't smile. He sneers.

For years, Dahli had ignored the attention and flattery of other men. She had not given in to that temptation. Her family remained her north star, even when she'd felt pulled toward something bigger.

Something fateful.

Her yearning had shifted her frequency. She was a magnet, and Weston Moss was pulled toward her, closer and closer over the past year.

Next to the bed, the image of Weston glowers at her. Just as he had after that last dinner when she'd foolishly followed him to a hotel room at the Bennett. She had not given in to his advances.

But her refusal of him hadn't been because of her family. It had been because of another man.

She had rejected him. Embarrassed him.

Weston Moss does not take the word 'no' lightly.

She gazes at the quavering image of him beside the bed. The image trembles and distorts. Its sneer remains fixed on a face that shifts into a younger version of the man—leaner, fitter. Meaner. Familiar.

She pleads with the vision to let her go, but the man refuses to meet her eye.

A panic takes hold of her. Had Weston abducted her to keep her for himself? Or was it cruel revenge? Did he plan to leave her to suffer and perish slowly in this secret location?

She tries to catch a hazy memory. There is pain in her head. A violation of her body.

Now, in her delirium, she can't be sure an assault had actually happened.

Surely, a man as controlled and refined as Weston would not stoop to such a level.

Her mind is toying with her. Deceiving her.

Dahli has become a liability to everyone in her life. She wants to die.

An image of her son reappears in front of her sightless eyes. *Oh, Luke*, she thinks as emotion floods her body. For a while, her children had been enough to keep her tethered to this reality, but she is so tired. *So tired.*

A sob bursts from her chest, and she gags against the cloth in her mouth.

As if she's watching a screen flicker across her dark mind, Maeve's elven face appears next. Her daughter is barely aware of her mother's absence. But when Dahli thinks *Maeve!* as loud as she can, the girl looks around with surprise and expectancy. Dahli can feel the connection.

Her children. Her world.

They will be fine without her.

People would be there for them. Her mother. Jeremy. Candace.

Candace.

She wishes she could go back in time and relive her last interaction with Candace. Dahli had told her friend too much. She'd shared too much—the chance for a fresh start, a new romance. Dahli expected Candace to be happy for her. But Candace's face had turned stormy and unpredictable.

She will not meet Dahli's eyes, and it fills Dahli

with shame and confusion.

Candace coolly sips a mimosa, as she had during their last interaction. But Dahli sees something else in the image. Pain. Regret.

In Dahli's delirium-addled mind, the golden liquid slides down Candace's throat—she can see the fluid pass through her friend's semi-transparent body. Anger sparks like static from the image.

Candace, she whispers in her mind. Again, she reaches out. The object of her imagination turns away.

Dahli has ruined everything.

I loved you. The words emanate from Candace's being. The accusation sits in the dark between them.

Dahli is selfish.

All the figures appear before her again: Jeremy, her children, Weston, Candace. In her fever dream, the specters morph, shift, fade, and reappear. They are angels. They are monsters. Candace tries to turn away, but she can't.

She's fastened to the vision, forced to experience the interactions from the perspective of the others. It's a punishment for thinking of nothing but herself in life.

It's not true…is it?

Dahli had been selfish. Now, she is desperate.

I've done nothing but live for others, she thinks. She's created this life, but she hasn't created it alone or for herself.

It's only recently she's allowed herself to have true feelings for another. The image of Carter Brooks fills her being.

He gazes at her sadly. He pities her.

Because of their situation, Carter is unable to express the sorrow he might feel about her absence.

Startled, she realizes that perhaps their relationship had not been as deep and strong as she'd thought it was. Carter will move on, nearly unscathed. He may even be relieved.

She'd been a complication for him, she realizes. The baggage she brought—Jeremy, her family… It's not something a successful man like Carter needs in his life. What he'd wanted was a beautiful companion.

She's weighed him down.

She's been foolish.

In her mind, they are no longer indoors, but running beside each other in the cool morning air, inhaling the smell of fresh dew. Suddenly, she veers off onto a forest trail, and Carter continues along the road. He holds up a hand in acknowledgment of their parting, but he doesn't stop.

Dahli leans forward, her hands on her knees, breathing heavily. She gasps for air and her lungs burn. She feels as if she's going to suffocate.

Her reality shifts from the cool outdoors and back again to her prison, where the distorted images of her reality play on.

Hello, Dahli. The words fill her mind, and she giggles. Her father used to sing a song with the same title to her.

She belongs in this room, gagged and bound.

Dahli sucks air in around the cloth blocking her airway. She can't get enough oxygen into her lungs. Her throat gurgles as she struggles, and her vision starts to close in around her.

She is going to die.

The upbeat melody plays in her mind, and the music envelops her. It vibrates around her and through her.

She hums the familiar tune and feels a sense of calm.

They will all be okay, she thinks. Distantly, she's aware of her earthly body trying to stay alive. Distantly, she senses herself struggling against the pull of the ultimate darkness.

But she's ready. She succumbs and begins to drift far, far away in a golden, hazy light…

And then there is pressure, commotion, and urgency. Hands are upon her, ripping at the cloth in her mouth.

Oxygen rushes into her lungs.

She tries to cough, but it hurts.

The cloth is gone from her eyes, and the light is too much. She squints, but can't see. Her mouth free, she moans again, and her voice makes an inhuman sound.

Finally, she can make out the face of the person above her. Her brows draw together. This can't be right.

She wills her vocal cords to work.

Her voice is hoarse when she whispers, "Aiden?"

CHAPTER 30

Candace pulls out her phone to dial Detective Ballard's number, but there's no service. She considers using its SOS feature, but an inhuman moan—weak and desperate—from the second floor causes her to abandon the task. Instead, she creeps up the back stairs.

A male voice pleads, "Come on. Come on," over and over again. "You're still here. You're okay…"

Candace edges quietly to the doorway and peers inside. The slim back of a male figure leans over the prone figure of a woman.

An audible gasp escapes her lips, and the head of her young cousin swivels around, surprise and fear painted across his face.

He's cradling a disheveled and pale Dahlia Reed.

"No…"

Candace rushes forward and kneels next to Aiden. Dahli's lips are white, and while her eyes are open, they loll back in their sockets. She's wearing what Candace assumes are the running clothes she'd had on when she disappeared. Her hands are bound behind her back.

Two black scarves lie next to her on the bed.

Candace swallows and tries to remain calm. "We need to get her to a hospital."

"She just… She needs to drink something," says Aiden.

Dahli floats in and out of consciousness. It's not too late.

What other horrors has her friend endured? She nudges Aiden out of the way and cradles Dahli's head against her chest. "We're going to get you out of here," she murmurs.

Dahli does not acknowledge this promise.

"Help me carry her to the car. We need to find the nearest hospital."

Aiden doesn't move.

"If we don't help her, she's going to die. I know you don't want that."

Her cousin shifts forward, looking unsure and confused.

"Look, Aiden, I don't know how she got here, and I don't care. We can figure that all out later. Right now, though, we need to get help."

"I-I can't do that," he stammers, his voice barely more than a whisper. "It wasn't supposed to be this way."

Candace wants to scream at the kid, but she takes another breath. "Has she seen your face?" She tilts her head toward the scarves she assumes have been used to cover Dahli's eyes.

He nods. "Just—just now," he whispers. He looks as if he might cry.

"We'll make something up, and I'll corroborate your story," Candace says. "Family first, always." She can see the shift in his expression. "But we need to get her help. Okay?" At this point, she'll say just about anything to get Aiden to act.

He nods and steps forward. A wave of relief washes over Candace.

Then he stops again. "I'm just not sure—"

Candace shuts her eyes. "I'm not asking, Aiden. This needs to happen now." Her voice has increased to a shout. The edges of her nerves shoot static around her. She has had her limit of nonsense.

Still, Aiden doesn't move. Instead of fear and un-certainty on his face, his expression has shifted to one of stubborn resolve. He reminds her of the ornery little boy she'd known two decades earlier. He says one word.

"No."

She doesn't argue. Instead, she turns back to her friend. She'll take care of this herself.

Straining, she attempts to lift Dahli. But though Dahli is small—and smaller still in her diminished state—Candace is not much larger, and her friend is a dead weight. Candace can only get to her feet by the surge of adrenaline that courses through her.

You can do this, she tells herself.

But Aiden steps into her path.

Barely able to keep Dahli in her arms, Candace manages to seethe, "Get out of my way."

"I can't let you go."

She tries to sidestep him, but she's slow with her extra encumbrance, and he easily blocks her again. She's about to shout, when she notices the bulge beneath the hem of the sweatshirt bearing the name of his college.

Aiden has a gun.

Why does he have a gun?

She pauses and blinks. She tries to keep the strain out of her voice when she says as calmly as she can manage, "Aiden, I told you—I'm not going to let anything happen to you. I just want to keep Dahli alive. That is my only goal in all of this."

"But she…she's not supposed to be alive."

Candace's arms burn, and she shifts the weight of Dahli in her arms. She won't be able to stand for much longer. "We can save her." Her voice is consoling, pleading.

"Maeve?" Dahli asks, her eyes snapping open in a moment of lucidity.

"We're going to get you some help," Candace says to her friend, who stares at her intensely then fades back into her delirium.

Aiden shakes his head. "I was supposed to take care of her."

"And you can do that now. *You* can save her."

"It's too late," he says, his voice breaking.

Candace takes advantage of his emotional state and attempts to move past him again. Just when she thinks she'll make it to the door, he moves quickly to the exit. "She's supposed to be dead." He sounds forlorn.

Another chill rushes through her, but she says, "Thank God she isn't. There's still time. We can make this right."

He doesn't budge. "My mother…" he says, then abruptly shuts his mouth. His hand shifts to the waistband of his pants.

Candace's skin prickles.

"I need to do what I should have done in the beginning."

"Aiden…" Her words trail off. Time moves in slow motion.

Candace thinks about her Aunt Josephine. Candace's mother had always commented that Josephine didn't understand the meaning of the word 'consequences'—that she'd always felt as though she could do whatever the hell she pleased. And usually, she got away with it.

Candace remembers Josephine's appearance at the press conference for Dahli. She recalls the woman's unhinged accusation that Weston Moss had killed Dahli.

And now, here they were—in a house the Mosses

owned—with Aiden, who'd do anything for his mother, a woman whose suffocating hold on her son had always been evident to others.

What Josephine may not have realized was Aiden's strong feelings for Dahli.

"What have you done?" she whispers, as her arms give out. She sinks to the ground, laying Dahli on the hardwood floor.

The gun is now in Aiden's hand. It glints silver in the dim light streaming in through the window. It hangs from his fingers, and Candace doesn't take her eyes off the weapon.

"Think about what you're doing. Think about your future," she pleads.

"It's too late for that."

"No, Aiden. We can figure this out. Please."

He shakes his head again, and the gun comes slightly up. While not pointed at her, it is aimed in her direction. She wants to glance around the room for an escape, but she can't tear her gaze away.

"*She* won't understand. She told me to take care of Dahli. She told me to dispose of the body out here in the woods." He runs his left hand through his sandy-brown hair. "I couldn't bring myself to do it." His voice cracks. "I thought I could keep her here—keep her safe. I thought she could be mine."

Keep him talking, a small voice inside Candace's head orders, and she swallows. "Your mom wanted

Dahli out of the picture?"

He nods. "She thought Dad was sleeping with her. She thought this was the woman he would finally leave her for. She couldn't..." A sob bubbles up from his chest. "...She couldn't stomach the embarrassment."

That may be true, but Josephine Moss likely had other motives—like revenge. And money.

Candace keeps her voice light when she says, "Aiden, this isn't your fault. We can explain all this to the police. Sweetie, it's not too late."

Aiden is crying now. "I've let everyone down."

She meets his eyes, beseeching him with every ounce of energy she has. "No, you haven't. In fact, no one ever has to know." With every ounce of strength she has, Candace manages to smile at the boy.

He returns her gaze as he lowers the gun to the floor, and Candace lets out a quiet breath. She just needs to keep talking, keep convincing him. But there isn't much time. Dahli has stopped moaning; Candace is sure she's slipping away.

There's a sound—an engine accelerating up the drive, the spinning of fast tires on gravel.

Aiden's tears stop and his head snaps up, along with the gun. "Who did you tell?" he demands.

Candace shakes her head. "No one." But that's not true. Miriam Ballard knows she's here.

Aiden whispers, "It's her. It's my mother."

Candace realizes her mistake. "It's not her, Aiden."

But it's too late, the gun comes up—the barrel points at Dahli Reed who lies oblivious on the floor.

Candace leans over her friend. Dahli has too much to live for. It's Candace who's expendable—alone with no family, no children, no connections. She will do this for Dahli. She will make it right.

A car door thuds closed, then footsteps pound up the outdoor stairs. The front door opens, and a female voice calls out.

"Candace?"

Aiden lets out a whimper, and Candace realizes what's about to happen a millisecond before it takes place.

"Aiden, no!" she screams.

CHAPTER 31

The crack of the gunshot reverberates throughout the house. Miriam freezes for less than a second before unholstering her weapon and bounding up the stairs to the second floor.

She isn't prepared for the sight: Candace on the floor, screaming and crawling toward the body of Aiden Moss, blood seeping onto the floor around him.

Dahli Reed lies unconscious next to Candace. Her hands are still bound behind her back, and her eyes are closed. There is no movement, and Miriam can't tell if she's alive or dead.

Miriam holsters her gun quickly and moves toward Dahli while Candace lifts the young man's ruined head into her lap and leans over him. "Aiden, no," she wails. "You didn't have to do that. You didn't have to do that…"

Miriam feels for a pulse at Dahli's neck. It is faint, but it's there. Backup is on the way, but she lifts the portable radio from her belt and calls for an ambulance.

Candace looks up at her with wild eyes. "We have

to save him," she says.

Miriam nods, but the boy is already gone. "We'll do what we can."

A moment later, the unit she'd called is at the house, and soon afterward, the ambulance arrives along with more officers.

It's only a matter of time before the news crews get here, though no names have been mentioned over the radio. But someone in the department will 'accidentally' let information slip. It's just the way it goes.

Soon, an officer escorts Candace out of the room and covers the body of Aiden Moss with a sheet, while two emergency technicians carry Dahlia Reed down the stairs on a stretcher. They put her quickly in the ambulance, and Miriam watches them start an intravenous drip to get some fluids into her. They'll take her to the local hospital to be stabilized and examined before she's likely transferred closer to the city.

Miriam doesn't know what kind of injuries may have befallen Dahlia, but she needs to believe the woman will make it.

It's too late for Aiden Moss.

Candace Witten sits sideways in the back seat of a patrol car, a blanket around her shoulders. She's still trembling when Miriam approaches.

Another unmarked car comes careening up the driveway. Arthur Hill parks crookedly in the yard and rushes out with Kristie Kaylor in tow.

He walks quickly toward her, and Miriam holds up a hand. Her partner's face is grim, but he stays back and prevents Kristie from approaching. They go to talk to one of the patrol officers instead.

Miriam crouches down so that she must look up at Candace. The woman's face is nearly white, and Miriam thinks she might also need to be checked out at the hospital. She looks at Miriam with a haunted expression.

"Where is Aiden?" she asks. "Why haven't they brought him down yet?"

"They will," Miriam assures her. "They're taking Dahli first, okay?"

Candace's teeth knock together, and she nods.

"You saved her, you know," Miriam says gently. "She wouldn't have made it out of here if it hadn't been for you."

Candace doesn't react to that.

"How did you know she was here?"

"I don't know," Candace whispers. "I remembered being here a long time ago, and I…I couldn't stop thinking about the place. Maybe it was my mom, guiding me here." Her voice trails off, and she looks up at the house. "Where is Aiden?" she asks again.

"Aiden's coming," Miriam says. But it will be a while before they bring him down. The crime scene technician has just arrived, and the medical examiner is still enroute. She suspects Candace knows Aiden hasn't survived, but that her mind won't allow her to accept it.

Miriam won't break the illusion yet.

"Can you tell me what happened in there?" She makes her voice as gentle as possible.

Finally, Candace looks at Miriam. "He was keeping her."

"After he kidnapped her?" Miriam frowns. She'd have to check with the timing, but she was almost positive Aiden hadn't arrived in town until after Dahli had been abducted.

"I don't think he was the one who took her."

"Was it Weston?"

Candace shuts her eyes, then opens them again. "Josephine."

Miriam presses her lips together, and doesn't immediately respond. "Are you…sure?"

"I'm not sure of anything. But he said…" Her words break off, and a sob escapes her throat. She swallows down the emotion and takes a few breaths. "…he said he was supposed to kill her."

Miriam glances over at Hill, who's watching her from the corner of the front porch. "Josephine wanted her dead," Miriam says.

"Aiden would have done anything for his mother, but I don't think he could bring himself to do that. He loved her." She's not talking about Josephine, Miriam knows.

Candace brings her hand to her forehead. "We all loved her." She's quiet for a second, then she says, "He's not okay, is he?"

It's not quite a question, and Miriam places a hand on Candace's knee. "No," she says softly. "He's not."

"It's all my fault." Candace raises her hands to her face and sobs.

"It's not your fault." *It's Josephine Vance Moss's fault.*

A few minutes later, a vehicle races up the drive-way, spinning gravel behind the parked cars of the first responders. Josephine Vance Moss climbs from the cherry-red Maserati. "I received a call that there's been an incident at our property," she demands to no one in particular. "What's happened?" She glances at Aiden's vehicle still parked in the driveway. "Where's Aiden?" She points to her son's car. Then she notices Candace, who is now crying softly. She turns a feral gaze on Miriam. "What is she doing here?" the woman demands.

Miriam stands and pulls Josephine off to the side as another vehicle arrives—this one transporting Chief Vincent Manning. "Let's talk over here," Miriam says, forcibly guiding the woman away.

Josephine stands firm, but Miriam is firmer. And when they were out of Candace's earshot, Miriam says, "Your niece called me with a theory that Dahlia Reed might be here—at this property owned by you and your husband, Mrs. Moss."

Josephine's eyebrows shoot up. "Well, that's just impossible. Who are you, by the way?"

"My name is Detective Miriam Ballard. I was investigating this case."

"The one from the press conference," the woman says with a wave of her hand. "Disastrous. You need to look at my husband if you want answers. You and your incompetent colleagues have not done your jobs."

"We'll look at everything," Miriam assures the woman. "But it turns out Candace was right—Dahlia Reed *was* being kept here."

The statement erases the superiority from the woman's face. She opens her mouth and shuts it again before regaining some of her composure. "That's impossible," she says. But her voice has lost its conviction.

"She's just been taken to the hospital. She's unconscious, but I think she'll live. We'll want to question her just as soon as she's awake and stabilized. We're hoping her memory hasn't been affected." Miriam watches the other woman's expression closely as she takes in this new information.

Josephine glances up at the house. A shadow crosses her face as she clenches her jaw tight.

"Is there anything you'd like to tell us before we speak with Dahli?"

Josephine clears her throat. "My husband was obsessed with her. And she, with him. Whatever lovers' quarrel they may have had, you'll need to keep their relationship in mind as you're speaking with her. I'm not sure whatever she'll have to tell you will be reliable. You take those types of things under consideration, I'm sure."

When she waves her hand in front of her, Miriam notices the tremble.

"Aiden didn't seem to think it was your husband who kidnapped Dahli."

In the silence that follows, Miriam keeps her eyes on Josephine.

"I'd like to speak with my son now."

Miriam inhales. No matter what Josephine may have done, this part gives her no pleasure.

"I'm afraid you can't speak with him, Mrs. Moss."

"Is he under arrest?" she asks. "Because I'm sure we can clear this up." She looks over at Vincent Manning who's talking with one of the officers on the front porch. Josephine begins to summon him over.

"Mrs. Moss," Miriam says softly. "Aiden is dead."

Josephine's hand drops, and there is a split second of absolute stillness before her face falls. She makes a noise at the back of her throat, and then whispers, "What kind of sick joke is this, Detective?"

Miriam shakes her head. "I'm afraid it's not a joke. He..." She pauses and blows out a soft breath. "It appears he took his own life. I'm sorry, ma'am."

The older woman's eyes dart around. "No…" she says faintly. She looks at Candace and points a long, manicured finger in her niece's direction. "It's her. She's always been a bad influence on Aiden. This is her doing."

Sensing the attention, Candace raises her tear-streaked face.

Miriam steps between Candace and Josephine, providing an obstacle to the woman's view. "Mrs. Moss, I think you kidnapped Dahli Reed and told your son to kill her."

"No. That's not true."

"And then you tried to frame your husband for her disappearance."

"It was Weston," she says. "Check the security footage. I'm sure you'll find his vehicle in the vicinity." She starts to walk away. "I want to talk to my son now."

Miriam steps in front of the woman. "Ma'am, you can't go in there."

"It's my house, Detective. I can do whatever I please. Now, let me see my son."

Miriam steps in front of her again. She can't yet arrest the woman, though she has probable cause to do so. First, she needs a warrant.

Chief Manning, however, sees what's happening and approaches.

"Mrs. Moss," he says. "I'm sorry about…all of this."

"I should hope so." Her voice is high-pitched and

quavering. Desperate. "This *woman*," she says with emphasis, "will not allow me to see my son."

Chief Manning presses his lips together and bows his head. That slight movement seems to drive the reality home for Josephine Moss.

"No…" she whispers.

"I'm sorry."

"No!" she yells. "No, no, no!" The words are a primal scream, and all other conversation and movement stop in deference to this mother's profound pain and suffering.

Chief Manning gently takes her by her shoulder and exchanges a look with Miriam. He's been filled in on the afternoon's developments. He nods once to her, giving her the permission she needs to continue. Then he says to Josephine, "Why don't we get you down to the station in town, and we'll continue this conversation away from this scene."

Her legs give out, and he supports her as he guides her to his car.

Miriam watches them go, her heart twisting.

A moment later, Arthur Hill approaches.

They stand side by side without speaking.

Finally, Hill clears his throat. "Looks like we were way off with Jeremy Reed," he comments.

Miriam lifts a shoulder. "Well, he was the most likely suspect."

"You think Josephine is really that vindictive?"

"It would seem that way," Miriam answers. A woman like that isn't used to being questioned, denied, or rejected. Even though her husband probably hadn't been sleeping with Dahli, she'd felt threatened, and decided to take matters into her own hands. "I hope Dahlia can provide her testimony when she's up to it."

"Listen, Miriam. You were right. And I didn't want to listen. I owe you an apology."

Miriam shakes her head. "I didn't believe it was Jeremy, but it was Candace who broke the case. Not me."

"I was so sure it was the husband."

The statement clangs through Miriam's mind. She'd been there, with her own husband, no less. She'd been so sure Mark had killed Erica Abington that she'd been unable to consider any other possibilities.

She'd thought solving this case would absolve her of that guilt, but she still feels shitty all around. A boy is dead. His mother is heartbroken and guilty. A family is shattered.

And now, Dahli Reed must recover and go home to her own broken family. Miriam is glad the woman is alive, but there isn't much more to celebrate today.

She looks over at Candace Witten who's resting her head against the back seat of the patrol car.

"The situation is rarely what it seems on the surface," Miriam mumbles. "There's so much more to life than what first appears."

"Yeah, well, I don't think I'm so great at seeing those shades of gray," Hill responds. "That's why we need you so much."

She smiles at her partner. "I need you, too."

Her phone vibrates at her hip, and she startles. Despite the lack of cell service, she must have somehow caught the signal. A text message flashes onto the screen. From her daughter, Samantha.

—News is reporting Dahli Reed has been found alive. Hope you're safe. Thinking of you.

The message finishes with a heart emoji, and Miriam nearly drops the device. Her own heart squeezes in her chest. Perhaps this is the first step in healing their relationship.

Hill says quietly, "You okay?"

Miriam blinks away tears of hope and takes a shaky breath. "Yeah." She slides her phone back onto her belt. "News travels fast," she quips, before asking, "So what about Jeremy Reed?"

"As soon as we finish up here, we'll release him. He's lawyered up anyway. We need to bring in Weston Moss for questioning."

Miriam nods. "I'm going to head to the hospital. Check in on Dahli."

"Hopefully, she'll pull through."

"She will," Miriam says. "We need her to tell her side of the story."

"It's not a happy story."

"We got Dahli back, Hill. And that's enough for me." Miriam isn't sure it makes up for Erica Abington or Mark Edwards, but she'll take the victory.

And she'll take the rest of her life and career, one step at a time.

CHAPTER 32

Dahli stares out the passenger window of the car as it turns down Linden Lane. She thinks about the last time she'd been on this road—during her regular morning run. It feels like it's been months, though in reality, it's been just over a week.

She's a different person now than she was then.

She glances over at her husband, whose face is set in a grim line as they drive home. Local, state, and national news crews line the street. Random people point phones at the car and smile, wave, and cheer.

A muscle ticks in Jeremy's jaw as he steers carefully through the crowds.

How had they known she was coming home today?

"Everybody fucking talks," Jeremy mumbles as if reading her mind.

He'd been released from prison the day Candace had found her in the house near the national forest. The house Weston Moss owned. The house where Weston's son, Aiden, had held her captive, starved her, and violated her.

She shivers and wraps her arms around herself.

Jeremy glances over. "Okay?" he asks.

She nods. But she's not okay. She's not sure she'll ever be okay.

She hasn't seen her children since the incident. She should be excited, but she's inexplicably nervous. She turns her head away from the windows so that the cameras and phones can't see her face. She has become an internet sensation—a survivor, a heroine.

But she is no hero. She is filled with shame and regret.

Jeremy swears as they inch through the throng of people outside their home.

They cheer and call her name. "Hello, Dahli!" they yell, and someone is blasting that song, which causes her to hunch over the center console and hold her hands over her ears.

Jeremy glances at her with a frown, but he doesn't say anything. There's a lot she hasn't told him about her time in captivity. Maybe the detectives have told him what has happened to her. Maybe the news crews have reported it.

People yell questions—muffled but audible.

How does it feel to be free?

How do they think it feels?

Do you have anything to say to Josephine Vance Moss?

She'd just as soon forget the woman existed.

What do you think of Aiden Moss's suicide?

When she'd heard Aiden had taken his life, she'd wept for the boy he'd once been and the monster he'd become.

Have you spoken to Candace Witten?

Not yet, though she had no idea what she was supposed to say to the woman who'd saved her and lost so much in the process.

Were you sleeping with Weston Moss?

No, but she'd been sleeping with someone who wasn't her husband.

She can't bring herself to look at Jeremy. She knows he's heard the question, too, and his thoughts are likely parallel to hers.

They're going to need to talk.

She will not give interviews to the media. Maybe someday when things have settled, she'll grant a sit-down with an outlet so the public can close out this case and leave her alone. But that's a long way off. She has much healing to do.

Two Hanahan squad cars sit in front of the house, and the officers hold the crowd at bay as Jeremy navigates into the driveway. He presses the button for the garage door opener and drives into the bay. The door closes behind them, and they sit for a minute in the dim light of the space.

He's breathing heavily, and Dahli's heart is thumping in her ears.

"Your mom and dad are excited to see you." His

voice is flat.

Dahli hasn't asked many questions about the days she's been gone, but she suspects her parents were not supportive of her husband. Especially after he'd been arrested for her suspected murder.

She shivers again.

Even though Jeremy had done nothing wrong, it hadn't stopped everyone in their lives from suspecting him. Even *she'd* wondered if perhaps her captor had been her husband.

There's something wrong with that, she thinks. How can she ever share a bed again with someone she'd thought capable of such an act?

Jeremy exits the driver's side of the car and walks around to her door. He opens it and offers her a hand, which she accepts.

Outside, the crowd clamors, her breathing comes quickly, and Jeremy tightens his grip on her arm.

She's grateful for the support.

When they open the door to the house's interior, Leo and Sherri Darling are waiting for her with hopeful expressions. Sherri grasps a handful of ribbons attached to mylar balloons that spell out 'Welcome Home' in a fat, cheerful font, as if she'd been away at college or on a vacation.

"Oh, Dahli!" Sherri Darling cries and abandons the balloons, which bounce and float above them. Sherri flings her arms around her daughter. She squeezes

Dahli tightly, and Dahli tries not to pry herself away.

Her father, who'd flown in a day earlier, is more careful.

"It's going to be okay," he whispers into her ear.

She chokes back a sob.

Other than Jeremy's tentative helping hand, the embrace with her parents is the first physical contact she's had since her abduction, and the sensation feels foreign to her. Part of her wants to lose herself forever in their hugs, but another deeper part of her wants to tear herself away and hide in shame.

When they let her go, she sees her children standing cautiously in the doorway. Maeve's thumb is between her lips—a habit her daughter had outgrown years ago.

Dahli's mother scolds, "Maeve, what did I tell you about your hands in your mouth?"

But Dahli understands. "Come here," she says to her daughter, who looks unsure.

Finally, she approaches slowly, presses herself against Dahli's side, and looks up at her.

"Did you die?" she asks.

"Of course she didn't die," Sherri answers. Dahli ignores her mother.

"Someday I'll tell you all about it," she says to Maeve. "But not today. Today, I'm just happy to be with you."

Sherri makes an exasperated sound. "You're not

going to tell her about it."

Her father says, "Sherri," in a quiet warning tone. She makes the frustrated sound again but doesn't say anything else.

Jeremy stands apart from the rest of the family, watching.

Luke doesn't approach Dahli. Dahli wonders what he's seen and heard. She holds out a hand, and he stares at it for a second before he walks away—down the hall and to his bedroom. The sound of the door closing is the loneliest sound she's ever heard.

"He just needs some time to come around," Sherri says. "I'll go to him."

Before her mother can leave, Jeremy steps in. "No." His voice is firm. "I'll talk to our son."

"Fat lot of good that will do," Sherri quips as Dahli's husband walks down the hall. When he's out of sight, Sherri beams. "We're so glad you're home, sweetheart. I know you've gone through a lot—before and after. Eventually, you'll need to decide what you want to do about..." She glances at Maeve as her words trail off, and jerks her head in Jeremy's direction.

"Mom, please." Dahli's voice is quiet but insistent. "This isn't the time."

Sherri shrugs a shoulder. "I'm just saying. I've always thought you were too good for him. Now I know for sure."

The accusation isn't fair. Jeremy has been through

hell, and not only because of Dahli's disappearance. He's been publicly accused and humiliated. A lot of that has been Dahli's fault.

Leo says to his wife, "Let's lighten up a bit on the guy, huh?" He doesn't wait for a response before he shifts his gaze to Dahli. "A lot has happened in the past few days."

She manages a smile. "Tell me about it."

Sherri moves to the kitchen. "Let me fix you something to eat."

For that, Dahli is grateful.

The blinds are drawn in the living room, and she can hear the sound of voices outside, but at least the music seems to have stopped. She curls herself onto the sofa and shuts her eyes. A few minutes later, she feels a soft pressure against her stomach. Maeve tucks her small body in beside Dahli, and Dahli smiles and drifts off to sleep.

Dahli wakes with a gasp and stares up into the face of the man whose hand is on her shoulder. For a split second, she doesn't know where she is. She presses herself back against the cushions and makes a soft keening sound. She is perspiring and trembling.

The recognition of her husband comes quickly, but her heart reverberates. Whatever she'd been dreaming of immediately fades from her mind, and she's glad for that small blessing.

"You were whimpering," Jeremy says. His tone is neither harsh, nor gentle. He is simply stating a fact.

She nods and sits up against the pillows. Maeve is no longer tucked against her, and Dahli misses the solid weight of her daughter's body. "Where are the kids?"

"Your parents took them to see a movie. They thought it might be a good idea to inject some sense of normalcy back into their lives now that you're home."

She twists around to glance out the window at the crowds of people still milling on the street across from their lawn. "Is it safe for them to be out?"

"Detective Ballard made arrangements for an escort. They'll be fine. And I'm pretty sure when it comes to any intrusions, your mother can hold her own."

Dahli doesn't think he means it as a compliment, but her lips raise in a half smile anyway. Despite her mother's overprotective nature, the woman only wants the best for her family. Dahli is thankful to have her.

She's also grateful to Detective Ballard, who'd been a frequent visitor to the hospital. Despite protests from the doctors and nurses, Dahli had wanted to give Detective Ballard a statement as soon as she'd been able.

When she'd regained consciousness and was certain she was safe, the memories had come flooding back.

After she'd left the Marrington Trailhead, a car had approached slowly behind her as she ran. She'd recognized Weston Moss's black luxury SUV.

Then the window had come down, and Dahli had been shocked to see, not Weston, but a woman. It took her a moment to recognize Josephine Moss behind the wheel. Her silver-blonde hair was not elegantly styled as normal, and she didn't wear the sophisticated clothing in which Dahli was so used to seeing her.

Instead, her hair was pulled away from her face and threaded through the back of a black ballcap. She wore an oversized black sweatshirt and dark pants. Despite the casual outfit, her face was smooth, plump, and unlined. She was a stunning woman.

"Hello, Dahli," Josephine had said breezily, and Dahli was shocked that Josephine knew her name.

Dahli had tried to mask her surprise, but it'd never occurred to her she was in any danger. Though Dahli couldn't think what Josephine could possibly want to talk with her about, she'd climbed into the car, oblivious and eager to please.

On that deserted road, Josephine remained in park. She shifted her body to face Dahli who was tired and perspiring from the exertion of her run.

"You may have been expecting Weston," Josephine said.

Dahli blinked. "When I saw the car, yes."

"You're disappointed."

"No," Dahli said, confused. "I'm not…" She didn't finish the sentence. She wondered why they weren't moving. "Did you want something from me?" She started to feel uneasy.

"You think I don't know." Josephine's voice escaped in a hiss. "You think I'm a fool."

"I… Of course not." It dawned on Dahli where this conversation was heading. Josephine thought she was sleeping with Weston. She wasn't the first person to think that, unfortunately, though it wasn't true.

"I work for your husband. That's all."

"I highly doubt that's *all*." Josephine gave a small, bitter laugh which turned into a sneer. "Do you think you're the first tramp with designs on him? The first one to think you could make him leave me?"

"I've never wanted that." The air conditioning was blasting arctic air through the car, and the sweat cooled rapidly on Dahli's skin. She shuddered.

"Lying will get you nowhere, my dear."

It was useless to keep arguing with the woman. Obviously, she had no intention of believing anything Dahli had to say. So Dahli kept her protests to herself. The truth was, Dahli's mind had been on Carter Brooks that morning, not Weston Moss. At least, not beyond the question of whether Weston might be getting ready to fire her for rejecting him after dinner the week before. She had no intention of telling Josephine *that* either.

"Slut." The word snaked from Josephine's artificially full lips.

Dahli had never been called such an ugly word to her face. She'd made a mistake in entering the vehicle.

She reached for the door handle to exit the car, but before she could pull it open, Josephine hit a button, and the lock snapped shut.

Dahli fumbled with the useless handle. Josephine laughed.

"I'm certain you were laughing at me as you were fucking my husband, but unfortunately for you, I will have the last laugh. I always do."

When Dahli thinks back on the words, she recognizes them as a threat. But at the time, she hadn't considered that. She'd been offended and angry. But she hadn't been afraid.

She reached out to manually click back the door's latch. She remembers a quick movement in her periphery; a black shadow rising up. There had been a rush of air, and then nothing. Blackness. Until she'd woken with her hands and feet bound, her eyes covered and her head pounding.

Now, in her living room, Dahli barely notices when her hand absently reaches up to touch the still tender spot on the side of her head where she'd been struck with the hammer. The doctors told her she was lucky the blow hadn't cracked her skull.

Apparently, Josephine claimed she wasn't trying to

kill Dahli.

But Dahli doesn't believe that. She thinks she may have jerked her head back at the last minute, causing the head of the hammer to glance off her skull while rendering her unconscious.

She believes Josephine found it too distasteful to finish what she'd started. She didn't have the guts.

It remains to be seen what Josephine's defense will be. Detective Ballard has told her the woman is devastated over her son's death. Josephine likely considers Aiden's suicide Dahli's fault, too.

Perhaps Josephine would be too aggrieved to fight the charge of abduction and attempted murder.

Josephine had made a fatal error in overlooking Aiden's connection to Dahli. The woman hadn't known about the text messages and the phone calls. She hadn't known Aiden had followed Dahli to the Hotel Bennett just two weeks earlier, and had begged her to give him a chance after she'd rejected his father.

Aiden, too, thought she'd been sleeping with Weston, but unlike Josephine, the boy's anger had manifested in a crazed desperation. He begged Dahli to leave town with him, spinning an insane plot to disappear together.

Dahli had tried to let him down gently, promising if she were just a few years younger and he just a few years older, it might work out. If only she hadn't been saddled with a family, and he with classes…

She realizes now, she'd given him the motive—the hope—he'd needed for her kidnap.

When Josephine directed him to finish what she'd started and make Dahlia Reed disappear, he'd thought he could keep her for himself.

She wonders how quickly he realized his mistake—that he was angrier than he thought. That he resented her more than he loved her. That he didn't have the time or the resources to take care of her. That he wouldn't be able to make her stay put like some dutiful child.

She wonders if he would've tried to forget about her; left her alone in that house to waste away.

She tries to hold on to the anger she feels, but at the back of her mind there's the twitch of sympathy. Despite what he'd done to her, he was a boy, and with a mother like Josephine, he was only looking for kindness and understanding. Dahli supposed she'd offered him that during his time at Mosswood. She supposed he'd been confused by his feelings for her.

That doesn't excuse his actions, and Dahli has every right to be angry. But she didn't want him to die.

She grieves for Aiden, but more than that, she grieves for Candace, who'd loved her cousin like a brother. In saving Dahli, Candace had lost what little family she'd had left.

Dahli has been so involved in her reverie, she's forgotten her husband is still in the room. He has been staring at her while her mind had been miles away.

"We should talk," he says. His eyes are somber, his mouth grim.

"I'm not sure I'm quite up for that yet." She doesn't want to meet his eyes.

"This didn't just happen to *you*, Dahli."

She has been the one beaten, bound, starved, violated. But he has been the one accused, vilified, arrested, imprisoned. It isn't a competition, but maybe they owe each other a conversation.

He sits across from her. His hands hang limply between his knees. He looks thin and tired. "During the search for you…" he starts, before his words trail off. He stares at the photograph of the two of them on their wedding day. They look young, beautiful, and full of hope. "During the search," he tries again, "I spoke with Carter Brooks."

Ice rushes through Dahli's veins, and her stomach drops. She does not want to have this conversation. Not now. Not yet. And not like this.

"I know it's him, Dahli. The early morning texts. The late-night dinners."

She wants to protest, but what would be the point? Instead, like a coward, she says nothing.

"Are you in love with him?"

He asks it as though it's a simple question, but there are no simple answers. She exhales slowly. Because Jeremy deserves the truth, Dahli says, "I thought I was." Now, she's not so sure. It feels like everything has changed.

"He hasn't called, you know." Jeremy's voice is tight. "Maybe he's giving you space. But he hasn't called."

Dahli considers this. Carter is a kind man. A good man. And he wouldn't have wanted to get in the way of her healing, she thinks, excusing him.

But she's not sure how committed she can be to him after everything else that has happened. She needs time to explore her feelings, not only for Carter, but for herself. She doesn't try to explain this to Jeremy. She can't expect him to understand, and it would be unfair to ask him to try.

"Your parents have agreed to stay here until you decide what you want to do."

Dahli glances at him, and his throat bobs when he swallows. Her gaze slides away again.

"I'm going to move out for a while."

A deep sadness fills her. "You don't need to do that."

"Yeah, Dahli. I do. I'm not sure where we went wrong." He glances back at the wedding portrait. "But neither of us are going to be able to move past this if we ignore how we got here in the first place."

She knows he's right, and yet…

"Maybe we should try to work through it together. As a family."

He shakes his head. "I'll just end up angry, and you'll just end up resentful."

This time, she doesn't argue. "What about the kids?"

"I'll get an apartment close by."

A tear slides down her cheek and she brushes it away. "They've been through so much."

He nods. "They have, but they nearly lost us both. Thank God that didn't happen. And in the long run, it'll be healthier for them to have two whole parents separately than two incomplete parents together."

Jeremy is absolutely right. She wishes she'd always had this logical and wise version of her husband.

"We'll work together to make sure they come through this okay," he says, and his voice is so utterly sincere that a swell of emotion bubbles up from deep within her soul. She looks at her husband through the well of tears that now spill over, making hot tracks down her cheeks. Her nose starts to run. He hands her a box of tissues.

While he is not crying, he looks as miserable as she feels.

She wrestles with a deep sense of regret. "I'm so sorry," she whispers.

He manages a small smile and a shrug. "I'm sorry, too, Dahlia Reed. You were the love of my life."

In the midst of the pain and the sorrow, there also burns an ember of hope. Perhaps, with some time and distance—with some space—they can find their way back to each other. She's not sure she wants that, but her appreciation for her husband has never been more intense than it is right now.

A knock at the door interrupts their conversation, and Jeremy stands.

"Don't get that," she says. "I don't want to talk to anyone."

"It may be the detectives. The police are the only ones allowed past the perimeter."

When Jeremy opens the door, it's not the police. It's Candace Witten, accompanied by an officer.

Dahli looks at her friend and feels a fresh surge of emotion. This is the woman who somehow, against all odds, has brought her back from the dead.

Jeremy, who now seems to be acquainted with Candace, says quietly, "I'll give you some privacy." He disappears down the hallway.

Candace stands awkwardly next to the sofa. Dahli's not sure if she should rise.

"I'm sorry to intrude," Candace says at the same time Dahli asks, "Are you okay?"

They both laugh nervously, and Candace nods. "I'm okay," she responds as Dahli says, "It's not an intrusion."

This time, they laugh for real, and it cuts through the tension. Candace takes the seat Jeremy has just vacated. "I won't stay long. I just needed to see you alive and well with my own eyes."

"Thanks to you."

Candace offers her a small smile. "I wasn't sure how much you remembered."

"I don't remember anything from the day of the…rescue." Dahli chooses her words carefully. While she'd been saved, not everyone had been so lucky. "Detective Ballard filled me in."

"Neither of us might be here if it hadn't been for Miriam Ballard," Candace says. "She listened to my crazy hunch and took me seriously. She arrived just in time, too. Aiden was considering shooting us both."

"He wouldn't have done that to you."

Candace raises her eyebrows. "I'm not so sure. If he'd thought he could get away with it…"

They would never know Aiden's intentions.

Dahli says, "I'm sorry you lost him."

"I'm sorry for what they did to you. All of them."

"How did you know I was there?"

"I have no clue. I'd been at the trailhead during the search they organized for you, and I just knew you weren't there—at Goose Creek. After they arrested Jeremy, I had this random memory of the Moss cabin. It felt like the memory had buried itself in my mind and wouldn't break free. Then when I called Aiden to ask him about the location, his reaction…" Her words break off. "I knew I'd stumbled onto something. Ballard helped."

Whatever had led Candace to think about the place in the forest, and Ballard to further risk her career by going along with it, Dahli was grateful.

"I actually came by to apologize for our last lunch together," Candace says. "If I'd acted differently that day, maybe none of this would have happened."

Dahli isn't sure how the outcome of their lunch would have altered the course of fate, but she waves her hand in front of her. "We don't have to talk about that now," she says, recalling Candace's declaration of love for her. That was a conversation to have over a long lunch when their emotions weren't so raw.

And unlike Jeremy, who'd wanted to rehash everything today, Candace looks relieved. "Raincheck on that conversation. But it might be a while. I'm going to take some time off. I've made arrangements to spend time with friends in Seattle."

Dahli is both pleased for her friend and sad for herself. Candace had been a constant for her. Fresh tears gather in her eyes, and she fights against the sense of abandonment.

"Oh, honey," Candace says. "Don't cry over me. We'll stay in touch."

Maybe they would, but maybe they wouldn't. And it isn't the reason Dahli's crying anyway. She dabs at the corners of her eyes with the tissue Jeremy handed her earlier. "When I was being held, I thought if I ever made it out and came home, it would be a happy ending. Instead, it feels like everything is falling apart."

"Sometimes things need to fall apart so they can be put back together the right way."

"What about Mosswood?" Dahli asks.

Candace huffs out a breath—a half laugh. "I've decided not to work for them anymore. I need some distance."

Dahli supposes she'll no longer work for the company either, though she hasn't had that conversation with anyone yet. That, too, is a problem for another day.

"What's Weston going to do?"

Candace shrugs. "He's grieving his son right now, and coming to terms with what Josephine has done. I suppose he'll go back to the company eventually. It's got his name on it after all." She smiles. "Weston Moss hasn't become as successful as he is without being persistent. He's a survivor."

"That he is," Dahli agrees. She never wants to see him again. But she knows she'll have to face him at some point. At the very least, she'll encounter him at Josephine's trial within the next year. The woman had just been arraigned, so Dahli has a little time to prepare herself.

"He's not going to let Josephine get away with ruining his life."

They both fall silent, each lost in thought about the events that have just transpired. Then Candace stands.

"My car is packed. I better get on the road."

Dahli makes a move to stand, but Candace motions her to stay put. "I'll text you," she says.

"You better."

Her friend smiles again and walks to the door. With her hand on the knob, she turns.

"I almost forgot. You know the creepy guy who sat outside your office? The one who stalked you around town? The one who *stank*?"

Dahli blinks. "Eugene Ryan," she says. "I was supposed to talk to him about his behavior the day everything happened."

Candace looks surprised, then she hesitates. "I hate to give you another shock, but they found his body a few days ago."

Dahli's hand flies to her mouth. "Where?"

"Oddly enough, at a cabin near Kingstree on the Cedar Swamp."

"Do you know what happened?"

"He took his own life, just like Aiden did." She breathes in deeply and lets it out slowly. "He was searching for you that day at the trailhead," says Candace. "I saw him lurking around. Honestly, I thought he was the one who abducted you. He was obsessed."

Dahli shakes her head. "I tried to be kind to him."

"That's all it takes, isn't it? Someone to be kind to us. Someone to see us. It makes us fall in love."

Candace meets Dahli's gaze, and she says, "You're a special person, Dahli Reed." She opens the door and says over her shoulder, "I'm glad you're back where you belong."

Before Dahli can answer, Candace is gone.

Dahli sits alone, listening to the silence of her own home. Despite everything, she knows Candace is right, and she is at peace.

I'll never go away again.

THE END

NOTES AND ACKNOWLEDGEMENTS

As always, thank you to each and every reader who took time and energy out of a busy life to spend time with the characters from my imagination. This is my first psychological thriller, and I hope you enjoyed the twists, turns, surprises, and resolutions.

I'll admit, throughout the writing process, I didn't always like the behaviors of the characters, but I certainly understood them. They are all deeply flawed personalities, and I was showing the very worst traits of all of them in a deeply challenging situation. Hopefully, I managed to illustrate the characters (with words) through a holistic view of their pasts, hopes, fears, and demons, along with their desperate attempts to move forward.

I've frequently been asked where the ideas for my books originate. Sometimes, they start with a dream or a place or a vision or an inspiration. 'Hello, Dahli' started with a song. Of course, the plot of this novel doesn't coincide with the lyrics of the song of a similar name, nor does it align with the familiar musical. Once a general idea for a plot presents itself—in this case, a woman goes missing while on an early-morning run— the story takes on a life of its own. I very rarely know what the plot twists are going to be before I type them, and at the outset, I almost never know who the killer or perpetrator is in my novels.

When I started writing *Hello, Dahli*, I knew Dahli's marriage was an unhappy one, and I knew this was due, in large part, to her own dissatisfaction. Dahli is not a perfect, angelic character. She's made mistakes. But those mistakes should not beget what befalls her. In fact, Dahli is doing the best she can as a kind, attractive, intelligent woman in a male-dominated workforce.

Likewise, the rest of the characters (at least, most of them) act as well as their pasts and circumstances allow. I do hope that is apparent.

A special thank you to my daughter Rachel, whose diligence and commitment to her running and training regimens helped to inspire Dahli's initial actions and circumstances. Appreciation also for being an early reader of all of my books, except for the romance novels.

And thank you to Noah and Adam, who are simply the best.

I am grateful to everyone in my life who is supportive of my hobby, and all those who have helped to spread the word about my writing or offered me kind words and support. I appreciate you all more than I could ever express. Your feedback, contact, reviews, and sharing has meant so very much to me.

To my new proofreader, Sarah Michalowski. Thank you for reaching out and agreeing to take a look at my work. Contact her at sarah.editingservices@gmail.com if you're in the market for editing, proofreading, content strategy, social media management, etc.!

And last, but certainly not least, to Paul Carson at Seminal Edits. Thank you for your thoroughness, honest feedback, and encouragement. I throw a bunch of genres at you, and you take them all on cheerfully and tell me what I need to hear. Contact Paul at seminaledits@mail.com if you're in the market for someone who is going to make you a better writer.

As always, reach out to me at sarah@sjcunningham.net if you'd like to discuss this book or any of my other works. I'm always happy to have a conversation about writing.

Until next time, my friends. Hope to see you at the Ramsay Castle in a few months!

www.ingramcontent.com/pod-product-compliance
Lightning Source LLC
Chambersburg PA
CBHW061043310726
48969CB00004B/1063